FAWN

FORGOTTEN HEIR CHRONICLES

LAURA ELIZABETH

Book Cover and Chapter Headers by Athena Bliss

Map and Internal Art by Anastasia Campo

Editing by Nikki Bulman and Alessia Quaranta

Proofreading by Holly Smith

Formatting by Brittany Uller at The Author Experience

ISBN: 978-0-473-72500-6 (ebook)

ISBN: 978-0-473-72497-9 (paperback)

ISBN: 978-0-473-72498-6 (hardcover)

Fawn, 1st edition 2024

For the little girl
who desperately wanted to disappear into her books.
Haven't you figured it out yet?
Magic's all around—just look a little closer.

CONTENT WARNING

Even though this is classed as a Cozy Fantasy, it does contain several darker themes.

If you have any sensitivities or triggers then please visit
lauraelizabeth.online
for a list of content warnings.

PRONUNCIATION GUIDE

As an avid reader of many fantastical books with hard-to-pronounce names, I am a firm believer in taking those weird and wonderful fantasy words and absolutely butchering them in your head.

I encourage you to take the names in my book and give them their own unique spin, turning them into whatever your own mind creates.
(If for some reason you desperately would like to know how I pronounce them, then feel free to contact me and I will let you know.)

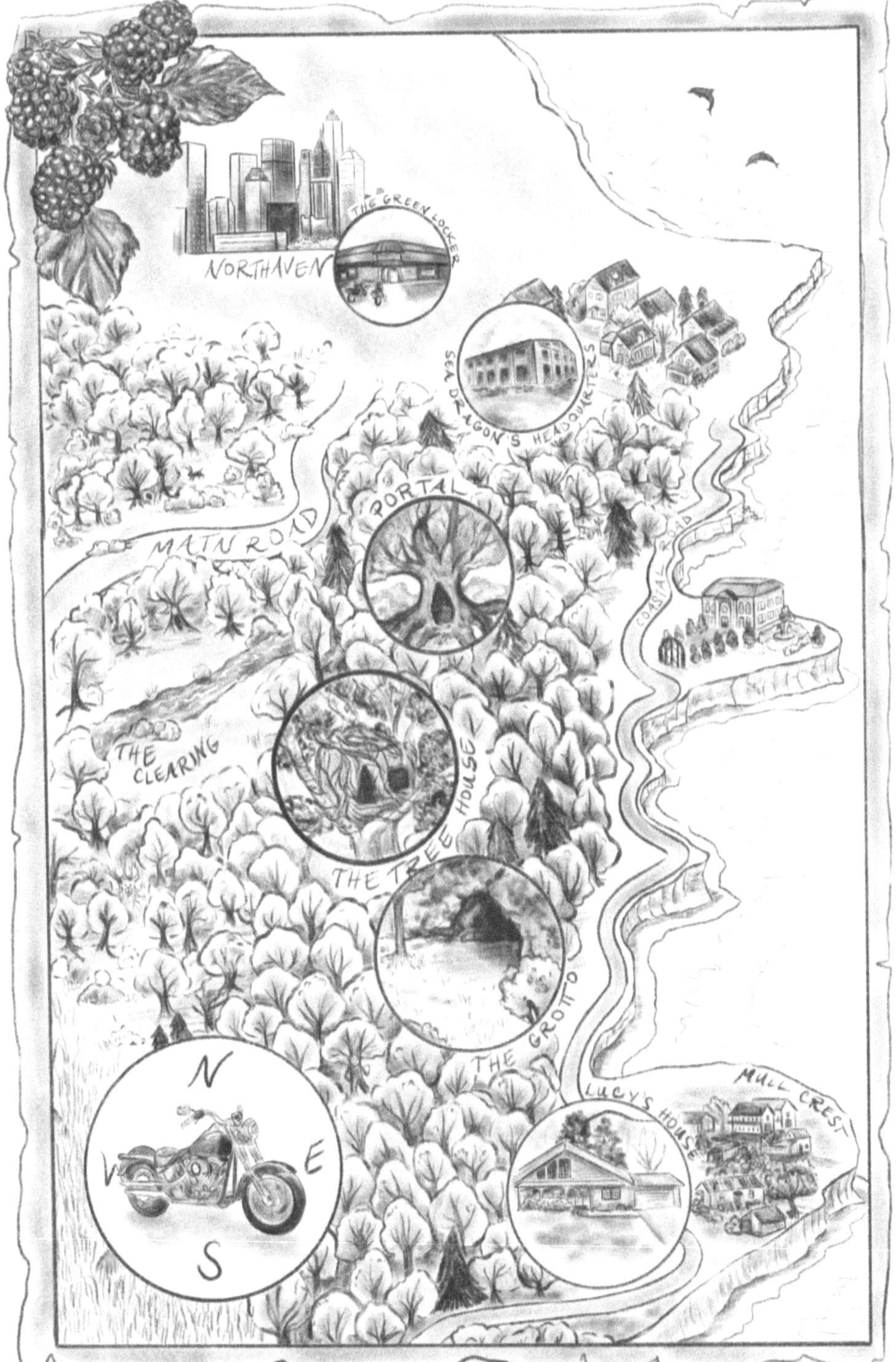

NORTHAVEN
THE GREEN LOCKER
SEA DRAGON'S HEADQUARTERS
MAIN ROAD
PORTAL
THE CLEARING
THE TREE HOUSE
COASTAL ROAD
THE GROTTO
LUCY'S HOUSE
MULL CREST
N
W E
S

There are two realms.

Earth, which belongs to the Humans, and Amaranth, the realm of the Fae. Unseen, Amaranth lies parallel with Earth, draping over the world like a blanket. They are a mirror image of each other—one world filled with magic and one world without it.

For many generations, the long living Fae, with their powerful shape-shifting magic and ability to jump between realms, walked the earth. As they experienced the wonderful fragility of the short human experience, they found, to their surprise, their power and strength was increased from the contact. After a time, they brought several humans back into Amaranth, not knowing the action would start a chain of events that would change the very foundation of Fae civilization.

A new race of Fae emerged.

They called themselves High Fae. They quickly spread throughout Amaranth, reducing the original Fae to the 'Ancient Fae' and carving out Kingdoms and territories of their own. However, they were unable to jump realms and found themselves limited to Amaranth. Due to this, they convinced the Ancient Fae to use their magic to form portals where the realms touched - portals any Fae could use.

—Excerpt from the *Histories of Amaranth,* Vol. 1

PROLOGUE

SOLANINE

The soft shuffling of velvet-slippered feet was the only sound that could be heard that morning. Usually, the air was filled with the sounds of birds waking and the distant roar of waves surging into the nearby bay, but this particular morning was silent. It was as if nature itself could sense the dark intent of the lone Fae walking down the deserted corridor.

Solanine prowled through the wing of the palace, the sconces casting a flickering shadow as she passed by each flame. There was no one to stop her, no one awake or aware of her at all. The anticipation of finally achieving what she had been working towards all these years had a deep chuckle bursting from her mouth. She quickened her pace and turned the corner, nimbly skirting a guard splayed out on the marbled floor. With no hesitation, she pushed open one of the double doors and slipped into the nursery.

Pausing for a moment at the edge of the room, Solanine surveyed the space. Warm, beige walls with intricate paneling gave way to a high, vaulted ceiling supported by dark wooden beams. Across from where she stood were several large french doors lining the exterior of the room. The nursery stretched out to her right, the empty space built with the hope of more children. She scoffed lightly.

As if the Fae can overcome their inability to conceive.

Even so, there were two children currently residing in the room. Her eyes cut to the curly-haired boy frozen in sleep on a small wooden bed along the left wall. He was too pale and still for it to be a natural sleep. Although she'd ensured he wouldn't wake, much like the rest of the palace's occupants, she still walked over and brushed the chocolate hair off of his forehead, tucking a strand behind one of his slightly pointed ears. As her fingers curled behind his ear, she grasped it and gave it a firm pull.

The boy, her brother, didn't stir at all.

Straightening, she let out a satisfied breath. There had been no need to test her enchantment. She was the strongest and most gifted Fae born in millennia. Nevertheless, she couldn't have anything go wrong today. Her future depended on it, and things had gone wrong before.

Solanine let the dark tendrils of her magic creep out of her as she turned towards the second bed in the room. Her smokey webs stretched up, pressing against the delicate cot sitting under the window a few steps from her brother's bed. It rocked slightly, blown by a warm breath of air, even though there was no open window in the room.

Her teeth ground together as she peered down over the sleeping child nestled inside. Revolting! The rounded ears, the dull skin, her stubby little fingers. Horrible, tainted child.

The righteousness of her mission made Solanine's chest swell, leaving her even more sure of this decision. She was the only one pure enough and with the strength needed to remove the scourge of the lower fae, and no one, not even her own niece, was going to stop that from happening.

Her magic reached out and covered the girl's face. As the child inhaled, the dark smog disappeared down her throat, breaking Solanine's enchantment. A moment later, large blue eyes still cloudy with sleep blinked open and shifted around until they landed on Solanine.

Swallowing her disgust, Solanine leaned down and pulled her niece from her bed, forcing her lips into a disarming smile.

"Morning, Faunella."

AMON

Amon winked into existence, appearing between two massive redwoods spearing up through the dark soil of the South Forest. Breathing deeply, he tasted the air, his wooden brow creasing with displeasure. He hadn't been back on Amaranth for nearly two hundred years, and in that time, the forest had changed. Amon flexed his roots and pressed them into the ground, feeling and tasting the knowledge in the very earth around him. Something was wrong; the vibrancy and wild energy of the forest had grown dark and weak.

I shouldn't have waited so long before coming back.

Retracting his roots from the soil, Amon straightened his large body and strode forward on thick limbs, picking up speed with every step. His leaves quivered at the tips of his branches, reacting to the empty hollowness he sensed throughout the kingdom.

Tasked with keeping the Ancient Fae connection to Earth, Amon and several others had been residing in the human realm for millennia, hibernating in their nature forms for a century at a time to survive. Since waking less than a week ago, they had discovered they were unable to fully transform back into their Fae forms. His brow furrowed deeper as he glanced down at his rounded trunk, wondering, not for the first time, if his inability to release this form had something to do with his kingdom's deterioration.

Skidding to a halt, he arrived at the Tree of Conalt and was startled to see that instead of the usually barren branches, the tree was in bloom, indicating there was a message waiting for him. Fusing his wooden fingers over the closest branch, Amon closed his eyes and opened himself up to the tree's vibrations. The flowers wilted one by one as the tree revealed its words, and when the last petal withered and fell to the ground, the final pieces of the message echoed through his head.

The King is dead. Stay the course.

Dazed, Amon jolted back. It wasn't just this territory that was deteriorating—all the Ancient Fae kingdoms were slowly fading. Their life and magic was rotting and growing dim.

The news of King Chalaonar's death made the Fae's fixed state clear: the resulting loss of magic cut off their gift of transformation and was slowly stripping their lands and people of power.

Too distracted to leave his update about the humans' massive social and technological advancements, Amon brushed his twigs over the trunk of a nearby tree, grimacing when his hand came away covered in putrid sap. Once again, he formed roots and dug them into the soil, thrusting them deeper into the land until he was connected to the whole forest. As he tasted the expanse of decay, he slumped over, his trunk weakening with grief.

How long have our people been without a ruler? he wondered. *How much longer can we survive without one?*

A sudden pulse of life flickered from the magnitude of land, cutting through the darkness and beckoning like a beacon through the night. Heart pounding, Amon focused on the light. There shouldn't have been any life left within the forest. Only a new ruler could coax the land to breathe again. Saturated with hope, Amon gathered himself and raced towards the boundary to investigate.

The life Amon sensed was a child—a tiny girl who couldn't be more than four years of age. His eyes drank her in, wondering what drew him to her. Her haphazard curls stood out starkly amongst the trees, their fiery red color a sharp contrast to the dark-haired Fae with her. Treading with caution and never more grateful for his nature form, Amon moved closer, watching what was happening between the child and the Fae with her with increasing concern.

The Fae stood tall, her beautiful face distorted by the venomous words spewing from her painted lips.

"You didn't really think anyone loved you, did you? How could anyone ever love a disgusting brat like you? Why do you think your mother and grandmother left together? They left so that I could take you away, so they would never have to see you again. Nobody wants you here."

The child stumbled backwards, squeaking out the identity of the female Fae. "Aunt Sol?"

Disdain thrummed through him. They were family.

He glanced towards the flickering sunlight that shone in thin slivers behind the two Fae.

They must be from Madivyre, he guessed.

If they were trespassing from the Kingdom of Madivyre, they had to be High Fae, not Ancient Fae.

Disappointment flooded his body. But then, why did the child draw him to her like a moth to flame? Standing still, he solidified his body until he no longer had any movement besides the organic swaying and creaking of his long branches. His two wooden limbs fused together into one round trunk, and his face smoothed out into nothing but bark, finishing his final transformation into a tree.

Using his senses, he felt for both Fae, inwardly recoiling when he touched the older Fae's aura. Her essence tasted toxic to his senses, leaving the bitter taste of poison in his leaves. Completely unaware that they had an audience, the duo continued their interaction freely, giving Amon the opportunity to study the girl. Her lackluster skin and rounded ears told him she was a lower fae. He probed deeper, feeling a light in the girl that shone right into his very being. He didn't know why, but somehow, this child was important.

So focused on her essence, he didn't notice the moment the female struck the child, only feeling her pain and fear as she collided heavily into a tree. The shock had his body jolting back, leaving him staring in horror as she turned and ran for her life, delving deeper within the ancient forest.

Her aunt smirked and tossed her hair back, then stalked after the child. With dread pooling in his core, Amon followed them, staying back to keep himself hidden. Even though the King was now dead, their orders had not changed. Having a Fae from another kingdom learn of their continued presence on Earth could put their already vulnerable kingdoms at further risk of attack.

Amon trailed them for hours, keeping his movements still. His chest grew tighter and tighter as the child weakened, her pace slowing after each whimpering cry. It wasn't much longer before she began to weave, her bloodied feet dragging over the forest floor, until she finally crashed onto the ground.

The urge to run to her was so strong that Amon had to thrust his roots into the ground to stay in place. His desire to remain hidden wavered with each passing moment.

The High Fae suddenly split off from the girl, heading directly towards where the old Earth portal stood. Confusion pulled at him. Stretching his roots though the dank soil, Amon felt a heavy, swirling mass of dark magic pulling the portal open once more. He jerked back as if he was burnt. The repulsive magic mixing with the remnants of the ancient spell was repugnant, warning him within the depths of his soul. Somehow, this High Fae had managed to open a portal to Earth. His heart pounded through his chest. This was bad.

Amon quickly turned his attention back to the child, finding her unconscious. A deep surge of familial protectiveness overwhelmed him, pushing him forward. Ignoring his better judgment, he reached his leafy arms down to attempt to rouse her and, at the same time, harnessed his power to observe her recent memories. The events from earlier in her day painted a clear picture of the High Fae's treachery. Amon was sickened.

This poor child.

She stirred, blinking wearily as she gathered her remaining energy. Still needing to hide his presence, Amon drew back, standing between her and the path to the older Fae. Concentrating, he stretched his arms out, creating more branches and weaving them tightly together until they formed a wide screen.

Satisfied that would be enough of a deterrent to turn the child around, he morphed back into his full tree form, hiding his sentience. He watched her unobtrusively as she stood and faced him. Instead of turning around as he expected, she blinked wide blue eyes up at him, her small pink lips popping open in wonder. Agony shot through him. Those eyes, so bright despite her pain— they took him back to a time he had sworn never to remember. His mind continued pulling him away from the present, wholly focused on choking back the sharp sting of loss her innocent gaze had provoked. Soft fingers ran over his bark as she trailed her hand along his branches. Her tender flesh, already grazed from her frantic dash through the forest, left traces of blood behind. Distracted by the ache in his heart, Amon absorbed it, unconsciously drawing it into his body.

The information the blood contained jolted him out of the past and left him reeling with shock. The girl stepped around his edges and continued towards her aunt's dark magic, leaving Amon lost in a maelstrom of feelings. Something in her blood called to Amon in a way he hadn't felt in ages. If what he thought he felt was true, the discovery could change everything.

His mind ran over the implications of what this meant and what would happen if the child didn't live. Now panicked, he shook himself out of his trance and swung around as quickly as possible. But before he could take a step, a loud thwack rang out through the air, followed by a low cry. His blood ran cold as bright light, and the familiar tingling draw of portal magic pulsed through the trees.

He was too late.

PART ONE

As the High Fae continued to take over, they saw themselves as the controlling Fae on the planet, overlooking the quiet, more elemental Ancient Fae and the Humans who continued to flood in from Earth. All seemed well on Amaranth until the High Fae evolved again: their offspring with the Humans no longer held any Fae characteristics.

This created a third race of Fae. They were dubbed as lower fae.

Coming in many different hues and sizes, their features were unique, like that of the humans, making them easily recognisable to the tall, pale High Fae. Despite this, the humans and the Fae continued to procreate, until at last they noticed the magic was beginning to fade in their Kingdoms–the High Fae Kingdoms. The influx of non-magical humans was starting to turn the tide and outnumber the magical Fae.

The reigning monarchs at the time gathered together from their individual territories to discuss finding a solution to the growing problem. Among other things, it was decided that the portals between realms would be destroyed, permanently closing the bridges to Earth.

The Ancient Fae King, whose people drew power from both realms, refused to take part in the discussion. Their shape-shifting and realm jumping abilities helped them disappear from civilization. They drew back from the eyes of Fae society, closing the borders of their many territories scattered throughout the land. Some of the Ancient Fae stayed hidden on Earth in their nature forms, but the others stayed deep within the wild places of Amaranth, growing in strength as they kept to themselves.

—Excerpt from the *Histories of Amaranth,* Vol. 1

EARTH

CHAPTER ONE
FAUNELLA

FAUNELLA WOKE TO THE cool feeling of water trickling past her cracked lips. She widened her mouth despite the ache in her jaw, her entire being focused on relieving the dryness that burned down her throat. The water stopped flowing before her thirst was quenched, and she let out a keening cry, opening and shutting her mouth in a weak attempt to get more of the refreshing liquid. A rough container was gently placed against her small lower lip, and she opened her mouth gratefully as more water slowly poured onto her parched tongue. It didn't take much before her shrunken stomach was full, and she sank back into the soft material under her. As the liquid refreshed her, it sharpened her awareness.

Letting out a long breath, Faunella cracked open her eyes, blinking against the mid-morning light that shone in her face. When her vision cleared, a wave of confusion flooded through her.

Where am I?

Faunella carefully propped herself up on her arms, crying out when a sharp bite of pain throbbed in her temple. Reaching up, she discovered a thick band of fibrous plants wrapped tightly around the back of her head and her forehead.

Who did that? she wondered, glancing around as the scenery surrounding her spun dizzyingly.

When her vision cleared, it revealed a bright clearing, the large space almost a perfect circle surrounded by dark trees. A wide stream gurgled beside where she lay, emerging from a rocky formation in the earth before flowing away through the trees on the opposite side of the clearing. Sitting up fully, she widened her eyes and looked around the space again, searching for another person. She couldn't have imagined someone being here—the bandage on her head was proof enough that she had been cared for, and she could still feel the water on her lips.

"Hello?" she called out, glancing around several trees directly beside her.

Pushing herself onto her knees, Faunella braced against the large boulder by her feet and attempted to stand. To her surprise, the rock twitched and rolled heavily a few steps away. Faunella let out a cry, scooting back on her bottom, her eyes round with shock. The rock rippled, changing shape while she stared on, frozen with horror.

The thing had come alive, but it was like nothing Faunella had ever seen before. She clapped her hand over her open mouth, stifling a scream as the creature settled into its final form. Its rocky body was a choppy oval shape, with rough arms and legs. An assortment of different-sized stones made up the short limbs, with no obvious material keeping them connected. A rounded head emerged from the top of the body, and two dark eyes blinked from a roughly carved face.

Faunella's heart pounded in the split second it took to register what was happening. The creature, though not quite double her height, towered over her as she cowered in place. Racking her brain, she hunted for answers, but with mounting worry—she found that she couldn't grasp a single memory. Her mind remained blank, leaving only a frightening darkness with no clue where or who she was.

"Who are you?" she choked out, hoping for a reassuring answer. A short rumbling reached her ears in reply and Faunella vaguely realized that the sounds matched the movement of the creature's mouth-like protrusion.

"W-what?"

Her heart sank as the creature yet again uttered a soft rumble. Faunella's eyes prickled, but before the tears could form, the rock gestured wildly, letting out a hurried crackle as his eyes locked onto something above her.

Turning, Faunella stiffened in terror as the space around her exploded with movement. The few trees dotted inside the clearing waved their branches, their trunks splitting in two. Bushes and flowering plants began to grow and morph, forming vaguely humanoid bodies of their own. The nearby stream bubbled wildly before shooting up a huge jet of water that landed on the bank in the shifting form of a translucent entity.

Faunella felt a tickle around the wrist of the hand that was bracing her on the mossy ground. Looking down, she let out a high-pitched cry as a portion of the moss separated from the patch she had been lying on, puffing out stubby arms and legs before turning a softly textured face to study her. It drew itself up beside her and reached out its arm to brush gently against her shoulder.

The touch snapped her out of her shock. Bursting into tears, Faunella hugged her legs to her chest, burying her face against her knees as she cried out in fear and pain. The moss creature immediately removed its hand and shuffled away, leaving Faunella alone once again.

Time stretched out, seemingly endless—an eternity in a day. Utterly consumed, Faunella's confusion grew, rising with the blood pulsing under her skin. Eventually, her breathing slowed, and her tears came to a sniffling stop, leaving her with nothing to do except listen to the noises around her—the creatures' noises. Nerves overcame her body, making her skin quiver with unrestrained energy. She wanted to ask where she was and who these creatures were, but she couldn't bring herself to speak again, to look into their strange faces. So, she kept herself tucked away and just listened.

That's how they talk, she realized after a few moments. Screwing her eyes shut, she tried to understand their sounds, but the noises flowed with seemingly no rhyme or reason.

Desperate to hold on to something tangible, she searched her blank mind. Snippets of memories swirled around—a smiling boy, the warm hands of a female wearing a pink dress. Faunella tried to hold on to those images, but the female's face began to fade, leaving her whispered words full of love echoing through the darkness. "Faunella, my little Fawn."

Fresh tears pricked at her eyes, and her heart swelled. Longing for more, Faunella chased the voice, pulling at the memory. Suddenly, a pair of vicious dark eyes flashed into her head, sending the smell of rot and a crash of terror roiling through her body. With a gasp, Faunella snapped her eyes open, crying out in alarm. As one, the creatures rushed forward, murmuring gentle sounds of worry and concern. The moss creature reached her first, extending its arm towards her again. Before it could touch her, it stilled, hesitation filtering across its mossy face.

The concerned look in its eyes had Faunella's panic stilling, her cloudy mind considering the possibility that these creatures, for all their fearsome looks, could help her. Unclenching her muscles slowly, she reached out and tentatively stroked the creature's springy texture. A soft whispering of sound emerged from its mouth, calming her further. Faunella didn't know what these things were or what they were saying to her, but they hadn't hurt her, so maybe they were good. Looking back around at the assortment of creatures standing over her, Faunella swallowed past the lump in her throat, giving them the only thing she knew with any certainty.

"I'm Faunella."

At her words, the moss let out a trilling purr and climbed into her lap. One of the other creatures, a tall willowy tree with vibrant leaves, came slowly around to stand in front of her. The tree opened its mouth and let out a long creaking sound, followed by a quick rustle. Looking up at its face, Faunellas brow furrowed, her fear only just held at bay.

"I don't understand."

The tree curved its body in half, bending without breaking, as it lowered itself down to her level. She stared at it in trepidation, clutching at the moss on her lap, her small fingers kneading the springy substance for comfort. Reaching out a branch, the creature repeated its creaking sound and brought the leafy tips of its arm close to Faunella's head. A hint of fear ran through her, and she leaned her head away, afraid of what the tree was doing. The leaves followed her retreating head and gently made contact with her brow.

All at once, her mind was invaded with pictures and feelings that were not her own. Faunella gasped and scrambled backwards, her mouth opening and closing in disbelief. Her heart beat a sharp staccato, thumping so hard she was sure it would burst from her chest. The moss creature stroked her arm and emitted small rhythmic sounds. Faunella whimpered, her eyes as round as saucers when the tree shuffled closer, offering his branch again. Overwhelmed, but not sure what else she could do, she nodded and closed her eyes, swallowing back her choking cry when he once again took over her mind.

A vivid scene played out, momentarily obscuring her fear and filling her with a bright feeling of happiness. Lost in the sensation, she watched images of the creatures interacting. They moved together through the forest making various noises, joking and pushing each other around. She sucked in a breath when the scene cut to another image of a girl so battered and dirty that it took her a moment before she recognized herself. The emotion that accompanied this picture filled her with sorrow, compassion, and a thick undercurrent of anger.

Faunella's eyes flew open, and she began to cry, unable to sort through the mess of emotions coming from both her and the tree.

The moss lowered itself back onto the matching ground as the tree removed its twiggy hand and placed it at her side. The branches on both sides of its trunk morphed and grew, stretching out to scoop her up. Drawing her close, the tree stood and cradled her against his body.

Faunella choked and hiccuped, her distress making it impossible to shy away from the creature's firm embrace. She placed her arms around its smooth trunk, pressing the side of her face firmly into its bark, and erupted into yet another round of tears. Keening quietly, she stayed locked in the tree's arms as it moved through the forest, swaying slightly as it walked.

When her tears slowed into little hiccuping sobs, Faunella lifted the front of her nightgown and used it to wipe her wet face and streaming nose. She raised her head to look around, taking note of the new part of the forest they were traveling through. Breaking through her distrust, her natural curiosity came out and she quietly whispered up to the big tree.

"Where are we going?"

At her words, the tree formed a small branch out of one of the limbs currently holding her. The leaves stretched out towards her and paused, as if waiting for her permission. Faunella nibbled on her lower lip, remembering the way it communicated with her the last time. She was unsure if she wanted to experience that again. As the tree waited patiently, she took a deep breath and pressed her head forward, closing her eyes as she connected with the tickling fronds.

The image once again showed her the scene of the group of creatures. They were traveling together and had arrived at a small clearing in front of a large cave. They entered the cave, and in their own strange way, seemed to settle in for the evening.

Opening her eyes, she pulled away. "A cave?"

The tree vibrated its assent. Pacified by its answer, Faunella lay her head back with no choice but to allow the creature to carry her back to its home.

CHAPTER TWO
AMON

TAKING A STEADYING BREATH, Amon clutched the girl closer to his chest. His eyes gentled as he stared down at her messy auburn curls.

Faunella...Fawn.

The spotted animal flashed in his mind, its innocent curiosity apparent. He chuckled softly. She was named well.

"Well, that wasn't as bad as it could have been."

Amon glanced down at the boulder ambling along beside him, his severe face pensive.

"Huxley has a point," muttered Violetta, rising up on her toes to flash a smile at the wide-eyed girl in his arms. "She's not much more than a baby and obviously scared of us. So, why isn't she crying for her mother or asking to go home?"

Amon's brow drew down as he pondered the water Fae's question. Faunella shifted in his arms, her head swiveling to take in everything around them. Her movement gave him a dawning understanding when his eyes caught on the thick bandage fastened around her head. It also renewed his anger over the abuse still fresh in his mind.

"The wound to her head may have affected her memory," he said between gritted teeth.

The Fae around him murmured their agreement, making varied sounds of pity and concern. However, Amon's sadness and anger soon morphed into something else.

"You know, this could be a good thing."

He winced at the horrified silence that followed.

"No, no. Let me explain." He took a breath and gauged the distance to their home. It would be a lot easier to relay all that happened once they were settled in the grotto. A hollow gurgle rattled against his trunk, and Amons lips twitched. He wondered if the child would be brave enough to voice her hunger. He turned his attention back to the Fae.

"With the urgency of healing Fawn, I haven't had a chance to tell you what's happened on Amaranth."

"Fawn?" Huxley asked, the divots in his face deepening.

"I think it's cute," chirped Erwin from his position on Huxley's back. He unfurled his mossy limbs and clapped his hands to his face, rubbing his cheeks as he gushed over how sweet Faunella was. "Fawn for Faunella. I get it."

Huxley grumbled, "You're too soft, kid."

The tension from the information Amon carried lessened at his friend's display, giving him a brief moment of joy before responsibility came crashing back down on him. From further behind, a hoarse voice brought the seriousness of the situation to a head.

"Tell us how this came about, Amon. A lower fae child arrived near death through a portal long since dismantled. That is something I never thought could happen. Has King Chalaonar finally defied the High Fae rulers and reopened the portals, with our borders along with them?"

Lothian couldn't have gotten it more wrong. Amon inwardly winced and prepared himself to answer the aged tree Fae's question.

"Our borders are still closed, and to my knowledge, the portals remain sealed." He frowned, wondering how long the South forest had been unguarded. Shaking away the thought, Amon continued. "When I reached the Tree of Conalt, there was a message from Chancellor Petrov waiting for me." He braced himself, stepping through the trees into the sunlit clearing before turning around to face his fellow Fae head on.

"He has died. King Chalaonar has passed from our realm."

The Fae gasped, mouths dropping in shock. Some fell to their knees in disbelief.

"When?" came the resigned voice of Lothian, who had seen several monarchs come and go—although King Chalaonar had lasted longer than most.

"He didn't say, but I'd assume at least a century," Amon said as he placed Fawn on the ground and shook out his leaves, knowing the worst was to come. No one spoke for a moment until Flavire stepped forward, his bright floral robes eliciting the first hint of pleasure from Fawn.

"Who is our next king then? Or queen?" he added as an afterthought, tossing his long leafy locks behind him when Fawn hesitantly reached up and tugged at a flower.

Steeling himself, Amon guided Fawn away from Flavire and said the words that would change everything. "We don't have one. He had no children."

Noise erupted from the clearing they were in. The Faes' sorrow was immediately forgotten as they exclaimed over the impossible news. Throughout the chaos, Erwin spoke out. "So, why haven't the king's advisors tested our people to uncover an heir yet? If it's been over a century, then surely that's more than enough time?"

"Maybe the royal line has died out?" speculated Violetta, one of the female Fae, conscious of their struggle with fertility.

Amon raised his branches up to quell the questions and to get his friends' attention.

"The message also contained an answer of sorts. It seems that Chancellor Petrov has seized power over our kingdoms. He has studied the royal genealogy charts and found that the royal line has indeed failed. Confident with his findings, he decided to not search for an undocumented heir, instead resolving to continue ruling our people in place of a monarch."

"But what of our lands?" questioned Huxley, his rough voice not quite gruff enough to mask his frustration. "You were there, Amon. What did they look like? Is the Chancellor enough to keep our lands from fading?"

Nine sets of eyes stared unblinking at him as they awaited his answer.

"The South Forest is already dying," he confessed, his heart sinking as he uttered the words. "The magic is barely hanging on. What I could sense was weak and dull."

"But the portal sent this child to us, despite being closed. How could that be if the magic has faded so much?" exclaimed Venek, his thick green vines quivering with feeling. He gestured to Faunella, who watched their rapid discussion with wide blue eyes. "How is this possible?"

"I'm hungry."

Amon startled at the high-pitched words, then a wide smile broke out on his face, pleasure filling him at Faunella's confidence. She frowned and chewed on her lip, obviously still not aware that she was safe with them. Amon clapped a hand to his forehead, cursing himself for getting caught up in the troubles in their home realm and not spending every moment tending the traumatized child at his feet. He swiveled his head, brow drawn tight, until he spotted the little bushy Fae quietly tucked in between Baol and Baeroot.

"Ah, Laurel." He gestured her out from behind the two trees and towards Fawn. "Could you?"

Laurel crept forward, her dark glossy leaves erupting into delicate white flowers. With each step, the flowers changed, wilting and forming tight green buds. By the time she had reached Faunella's side, her body was heavy with large purple berries. She plucked one from her body, shyly handing it to Fawn with her flexible branches.

Amon's heart grew warm at Faunella's awestruck expression. She uttered a quick thanks as she accepted the berry, moaning in delight when she bit into the food. The warmth almost immediately hardened to ice as he turned back to answer Venek.

"The reason the child is here is because her High Fae aunt used strong, dark magic to rip open our portal and send her through to die."

The Fae drew back, mirroring Amon's disgust. To use dark magic was an affront to life, and to use it to kill a child was the worst crime of all.

Amon shook his head, looking down at the girl happily munching on the fruit, her mouth and fingers stained purple. "I have never sensed as much animosity from anyone as I have from this Fae."

"Do you think it's because she's a lower fae?" considered Venek, reaching out and tenderly touching one of Fawn's obviously rounded ears. Faunella jumped at the contact, but then a tentative smile tugged at her lips, and she grasped his limb with her sticky fingers. "That tickles."

Lothian came closer to Fawn. "If I may," he started, bending down for a closer look. "I can't see why anyone would hate a child simply because they contain human blood. The lower fae are an integral part of our society now, and not all of them stay that way."

Fawn's face fell from Lothian's close proximity. She let out a cry, her renewed fear piercing Amon sharply. Lothian straightened and cleared his throat, unbothered by her reaction. "The child has every chance to grow into a High Fae when she reaches her second puberty, and from that moment, she will be indistinguishable from someone born that way."

"But what if she doesn't?"

Amon ignored Erwin's question and stretched out to scoop Fawn back towards him, tucking her under the sheltering canopy of his body.

"If she doesn't," answered Lothian, turning his wizened face towards Erwin, "then she will remain similar to the way she is now. A watered down version of a High Fae—still essentially human, but with a slightly longer life span."

Amon shifted uncomfortably, his roots shuffling over the grass. "I really hope that's not the case."

"Amon?" growled Huxley. "What aren't you telling us?"

Holding Fawn out of the way, Amon stretched out several branches, seeking out their forms. When each Fae accepted his connection, the truth he had seen flowed jerkily from his thoughts and into their minds.

"Holy hell!" barked Huxley, yanking back once the memory ended. "This changes everything."

"Indeed it does," Lothian mused, leaning in closer once again.

As if in unison, the Fae turned their attention to the child tucked behind his legs. Fawn peered around his trunk, a crease between her brow as she warily studied Lothian's petrified face. Her serious expression had Amon's lips quirking upwards, despite the gravity of the situation.

"What are we going to do with her?" blinked Baol with wide eyes. "Surely we can't keep her here? Not with the humans so close by."

Amon grimaced, his mind conjuring images of the humans entering the forest and finding Fawn, the fae child looking no different than their own young.

"They would try and take her," he whispered, his limbs instinctively tightening around Fawn's small body.

"I'd like to see them try," growled Huxley, sending shards of rock flying with his tightly clenched fists.

A whimper escaped from Fawn's mouth, cutting through the tension forming in the clearing. Amon took in her pale skin and the way her body drooped. Protectiveness surged through his chest. He wanted to keep her safe by his side, never to be touched by either human or Fae.

"It's been a long day," he said in a tone that left no room for argument. "Fawn has been through enough and doesn't need us deciding her fate right away. Let her heal fully before we decide what is to be done with her."

The Fae murmured their agreement and slowly dispersed from the clearing, giving Amon and the girl some space. He pulled her into his arms, hoping that, with time, she would understand that she had nothing to fear. He rocked her gently, humming a soothing melody until the tension left her body and her eyes fluttered shut. Laurel and Erwin had remained with him and busied themselves making a small mossy bed about five feet into the cave.

However, Amon's mind was still a jumble. This was the first time he had ever considered breaking his oath and taking a different path. He sighed, never guessing he would be faced with such a dilemma. He studied the child nestled in his limbs, her dark lashes fanning over the deep shadows under her eyes. With his own kingdoms in turmoil, and Fawn's family trying to kill her, there was really no other option but to keep her on Earth. He smoothed an errant curl stuck to her lip and tried to repress the apprehension creaking up his spine.

In all his years observing and learning from the humans, there was one thing he could say with utter certainty.

The humans were dangerous.

CHAPTER THREE
DERICK

EVEN WHILE STANDING STILL, the balaclava slowly twisted itself around. The black nylon seemed to have a mind of its own, constantly moving and bunching up from the moment Derick had first pulled it over his shaved head. He adjusted the thick material, taking a moment to scratch at the persistent itch on the underside of his jaw.

Damn, this material is itchy.

Lowering his arm, he reached around, placing his hand on the gun tucked down the back of his jeans. Tapping it nervously, Derick reassured himself that he was still armed, even though he hadn't done anything that would have dislodged the weapon in the five minutes since he last checked. He took several deep breaths of cool night air and tried to calm his pounding heart.

Despite the chilly temperature, beads of sweat trickled their way down his back. Shaking himself out of his nervousness, he once again brought his hand up to his covered face. Reaching under the stretchy mask, he rubbed his fingers over the soft fuzz that had been slowly growing over his chin in the past few months.

After tonight, I'll be a man—a real man. Tomorrow, I'll shave all this off.

Cloaked in shadows at the rear entrance of the downtown jewelry store, Derick puffed up his chest and peered up and down the alley. His father had decided that, at almost thirteen, Derick was old enough to be initiated into the gang. He handed him a gun and radio, telling him to alert the men inside if anyone came along.

Derick's stomach churned; he couldn't mess this up. His dad, Frank, was the leader of the gang, and Derick knew that he was expected to take over one day. Desperate to do a good job and make his father proud, he stayed vigilant, his hazel eyes swiveling back and forth, looking for any movement.

The temptation to radio and ask how much longer they would be gnawed at him. It was getting harder and harder to tamp down his rising anxiety. He wiped his damp hands onto the front of his hoodie, needing to distract himself.

The other men had been inside for close to twenty minutes now, and all was quiet in the alley. This area wasn't very well traveled at night, so it was an easy target. The driver of the getaway van had pulled up at the mouth of the alley and let them out before speeding off, the wheels squealing on the dew-slicked pavement. Then it was a simple matter of shattering the dim light bulb that lit up the rear door and cutting the two padlocks that held the door shut.

The quiet was interrupted by a scuffle coming from the street. Derick's heart leapt into his throat, and he quickly dropped down behind a pile of cardboard boxes filled with rubbish. Peering out through the darkness, he looked towards the lit-up street as the shuffling turned to heavy footsteps. Fumbling for his radio with sweat-slicked fingers, he grabbed it and brought it to his face, pressing the talk button twice in his haste. The sharp buzz of static echoed through the air right as an overweight security guard stepped into view. All the air left Derick's lungs as his world narrowed to just him and the guard.

Oh my God! Oh my God! He knows I'm here. He's going to catch me, and I'm going to prison.

Derick seized up, his mouth going dry as his heart pounded frantically. The guard stopped when he heard the static and was squinting into the gloom, unable to see anything due to the blown-out light. The man took a hesitant step into the alley, then another. Frozen with fear, Derick kept silent, not daring to use the radio again. A noise from behind had him turning in horror. The crew, led by his father, opened the door into the alley and emerged, their arms laden with bags of stolen jewelry.

"Hey you, freeze!" shouted the guard, the light from his torch flashing over the stunned men.

Frank's shocked eyes, visible through the holes in his well-worn mask, shot from the tubby guard to where Derick cowered, understanding and irritation flickering in their dark depths. Without hesitating, he snatched up his radio.

"Get to the other end of the alley!" he barked to the getaway driver, his crew behind him following the same command.

Derick watched everything play out as if in slow motion. The security guard was yelling into his radio, calling for backup as he fumbled with the gun in his holster. His father's crew were taking off towards the other end of the alley, the glow from the street blocked by the familiar van's side door whipping open to admit the fleeing men. Derick could hear his blood rushing in his ears, his panic causing him to freeze up, muting the noise around him.

Crack! Crack!

The shots that rang out permeated the haze he was in. His father was shooting at the guard, his bullets embedding into the bricks on either side of the alley.

"Derick, move your ass!"

Belatedly, Derick realized it was not the first time his father had called his name, and he readied himself to run to his side. Launching out from behind the boxes, Derick stayed low, ducking as the whiz of bullets flew over his head.

"Argh!" Frank cried out, clutching his thigh as he stumbled to the side. "Derick, help me."

All the blood left Derick's face. He raced to his dad's side, bracing his arms around his solid waist. Derick had already lost his mother; he couldn't lose his father too.

"I've got you."

They backed away together, Frank firing wildly at the guard as Derick struggled to keep him upright. They were only halfway down the alley when a second bullet clipped his father's shoulder. Frank dropped to the ground, blacking out from either shock or blood loss. Derick bowed under his weight, unable to carry his father alone. He craned his neck to look behind him.

The rest of the men had reached the van and did nothing more than yell out for them to hurry. The van revved its engine amidst their hurried calls. At that moment, Derick had a revelation. For all the men's talk of comradery, when it came down to it, there would be no one but himself to rely on. He was on his own.

Fighting the fear and bitter disappointment flooding through him, he turned back to the guard and continued trying to drag his father towards freedom. He narrowed his eyes, breath coming heavy. He wouldn't be like those men. He would stay and get his father to safety. The guard was still shooting, causing Derick to flinch and duck with each pop of the firearm. Desperate to escape, he took one arm from around his father and reached behind him to the gun he had been given.

Gripping the cold metal in his shaking hand, he drew it out, wildly swinging his arm around and pointing the barrel towards the mouth of the alley, hoping to hold off the man who was preventing their escape. Squeezing his eyes shut, he pulled back on the trigger, *Pop! Pop! Pop!* The gunfire rang out loudly, the gun vibrating in his hand.

Hearing no return fire, Derick opened his eyes, slowly looking at where the guard once stood. His heartbeat stilled. The guard was flat on his back, a dark pool of blood slowly seeping from under his large body.

I've killed him.

The thought echoed through his mind. Before he could come to grips with what he had just done, two police cars came screeching to a halt on the street behind the dead guard. Fear churned through his gut, flooding his mouth with acidic saliva. Derrick clamped his mouth shut, violently trying to tamp down the sickness that threatened to emerge. His hand shook on his father's body as he desperately tried to hold on to the promise he had only just made to himself. But as the cops emerged from the cars and raised their weapons at him, he felt himself let go. Cursing his cowardice, Derick dropped his father to the ground and bolted for the van—tears streaming down his face as he ran.

CHAPTER FOUR
FAUNELLA

"ROCK?" FAUNELLA CALLED OUT, her high voice ringing around the clearing. "Where are you, silly?"

She skipped out of the mouth of the cave with the moss creature riding on her back like a cape. Not seeing any sign of the large rock outside, Faunella ventured further on the dew-soaked ground, her bare feet growing slick with the moisture.

"Roooock?" she tried again, stretching his name out earnestly. Her lower lip protruded as she pouted her displeasure. "Where's Rock?" she asked the moss as she gestured wildly around the clearing.

The small creature quivered and pulled her shoulders back in the direction of the cave. Even though it was too early to be up and most of the other creatures were still asleep, Faunella didn't want to go back to bed. She had spent so much time resting over the last week and was now eager to play.

"No! Fawn find Rock," she protested as her little foot stomped the ground, leaving a small depression in the earth. "Fawn go look."

The moss let out an airy sigh and wilted down in acceptance. No longer feeling resistance from her friend, Faunella let out a triumphant smile, stuck out her chin, and marched through the first layer of trees that surrounded the clearing.

The forest remained dark this early in the morning, only lit with the faint beams of light that shone through from the canopy above. Wisps of mist swirled among the shadows, not yet dissolved by the still rising sun. Faunella walked determinedly through the cooling fog along a nearly invisible path. It was one of many made by the Fae as they traveled to and from their home in the grotto. Faunella instinctively followed one of the roughly formed trails, her unprotected feet finding the path of least resistance.

Reassured by the moss's comforting weight around her neck, she hummed a little tune as she walked, thrilled to be finally exploring some of the area away from the cave.

Before long, a mossy hand tapped her left shoulder. Faunella glanced to the side, her eyes scanning the undergrowth. There was no movement, but a grinding rumble started up, growing louder by the second. Faunella backed away, her brows drawing down in concern. Maybe there was a reason the creatures wanted her to stay in the cave. A moment later, the brush opened up to reveal the very rock she was looking for. Worry forgotten, Faunella danced on the spot, letting out a triumphant squeal.

At Faunella's cry of delight, the large creature's placid expression grew stern, but he was gentle as he turned her around to face the way she had come.

Happy to have found him, Faunella skipped along, jabbering enthusiastically in a one-sided conversation.

"I wanted you, but you not there," she frowned briefly before brightening up again. "So Grass and me look. And found you!"

Laughing excitedly, Faunella clapped her hands, then reached out to take hold of his rocky arm. Smiling up at the surly rock, she looked on expectantly, waiting for a response of some sort. The rock glanced down at her before opening his mouth and letting out a series of sharp clacking sounds. Faunella nodded seriously, imagining that he must have said something very important.

"You pretty happy to see me," she replied in return, which made the moss let out a humming sound against her back, mimicking the pattern of laughter. Sensing that he was laughing made Faunella feel like laughing too, and she let a little giggle come bubbling up out of her mouth.

She was buoyant with contentment and swung the rock's arm wildly as they walked back to the grotto together. It wasn't until they had stepped into the now bright clearing that she had a thought.

"Where you go?"

She had noticed many of the creatures leave the clearing during the day, but they always came back as the sun set, never going out at nighttime. Rock had now broken this pattern.

The creature in question paused before removing his arm gently from Faunella's hand. His gray cheeks darkened slightly, and he looked away, refusing to meet her eyes.

Sensing an answer, Faunella clasped her hands in front of her and jumped up and down.

"Where? Where? Where?" she sang, reveling in the rock's halting embarrassment.

He reached up behind his right shoulder, withdrawing a woven bag that had gone unnoticed until now. He held it out to Faunella, and when she made no immediate move to take it, he pressed it to her chest. Staring at the bag in surprise, Faunella clutched at the soft bundle, her mouth popping open in wonder.

"For me?"

Rock's eyes darted down to meet her questioning face. He made a dismissive noise and gestured up and down her body, pausing his hand to reach out and touch one of the dirty sleeves that had been nearly torn from her nightgown. Then he drew back, shrugged, and stepped quickly around her only to hurry away, disappearing into the cave.

Faunella watched him leave before whipping her attention back to the bag in her arms. She knelt down in the cool grass and reached her hand into the opening, swirling her arm around until her fingers closed around a piece of material. She removed it and used both hands to hold it up flat.

It's clothes. Strange clothes.

Faunella eagerly wrenched the remaining contents out of the bag, spilling the assortment of clothes onto the ground. The items heaped up in a jumbled pile at her feet were a multitude of colors and textures. Faunella's attention was captured by a particular piece, the vibrant pink standing out from the other more muted tones. Reaching out her hand, she stroked the fabric. The color tickled something inside her mind, and she had to press her fists to her eyes to relieve the sharp ache of tears that threatened to emerge.

The moss creature moved from where he had been clinging to her back. Dropping down, he came around to sit on her lap and gently tugged her fist away from her face. Sniffing, she lowered her other hand and looked at him with stinging eyes.

"I'm sad," she whimpered, her forehead furrowed with confusion.

Stretching up, he placed his small hand on the side of her face, caressing her cheek while murmuring unintelligible sounds of comfort.

Faunella let herself be comforted by her small friend, and the two of them sat quietly for a moment. Although she was grateful to not be alone, she couldn't shake the feeling that she was missing something.

A groaning sound broke the silence. The tallest tree creature was emerging from the cave, followed closely by the rock. They made their way over to where she knelt on the ground, concern evident on the face of the tall tree. Surveying the scene quickly, the tree looked at Faunella's upset face and the bundle of clothes still piled on the ground. Extending an arm, he reached out and picked up an item. It was a green suit with holes for legs and little straps that buckled over the shoulders. Rumbling in confusion, he first looked to the moss, who shook his head and pointed over to the large rock currently hiding halfway behind the tree's trunk.

Holding the overalls out to the creature behind him, the tree let out a stream of sharp sounds. Rock looked sheepish and responded by pointing to Faunella.

Faunella couldn't understand what was going on. It seemed like the tree was upset about something.

Is he mad at Rock?

Getting to her feet, Faunella strode over to Tree and jumped as high as she could, just managing to grab the dangling item from his proffered limb.

"That mine," she cried indignantly. "Rock got for me. Don't you be mean to him!"

Walking around to her rock friend, she didn't notice the shocked expression on both their faces, nor the wry amusement on the moss creature's. Coming to stand in front of the rock, she reached her arms as far around his stout body as she could, squeezing the Fae with all the gratitude and protection she could muster.

"Thank you, Rock. I love you."

Rock tentatively snaked his arms around her back, giving her a light squeeze and a pat in return before stepping away to give himself some room.

Faunella smiled and dug back into the mound of clothes, so engrossed that it took her by surprise when she looked up and saw that the whole group of creatures had gathered around her. Her eyes kept straying towards the pale bent tree. She chewed her lip nervously. There was something different about it - the way it looked, or maybe smelled. Despite the strangeness of these creatures, the pale tree stood out as something *other*.

"Tree?" she whispered, turning her face up to the tall tree she felt safest with.

He gave her a gentle smile and offered her one of his leafy limbs. After a week with the creatures, Faunella was getting used to the tree's pretty pictures. She looked up with one more cautious look at the pale tree before eagerly grasping his offered limb.

"Lothian will be pleased with the King's decree. He has spent the most time on Earth out of all of us. It would have killed him to be separated from his beloved humans."

A deep manly chuckle came from her own mouth, and Faunella brought her hands up to her face in the real world. Satisfied that it wasn't her voice, she tuned back into the vision.

"None of us like the decision to close the portals," continued the voice. *"The King made the right decision to break away from the High Fae territories. Realm jumping is who we are, and giving it up is too much to ask."*

"Yeah Violetta, don't pretend that it's just Lothian who will miss the humans. I know how much you love swirling around the waterways hoping to catch a glimpse of human men bathing."

The new speaker was a dark-haired male with heavy eyebrows. His face, though beautiful, was streaked heavily with frown lines. Currently, his mouth was drawn up in a smirk, and his eyes held a teasing glint.

Faunella watched with fascination as the female Fae, Violetta, reached over and smacked the dark-haired male on the arm.

"Cut it out, Huxley! You're such a tease. That only happened once or twice, and you know it." She turned away, a blush staining her pretty cheeks as the whole group erupted into laughter.

Faunella screwed up her nose. *What was a human?* she wondered.

The laughter faded away as the scene cut to a different place. It must have been another day because the group of Fae were dressed differently. They stood just outside a dense forest, their bodies dwarfed by massive trees. Somewhere in the back of her mind, Faunella felt a vague familiarity, but as soon as the thought registered, it fluttered away.

The group spread into a large circle, then stared expectantly at the Fae that Faunella was seeing through. He looked at a slender male before nodding and calling out a name.

"Baeroot."

Upon hearing his name, the Fae started to morph and quickly transformed into a tree. Before Faunella could understand what happened, the tree vanished. Turning slightly to look at the next Fae, he called out again.

"Baol."

This Fae also turned his body into a tree before winking out of existence. The Fae male continued to call out names as he looked around the circle, and one by one, the Fae transformed into various natural things. Faunella stared on blindly as she realized what her tree friend was showing her.

Her young mind couldn't grasp the complexities of the situation, but the visual sight was enough to show her who and what the creatures were. A word danced on the edge of her consciousness, and Faunella stuck the tip of her tongue out until it became clear. These beings weren't creatures. They were Fae.

Paying closer attention, she watched as the last few Fae were called.

"Erwin," the voice called out.

Erwin was much smaller than the others and had a kind, happy face still soft with youth. He bounced around on his toes for a moment before scrunching up his eyes and rapidly shrinking down into a small pile of green moss.

Faunella perked up, recognizing the mossy creature, and ran his name over in her mind so she wouldn't forget.

Erwin, Erwin, Erwin.

Next came the beautiful Fae female, Violetta. She remembered before the female's name was called out. Violetta's transformation was the smoothest Faunella had seen. Her skin rippled delicately as she grew translucent, her body turning into an exact replica of herself, only made of water. Faunellas' skin prickled with delighted recognition. The beautiful water creature was Violetta.

There was only one other Fae standing in the vision with her now. His severe face lifted to look up as he cocked a thick dark eyebrow.

"Just you and me now, Amon? Saving the best for last, are we?" The voice let out a little laugh.

"If that's what you need to tell yourself, Hux, then go right ahead."

Huxley's mouth opened into a toothy smile before he jumped into the air and landed as a heavy boulder. As Huxley disappeared, Faunella felt her vision-self start to vibrate, her bones getting heavy and thick until suddenly she shot up, her vision obstructed by familiar green leaves that dangled in the corners of her eyes.

The pictures left her, and her sight returned to the dim blackness of her closed lids.

Overwhelmed with all the new information, Faunella kept her eyes closed for a few beats before taking a steadying breath and opening them to find herself staring into Violetta's watery face.

"Violetta?" Faunella said hesitantly.

Violetta immediately broke into a beaming smile and vigorously nodded her head, her watery locks sending a misty spray in Faunella's direction. The sides of Faunella's lips pulled up tentatively, and she looked up at the tree beside Violetta.

"Amon?"

The tree also formed a relieved smile and reached out to wrap a branched hand around Faunella's small one, giving her a gentle squeeze. Feeling happier and more confident, Faunella looked around, trying to recognize the other Fae in the clearing. Her whole world was full of possibilities with the simple knowledge of the strange Fae's names.

CHAPTER FIVE
AMON

"**S**O WHAT SHOULD WE do with her?" Baol asked carefully, obviously worried that it was still too soon to discuss the girl.

"We need to do what's best for her," Amon finally replied, tearing his attention away from Fawn, who had gone back to gleefully pawing through the clothes from Huxley.

"And what's that, Amon?" drawled Flavire. "It's been a week now, and I get the impression that you'd rather bury your roots permanently than let her leave your side."

Amon frowned at the antagonistic Fae, a flush heating his face. While Flavire technically wasn't wrong, it still galled him to admit he was right.

"I don't want her to leave either," said Erwin, with confidence he obviously didn't feel.

Amon cleared his throat to hide his smile. "It doesn't matter what I want. All that matters is that we keep her safe from anyone or anything that might harm her."

"We should just jump her back to Amaranth and let Chancellor Petrov care for her until she is of age."

Amon swung around to face Venek, stuttering in his haste to explain the way his bark crawled at the thought of a Fae such as Petrov being entrusted with Fawn.

"He is—we can't," He closed his eyes and took a deep breath, trying frantically to come up with some proof to his unfounded suspicions.

"I don't think the Chancellor will be happy to have her turn up."

The tension up his back lessened with Lothian's careful words. Maybe he wasn't alone in his feelings. He glanced back to Fawn and caught her warily flicking her eyes up at Lothian. She might take a while to warm up to the elderly Fae, but he couldn't blame her. Even among the ancient Fae, Lothian's appearance was concerning. His age had changed him, degrading him to the point of petrification.

"But why?" questioned Erwin. "A good ruler should protect everyone, even if they're different."

Amon's attention snapped back to the conversation at hand, watching as Huxley rolled over to the innocent Fae. "You're too trusting for your own good," the rock murmured while fondly roughing the top of Erwin's head. Erwin smoothed back his fluffed up moss, looking from Huxley to Amon in confusion. Amon blew out a sigh, grateful to have the large rock on his side as what he was about to say could be considered treason.

"I don't think Petrov is a very good Fae," he said as he glanced around. When no one jumped up with outrage, he continued. "Not testing our people as soon as the king died, letting our lands waste away, and seizing the kingdom for himself makes it seem like he would do almost anything to keep power in his grasp." He reached down to ruffle Fawn's hair, tenderness lighting his eyes as she shoved a bright pink beanie onto her tousled red curls. "A Fae like that wouldn't be a good protector for Fawn."

"He speaks the truth," Lothian asserted. "There is no reason other than greed and the desire to rule that would stop a true loyalist from searching out a royal heir. To have let it go on for so long and blindly ignoring our people's decay would indicate Petrov's selfish ambition to remain in power." Staring sadly at the girl, he shook his head. "This child would only be used as a pawn to further his control."

The Fae studied Fawn, their bodies drooping with despair as they got lost in their own thoughts. Huxley's rock fists ground together, sending fine dust swirling to the ground. He turned around and kicked out angrily at a slender tree.

"Ah, ouch!" cried Baol, flinching away with a scowl on his face.

"Oh, sorry. I didn't see you there, Baol," Huxley mumbled, gray cheeks darkening. Baol rubbed at his trunk and retreated several steps away from the volatile rock.

"What if we sent her back to her kingdom?" voiced Violetta, her sheer body undulating as her water nature shifted her appearance from one mood to another. "Madivyre, wasn't it?"

"No, we can't do that," Amon interjected. "Don't forget, it was her blood relative that caused these injuries, and it's highly likely the rest of her family were in on it. What's to stop them from successfully killing her if we send her back?"

Murmured agreements rang out from the group. It seemed like Fawn wouldn't be safe in either kingdom.

Faunella jumped to her feet and skipped over to Flavire, eyeing Lothian warily as she passed.

"Flavire?" she said hesitantly, touching one of the Fae's pink flowers with her dirty fingers.

Flavire's face softened, and he reached out to touch the hat on Fawn's head that perfectly matched his flora.

"She is pretty cute," he admitted. "It would be a shame sending her off to get hurt."

Oblivious to his words, Faunella's smile grew into a wide grin, excitement filling her eyes as she gazed around at the other Fae in the clearing. Amon kept quiet, wondering what she would do. When her eyes landed on Huxley, she gave a small intake of breath and lifted her finger to point at him.

"Huxley," she exclaimed then swung her small finger to Erwin, sprawled on Huxley's stone back. "And Emran?" she questioned, still pointing towards the two Fae.

Amon grasped her hand and quickly repeated the clip of him in his ancient form calling out the young Fae's name, right before he transformed from a gangly teen Fae into his mossy nature form.

"Oh, Erwin!"

"What if she stayed here with us?" blurted Erwin, his hopeful gaze looking around at his fellow Fae. "We could look after her and help her grow big and strong until she's old enough to protect herself."

Amon's breath caught at his friend's suggestion, the idea so similar to the hope in his heart that he couldn't move for fear that the others wouldn't agree. Technically, they could consider sending Fawn to one of the other High Fae kingdoms to ask one of the many High Fae rulers to grant her asylum. It didn't have to be between the kingdom of Madivyre or one of the ancient kingdoms. Amaranth was divided into many territories.

He clamped his mouth shut, not willing to offer another suggestion. There was a connection between him and this lower fae child, a connection he wasn't willing to sever.

"Hello, Erwin." Faunella giggled. "And hello, Huxley." She beamed up at the grumpy rock, who gave a crackling huff in return. Erwin scrambled down and launched himself back into Faunella's lap.

"If we keep her, I won't be the youngest anymore."

"Hmmm," rumbled Lothian, tapping his pale branches against his trunk in consideration. "It could work. We could keep her on Earth until she reaches the age of transformation. She will either develop into a lower fae body or she will emerge as a High Fae, strong enough to protect herself when she returns." He looked around at the Fae surrounding him. "We all need to agree. The decision needs to be unanimous."

"I agree," said Amon immediately, his assent quickly echoed by Erwin, currently being smothered by Faunella's loving arms. One by one, the Fae gave their consent, finalizing the decision that the child would be their responsibility.

Pride swelled in Amon's chest. None of the Fae had let him down. Fawn was now theirs to care for, teach, and protect. Despite his elation, a dash of fear wormed through his mind, bringing with it the image of the humans surrounding their peaceful forest. Amon gritted his teeth. He'd keep her away from The Edge for as long as he could. Fae had no business interacting with the humans, and Fawn's time on Earth was limited. As soon as she was grown, they would take her back to her rightful place in Amaranth.

"So what now?" questioned Huxley.

"Now," replied Lothian, "we raise her and hope nothing goes wrong."

PART TWO

A lower fae contains nothing of consequence. They have no power and no magic to speak of. From what we have observed over the past few centuries, the lower fae are completely unremarkable.

Once these fae reach adulthood, they live out a human length lifespan, in which they have no increased strength, no advanced senses, and no amplified healing abilities.

It bears repeating that one must not judge a lower fae child too harshly. Unlike the fully grown low fae, these children may end up going through a change, a second puberty of sorts, in which the Fae blood takes over and transforms them into worthy members of our society—High Fae.

—Excerpt from *Amaranth, a New Age*

SEVEN YEARS LATER

CHAPTER SIX
FAUNELLA

Faunella's eyes flew open, and she blinked past the blur of sleep still clouding her vision. The dream had been so real. Raising her arm, she brushed away the long strands of hair tangled over her face. The long-ago memory of her early days in the forest remained swirling around in her mind and filling her with a deep sense of nostalgia. *How long has it been?* she pondered, counting back the years since her life in the seemingly endless woodland began.

Shock filled her. She held her hands out in front of her, counting away each year with the flick of a finger. *Has it really been seven years?* Rolling out of bed, she landed lightly on the balls of her feet, her toes scrunching on the smooth planks of wood carefully grown from the bodies of Baeroot and Baol. She thought back over the past. The seasons passed so quickly. After waking up frightened and injured all those years ago, she had settled in quickly among the Fae. However, her natural exuberance and curiosity had soon emerged, and it wasn't long before the confines of the Fae cave became too small for her.

Faunella smiled, walking across to a woven wall and flinging back the richly scented floral covering to reveal her favorite view. The early morning sun was just cresting over the ocean of trees surrounding her home, turning the sky a vibrant gold that highlighted the deep shadows of the unbroken greenery. Closing her eyes, she breathed in the crisp air, feeling the first rays of light flicker over her upturned face.

45

The Fae banded together and built her tree-top home several seasons ago. She giggled, remembering how Huxley had huffed and complained about the change, unable to climb the large tree in his rock form.

Faunella's happiness was abruptly pierced with a strange feeling of emptiness. She frowned. The sensation was happening more and more, coming over her at the most unusual times. Brushing off her restless energy, she stepped back from the window and rushed to get dressed for the day.

There was a bite in the air, so she dressed warmly, pulling on the top and leg coverings the Fae had recently procured for her. Her lips turned down as she surveyed her body. The clothes revealed a fair amount of her wrists and ankles, even when she tugged them down to cover her skin.

When did I get so tall?

Knowing there wasn't anything she could do about her growing body, Faunella left her house and scurried down the towering tree with ease. She debated heading to the grotto for some company but found her legs taking her in the opposite direction, her strides quickly putting distance between her and the Fae.

As she passed over some decaying foliage, a small patch of mushrooms caught her eye. Her hollow stomach echoed loudly, a clear reminder to eat. Wrinkling her nose at the fungi, she found herself brightening up and slightly changing her course to the berry bushes.

Content with her decision, Faunella climbed nimbly over a fallen tree, carefully gripping the slippery wood so she didn't slide down the trunk. Spotting a bright flash of green, she felt a quick flare of satisfaction and hopped over to the patch of small ferns, kneeling down and breaking several flared fronds from each plant. She made sure to not damage the remaining plants, conscious of the need to safeguard the forest.

"Never take more than you need," Amon's creaking voice echoed in her head as she remembered the times he had taken her foraging. She could not understand the words he spoke, but the meaning was clear from his actions and the emotion behind his now familiar tree sounds. Faunella

stood and stacked the picked ferns into her hand, then carefully tucked them into the waistband of her pants, leaving her hands free to navigate the thick undergrowth.

The rest of her journey passed by uneventfully. By the time she reached her destination, her skin was covered in a thin layer of sweat, the coolness of the morning now desired. The sun had broken through the gaps in the trees, warming the air that pressed in on her as she walked. Stopping in front of prickly vines that housed the abundant fruit, Faunella was tempted to take her warm clothes off and just pick the berries in nothing but her underwear. She eyed the sharp thorns warily and quickly decided she would rather endure the heat than suffer the sharp pricks from the plant.

Popping a berry into her mouth, she chewed slowly, enjoying the feeling of the sweet liquid running over her tongue.

"Mmmm," she moaned, savoring the taste for a moment before her lips stretched over her teeth in a cheeky grin. Her hands shot out again in a blur of motion as she picked as many berries as she could, shoving them into her mouth greedily.

After steadily eating for a time, Faunella's hands stilled. A queasy feeling began deep inside, creeping upwards with an uncomfortable pressure. Sinking down to the ground, she placed her stained fingers over her stomach, gingerly rubbing her aching belly. A cooling breath of wind came out of nowhere and blew past her flushed face, easing the worst of her sickness. She let out a relieved breath and pulled the ferns free, absentmindedly weaving the fronds together.

Something broke her concentration, marring the quiet of the day. Faunella cocked her head to the side and paused to listen. Not hearing anything, she continued her work, her hands only stilling when she heard the sound again. Faunella froze and strained her ears, listening for the sound to repeat. A weak rustle sounded a little to the right. Curious as to what could be making the noise, she crawled over and peered into the thick tangle of brambles. This time, movement caught her eye, and she carefully pushed the vines aside, revealing the cause of the rustling.

"Oh!"

Hanging from one of the twisted branches was a small bird. Dropping her makeshift basket, she reached in and grasped the surrounding vines, snapping them with care to make sure they didn't swing back to hurt the struggling bird.

"Now, now, it's alright. I've got you."

As her hand came close to the bird, it let out a little chirp, frantically scrambling to get away until Faunella grasped its small body. Her fingers tightened securely, making it impossible for the bird to move. Realizing that she would need her second hand to free the bird, she sighed and turned her face to the side before she pressed into the mass of green leaves and sharp thorns. Using touch alone, Faunella felt along the bird's soft feathers, feeling for the vine that was wrapped around its body and leg. The bird let out a pained cry when she drew the vine over its foot, and Faunella's eyes burned with tears. The appendage was bent at an unnatural angle. She pushed back from the berry bush in a rush, her concern growing.

She stared down at the injured bird in dismay. While she had saved it from the tangled plant, it was in no way out of danger. The bird lay on its side in her hand, a streak of vivid red blood standing out starkly against the pale white of its underbelly. It watched her, eyes dull against the black and white feathers on its head. Using one finger to stroke at its gray back, Faunella let her tears fall, her heart aching at the creatures suffering.

"I'm so sorry." She sniffed, cradling the bird, its small body fitting easily in her hand.

I think it's just a baby. The thought brought a fresh wave of tears to her eyes, and she keened at the inevitable loss.

Then a thought jolted her from her despair. *What if I can help it?* Now hopeful, her mind worked quickly, running over her options. The first thing she would have to do is to get the bird back to the grotto as soon as possible. She didn't know how long it had been trapped, and it already looked very weak. Then she would have to figure out a way to heal its injuries. It had a wound somewhere on its stomach, and its leg looked really bad.

Faunella suddenly remembered that whenever she had hurt herself in the past, Violetta's water had always made her feel better, taking her pain and dulling it until it was more manageable.

"That's it! Don't worry little bird. I'll help you." Cradling the black and white bird to her chest, she got to her feet and headed for home, the makeshift basket forgotten.

CHAPTER SEVEN
FAUNELLA

B Y THE TIME SHE reached the clearing in front of the cave, Faunella was a sweaty mess. Fearful at hurting the bird, she had cradled it with both hands, making the return journey take twice as long. Stumbling through the final trees, she swayed, her body heavy with relief.

"I found a bird, and it's badly hurt," she called out to no one in particular, hoping that anyone would take charge. She peeled her hands away from her chest, glancing down to check on the bird. She felt a flare of alarm when she saw that its eyes were closed.

"Someone, please help me! It needs help."

Eyes wide, she frantically scanned the clearing, her panic lessening when Huxley, Laurel, and Baol rushed over to where she stood. She thrust her arms out in front of her and showed the Fae the wounded bird, hopeful that they would be able to help. Faunella watched them study the tiny creature, her heart in her mouth. Baol glanced at Huxley, his face morphing from concern to deep sympathy. Faunella gasped and pulled back her hands, hiding the bird from view.

"I thought Violetta could help. She could give it some of her magic water," she pleaded, her voice choking on the last few words, her throat thick with tears. She turned to Huxley. "Please, Huxley, can we try?"

The rock looked at her with his dark eyes for a moment before letting out a grinding sigh and swiveling to look up at Baol. Giving the tree a crunching message, he sighed again, then turned back to Faunella and guided her to sit down in front of the cave. Laurel joined her as Baol headed for the treeline, his pace steady until a sharp crack from Huxley had him leaping into a loping run. Reassured that something good was happening, Faunella ran the back of her hand over her wet eyes and tried to stay calm while waiting for help to arrive.

Before long, Baol strode back into the clearing, followed closely by Violetta. When Faunella saw the water Fae, she shifted to her knees, her eyes hopeful. The Fae rushed over, lowering herself to mirror Faunella's position, the motion creating damp spots on Faunella's pants as their knees pressed together. Unbothered, Faunella lowered her hands to show Violetta her rescued bird.

"They didn't want to help, but I thought you could use your magic to heal it." She stared up into Violetta's face, scanning the female's eyes intently as she watched the thoughts wash over the Fae's expressions. Holding her breath, she didn't move while the Fae deliberated, not wanting to do anything that might cause her to say no.

After what seemed like forever, Violetta looked up from the bird, her eyes softening as she took in Faunella's purpling face. Smiling her approval, Violetta nodded once, then laughed when Faunella let out her breath in an explosive burst. "Thank you, thank you, thank you!"

The Fae motioned for her to keep hold of the little bird, showing her how to cradle it gently with two hands. Once the creature was secure, she held her finger over the crooked leg, letting a gentle stream of water wash over the break.

Faunella gasped when the water dripped off the bird's leg onto her hand. The liquid was warm and light, tingling her skin where it landed. As it rolled off her palm, it left a sparkling clean streak through the dirty skin. Marveling at the sight and feeling of the water, she almost missed the moment the bird opened its eyes. A wiggle against her palms reminded her to keep gripping the bird securely. Warring feelings shot through her as it returned to consciousness. She was concerned that the animal would hurt itself more from struggling but felt relief that it was awake and no longer looked seconds from death. Faunella eyed Violetta desperately, hoping for further instruction. The Fae turned to look at Baol and let out a splashing sound, holding up her thumb and her finger to indicate something very small.

Turning her attention back to the bird, Faunella stared into its shiny eye. A deep longing for the bird to be healed filled her. She wanted it to understand that she was trying to help. Sliding her tongue out, she wet her lips, pressing them together to let out a gentle whistle, hoping to connect with the bird in some way.

At her chirp, the bird cocked its head, looking up at her with a focus that belied its injuries. As the moment stretched out, a warmth grew deep within her stomach, strengthening the longer she kept her gaze connected to the bird. The tingling built up, pressing against the inside of her skin with a writhing energy that begged to escape.

Captivated, she maintained eye contact, hardly daring to blink as she focused on the foreign sensation that she instinctively knew was nothing to fear.

Without warning, the feeling pushed out from beneath her skin, spearing out in a powerful wave that headed directly for the bird.

The tiny creature chirped in surprise, a noise Faunella echoed as a warm embrace of tender magic wrapped around them, tethering them together in an unbreakable connection.

Her mouth fell open, her mind barely able to wrap around what had just happened. The fear from the bird roiled inside her, as if it were her own body conjuring the emotion. Unable to help herself, she fell deeper into the sensation as instinct took over. The cloying feeling was thick and unpleasant, filling Faunella with a shuddering sympathy. The bird was almost completely overtaken by fear. She resisted the urge to let go and release herself from the emotions that were not her own, but a bigger, stronger part of her couldn't let her leave the creature, needing her to stay with the sensation.

She closed her eyes, breaking her visual connection with the bird, allowing her to strengthen the emotional connection between them. She took a deep breath and conjured up her own feelings of peace and safety, holding the emotions in her mind for a moment before sending them out through the thick tether holding the two of them together. Faunella wasn't sure if it would work, but her desire to help the bird was strong enough that she would try anything.

She kept pushing the reassuring emotions into the bird, occasionally feeling for the bird's fear. Before long, the fear was replaced with a cautious curiosity. Faunella opened her eyes and grinned down at the little bird, elated with her success.

"It's okay, little bird. I'm your friend now."

The bird tilted its head at her, its glossy black and white feathers reflecting the sun. It opened its beak and let out a call, its meaning made clear through their connection. The questioning swirl of warmth and safety coiled its way into her belly, and Faunella sent back her confirmation. Satisfied that the bird was calm despite its physical pain, Faunella looked up at Violetta, ready to accept more of the Fae's help. To her surprise, the four Fae gathered around were staring down at her in shock.

"What?" she asked, a little concerned by their reactions. Her head moved around the group, trying to figure out why they were so still.

Oh, maybe they didn't expect Violetta's magic water to work so well.

Faunella grinned up at them smugly. "I told you Violetta could help," she pursed her lips as she reveled in being right. "She only used a little water, and the bird is feeling much better. I didn't know her magic could do all of that though," she added as an afterthought, still amazed by her interaction with the bird.

At Faunella's words, the three Fae looked to Violetta, who was still kneeling in front of her. Huxley let out a questioning crunch, to which Violetta shook her head and pointed her finger at Faunella's chest. Oblivious to her friend's interaction, Faunella, impatient to continue tending to the bird, spoke to Violetta.

"What do we do next?" She held the now calm bird out to the water Fae and looked at her expectantly.

Shooting a bewildered glance at the other Fae, Violetta held her hand out to Baol. The tree passed her two identical twigs, both the same length and thickness of the bird's delicate leg. Motioning for her to hold the bird still again, Violetta mimed that she would have to straighten the broken leg before attaching the supporting pieces of wood.

Faunella bit her lip, sure that the Fae's actions would cause the bird more pain. Trusting the older Fae to know what was best, she secured the bird again, closing her eyes as she attempted to warn what was coming. Even with her warning, the bird still let out an agonized squawk when Violetta straightened its leg. Faunella stifled a small gasp as the matching pain flared in her own leg.

Violetta's hands were swift as she quickly attached the supports to the bird's injured leg. Humming under her breath, Faunella blinked back tears, sending good feelings through to comfort both the bird and herself. Violetta sent her water over the bird's leg again, this time also cleaning the wound on its side. The water washed over the blood-stained feathers until the downy plumage was once again a creamy white.

"Are you finished?"

Violetta cupped her hands in response, bringing them to her mouth to indicate that the only thing left was for the bird to have a drink. Faunella imagined opening her mouth and feeling cool, refreshing water sliding down her parched throat. She sent the feeling to the little bird, holding it with two hands and turning it right side up in preparation for its drink. Looking up to Violetta, she nodded that they were ready.

The water Fae held her hand in front of the bird's face, allowing her water to fill her cupped fingers. The bird hesitantly lowered its beak into the healing liquid, watching Violetta warily as it lifted its head to swallow.

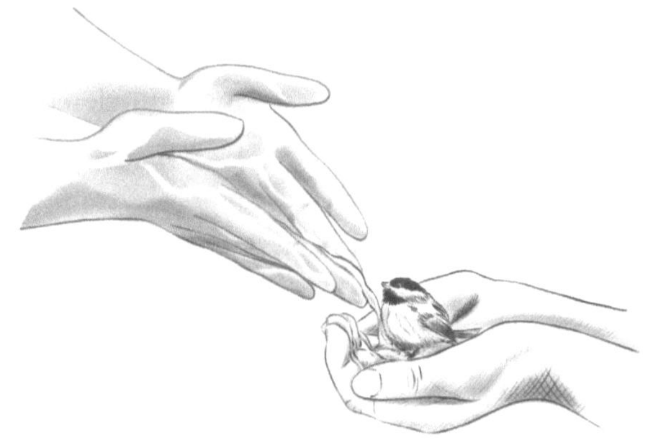

"That's it, good job bird. Have a bit more." Encouraged by Faunella's words, the bird dipped its head several more times, drinking more quickly as its pain lessened and its thirst was quenched.

Faunella looked on happily. The knot of anxiety for the bird was slowly starting to disperse. The bird finished drinking and shook its head to remove the droplets of water still clinging to its beak. Waves of contentment and tiredness flowed from the creature, and she loosened her hands, watching as the little bird tucked its head and its uninjured leg before it settled down to sleep.

"Thanks, Violetta. It's going to be alright now."

Trying not to jostle the bird, Faunella awkwardly got to her feet, stumbling when she was hit with a wave of exhaustion.

"Oh," she breathed, her mouth breaking open in a huge yawn. She hadn't been this tired in a long time. Studying the bird with heavy-lidded eyes, she resolved to figure out how to disconnect from it, convinced it's sleepiness was the reason for hers.

Cradling the sleepy bird to her chest, she made to walk home but quickly realized she couldn't make it that far. She swayed in place for a moment when a soft hand stopped her. Her confusion turned immediately into a grateful smile as Violetta turned her, gently leading her into the cave at her back.

"I think I'll just have a little sleep," she murmured, settling down on her old bed, her mind barely able to grasp reality.

With Violetta's help, she uncovered the mossy layer under the blanket and ripped off a chunk. Molding a slight hollow in the springy plant, she arranged it at the back of a rocky shelf, placing the now sleeping bird in the makeshift nest.

After Violetta left, Faunella lay down, her eyes tracing the cave that had once been her home. As her eyes fluttered shut, she thought of the hollowness that had slowly grown over the years. She wondered if the feeling of missing something was the result of leaving the cave to live on her own, and she hoped that maybe the bird's arrival would fill that place.

CHAPTER EIGHT
DERICK

THE HEAVY THUD OF fists hitting flesh rose above the raucous laughter and jeers of the men around him. Derick stood tall in his place in the circle, face impassive as he waited for their latest recruit to be shoved in his direction. He tightened his fists, mouth grim as he braced himself to hurt the already bloody young man currently stumbling from person to person.

Each initiation he took part in brought back memories from his own recruitment. It was only after several that he realized the men had gone extra hard on him. His father's second, a man named Shaun, had taken over after Frank had been tried for murder and sentenced twenty to life in prison. He rubbed his jaw absentmindedly, feeling the hard ridge of bone from the break he had suffered almost seven years ago after his welcome to gang life.

Motion had him snapping back to reality just in time to see Rhett trip towards him. Before Derick could swing his arm back and take a jab, Shaun's son stepped out of place and roughly kicked Rhett in the side.

"Nice one, Jarred!" called out several of the younger men in the gang, their eyes filled with admiration as they stared at the hunched over Rhett, wheezing on the blood stained basement floor. Jarred puffed out his chest and smoothed back his blond hair before stepping forward again and swinging his fist into the side of Rhett's head. Blood spurted from the new gash on the teen's temple, and he fell to the ground. He raised his arms weakly to try to defend himself against the unrelenting attention Jarred poured on him. Derick swallowed back bile. Seeing people get hurt never got any easier. He stood stiffly in place, watching Rhett whimper with each punch.

He had tried befriending Jarred a few months after he turned sixteen, but unlike him, Jarred had thrived in the gang life, sneering at the softness he detected in Derick.

Jarred straightened up, panting as he gave Rhett one last kick to the stomach.

"Get up, you shit!" he barked, smirking down at the cowering figure. "Initiation's only just begun." Jarred's eyes lit up, and he raised his booted foot, intending to bring it down on Rhett's knee. Unable to witness anymore, Derick launched himself forward, shouldering Jarred out of the way. Unsteady on one foot, Jarred's wiry body crashed heavily to the ground, drawing out pealing laughter from the surrounding men. Ignoring him entirely, Derick sank behind Rhett's back and wrapped him in a headlock, squeezing tightly. Within six seconds, he was out.

Stilling his quivering limbs, he released the unconscious teen, letting him slump to the ground. Then, carefully erasing any trace of his true feelings off his face, he stood.

"I'm sorry," he shrugged, nonchalantly wiping a smear of blood off his forearm. "Those pathetic noises were giving me a headache." Raising his eyebrow, he stared down the circle of men, hoping that no one would hear his frantic heartbeat. When he met Shaun's gaze, he was startled to see a hint of admiration pass over his weathered face.

"What the fuck was that?"

Derick turned to Jarred, holding back a groan at the livid expression on the other man's face.

"What was what?" Derick bit back, spreading his legs and drawing himself up to his greater height. At nineteen, Derick was taller and broader than most of the fully grown men in the Sea Dragons gang, and still growing. His mother had been slight, and his father was short and stocky, so Derick often wondered where his size had come from.

"You pushed me!"

The men around them snickered, and Derick let a sly smile grow on his face. Jarred had left himself wide open, giving him the perfect opportunity to put him in his place.

"I pushed you?" He turned away, shaking his head in disbelief. "What are you, five years old? Grow up, Jarred."

As expected, Jarred went bright red and lunged towards his turned back with raised fists. Nimbly stepping to the side, Derick stuck out his foot, tripping Jarred and sending him to the ground for the second time that night.

"All right boys, that's enough."

Shaun stepped forward, glancing at Jarred with disgust as he scrambled to his feet, shuddering with undisguised fury.

"Jarred, head outside and cool off before you embarrass yourself any further."

"But Dad!"

"I said fuck off!"

Derick swallowed dryly and ran his hand over the brown curls on top of his otherwise shaved head. Perhaps he shouldn't have riled up Jarred the way he had. He kept his face blank as Jarred stormed past and shot him a venomous glare that promised retribution.

Shit.

"Initiation's over. Get about your business."

At Shaun's words, the men quickly dispersed, heading out into the night to either drink, steal, or fuck. Probably all three.

"Shaun, I—" he started, intending to make up some story that might convince Shaun he was as cutthroat as any other member of the gang and deferential to Shaun's leadership, but Shaun raised his hand, cutting off any of the words he might have spoken.

"I took you under my wing when Frank got put away," Shaun started. "Out of respect for your father." His eyes were cold, staring hard at him in a way that sent a shiver down his spine. "I've treated you like my own son. But, I think you've forgotten one important thing." He paused, stepping close enough that Derick could see the salt and pepper in his hair. He wrapped his hand around the back of Derick's neck, gripping it firmly. "I know you've been visiting Frank every month, but this is my gang now—not your father's, and not yours. If you can't remember that, then you're no good to me."

The pressure from Shaun's hand felt like a collar around his neck, reminding him that no matter what he did, he was tied to this life. He attempted to tamp down his resentment, keeping his voice carefully neutral as he answered.

"Of course, Shaun. You're the boss. I'd never question that."

He bowed his head to hide his flashing eyes, lowering himself in submission to the man who held his life in his hands. He'd seen what had happened to people who were no longer useful to Shaun.

"Good."

Shaun let him go and walked over to where Rhett lay on the ground.

"I think you can be in charge of making sure our latest member gets cleaned up. After all, you were the one who stopped his initiation early."

Spinning on his heel, Shaun sauntered off, leaving Derick more alone than ever.

CHAPTER NINE
AMON

A MON STUCK HIS HEAD into the cave for the third time in the past hour. Fawn was still curled up fast asleep, her hand pressed under her cheek. She was likely drained from the massive amount of power she had produced earlier that afternoon. He couldn't believe Fawn manifested magic.

He looked up at the shelf above her bed. The young chickadee Fawn rescued was awake. Unmoving, it gazed down at Faunella, totally unafraid and making no move to escape. Shaking his head, he left the cave, making a mental note to get the bird something to eat if it stuck around for much longer.

Amon rejoined the group who had assembled under the starlit sky in the clearing.

"She's still asleep. I think she will stay like that all night if you're right about how much power you felt coming from her."

"You wouldn't doubt it if you were here when it happened." Violetta shook her head in disbelief. "I've never seen such a display, not from the Ancient Fae children or the High Fae's young."

"But she's a lower fae. Lower fae don't have any powers."

Baeroot ran his branched hand across his face, still in disbelief despite the reassurances from Baol beside him.

"Violetta's right," Huxley said. "Laurel and I both saw it as well. Fawn was staring at the bird when a surge of power pulsed out of her and into the creature. You could almost see the connection between them. She closed her eyes, and the bird calmed down, allowing Violetta to put a splint on its leg." Amon looked at Laurel, who nodded her agreement.

Lothian shuffled over and clasped him on the shoulder. "I don't think you can deny that Fawn has magic much more powerful and advanced than what she should have as a lower fae." He drew Amon forward until he and the other Fae formed a large circle. "The moon is full, and we had planned to gather tonight to discuss what to do about the child's speech."

Amon stood quietly, allowing Lothian to take charge for now. He had been thinking over the past fortnight about what they could do to improve Fawn's speech. The years hidden away in the forest with only the Fae's nature sounds to listen to had given Fawn an unintended speech impediment. She had slowly begun to incorporate their sounds within her normal words. The Fae could understand her perfectly, but when she eventually returned to Amaranth, she would be at a disadvantage. He ran his hand over the leaves on his head. Now, they also had the unexpected complication of her power.

Lothian blinked his cloudy eyes at each of the waiting Fae. Despite Amon's objections, the time had come to decide if they were going to allow Fawn to observe the humans.

Amon steadied his nerves and took a deep breath, reminding himself that whatever they agreed on, Fawn's life was not only his responsibility. He had to try to relinquish his need for control.

"However," Lothian continued, "I believe the appearance of a magic she shouldn't possess warrants gathering more information regarding her heritage. We need to return to Amaranth."

Amon's mouth fell open. Of all the things Lothian could have said, returning to Amaranth was the last thing he expected.

"Why Amaranth? What good will that do?" His heart pounded. "We would be actively disobeying Chancellor Petrov."

Huxley coughed into his hand and mumbled, "You mean usurper Petrov."

Erwin snickered, the sound abruptly cutting off when Amon shot him a sharp look. "This is nothing to joke about, you two. Are you telling me that you believe Fawn would be safe back on Amaranth, either with Petrov or her own family?"

"Calm down, Amon," drawled Flavire, seemingly unbothered by the tension that flooded the clearing. "After hiding her away for seven years, we're not about to throw her back into the arms of her abuser," he scoffed. "There's no way any of us would put Fawn anywhere near the Fae responsible for allowing our own lands to wither away."

Lothian held up his pale branches, gesturing for silence.

"There was never a question of returning the child to the kingdom of her birth or to our own lands. The fates allowed this century's hibernation to end at precisely the right time for Amon to check in back on Amaranth, where he discovered King Chalanour's death and the seizure of power by usurper Petrov."

Huxley snickered. "Usurper Petrov. See? It has a nice ring to it." He bumped his shoulder into the tree next to him, flushing hotly when instead of the tree Fae he expected, he discovered a regular Earth trunk. Too anxious to find amusement in Huxley's display, Amon rolled his eyes, then turned his attention back to Lothian, who continued as if nothing had happened.

"For this to happen at the same moment that a child from another kingdom was being violently attacked? It was meant to be."

Amon let out a breath, his leaves standing on end at the timing of it all. He could still feel the toxic soil on his roots from the moment he had jumped back into the South Forest all those years ago and the horror of discovering their king's death, subsequently leaving the Ancient Fae with no true ruler to hold the life force of their lands or people in check. He shook his head, clearing away the memories, and thanked the fates that he had been sent Faunella.

"A lower fae child should have no power. None at all. But she does." Lothian's voice held a quizzical tone. "We know barely anything about her early years. We only know what Amon revealed to us the day she arrived, and that should have no effect on this unexpected magic." A high-pitched groan left his body as he adjusted his position. "Though, she is from the Kingdom of Madivyre." He frowned slightly. "I want to know who her family is. It might give us a clue to why she's so strong." He looked around the group, his filmy eyes probing. "Only one of us is needed for this mission."

A heavy weight settled low in Amon's center. The Fae around him murmured quietly to themselves, excited for one of them to return to Amaranth for something other than reporting information to the Tree of Conalt. However, he shifted uncomfortably, wondering how it was possible to have made such an oversight.

"Are you okay?"

Huxley's voice had the unfortunate effect of drawing everyone's gaze to him. Amon gave a nervous chuckle, feeling a hot flush of embarrassment run over his body.

"I said there was something special about her. Something marked her as different."

All he got back were blank stares.

"I didn't think it mattered, but perhaps it's part of the reason she has power."

Huxley frowned at him and swung out an arm, giving the side of his trunk a quick jab.

"Get to the point, Amon. What do you know?"

Giving a weak, lopsided grin, Amon closed his eyes, cursing himself for not looking into it years ago.

"Fawn came from the direction of the palace and might be some sort of relation to their royal family."

The cries of disbelief made Amon flinch back.

"I know, I know," he cried, holding out his twig-like hands. "I'm sorry. I thought I had mentioned it, but with everything that happened that night, it didn't seem important."

"How do you not mention something like that, you great lump of wood?"

Huxley threw up his arms, small chips of stone splintering and flinging from his body.

"It's okay," piped up Erwin, giving him a small smile. "You just forgot. Anyone could have."

Lothian wearily shook his head. "Even so, royal blood should have no impact on a lower fae's abilities. Low fae have no magic. Though perhaps there is something..." He trailed off, lost in thought. As the silence lengthened, Flavire snickered, his floral body bobbing up and down. Even with the gravity of the situation, Amon felt his own mouth twitching. Lothian was showing the effects of his lengthy life. Giving a little cough, Amon subtly reached out a limb and placed it on Lothian's trunk.

"Lothian?"

"Ah, yes. Where was I?" Lothian shook himself and looked around the group. "We should still send someone to confirm." His eyes landed on Violetta. "Since we will have to venture into Madivyre, I would suggest that you go, my dear."

"Me?" Her large, clear eyes blinked in surprise.

"Yes, you." His mouth curved up at the corners. "Stealth is needed, and your fluid form should be the most successful."

Violetta preened at the compliment, her lips pursing into a smug smile.

Amon bit back the argument that he should go instead. But as much as he would like to be in charge of the mission, he knew that Lothian was right. Violetta was the best choice.

"He couldn't have picked better." He stepped forward and clapped a hand on her shoulder. "Your journey will take hours, so while you're gone, we could discuss Fawn's speech. Could you quickly tell us your stance on the issue before you go?"

Her cheeks drew back into a wide smile. Darting her eyes around, she found Huxley.

"I'll side with whatever Huxley decides."

Then, with a saucy wink, she jumped from this realm, leaving nothing but a fine mist of water behind.

Amon couldn't keep the smile off his face as he turned to his friend. Huxley's gray cheeks had darkened with color, his eyes glued to the rapidly evaporating water Violetta left behind.

"Well Hux, now that you have the voting rights of two Fae, do you also have an opinion on what we should do about Fawn?"

Huxley swung his eyes to meet Amon's, grinning sheepishly up at him.

"Sorry, Amon. I know she needs to observe the humans to improve her speech, but as for how to keep her safe and when we should do it, I have no idea." He shrugged his shoulders.

CHAPTER TEN
Huxley

HUXLEY HAD NO IDEA how they expected him to think about anything after the look Violetta just gave him. He subtly moved over to the empty space left behind, closing his eyes as the soft mist touched on his heated rock.

A gentle cough caught his attention, bringing him back to the conversation at hand. He cleared his throat, hoping no one had noticed his distraction.

"Yes, Flavire? You have a suggestion?"

Amon's words were curt, his smile from moments before nowhere to be seen. Huxley's lips twitched at Amon's weak attempt at hiding his disdain for the floral Fae. His amused eyes found Erwin's across the clearing. The moss Fae cringed subtly, the movement unnoticeable unless someone looked directly at him. None of the other Fae had reacted, and Huxley wondered if he and Erwin were the only ones who knew Amon well enough to notice the snub.

Flavire nodded before turning and addressing the other Fae.

"When it comes to Fawn, I think Amon and a few others are being too cautious."

Huxley jerked back, his amusement evaporating. Flavire obviously meant him, but he wasn't known for being cautious. *Amon, on the other hand,* he thought as he took in Amon's tightening jaw.

"If we let Fawn observe the humans now, she'll have the benefit of being young enough to more easily learn their speech. If we wait, it will only be much harder for her." Several Fae voiced their agreement with Flavire.

Emboldened, he continued. "Also, we won't be letting her go to The Edge alone. One of us will always be with her." He flared his thick floral robe. "We can even figure out a unique way to hide her with our bodies and camouflage. Honestly, I'm surprised we haven't done that already."

A familiar tightness began growing through Huxley's body. He tried to ignore it and arched a brow at Flavire. The Fae made a good point, though there wasn't much Huxley could do to help Fawn. His hand clenched and unclenched, his power in the very foundation of his make-up. As the discussion swirled around him, he blew out a breath, restless from all this talk and unable to contain it any longer.

"This is all pointless," he blurted, the words escaping him in a rush. "All we ever do is talk."

The conversation stilled, the clearing going silent but for a choking snort from Venek. But Huxley couldn't care less.

"Look, Amon, I know you're worried about our Fawn. We all are."

In our own ways.

"But the fact of the matter is she needs more from us than we've given her. If she has any chance of living a successful life when she returns to Amaranth, then she needs to be able to talk." He paused, guilt momentarily overtaking his frustration at Amon's hurt expression.

"For that, she needs the humans," Amon finished for him with a resigned sigh.

Huxley crossed the clearing to his tall friend, knowing how hard that was for him to admit. He slapped his hand against Amon's wide back, hoping to convey the feelings he couldn't express with words.

"I'll leave the decision to the rest of you, but it's going to be a long night waiting. I need to move."

He strode for the treeline, eager to push his body, to release the tension that he never seemed to expel for long.

"Wait, I'll come with you."

Erwin darted towards him, his dark eyes worried. Without knowing it, the young Fae often helped Huxley through his dark moods. Giving him the space to do what he needed to do, accepting all his rough edges with a laugh. However, tonight he had a plan that he needed to complete alone.

Huxley waved him away, disappearing into the forest with a single-minded focus, and one word on his lips— Faunella.

The biting smell of asphalt was sharp and bitter, invading his senses as he inched across the quiet street. Huxley kept low, shaping his body into nothing more than a large rock. The moonless sky was a lucky coincidence, helping him hide from any stray humans but in no way impairing his own Fae vision.

"Finally," he grumbled under his breath. "That took forever."

The convenience store was dark, lit up only by the gaudy neon lights in the boxes that kept the humans' drinks cold. Huxley rolled the last few feet, straightening up with his back tight against the side of the building, his heart pounding in his chest.

Cocking his head, he took in the sounds from Northaven's city center, far away from his position on the outskirts. The hum and whir of distant traffic highlighted the desertion around him.

Huxley's tension melted away, his frown smoothing out into a crooked smile as excitement raced through him.

"Sorry, Amon, I know I said I wouldn't leave The Edge again."

With splayed fingers, he pressed his palm against the concrete wall, euphoria filling him as he accessed his power for the first time in years. He let out a tight breath, finishing the excuse that he would be forced to repeat later.

"But I'm doing this for Fawn."

The concrete began to shake, the minuscule movements vibrating faster and faster until the wall at his back was no firmer than a body of water.

Huxley eased backwards, melting into the building until he reappeared on the gray linoleum floor. The moment his body was clear, the wall solidified, returning to its original matter with no sign of tampering. He chuckled, wriggling his fingers as the remnants of magic faded.

"Too easy."

As the words left his mouth, a steady blinking to his right caught his attention.

He let out a crunching growl and dropped to the floor, thrusting his hands onto the linoleum with one frantic motion. *He* forgot about the damn cameras.

Power erupted from him, tearing through every molecule that stood in his way. He closed his eyes and let himself feel the matter around him, seeking out the electronic red eyes that recorded his existence. With a final thought, he turned solid to liquid, melting wires and allowing them to run freely until not even he could put the technology back into its rightful form.

The steady hum in the store cut off, all the night lights shutting down with a pop. Huxley opened his eyes, sheepishly gazing around at the evidence of his destruction. In his haste, he had destroyed all the electronics, not just the building's security system.

"Whoops."

Scratching his jaw, he slowly got back to his feet. "Amon doesn't need to know about this." He grimaced at a blackened puddle of metal pooling by the register. "I mean, it could have happened to anyone."

Passing through the rows of shelving, Huxley hurried to find what he was looking for, his internal clock urging him to return to the grotto in time for Violetta's arrival. He scanned each shelf, using his senses to smell for the present he knew Fawn would love. At last, he came to a wide display stacked high with brightly colored items.

Though it wasn't possible in this body, his mouth seemed to water. The familiar scent brought back memories of his time back on Amaranth, when he could indulge as often as he liked.

His mind snagged on Violetta, her shimmering curves and laughing smile. He shook away the image, convincing himself that the only reason he wanted to be able to access his Fae body was to enjoy the sensation of eating, not any other pleasure currently off limits due to his nature form.

Ready to leave, Huxley plucked his present for Fawn off the shelf, his cheeks heating with pleasure at the joy she would experience. Back in their realm, it was customary for Fae to receive a gift when they accessed their magic for the first time. He grimaced slightly at the thought. The present was usually gifted by the child's closest relative.

Closing his eyes, he pictured Fawn's bouncing curls and freckled cheeks. Though he wasn't her relative, they were connected, and no one could deny that.

A rhythmic rumble began at his feet, traveling through the earth before the sound registered in his ears. Unconcerned, Huxley moved to the side of the store, waiting for the traffic to pass by so he could leave unseen. It was only when the deafening motors reached a fever pitch, then abruptly cut off, that a surge of annoyance ran through him.

Humans were outside the store.

Glass shattered, sending thousands of shards pelting the floor in a crunching shamble. Huxley's eyes sharpened in the darkness, his focus entirely on the leather clad men shouldering through the fragmented door. His very being recoiled against their presence. He counted them quickly.

Three.

In the night behind them, the way looked clear. So when the third man stepped through the entrance, Huxley turned the side wall to liquid and left the same way he arrived, moving more quickly as early morning birds began to signal the upcoming dawn.

CHAPTER ELEVEN
DERICK

"I'M SO HUNGRY THAT I could eat a whole pig on a spit, right down to its piggy tail."

Rhett took off his helmet and ran his fingers through his dark waves before hanging it loosely on his handlebars. Derick chuckled, pausing for a moment to listen to the hollow gurgle in his own belly. He jerked his head to the three men with them, Jarred included.

"I'm so hungry that I can stomach Jarred's company."

Rhett followed his gaze, his blue eyes dark in the inky blackness.

"I still don't know why he hates you so much." He lay back on his bike, crossing his arms behind his head with a smirk. "You're only a piece of shit half the time."

"Asshole."

"Exactly!"

Laughing, Derick shook his head and dismounted, placing his helmet carefully on his seat. The night had been long but successful. Several of the gang had made their way to the next city over, completing a big job for Shaun. Surprisingly, things had gone smoothly, even with Jarred's involvement. In fact, things with Jarred had been a little too good this trip. He ran his hand up the back of his head and smoothed down the longer brown strands on top, trying not to let Jarred's lack of vehemence worry him.

"Okay, let's go before the others take all the good stuff."

Derick strode towards the broken door, pushing down the hint of guilt that flared for the damage and theft of the convenience store. He glanced back over his shoulder and called out to Rhett. "You coming?"

Rhett stood stock still, his entire focus on the side of the building.

"Rhett?"

His words finally registered. Rhett whipped his head around to face him, his eyes wide and face pale. Derick's top lip curled, amusement filling him.

"You look like you've seen a ghost. Surely one all-nighter hasn't addled your brain that much?"

Rhett didn't so much as blink.

"I saw—I could have sworn..." His voice cut off, and he swallowed roughly, whipping his head back to take another look. Bemused, Derick retraced his steps, walking past Rhett until he could see the entirety of the concrete wall all the way down the side of the store. There was nothing there.

"It's gone."

Derick laughed and threw his arm around Rhett's neck, dragging him back towards the front.

"The only thing that's gone is your sanity."

Rhett gave a weak chuckle and let himself be dragged along.

"You might be right," he shook his head briskly, as if banishing the image from his mind. "I was just so sure." He cut off, letting his mouth stretch into a wide smile as the two of them stepped into the store, their booted feet crunching on the scattered glass. "Nah, there's no way."

Now curious, Derick released Rhett and began picking through the confectionery, snagging several bars of his favorite chocolate.

"So, what did you think you saw?" he asked, glancing over to make sure Jarred was out of earshot. The last thing he wanted was for him to hear and have a reason to bully Rhett. As if sensing his gaze, Jarred's eyes met his, but like every other time tonight, Jarred smiled, the sinister grin so much worse than the glare he usually gave.

"I couldn't be sure, because it was pitch black, but..." Rhett ducked his head, color filling his cheeks.

"But?" Derick prompted, fighting to keep his face still.

"It was this man—this creature." The words tumbled from his mouth, almost frantic in nature. "One moment, there was nothing but a wall, and then there was this chunky shape." Derick's brows rose, unable to hide his surprise, but Rhett carried on without pause, his chest rising and falling quickly. "It started to run, its arms and legs swinging, and then, all of a sudden, it leapt. And when it landed?" His wide eyes finally met Derick's. "It was a rock."

"A rock?" This time he didn't fight his smile. "You've been reading too many comics."

A fleeting look of disappointment flashed across Rhett's face, covered swiftly by a sheepish shrug. Derick's smile wavered. He was sorry he'd asked. Rhett didn't usually let things get to him; his easy-going, light-hearted nature meant things often rolled right off his back. Derick was the serious one out of the two of them.

"Don't worry. I'll protect you if he comes back," Derick promised as he threw a candy bar at Rhett in an attempt to lighten the mood. The answering volley of items was proof he had succeeded.

"Come on you two. Shaun's waiting for us."

Derick nodded at the man and headed towards the door.

"Hold up," called Rhett. "I'm just going to check if there's any cash."

Pausing at the exit, Derick waited as Rhett jogged over to the register. Dawn was blooming on the horizon, so he was able to clearly see the moment the surprise returned to Rhett's face.

"What the fuck?"

Derick straightened up, trying to see what Rhett was studying so intently.

"What is it?"

"The register's fucked." He gave it a few slaps with his palm, utterly bewildered. "The damn thing is totally mangled. It's melted all over the place."

The bikes started up their roar from outside, a clear message to get moving. Derick waved them away, then casually scratched his head, lips trembling as he once again tried to hold in his laughter. He locked eyes with Rhett and finally let his cheeks spread, baring his teeth in the biggest grin he could manage.

"You know what happened, don't you?"

"What?" Rhett frowned, thoroughly confused.

Derick waited for a moment before methodically pulling his expression into one of total seriousness.

"I bet the rock man did it."

The deadpan look Rhett gave him had Derick throwing his head back and roaring with laughter. He ducked out the door, narrowly missing getting hit by the handful of items flung his way.

"How'd it go?"

Despite the early hour, Shaun was up and waiting, with no hint of fatigue on his face. Derick's shoulders automatically stiffened as he slipped in behind the other men, entering the oppressive building he called home. The night had been long, and although being away from Northaven had brought a sense of freedom, it also reinforced his distaste for the gang's activities.

Eager for sleep, Derick pushed to the front of the group, forcing his face into an arrogant smirk.

"It went well. We got the shipment and successfully split it up. It's now on its way to our distributors."

Shaun nodded, the assent more powerful than words.

"Any interference?"

Derick opened his mouth to respond, knowing once Shaun got the all clear, they would be released. However, Jarred beat him to it.

"No cops and no other gangs, but—" Jarred slunk his way to Derick's side, his gaze never straying from Shaun. "I couldn't be sure the drugs weren't tampered with."

Surprise lit Derick up from the inside. *Where the hell did that come from?* He turned to face Jarred fully, narrowing his eyes at the slender man.

"What makes you say that?" Shaun's voice was steady, calm even, if not for the bite behind his words.

Jarred's gaze shot to him for a split second, the barest hint of a smile tugging at the corner of his mouth before quickly smoothing back into a picture of innocence. A churning began in his gut, swirling tightness that intensified as moments from last night flashed through his mind - the calculating smiles, the shifting eyes.

Derick clenched his teeth together. He was innocent, but that wouldn't matter if Jarred had set him up.

"I don't want to point fingers." Jarred angled his head towards him more pointedly this time. "Maybe we should talk in private."

From behind him, Derick heard Rhett suck in a breath, which was immediately swallowed by the other men's confused murmuring.

Yeah, not so subtle, asshole.

Shaun had picked up on the accusation as well. He ran his hand over his face, then jerked his head towards the back rooms.

"You lot, piss off. Derick." Shaun's eyes bore into him, his mouth grim. "You and Jarred stay behind."

All the men but Rhett filed out instantly. His friend hesitated at the door, his pale face pinched with worry. Derick's heart softened, touched by Rhett's concern, but he couldn't show any weakness, especially not now. So when Rhett made to step back towards them, Derick hardened his face and shook his head. There was no way he'd let Rhett get dragged into this mess. However, Rhett kept coming, his face set in determination. He opened his mouth, his focus shifting to Shaun.

Derick's pulse hammered in his throat. Shaun did not take kindly to his orders being disobeyed. Rhett, the misguided fool, was about to bring a shit ton of trouble down on himself unless Derick did something.

"Rhett!" he barked, striding past Shaun to grasp Rhett's arm. "Get your fucking head on straight." Swinging the man around, he marched him back to the door, inwardly crying out for Rhett to understand and forgive him.

"When Shaun gives you an order, you do it with no questions asked." He thrust him through the door, cuffing him on the back of the head as he stumbled into the next room. "Got it?"

Derick didn't wait for an answer. He slammed the door in Rhett's hurt face and prayed that his little performance had been enough. But, the game wasn't over yet. Taking a deep breath, he swung back to Shaun and Jarred, smoothing his face into boredom.

Shaun chuckled, his brows raised high, while Jarred looked on with a sour expression.

Derick shrugged. "I like the guy, but he needs to learn some respect."

Jarred's face twisted into a snarl. "He's not the only one."

At that, all the humor left Shaun's face, replaced with an almost tired frown.

"What's this all about, Jarred? Stop dancing around it and get straight to the point."

Anxiety coiled through Derick's body as he waited for the axe to fall. He was under no illusion that this would pan out well for him.

"Before the shipment left, I saw Derick come out of one of the trucks. He was acting suspicious, so I followed him and saw him slip something down the side of his bike."

Derick closed his eyes, heart dropping. Theft of product was a death sentence.

"Derick?"

Sweat poured from his body, weakening him and leaving him dizzy. What should he do? Confess to a crime he didn't commit, or tell Shaun the truth and hope to survive?

In the end, it didn't matter.

He popped open his eyes just in time to see the fist before it smashed into his jaw.

"I knew I was too easy on you."

Pain arched through his head as Shaun followed through with a back hand, catching him straight across the cheekbone. Derick caught himself before he fell, straightening up and bracing for the next shot to his stomach.

Shaun hadn't even waited to find the drugs Jarred planted on his bike. He had taken his son's word as proof, not even considering for one moment that Derick could be innocent.

A hot surge of anger overcame his fear, fighting to override the instinct to bow down and take his punishment. Shaun must have seen the defiance in his eyes because instead of another fist, he slid a knife from his back pocket.

"Don't even think of doing anything funny." His eyes were cold, any admiration or fondness he had once shown for Derick replaced by pure steel. He gestured the knife at a ratty sofa along the wall. "Sit."

Derick collapsed onto the seat, keeping his chin high and feigning confidence he didn't feel.

"Jarred, watch him." Shaun jerked his head at Derick and left out the front door, leaving him alone with Jarred.

Derick knew he could overpower the other man easily. He was taller, broader, and stronger. But then what? His anger simmered. Where would he go? What would he do? He didn't know anything else but the gang. For all that he hated it, this was the only life he had ever known.

Jarred sneered at him, his eyes glinting maliciously.

"You think you're better than me. But after today, you won't be any-thing. You'll be dead."

Swallowing the fear of the truth of Jarred's words, Derick resolved to keep his brave front on, right until the last moment.

"Even dead, I'm better than you." He leaned back and crossed his arms over his chest, feeling the muscles flex. "You're just mad that Daddy likes me better."

Jarred's face turned bright red, and he lunged forward, intending to grab Derick by the shirt front. As quick as a snake, Derick whipped his leg up and kicked into Jarred's chest, sending him flying back onto the ground, gasping for air.

"What the fuck, Jarred?" Shaun stood at the entrance, disgust curling his lip. "I asked you to watch him for less than a minute."

Jarred scrambled to his feet, chest heaving. He adjusted his jacket and smoothed down the greasy strands of blond hair that fell over his face.

"He was trying to escape," he lied.

Derick ignored the jab. At this point, it couldn't get worse for him. He watched Shaun approach, trying to interpret the look on his face.

Holding up his hand, Shaun let the clear baggy dangle from his fingers.

"No one gets away with stealing from me. Not even you."

This was it. The knife glinted in Shaun's other hand, demanding his attention even as he fought to keep his eyes on Shaun. He pushed to his feet.

I'll die standing.

Maybe it was better this way, after all the hurt he'd caused - the death of that guard all those years ago, allowing his father to take the fall, and everything since. All of it.

He tried to quell the shaking in his legs and tamp down the desire to flee or fight. Even though he was innocent in this, he was guilty of so many other crimes.

Shaun stopped in front of him, so close that if he took a deep breath, their chests would touch. Derick's mouth went dry. He deserved punishment, but he didn't want to die.

"This…" Shaun's whisper was filled with gravel. He gripped Derick's shoulder and held him firm. "…is for your father."

Derick's body jolted, curving around the thrust of the knife before the pain registered. A gasp tore from his mouth as he sucked in a lungful of air.

Fuck.

His lungs were on fire, tearing him apart from the inside out. The white-hot agony cut through him, burning hotter and hotter with each ragged breath.

Without meaning to, Derick clapped his arm to his side, pushing against the wound as if the pressure could take away the flaming sensation.

Shaun stepped back, wiping the blood-streaked knife on his arm as he retreated.

"Don't worry," he breathed. "You'll live this time."

Derick jerked his head up, wondering if the ringing in his ears was affecting his hearing.

"But dad, he—"

"Shut the fuck up, Jarred." Shaun didn't take his attention off Derick as he berated his son. Instead, his eyes narrowed, and his words filled with ice, leaving Derick with no doubt that what he said was true.

"You get one chance. One more slip up, even a hint of disobedience, and the only thing you'll be good for is a wooden box."

Derick nodded, his pain fading to a steady ache with the knowledge that it wasn't a killing blow.

They left him covered in his own blood and bewildered at the sudden turn of events. He would heal, and things would go back to normal. Gritting his teeth, he inched his way to his room, trying to decipher the quiet feeling deep in his belly.

He would live—but for what?

CHAPTER TWELVE
AMON

Dawn had well and truly arrived by the time Huxley rolled back into the clearing.

"Is she back yet?" he blurted, scanning the area quickly.

Amon lay back against a neighboring tree, absentmindedly weaving pieces of grass with flowers. He kept his fingers moving steadily so as not to alert Huxley to his suspicions. God, he hoped he was wrong. With his attention on his work, Amon answered, trying to keep the frustration out of his voice.

"No Hux, Violetta still hasn't arrived." He drew in a calming breath, wanting nothing more than to demand to know where Huxley had been.

"Good." Huxley brushed himself down, glancing back over his shoulder casually before flicking his eyes over to Amon. When he caught him looking, Huxley gave a brisk chuckle, the nervous sound and shifting eyes confirming what Amon and the other Fae suspected.

"What's going on?"

Huxley finally noticed the stillness of the group. His gaze jumped from Fae to Fae, his obvious confusion growing when all he received were averted eyes, except for Flavire's face filled with disgust.

"What's wrong?" Huxley backed away with a frown. "Why are you all behaving this way?"

Amon let out a sigh. This had gone on long enough.

"Erwin."

He nodded his head north, sending the young Fae out to retrieve the proof. When the Fae heard Huxley drawing closer, Amon had honed in on his movements, intending to use Huxley's arrival as some sort of game to break up the monotony of waiting for Violetta. But as he relayed his positioning, Huxley made a sharp detour, pausing for a few moments before continuing onwards.

"Where did you go, Huxley?"

Huxley opened his mouth, then paused and scanned their faces one more time.

If it wasn't for the potential danger, Amon would have found it comical. Huxley's face tightened, switching from one emotion to the next in rapid succession—surprise, sheepishness, defiance, and then finally landing on anger.

"She has magic!" He exploded, throwing up his arms with a thunderous crunch. "You lot kept focusing on the fact that Faunella is a lower fae, and she shouldn't even have magic. Well, that doesn't matter to me." His arms came down to cross in front of his chest and he sent Amon a hurt glare. "She's just a little girl. She's our little girl, and she deserves something special to mark the occasion." He looked to the ground and mumbled, "Even if she doesn't understand the significance."

Erwin chose that moment to come bouncing back into the clearing with a chocolate bar held aloft in his small, stubby hand.

"I found it," he cried. "It still carries the scent from the city." He stopped short and gave Huxley a sheepish look. "Sorry Hux, I didn't want you to get in trouble."

"Well, he's going to be." Flavire swished his fauna angrily. "We all agreed to follow the rules when we came here. You can't just do as you please, and no one is allowed to cross The Edge. Especially not a reckless rock like you!"

Amon inwardly groaned. He absolutely hated agreeing with Flavire, but the Fae was right. When Fawn needed clothes or other items from outside the forest, they carefully planned and hunted for them along the forest's edge, usually sending Erwin or Violetta for the retrieval. Huxley was just too big. Amon tamped down his annoyance and tried to remind himself that while Huxley often broke the rules, his heart was in the right place.

"I've told you this before, Huxley," he began. "You can't just decide to leave The Edge, no matter your reasons. You've got to stop doing this. What if one of the humans saw you? You could be bringing greater danger down on all our heads, including Fawn's."

By the end of his speech, his tone had turned pleading, and if he was honest with himself, he'd admit that his annoyance and frustration were masking his real emotion - fear. He feared they would lose Fawn to the humans, and he would lose her.

"No one saw me," Huxley countered, clenching his hands rhythmically. "I was careful."

The gray of his cheeks darkened dramatically, contradicting his earnest expression.

"Huxley?" Amon growled, his branches quivering rapidly with renewed anger. "What happened?" If he was spotted or left any trace, then it was even more imperative that they begin to teach Fawn to camouflage. She needed as much protection as they could give her.

"Nothing!" Huxley snatched the chocolate from Erwin's hand. "Nothing will happen to Fawn. I know I messed up, but can we just drop it?"

"I'm sure Huxley won't do it again?" Laurel questioned quietly from between Baol and Baeroot's trunks. The two tree Fae nodded along with her, their faces pinched with concern at the tension that had risen in the clearing.

Amon sighed. He was under no illusion that Huxley wouldn't repeat his ventures past the forest edge, but perhaps it was time to drop the matter. He pierced his friend with a sharp stare, promising that they would be revisiting this discussion at a later date.

"At the very least, you owe all of us an apology," he said instead. "Is there anything you want to add?" Swiveling around, he addressed Lothian, respecting him as their unofficial leader. But with a groan, Amon slapped a branch to his forehead. Somewhere along the way, the elderly tree had nodded off. He stood hunched over with his eyes closed, letting out small echoing snores.

"Lothian, wake up." Venek snaked out his arm and shook one of Lothian's pale branches with an awkward laugh.

"He's not going to do anything, Amon," Flavire huffed, still shooting daggers at Huxley. "You'd be better off asking the girl to punish him. At least she's got some spunk."

Amon's lips twitched. Fawn could be commanding at times.

"We're not going to punish—"

"Amon, look what I found." As if summoned, Fawn appeared at the cave mouth, her energetic voice demanding his attention and momentarily distracting him from his worries.

I guess all of that sleep restored her energy, he thought wryly, clearing his throat and pushing away the last of his negative emotions so he could focus on the gangly girl bouncing her way towards him.

"What have you found, Fawn?"

She held up her arms, stretching them above her head as close to his face as she could reach. Clasped between two hands, considering him carefully with calm black eyes, was the little chickadee.

"Her name is Beebe. She was hurt really badly, but Violetta helped me fix her." Fawn beamed up at him, pride obvious in her expression. Amon hid a smile.

"Good work."

Reaching out an arm, he gently stroked the head of the freshly named Beebe. Fawn looked around, a line forming between her brows.

"Where's Violetta?"

Worry wormed through his trunk. She should have been back by now. A quiet murmuring spread through the group, Huxley's indiscretion forgotten.

"Should I go after her?" Huxley's eyes widened, concern flowing from him in waves.

"Calm down, everyone, " Amon said with a forced smile. "Let's give it a bit more time." He stroked Fawn's tousled curls, carefully covering her ears in case she picked up on some of their words.

Faunella lowered her arms and leaned into his touch with closed eyes, unaware of his inner turmoil.

She thinks I'm giving her a memory.

I guess now would be as good a time than any to prepare her for lessons at keeping hidden. Taking a moment, Amon searched his memories for something, anything that would help prepare her to one day leave The Edge. Her speech was becoming less words and more nature sounds as the days wore on. Deciding on a scene, he allowed his thoughts to flow into Fawn's mind and made the connection, waiting while they played out.

"Okay everyone, today we are going to be working on our transformations. You have all begun to show the signs of being able to access your natural states, and it is my job to guide you into doing that safely and correctly."

Bubbles of excitement fizzed in Amon's body as he waited for the Fae to begin teaching today's lesson. He had been feeling an itch under his skin, which his mother assured him was a sign that he was ready to embrace his nature form. He looked around at the other Fae his age who also started the process. There weren't many of them, only five children including himself. His gaze kept straying back to one child who had a thick green vine sprouting out of his head. The boy reached up and itched uncomfortably at the protrusion. Grimacing at the sight, Amon turned back to the teacher, ready to get started.

Over the next hour, the teacher led them through various exercises, designed to get them to tap into their magic center. This allowed them to transform parts of their bodies. Amon focused intently on the tight feeling inside, and, to his delight, his arms erupted into wooden limbs, his fingers now twigs covered in bright green leaves. He waved them around slowly, marveling at the feeling of his new extremities. Closing his eyes, he once again drew on his magic, this time feeling a slight implosion before his body rippled and changed. Opening his eyes, he was shocked to see that he now looked down on everyone from a much taller height.

"Well done, Amon!" came the voice of his instructor at his feet. "Look, class. Amon has successfully transformed into his nature form. The next step, which we will attempt another day, is to learn how to take it to the final level of becoming the very thing this form emulates. In this final form, you will be indistinguishable from the nature around you."

Pride filled him from the older Fae's words. He couldn't wait to learn more, and he was also excited to hide from his mother when he didn't want to do chores. Being able to disguise himself would be fun.

He drew the vision away from Fawn's mind, pushing past his grief at being unable to transform back into his Ancient Fae body. Turning his attention back to Fawn, he hoped she would understand what he was trying to tell her.

Her bright blue eyes opened to look up at him, and her lips curved into a sweet smile.

"That was the first time you transformed." She spun around carefully, still mindful of the bird she carried. "Oh, I wish I could do that. What do you think I would be? A flower, some vines, or maybe a tree like you?"

Amon smiled at her enthusiasm. There was no way Fawn would be able to transform like one of them. The chances of her being able to tap into any transformative powers were slim to none.

Shaking his head, he motioned for her to follow him out of the clearing, he didn't want her to be there when Violetta got back...if she got back.

When he saw she was bringing the chickadee, he stopped and pointed to a nearby tree.

"Leave the bird behind."

Fawn stopped, looking towards the tree and then back at him.

Oh no.

Amon tipped back his head and sighed. He knew that look. The blue in Fawn's eyes had turned glacier, crinkles forming on her forehead as her eyebrows came down to almost touch.

She raised her chin stubbornly and glared at him. "I can't leave Beebe behind. She'll be scared if she's all alone. Why would you want her to be scared?"

Amon racked his brain to come up with a good enough reason to leave the bird in the cave, but every time he opened his mouth to explain, Fawn would catch his eye and send her death glare straight through him.

He raised his hands to concede and shook his head, letting out a shallow chuckle. "All right then, you win. You can bring the bird." He could never say no to Fawn; the girl had him wrapped around her little finger.

Fawn's steely expression released at once, returning her face to its normal happy state. Amon shook his head gently at her instant mood change, thinking he probably shouldn't have given in so fast.

Next time. He made the unlikely promise to himself as he ushered Fawn ahead of him.

"Wait, kid."

Huxley cut her off, a deep frown marring his face. He stepped to her side and grasped her free hand, almost bashfully placing the chocolate on her palm. Faunella's eyes widened in delight.

"For me?"

Huxley cleared his throat and nodded at the bird.

"You did a good job. Now get out of here." He lightly tapped her on the bottom, his face softening when she let out a high-pitched chortle.

Without taking her eyes off the shiny item in her hand, Faunella disappeared into the thick forest, not a moment too soon.

There was a shift in the air followed instantly by Violetta collapsing on the dew swept grass.

Amon's heart leapt into his throat. They all rushed towards her, but Huxley reached her first, scooping her tightly against his stone body.

"Violetta, are you okay?"

"What happened?"

Amon's words overlapped Huxley's, but they didn't quite hide the panic in the rock Fae's voice. Violetta gathered her breath and shook her head, then rested it against Huxley's chest.

"I'm fine," she gasped. "I'm just not used to wielding that much power. I thought being in Amaranth would make me stronger, but it didn't help." Her eyes welled up. "The South Forest is so damaged. It hurt my soul just to be there."

Amon's heart went out to her. Out of all of them, he was the only other Fae in the group who had felt the decay. It burrowed into the depth of their being, but they had no choice other than to wait. They couldn't leave Earth yet. They still had at least a decade to go before Faunella's second puberty and her ascension to High Fae.

"What did you find out?" Erwin asked, placing his hand on Violetta's leg, worry filling his eyes.

She lifted her head and faced the gathered Fae. Amon braced himself, nervously tightening his roots in anticipation of what they were about to hear.

"It's true," Violetta breathed. "But she's not just part of the royal family."

She paused, as if gathering herself to finish the message. Slowly, she turned her eyes to face him, the knowledge of what this would mean to him shining in their watery depths.

"She's Queen Nyssa's great granddaughter."

Her eyes closed.

"She's next in line for the throne."

"She's next in line for the throne."

CHAPTER THIRTEEN
FAUNELLA

FAUNELLA HELD HER BREATH as the two Fae moved under the branch where she perched. The moment they disappeared from sight, she let the air rush out of her mouth, breathing easier. Shifting slightly, she shook out her cramped limbs while she lay in wait for the particular Fae she had been stalking all morning.

"Beebe, stop that. You'll give me away." Faunella swatted at the small bird flying around her head. Beebe chirped at the dismissal before darting two trees over to perch with her back towards Faunella, her feathers ruffled up in annoyance.

Turning back to the trail, Faunella stilled her body once more, hoping it wouldn't take much longer until her target wandered by. The tree she had chosen as her hiding place had thick, knobby branches covered in curtains of ribboned foliage that hung down over the edges of each branch. She had been planning this disguise for a while now and even made herself a dress out of the stringy green plant.

A tweet from Beebe had her dropping her head and becoming motionless. The slight crunch of leaves underfoot drew her attention back down to the forest floor. Her mouth curved into a wicked smile, and she stilled her heartbeat, her breathing becoming quiet and gentle. Faunella closed her eyes and focused on the subtle noises coming from the Fae, the thud of his heavy body striking the ground with each step, the scraping of rock against rock. When she judged that he was near enough, she popped open her eyes and tracked his movements as he passed under her tree. Tightening her muscles, she waited for him to take two steps away before springing to her feet on the wide branch and launching herself at his broad back.

"Gotcha!" she cried, a loud laugh erupting from her open mouth.

Huxley gave a sharp cracking shout and fell to his knees from the force of her attack. Faunella held on tightly as his body lurched forward, bracing herself with her knees and arms when he hit the ground. Laying still, he let out an exasperated sounding clack. She slid off Huxley's back, smiling broadly as he pushed himself up and turned to face her. He made the clacking sound again, which Faunella knew to be her name, followed by another string of sounds. She could tell he wasn't happy by his tone.

Not letting his gruff words affect her, Faunella reached forward to brush the dirt and leaves off his knees and hands. "There now Huxley, you're okay. Don't be mad that I got you good." She grinned at his solid face. "You know Amon's been wanting me to practice my camouflage." A snorting giggle escaped her mouth, and she gave up trying to contain her laughter. "I guess I'm getting better." Throwing her arms around Huxley's neck, Faunella squeezed tightly. "I love you Hux, but you'll have to do better next time."

Giggling, she darted out of reach as the moody rock reached out to bop her lightly. Sticking out her tongue, Faunella raced away, but not before she saw Huxley shake his head affectionately.

He loves me, too.

Satisfaction filled her. The successful disguise and her ability to trick the stern Huxley had her almost giddy with pleasure. Pursing her lips, she let out a series of melodic bird calls. A moment later, air brushed against her cheek as Beebe swooped down to perch on her shoulder. She ruffled her feathers and turned her back to Faunella's face, standing so stiffly that she almost fell off.

Faunella pursed her lips, wondering if Beebe was still offended from earlier. She reached inside herself to feel for the bird's essence. The connection pulsed between them, bright with strong feelings coming from Beebe in waves. As she suspected, Beebe was upset from the way she had shooed her away. She concentrated harder as Beebe sent her another feeling.

She thinks I treated her like she was any other bird. Faunella sighed. For such a small bird, she sure did have some big emotions.

"You aren't like every other bird, though. Huxley could have recognized you, which might have made him notice me." She reached out to stroke the black stripe under Beebe's neck. "How about we stop by the cave and see if Laurel will grow some berries for us?"

The change was instant. Beebe chirped, flaring her wings with delight. She hopped closer to Faunella's face and rubbed her feathered head against her jaw, clicking her beak softly. Faunella laughed, her heart feeling lighter now that her little friend was happy with her again.

"Hold on, Beebe." She filled her lungs with air. "Let's run."

Digging her feet into the ground, Faunella launched herself into a fast sprint. Her legs pumped up and down as she jumped over fallen logs and lichen covered rocks, stepping nimbly past any obstacles. She moved quickly through the forest, reveling in the feeling of the air rushing past her face. It swirled through her hair, soft and tangible, curling around the strands before turning around and pressing against her back. Faunella briefly closed her eyes as she raced through the trees, marveling at the feeling. Unable to hold on once Faunella started running, Beebe flew along beside her, wings outstretched as she glided along the air currents.

All too soon, they arrived at their destination. Faunella slowed her pace, beaming at Beebe when she returned to her shoulder.

"That was a good one, Beebe. It almost felt like I was flying." Her eyes fluttered closed to relieve the sensation. She often dreamed about taking to the sky and flying high over the forest. The idea had first come to her years ago. However, since finding Beebe, it had grown into a near obsession, soothing her when a recent quiet question would worry her mind.

Who am I?

Faunella's eyes flew open, and she shook her head to remove the uncomfortable feeling. It was so much more fun to be happy. Dismissing her musings, Faunella scanned the clearing, quickly spotting the Fae she was after. The pretty bush was over by the cave mouth locked in a discussion with Amon with a concerned looking Erwin standing by.

"What's going on?" she whispered, coming up to Erwin's side.

Before he could answer, there was movement within the trees. One by one, the Fae returned to the clearing. While this wasn't unusual during the day, what was unusual was the fact that they all returned together as a group. A moment later, Lothian emerged from the dark mouth of the cave, joining the circle his fellow Fae made.

"What's going on?" she tried again, this time causing every single face to turn to her as one. "Is everything okay?" Her stomach clenched with anticipation as the building silence became as strong as a deafening roar.

Finally, they all turned from her, looking expectantly towards Amon. The tree Fae took a deep breath and picked up his roots to make his way over to her. His face creased with worry. Faunella watched him approach, her head lifting higher and higher until she was looking straight up to where he towered above her. Unable to bear the tension any longer, she jerked her head down and backed away.

"Why are you doing this? I'm scared."

Ignoring her, Amon reached out his arm and wrapped it around her back, his resigned expression scaring her more than his worry. Pressing in, he stretched his other arm towards her head, pausing before he made the connection.

Faunella's heart thumped painfully in her chest, a warning that something wasn't quite right. She focused her attention on Amon's familiar face. She trusted him. He had never done anything to give her a reason to doubt him. So why was she filled with fear?

Amon watched her just as carefully. Whether he could see the thoughts on her face or not, he still gave her a small smile, nodding his head in reassurance. Swallowing thickly, she allowed Amon to place his branched limb onto her head, whisking her away to a memory of his choosing.

The scene Amon chose was very familiar. She frowned slightly as each Fae in the circle had their name called out, and they transformed into their nature state before disappearing.

This time, something struck Faunella as strange. It had never occurred to her when she was younger, but where were they disappearing to? Why did they never vanish now?

Mind whirling with the new thought, she paid close attention as the vision came to the end. However, the vision didn't cut out like it usually did. Instead, Amon inhaled deeply, pulling his body inwards and shrinking down until he was once again in his Fae form. Faunella was transfixed. She had no idea that the vision had more to it than she had previously been shown.

Striding forward, Amon tensed and relaxed his muscles, enjoying the feeling of his Fae body as he moved through the grass.

"I'll miss this." He sighed deeply, scrunching his toes into the warm grass. Spinning around, he walked back to his place in the empty circle, the flattened grass now the only proof that they had been there. His eyes gazed around the space, excitement now beginning to rise in his stomach. *"Goodbye, Amaranth."*

With a stomach-lurching jolt, Faunella felt herself fall through a kaleidoscope of color. The air pushed in on her, squeezing tightly until just before she felt she would be crushed. The pressure released, leaving her standing, gazing around the same vista as before, only dimmer and less vibrant.

"Hello, Earth."

Earth made no sense. Faunella racked her brain for answers. Finding none, she opened her eyes and shook her head to break from Amon's vision.

She looked up at Amon questioningly. "You were in a place called Earth?" The name swirled around in her mind, hazy like all other thoughts she had other than her memories of the forest.

Amon shook his head from side to side, pointing to her and then to the ground.

"I don't understand," Faunella stuttered. "Where are we? We are still on Amaranth, right? Just in the forest?"

Amon reconnected with her head, sending her back into the vision.

He ran to catch up with his fellow Fae, transforming once again into his tree form. They traveled through the forest as a group, laughing and talking with each other with their own unique sounds.

Distracted by the Fae's conversation, Faunella almost didn't recognize the clearing the Fae emerged into. Only the sight of the familiar rocky mouth of the cave garnered her attention, giving her the dawning realization of where she truly was.

Her throat closed up. "I'm on Earth," she squeaked, hardly managing to draw breath from the shock of her discovery. She looked up at Amon's towering form and saw the truth in his eyes, confirmed by the gentle nodding of his head.

"It's true? We've been on Earth this whole time?" Faunella felt like she had been tossed on unsteady ground. She couldn't catch her breath as her mind spun wildly.

Abruptly, a thought came to her. "Why didn't anyone tell me sooner?" Turning her attention to the circle of Fae, the image was so similar to the start of the vision that she was momentarily taken back. Recovering quickly, she shook her head, clearing her mind so she could focus on what was important - getting information, right now.

"Why couldn't I know we were on a place called Earth? Why are we here?"

She looked from face to face, desperate for an answer. Faunella had never been so frustrated with the lack of communication between her and the Fae. They always made do before. But this time, she needed real answers. She got to her feet, her body vibrating with excess energy. Fighting the urge to turn and race away through the forest, she began to pace back and forth in front of the waiting circle. She took several deep breaths, the air filling up her lungs and clearing her head. She pursed her lips, pushing past her confusion to work on solving the question of how she would get the information she needed from the Fae.

She spun around to face the group, steeling her face and placing her hands on her hips in what she hoped was a stern manner. "Here's what's going to happen. I'm going to ask questions, and you are going to give me yes or no answers. Is that understood?"

The Fae turned to look at each other out of the corners of their eyes before letting out the sounds of their assent. Satisfied that they would play along, Faunella returned to pacing, the movement helping her mind figure out its questions.

"First question." She faced the group again, her voice coming out smaller than intended. "This forest is all I've ever known. Is this all there is of Earth?"

Amon looked to the ground, his head shaking back and forth in an apologetic no. Faunella bit her lip. So why was she only allowed in this one place?

"You all decided together not to tell me that this was Earth?" All eyes shot to Amon before they uttered a hesitant yes.

"There was a reason you haven't told me before?" Another nod.

Amon called her name before she could ask another question, getting her attention. He placed an arm out low to the ground and slowly drew it upwards until it was around her current height. Understanding bloomed in her mind.

"You didn't tell me before because I was too little?" The nods and affirmative sounds from the surrounding Fae were accompanied by relieved smiles. When Faunella began to feel a bit calmer, she stopped her frenzied pacing and came closer to the gap she had left in the circle.

Thinking back to the past few years, Faunella thought of the times when she was allowed to be alone and the times when she would wander a bit further. Somehow, one of the Fae would pop up and convince her to come back home.

"Have you been keeping me from leaving the forest?" Their confirmation brought another wave of questions. "But why? Why are we even here and not on Amaranth? Where are the other Fae?" On the word 'Fae,' her voice broke. The question brought a wave of deep loneliness and longing for others like her. Swallowing past the lump in her throat, Faunella blinked at the Fae around her, their otherness suddenly standing out starkly. "Is that why there are no other Fae who look like me? Because we're on Earth?"

Lothian stepped forward and nodded at her, his eyes bright with compassion. He turned to talk to Amon, drawing the attention of the other Fae. Faunella took that moment to compose herself, her mind working overtime at what this meant for her. Over the past moon cycle, Amon shared the Fae's memories of Amaranth, showing her pictures of their world, teaching her names and the locations of its many vast kingdoms. Now, it all made sense. She furrowed her brows, feeling an uncomfortable tightness in her stomach.

Anger flared up hot and tight within her. She was frustrated about why she never questioned the way things were, only blindly accepting the life the Fae had shown her. What would life have been like if she were back in the Fae realm?

"I want to go back."

Ten pairs of eyes turned back to her.

Worry flashed across the assortment of faces staring at her. She looked up into Amon's wooden face. His dark eyes held a hint of panic, causing her to step forward as if to comfort him.

"Please, Amon. I don't understand why I must be alone."

The tree let out a pained cry, the sound piercing through Faunella's heart. He dropped to his knees heavily, shooting out his smooth limbs and drawing her into a tight embrace.

Confusion and regret flooded her small body. She never meant to cause anyone distress. Was it really so bad to want to return to Amaranth, to be with people who looked like her?

Lothian let out a dry *creak*, stretching out one of his gnarled limbs with firm movements and wrapping it around Amon's trunk. The younger tree sighed and leaned back from Faunella. He offered her his branched hand, reaching out and placing it on her head. She was shown a series of memories, all from Lothian's point of view. After another few moments, things became clearer.

"Humans," she breathed, mesmerized by the visions she was shown. "There are humans here?" All thoughts of leaving fled her mind. There were other people in this realm, people the Fae were tasked with observing - people who looked just like her.

Excitement coursed through her body, lighting her up with a joyous energy.

"When can I see them? Why haven't you showed me them before?"

Amon gently lowered his hand, then turned to look around him, uttering a short command. Instantly, every single Fae transformed until all that was left in the clearing were remnants of the forest.

"You don't let the humans see you?" Amon transformed back just as quickly, shaking his head sadly. Faunella looked down at her makeshift dress, a poor disguise compared to the Fae's nature forms. She deflated slightly, making the connection quickly. "But they would see me because I'm not like you?"

He nodded his head, and all of the Fae began to pop back to their more humanoid forms.

"Why can't the humans see us?"

This time, Huxley answered. He stepped forward and let out a crumbling, crashing sound. Faunella recognized the word.

"The humans are dangerous," she said.

The information surprised her. From what she had just been shown of the humans, they seemed just like her, and she wasn't dangerous. Though, if the Fae were right and they were a threat, that would explain why they never told her and why they didn't want her to see them.

Her head swung up so quickly that something twinged in her neck.

"Are you telling me now because I'm big enough to see them?"

Amon seemed to hold his breath. His eyes never strayed from hers, so Faunella could see the waves of emotion passing over his face - sadness, fear, then finally resignation. He lifted a limb and pointed to a path out of the clearing before he opened his mouth and let out a quiet rustle.

Faunella couldn't help the broad smile that erupted on her face nor the excited whoop that rushed from her open mouth. She surged forward, wrapping her arms around Amon's trunk and squeezed tightly.

"I'm going to see the humans."

CHAPTER FOURTEEN
AMON

"WELL, THAT WENT BETTER than expected." Amon let out a weary chuckle, his heart still pounding from their revelation about Faunella.

Princess Faunella.

Something inside him twinged as he watched her dart out of view, her red hair catching the sun and turning a burnished gold. It felt like she was running from him, as if the revelation of who she is coupled with the decision to show her the humans of this realm meant that she would one day be out of his reach. From the moment the words had left Violetta's lips, indecision warred within him. He had taken Fawn from her family based on the assumption that they all wanted her dead, a fact now obliterated by what Violetta recently discovered.

The right thing to do would be to take her back.

Amon stretched out his trunk and blew out a breath. He needed to stop mulling over their decision. Even with the news that Queen Nyssa had placed guards in the South Forest by the portal tree due to the slim chance of Fawn's return, the Fae had agreed to keep to their original plan of keeping Fawn with them until her second puberty. He shook out his leaves and nodded once to himself. Now that they knew this side of Fawn's heritage, it made total sense why her aunt had tried to kill her. She was making room to take the Madivyern throne herself. Amon tried to relax, forcing himself to believe that this was the right path for her, the safest path. Keeping Faunella safe was all that mattered.

"Erwin, Baol," he called out, his eyes never leaving the place Faunella disappeared from. "Can you both go with Fawn and make sure she heads in the right direction?" He turned back to the Fae. "We'll catch up soon."

"Of course, Amon." The two Fae started after Fawn, Erwin scrambling up Baol's trunk to catch a ride with the larger Fae. "We are taking her to the coastal town, right?" Baol called back over his shoulder, shortening his strides to wait for Amon's confirmation.

"That's right, but I thought we could stop by the South road first to show her the road and how to stay safely hidden."

At his words, Erwin popped up, punching his fist into the air. "Yes! She's going to love the cars."

Warmth filled him at Erwin's exuberance, and Amon waved them on. "You'd better hurry. You know how fast she can go when she's excited about something."

"On it!" Baol raced after Fawn, quickly disappearing from sight.

Amon studied the remaining Fae. The eight still in the clearing suddenly looked like quite a large group. Worry tickled at his leaves, and he considered them carefully. They generally didn't go to the Edge all together, instead staying in small groups of two or three.

"Does everyone want to come with Fawn for her first sighting of the humans, or would anyone like to sit out?" He scanned the faces of the group, taking note of the sheepish expressions on many of their faces.

"Of course we all want to go with Fawn!" burst out Huxley. "Your first time seeing a human is one you'll never forget, and I, for one, don't want to miss Fawn's first experience."

"Huxley's right," chimed Violetta, firing the rock a small smile as she stepped closer. "I think most of us would like to be present. And we don't have to worry about being noticed, Amon," she added, shooting him a sharp look. "We're all skilled at staying hidden. None of us will be seen."

His eyebrows flung up, surprised and slightly embarrassed that Violetta had read him so easily. "Of course you're all capable of staying hidden. I wasn't worried about that. Not really." The hidden smiles and muffled giggles told him all he needed to know about what the others really thought. "Anyway, if we are all going, then I'll save this conversation for later." He turned abruptly, meaning to leave the clearing before anyone could question him.

A loud cough made him pause. "Hold on now Amon," said Lothian, his branches held up in front of him. "We can take a few more minutes to hear what you wanted to say. We have time."

Amon gathered his thoughts, wondering the best way to present them to his fellow Fae. Ever since Lothian had sent Violetta back to Amaranth to infiltrate the Kingdom of Madivyre, he had been plagued with an idea.

"I want to go back to Amaranth," he plowed on hurriedly, despite the surprised looks on his friends' faces. "This mission was for our king—a king who is no longer with us. So, now our loyalty lies with Fawn."

"How does this help her?"

Amon smiled at Laurel. She had asked such a perfect question.

"We cannot all return to Amaranth until her second puberty, but there is nothing stopping a few of us from returning at some stage to gather things that might help with her learning."

"Ah, I see." Lothian nodded slowly, his withered branches croaking with the motion.

"What do you see?" Flavire asked, a bewildered frown etched amongst his greenery. When Lothian didn't reply, he reluctantly turned his gaze back to Amon. "Amon?"

Amon grinned, now even more sure of his idea. "The things Fawn will need most of all to successfully ascend the throne are books."

Leading the remaining Fae through the gap in the trees, Amon drew on his senses to follow the path the child had taken.

They headed south, moving at a quick pace through the undergrowth. Venek raced beside him, drawing on his magic to help them move unencumbered through the forest, subtly nudging trees and plants to the side with his snaking vines.

Amon flared his leaves, tasting the air for signs of Fawn. Once they cleared the southern stream, he veered left, Fawn's familiar essence growing stronger as they came closer. Before long, he heard the tell-tale signs of her presence. They rounded a few more trees as the excited chatter got louder.

Amon let out a deep chuckle as he took in the sight in front of him, suddenly very glad he had sent Erwin and Baol after Fawn. Erwin was wrapped around Fawn's leg, clutching a nearby root as he strained to keep her from moving forward. Baol had extended his body to form a wide barrier, which Fawn was now attempting to climb.

"Come on, Erwin, let go," she laughed, obviously enjoying the challenge of getting past them. "I don't want to wait for the others. Let's keep moving."

She reached down to pry at Erwin's arms, and when that didn't work, she gave the small Fae a gentle tickle. Amon slapped a hand to his forehead when Erwin let out a snorting giggle, immediately releasing his arms from around Fawn's leg.

The tickling gets him every time. How did she figure that out?

Now released from Erwin's mossy embrace, Fawn let out a triumphant cry and launched herself onto Baol's latticed barrier. She began to climb, nimbly dodging Baol's attempts at stopping her.

Deciding this had gone on long enough, Amon stepped forward, clearing his throat to get their attention. "What's all this?" Three sets of eyes shot to his. Erwin's green eyes and Baol's brown ones filled with relief at the sight of reinforcements.

"What took you so long?" cried Baol, gesturing at Fawn, who was perched halfway up his tall body. Fawn's blue eyes sparkled with mischief as she stared at him, a coy smile gracing her lips.

"She moved so fast that we could barely keep up. Erwin and I have been trying to keep her in one spot for ages now." Baol sounded out of breath as he spoke, more fatigued than he should have been.

"If you couldn't keep up with a lower fae child, then I'd say you need to get back into shape," Huxley scoffed, moving around him to walk over to stand under where Fawn perched. He raised his arms up as close to her as he could. "Come on down. We can go see the humans now."

Erwin brushed himself off, standing up next to Huxley's hard body. "Baol's right, Hux." He admonished his friend before turning his confused expression to face Amon and the others. "She's always been quick, but today she seemed to fly. It looked like her feet barely touched the ground, and the wind blew at her back, propelling her forwards." He shook his head, looking back at Huxley. "I don't think any of us would have kept up easily."

Baol nodded his head vigorously as he helped Fawn climb down, steadying her before she launched herself directly on top of Huxley. "Umph!" he huffed, stumbling slightly from her momentum.

Fawn let out a melodic laugh, giving Huxley a brief hug before sliding back onto the ground. "Can we go now?" she asked brightly, her feet moving up and down on the hard-packed ground as she practically vibrated with impatience.

"I don't see why not," Amon laughed and gave her a nod, which made her smile grow, exposing the bright whites of her teeth. She spun around as if to dash off again. Amon reached out to grasp her arm before she could run away. "Slowly, Fawn. Slowly." He spoke the words carefully, exaggerating them for her benefit.

"Slowly," she repeated, speaking in his tree language. The swishing sounds strange coming from her human-like body. "Slower?" she asked, confirming the sound meant what she thought. Amon smiled his approval, even though his stomach clenched at her ease of using his nature speech.

Shaking away his concern, he let go of her arm and smiled down at her, watching with fondness as she took stiff steps forward, her body tensing with the effort of holding herself back. They continued on as a group, only slowing further when Amon picked up steady vibrations from the cars traveling past on the road ahead.

"Start spreading out," he called to the group behind him.

The Fae dispersed, moving towards the rapidly increasing sounds. Fawn extended her head, cocking it from side to side as she strained to see where the roaring sounds were coming from.

Amon's body was a bundle of nerves by the time he reached the last line of trees separating them and the road. He gathered Fawn to his side, sprouting thick bushy branches to cover her body. Stepping into a gap between two dark pines, he tapped into his magic, stiffening until he was halfway between his current form and his full nature state. He didn't want to fully transform in case he needed to intervene if Fawn decided to do something reckless.

He needn't have worried. Fawn slowly crouched onto the hard earth and focused intently on the black asphalt several feet away. Pride filled him, stronger than any parent might have felt.

Soon, a humming sound began some distance to their right. Amon didn't need to look to see what was coming. Instead, he kept his eyes on Fawn, curious to see her reaction when the car sped past their location. Her head tilted as she looked to where the sound was rapidly increasing. Amon knew the moment the red sedan came into view by the small gasp of surprise Fawn uttered from behind tightly closed lips. He smiled down at her as her head swung quickly to the left, tracking the car as it rushed past.

As the fumes from the machine blew into her, Fawn wrinkled her freckled nose against the acrid smell. Her head whipped to the right again, drawn to the sound of another approaching car. Fawn leaned forward as the silver wagon rounded the bend and came into view. Amon flexed his branches, pressing her back gently, needing her to understand that she shouldn't do anything that might get her seen. He made sure she stayed still while he waited for the wagon to scream by. However, when a few moments had passed and the car still hadn't traveled past, he turned to look, his heart leaping in his chest. Instead of speeding past, the car was slowing.

It was too late to move Fawn away. Any sudden movements would surely alert the driver to their presence. Amon had no choice but to stay where he was, hoping Fawn would remain concealed.

The car eased past them, giving Amon a clear view of the man and woman in the front seats, their faces pinched with worry. Pulling off the road a little to the left, the wagon came to a stop. Almost immediately, the passenger door swung open, and the dark-haired woman emerged.

He heard Fawn take a sharp breath when she saw the woman. He tightened his hold on her in case she decided to move. The wagon was only two car lengths away from their hiding spot, probably right in front of Erwin.

The woman wrenched open the back door as the man emerged from his side of the car, rushing around to join where she was leaning into the side of the vehicle.

"Quick, I don't want it getting in the car!" he called out to her in a panicked voice.

The woman drew back quickly, turning towards them as she removed a pale toddler from the car. His hair was the same dark shade as the woman's, and the soft strands clung to the perspiration dotting his brow. Faunella's hands clutched at Amon's branches as the small boy came into view.

"You're okay, baby," the woman crooned as she took a few steps forward, squatting down and positioning the toddler in front of her, facing away. The boy's pale face blanched, becoming almost white, his skin contrasting starkly against his dark hair. He opened his mouth and started to cry, his eyes screwing shut as he wailed.

"It's okay. Mama's got you. Let it out."

His body spasmed, the cry cut off from the force of the vomit that erupted from his mouth. While the child emptied his stomach, the waiting man paced, running his hands through his dull brown hair as the woman continued to lightly stroke the boy's back, murmuring sounds of comfort.

Amon looked down at Fawn. She hadn't moved or made a sound since the toddler was pulled from the car. He wondered what she was thinking.

What an introduction to the humans, he thought wryly.

The man's voice brought his attention back to the scene.

"Thank God we stopped in time. It would have taken forever to get the stink out of the carpet."

The woman didn't take her attention from the child as she responded. "He was only sick because we didn't stop once." Her tone was edged with frustration. "Six hours is too long for a baby. He's only two." She brushed his hair back tenderly, pressing a kiss to the top of his head.

The boy had stopped being sick and was now starting to squirm in his mother's arms. She held her hand out behind her, opening and closing her fingers rapidly in the direction of the car.

"Wipe," she ground out, not managing to disguise her animosity.

"We were only ten minutes from town. He couldn't have waited ten more minutes?" The man crawled into the car, rummaging around until he emerged holding a few squares of wet tissue.

The woman didn't answer him as he handed her the wipes. Instead, she gently wiped the vomit smeared on the toddler's face before pulling the squirming child onto her lap.

A chorus of loud rumbles began, quickly increasing in intensity like an approaching hive.

"Can we keep moving now?" the man spat out, glancing in the direction of the threatening sound. His tone rubbed Amon the wrong way.

"His color is looking better," the woman told him, snuggling her nose into the boy's chubby cheek, causing him to let out a low giggle. "He should be okay in a minute. I'll sit in the back with him just in case."

The man nodded, his face tight with annoyance. He walked back onto the road and got back into the driver's seat, more concerned with the oncoming traffic that had just come into sight.

Amon felt a rush of compassion for the woman as she crouched there, sadness evident on her face. That was one thing he had noticed amongst the humans. They rarely appreciated what they had, treating their supposed loved ones with little regard. He hoped that one day the man in that family would realize the treasure he had in his woman and son.

Before she could get to her feet, a sleek motorbike sped past, followed by two more. The third narrowly missed the couple's car.

The woman let out a cry of alarm and pushed to her feet, clutching the little boy to her chest as she faced the biker gang descending on them. Faunella also shot to her feet, bracing her hands on Amon's branches.

There was too much commotion, too many people for Fawn to take in at once. He needed to get her out of there—now.

"Faunella, you need to slowly back away." He spoke the words quietly, but they were loud enough that she could hear him over the deafening bikes speeding past.

Faunella acted like she hadn't heard. Her eyes were wide, totally focused on the woman holding her toddler.

"Fawn, leave!"

Amon thickened his branches in increments, cutting off Fawn's view as the final bike came to a stop at the back of the car.

"Violetta," he ground out, knowing the water Fae was nearby. "She's covered. Get her out of here."

The dirt at their feet filled with water, turning into mud before Violetta surged upwards, returning to her female form. She tugged Fawn away, leaving Amon alone to witness the human family's interaction with the bikers.

CHAPTER FIFTEEN
FAUNELLA

*T*HEY LOOK LIKE ME. *Exactly like me.*

The thought kept swirling through her mind as Violetta tugged her away, taking her further from the human family.

Too dazed to do anything but follow, Faunella let herself be guided despite the urge to turn around, rip herself free from Violetta's embrace, and run back towards the ribbon of gray that snaked through the trees.

She craned her head to look back, her eyes searching for one more glimpse of the humans. Something inside beckoned her - a sensation, a quiet feeling. It felt like the tug from Beebe, but it was different, softer. Distracted, she stumbled over an exposed root, and when she adjusted her gait, the feather-light whisper disappeared.

"Wow," she breathed, bringing her hand up to rub her chest, soothing the warmth that pressed against her ribs.

Violetta smiled down at her, keeping a steady pace even as her eyes crinkled with shared delight. Faunella's face bloomed, her excitement finally coming to the surface and bringing her features to life. She had never seen anything that had touched her as deeply as seeing that woman with her child. The way her delicate face showed every emotion, clearly relaying the love she had for her offspring, and the sadness that the man had brought to light inspired her.

She ran her fingers over her face, tracing her nose and mouth with reverent strokes. Her hand traveled up to trace her rounded ears. Pinching her eyes shut, she let Violetta guide her, focusing instead on the question that always eluded her, flitting through her mind like a butterfly.

Who am I?

The familiar forest was a steady constant in her life, and those memories came easily. She skimmed through them, pacified by the unchanging Fae, but she needed more. Darkness rushed towards her, any hint of her early years hidden by an inky blackness. Faunella focused on the image of the human woman and her child, trying to use the feeling to access the hint of a memory she couldn't quite grasp.

What did the woman say again?

Words tumbled by, until the one that had struck a chord in Faunella's heart was revealed.

Mama.

Warmth filled her, then flitted away, leaving a strange hollowness that made Faunella's eyes flick open. She blinked rapidly and shook her head to dislodge the sting behind her eyes.

Violetta noticed and gave her hand a gentle squeeze, not understanding the reason for her shift in mood.

"Don't worry. You'll see the humans again soon."

Faunella forced a small smile to her face and nodded, forcing her attention away from the new thought that felt like a bruise in her mind.

Where's my mama?

CHAPTER SIXTEEN
DERICK

DERICK STAYED AT THE rear of the pack, trailing behind as the entire gang made their way north along the coastal road to Mull Crest. It was the furthest he could get from Jarred, who, of course, had to ride up front with Shaun.

Hidden behind his helmet, Derick let his facade fall, giving space for his conflicting emotions to play out on his face. It had been several weeks since Jarred had framed him and destroyed any goodwill Derick might have had with Shaun, but the damage still lingered. He took a turn in the road ahead, wincing when the wound on his side pulled. He gritted his teeth, anger flaring hot and heavy in his chest. If Jarred thought he would roll over and cower, he was in for a rude surprise.

The stabbing made him fear Shaun, did nothing for his increasing dissatisfaction with this life, and only strengthened the hatred he had for Jarred. The silver lining that came from his injury was the fact that he was given a few days respite from the usual gang activities. He had some space to breathe and a moment to think.

Trees swept past on either side of the road, the greens and browns only a blur in his peripherals. Even amidst his turmoil, the forest calmed him, their dark depths hinting at an escape. Derick eased off the throttle, creating more space between him and the bikes ahead. His days recovering alone were over, but his decision was not.

He couldn't leave the gang; he had done too much damage, hurt too many people. His mouth drew down into a grimace. The only way he would leave would be as a body in a ditch. Derick thought of his father and all the people who had suffered from the gang's actions—from his actions. He wasn't getting out of this alive, but he could try his best to atone.

Up ahead, the road straightened, revealing a silver car pulled over on the verge. Derick watched as the first riders shot past, swerving so close they almost scraped the side of the wagon. The corners of his mouth angled down. It was always something. He drew closer, only then noticing the dark-haired woman clutching a child to her chest. The man in front of him sped up, creating more distance between them as he joined in on terrorizing the woman. Derick chewed on his lip. He hated being feared. The woman's face grew clearer, and her face pinched with worry. Derick's heart stuttered. She reminded him of his mom.

Before he knew what he was doing, Derick slowed to a stop, pulling over behind the vehicle. The few memories he had of his mother were kept close to his chest, carried so tightly that it would be impossible for him to ever forget them. In his mind, she had a brow that was constantly lined with strain and a voice that wobbled with anxiety whenever his father would come home smelling of beer and cigarettes.

He cleared his throat, removing his helmet along with the weight of regret. He was only seven when she died, too young to understand and in no position to help.

"Sorry about that." He kept his tone even, not wanting to frighten the woman further. She backed towards the side of the car, glancing inside with furrowed brows. Derick ducked his head to see through the glass. There was a man inside, his angry eyes glaring at Derick through the rearview mirror. Disbelief floored him. How could a man leave his wife and child alone to their fear? He swung his leg off his bike, struggling to keep any anger from showing on his face. The woman didn't need any other reason to be afraid of him.

"Are you all okay?"

The toddler swiveled his head to look at him, curiosity shining in his eyes. Derick's face softened into a smile. The boy's dark hair, while plastered to his head, reminded him of Rhett.

"We're alright."

The woman stroked the boy's back, eyes shooting to the man again. When he made no move to leave the car, her face fell, sadness obscuring her features.

"You're not far from town. Are you having car troubles? Maybe I can help."

Derick hoped they weren't. As much as he would like to help, he had to catch back up before anyone realized he was gone. He ran his hand through the curls on top of his head, suddenly wondering why he even stopped. He glanced to his left, feeling eyes on him. The woman began putting the child back into the car, explaining the reason for their stop. Derick only half heard her response. A prickling stirred under his skin, filling him with a strange restlessness that demanded resolution.

A hand came down to rub at his sternum. Something tugged at him.

"Well, we'll be off now."

Derick jolted back to reality.

"Of course. I hope your day gets better." He forced the words out with a half-hearted smile, his attention still captured by the thick forest at his side. He barely even registered when the wagon started up and moved off in a cloud of smoke.

An internal warning forced him back to his bike, the sensation grown from years living on the edge of danger. But he couldn't seem to leave. His bike sat there, just waiting to take him back to the gang, and he knew that if he left now, he could catch up with no one the wiser.

He rolled his shoulders, fighting the itch at his back.

God, you're an idiot.

He gave up and spun on his heel, quickly striding towards the thick line of trees. The earth puffed up under his boots, dry, even with all the humidity this much greenery produced. Stepping between two large trunks, Derick squinted through the dappled light, trying to find what sent the strange sensation skittering across his body.

Tension built within him, sending his imagination into overdrive as the stillness around him intensified, amplifying the heavy thudding of his heart.

A crack sounded from his right, making him jump, his breath catching in surprise. A small bird flitted past, completely ordinary and taking no mind of him.

Derick lay his forehead on the tree beside him, closing his eyes as he chuckled softly.

"You're losing it, utterly losing it."

He was getting as bad as Rhett, who still mentioned the rock man every time he had too much to drink. It was time for him to go. He flicked open his eyes, but before he could raise his head to leave, his eyes snagged on something on the ground.

Derick stilled, sucking in his breath as his focus honed in on the small patch of mud at the base of the tree. It was the only moisture around the area.

"What the hell?"

He lowered himself into a crouch, hesitantly bringing out his hand to trace the footprint marked into the earth. Someone was watching him.

His head shot up, and he scanned the forest with renewed interest. But just like before, there was utter stillness. Whoever it was was long gone, as was the feeling under his skin.

Derick slowly walked back to his bike, no longer concerned with making it back in time to avoid suspicion. If anyone had any questions, he would handle it. He would do everything in his power to not show any weakness, any kindness. This was his life, and he needed to adapt—at least on the surface.

He mounted his bike and started the engine, taking one last look amongst the greenery. He should have been unnerved at the knowledge of being watched. He kicked off, opening the throttle quickly and bursting forwards. To anyone else, he was sure they would have been creeped out. But when Derick thought of the perfectly shaped footprint, all he felt was a burning curiosity.

CHAPTER SEVENTEEN
FAUNELLA

That morning, Faunella was awakened by the chirping of birds. The symphony of sounds permeated her mind, mingling with the dream she was in until she was roused to awareness. Rolling onto her side, she pressed her arm over her ear to block the noise as she tried to hold tight to the rapidly fading dream.

She crested the sandy hill, brushing past stiff grasses that jabbed into her skin. Small grains of sand stuck to her legs, and the sounds of birds rose up all around her, their loud cries mixing with the crashing waves against the shore. A bubbling laugh burst from her mouth as she launched herself onto her side, her body rolling over and over as she slid down the side of the dune.

"Faunella," a voice called, filling her with unbridled happiness. Scrambling to her feet, she ran a short distance away, crouching down behind a patch of longer grass. She giggled quietly as someone walked past her hiding spot, her chest tight with anticipation. "Gotcha!" the voice cried as two hands came swooping in to scoop her up. Faunella erupted into a riot of laughter, snuggling into the warm, soft body that smelled of sweet mint and salt.

The dream began to break up, the images distorting as they dissolved into nothing more than the first hints of sunlight pressing through her closed eyes. As the last of the dream faded away, Faunella caught the sweeping whisper from the woman who held her. *"I love you, my little Fawn."*

The tender words echoed in her ears as the last dregs of sleep left her body. Faunella flipped onto her back with a huff, her eyes popping open as her arms flopped to her sides. She brought her hands to her face and rubbed the sleep from her eyes. Touching her cheek gently, she ran her fingertips over the smooth skin. She could still feel the sting from the air.

Shaking her head at the bizarre sensation, she stretched her arms up, letting out a groan as she worked the kinks from her back. It had been almost three moon cycles since she had been exposed to the humans, and as a result, her room had quickly transformed into something new. The walls Venek had made using his vines to bridge the gaps between the original tree branches now sported wide shelves filled with dozens of curiosities.

Faunella rose and walked over to one of those walls. She ran her hand over the thick green vines, marveling at their creation. A flash of movement caught her eye, and she reached forward to pick up the distracting item.

She held the pink circle away from her, angling it until her own face stared back at her. She admired her soft, golden skin, marred only by a smattering of freckles and the occasional smudge of dirt. Her tangled copper hair curled over her forehead and tickled her nose. Wrinkling the appendage, Fawn tucked the curl out of the way, hooking it behind her ear. As she did, she watched her eyes shutter and felt an uncomfortable wave of loneliness wash over her. She clapped the disk shut, cutting off the image. With brisk motions, she placed the treasure back on the shelf and ruffled her hair, pulling it back over her smooth, rounded ears. Her human ears.

Shaking off that nagging thought, she moved along the dips and rounded edges of her room and crouched down in front of a large chest. Opening it quickly, she sorted through the items inside.

I won't wear human clothes today. They're too easily spotted.

She pushed past the bright pieces of clothing, instead reaching for some pants made from large leaves and a matching top.

"I think we should go to the suburbs today, Beebe," she called to her friend as she changed. "It's a fair distance, but I'm sure I can get someone to come with me to speed up the journey."

Beebe let out a happy tweet and flew in to nestle in Faunella's auburn waves. Propping open the leafy bush that covered the floor to ceiling opening, Faunella stepped out onto the thick knotted branch that laid just outside her door. Within a few minutes, she was safely on the ground.

Because it was so early, Faunella knew most of the Fae would still be in the cave. Her breath puffed out from her mouth as she walked, becoming visible as it collided with the chill in the air. The corner of her mouth tugged up into a crooked grin at the sight of the white mist whirling around in front of her face. She blew out a breath and tried to shape her exhalation, letting out a barking laugh when she saw the white, swirling image she had created.

"It looks like a man," she chuckled to the bird still nestled in her hair. Beebe let out a little squeak, sending her own small tendril of white mist wafting out to join with the quickly dissipating, life-like figure.

"Nice one, Beebe," Faunella said, stroking the soft black band under the bird's neck. Picking up her pace, Faunella hurried the remaining distance to the grotto. As soon as she arrived, she entered the cave, letting her eyes adjust. She looked around in the dim light and saw that all of the Fae were indeed still asleep.

"Morning," she called out in a sing-song voice as she skipped her way past the entrance. Beebe ruffled her feathers and flew back out into the clearing. Faunella made a beeline towards Violetta, her dry mouth urging her to get her morning drink.

"Violetta? Violetta," she whispered loudly, crouching down and placing her hands on Violetta's watery shoulder to shake her gently. "Wake up. It's morning."

Violetta rolled over with blinking eyes and let out a rough gurgle. Faunella caught the sound of her name and also something that sounded like '*go away.*' Using her inability to fully understand the Fae to her advantage, Faunella decided to ignore the *go away* part and instead leaned in closer, focusing on Violetta's squinted eyes.

"I want to go to the suburbs," she declared, her whisper causing Violetta to frown slightly and prop herself up onto her watery elbows. "I haven't had anything to drink this morning, and I'll be traveling a long way. Can I have some of your water? I'll need to keep my energy up so I can stay hidden from the humans." She spoke the last part slyly, knowing what buttons to push to get her own way.

Violetta sighed, morphing until she was sitting upright. She lay her head back to rest on the cave with her eyes closed.

"Violetta," Faunella whined, tapping the Fae's wet knee.

Violetta popped open her eyes and gave Faunella a reluctant smile. Looking away, she scanned the cave before a wicked glint appeared in her eyes. Her hand came up to form a swirling globe of water. Faunella's mouth popped open as Violetta sent the orb shooting over to the other side of the cave, and from the crashing crunch that came after the splash, Faunella knew that Violetta had woken Huxley.

The floor of the cave vibrated as the big rock jumped to his feet, chips of rock flying off him as he coughed and spluttered. Faunella's mouth snapped closed, but she couldn't help the giggle that came from behind her tight lips as he came stomping over. The annoyed sounds and gestures he made to his wet face clearly told Faunella what he was upset about. Violetta gave him a charming smile, craning her neck to look up at where he was towering over them, then gestured at Faunella as she let off a stream of sounds.

Faunella waited patiently for the two Fae to finish conversing. She was excited to get going but knew she needed someone to accompany her.

The other Fae somehow slept through Huxley's outraged awakening. Faunella smiled, pleased that her grumpy friend would be the one to come with her. Huxley was always more relaxed than Amon or Violetta.

"Can we go now?" she asked, looking from face to face. Huxley threw up his hands and stomped off towards the mouth of the cave. "So that's a yes, then?" She directed her hushed call at his retreating back.

His rough grumble was enough confirmation for her. She turned back to Violetta, and the two of them broke into fits of giggles. Still chuckling softly, Violetta held out her hands for Fawn to drink from, then nodded her head towards the mouth of the cave and waved her away. Happy to comply, Faunella jumped to her feet, ready to run after Huxley, but as an afterthought, wrapped her arms around the water Fae, heedless of getting her body wet.

"Thanks, Violetta. You're the best. Tell the others where I've gone, okay?" With that, she turned and hurried out of the cave.

By the time they reached the northern edge of the forest, Huxley's mood improved. The rock Fae was always quick to anger, but it never lasted long. As Faunella crept slowly through the thinning trees, she glanced up at the sun. They made good time, and it was only a little past midday.

Huxley curled himself up and slowly rolled the remaining distance to settle himself half-hidden under a fallen tree propped up by a nearby fir. Faunella reached for the thread connecting her to Beebe to let the bird know to stay away and not draw attention to her while she was on The Edge. From behind the large rock, she watched for his signal that said no eyes were on this area, and it was safe to get into position. A thick shard of rock about the size of a pine cone suddenly shuddered and broke off the side of Huxley's body.

That's it. All clear.

Staying low, she swiftly moved forward, jumping from a smaller rock onto Huxley's wide back. From there, she used him to pull herself up onto the slanted tree until she was crouched on the rounded trunk. Using her hands and feet, she climbed along the incline, working her toes to grip the soft bark and stop her sliding off. Once she reached the point where the two trees met, she settled down on the thin scratchy branch of the fir, letting the abundant green needles conceal her from sight. And not a moment too soon. The branches had only just stopped swaying from her movement when a door slammed open, and a young male voice called out.

Faunella's heart pounded with excitement as she looked out from her perch, honing in on where the noise was coming from. Several houses down, a thin, young man emerged from the back door of one of the dwellings that butted up against the edge of the forest. He walked into the grassy square and opened part of the barrier, walking through to the next dwelling area. Then, rapping his hand on the door of the new home, he called out a greeting and let himself in.

Faunella let out a huffing breath. *That wasn't very interesting.*

She scanned the first row of houses, stretched out in a long line that followed the curve of the forest. It didn't look like anyone else was out.

Tilting her head, she looked up at the thinner branches towards the top of the tree. A smile crept its way over her face. Glancing down at where Huxley sat, she briefly considered what he would say before dismissing any safety concerns and quickly scrambled higher.

She had been coming to the northern edge on and off since her first observation of the humans. She usually spent her time near the coastal town on the other side of the forest since it didn't take as long to get there, but this was her favorite place to go. She had heard it called "the suburbs" on her third visit by an angry man yelling at a woman. *"Why would I want to live in the suburbs when I have the option to live in the city?"* The woman had been crying and begging the man not to leave her. *"You can take this life and shove it up your ass!"*

Faunella had asked Erwin later what that word had meant, but the Fae's cheeks only darkened to a deep green, and he didn't answer her. When she had returned to the grotto, she asked the other Fae as well, but they also seemed reluctant to tell her. Huxley later informed her what the word meant. She shook her head. Why anyone would want to shove anything up there was beyond her.

Coming back to the present, Faunella clutched the thin branches as the fir tree swayed under her weight. The wind that traveled over the tops of the trees swirled around her, sending long strands of hair sweeping across her face. She closed her eyes for a moment, relishing the feeling of being caught up in the maelstrom of air. The wind picked up in intensity, tearing at the leaves of her clothes and sending her body careening back and forth as she clutched the top of the tree. Instead of being frightened, Faunella let out a breathy laugh, the untamed wind reaching deep inside and touching the recesses of her soul. She opened her eyes as the wind settled once more and looked out at the solid patchwork of hard shapes stretching out in front of her. In the distance, high buildings rose up from the smaller structures that surrounded them. The tops of the taller buildings seemed as tall as the tree she called home. From her observation, Faunella knew that most dwellings contained at least two people. The sight of so many homes and the thought of all of those people sent a shiver tickling down her spine. *What would it be like to walk amongst them?* she wondered, and not for the first time. With the thought, a heavy weight settled over her, washing away her contentment in one fell swoop. Her shoulders drooped as if the feeling was tangible, and with a small sigh, she began her descent.

Settling back on the lower branches, she prepared to wait for as long as she needed to. Some days, there were hardly any people around, but other days, the suburbs were busy with an abundance of humans. Those were Faunella's favorite days.

The back door the young man disappeared into opened again, and the gangly youth emerged, followed by another boy and a girl around the same age. Faunella perked up, shaking off her melancholy as she focused on the humans.

Luckily, they were in the row of houses that gave Faunella the ability to follow their conversation. The trio walked to the back barrier of the property and jumped the low structure. They walked along the narrow grassy incline that separated the edge of the forest and the wooden walls. As they drew closer, Faunella held her breath and studied the group intently.

The first young man had sandy blond hair and very pale skin. He had two circles that hung off his ears and sat in front of his nose. *Glasses,* Faunella reminded herself, thinking back to the few times she had heard them mentioned by other humans wearing the strange objects. The second, younger man had darker hair, a similar coppery shade to her own. His face spread into a wide grin as he ducked around his friends. The girl captivated Faunella the most. Her bluntly cut hair only just brushed her bare shoulders, and the ebony strands reflected the light with each sway of her body. Faunella stared, transfixed by the girl as the group walked past her tree. Her eyes were like no eyes Faunella had ever seen before. They were almond shaped, curving up at the outer corners into a delicate point.

She brought her fingers to her lips, touching the soft skin while she took in the unnatural shade of pink against the girl's fair skin. The girl let out a melodic laugh, a sound Faunella echoed quietly to herself. For a moment, Faunella could almost imagine she was one of them, something special—someone who belonged.

They slid down the rise and headed to a dwelling with a large pool of water set slightly back from the house. It was only then that she noticed the rolled-up lengths of cloth they all held.

One of the boys called out towards the dwelling as they began to remove their clothing. The boys both went shirtless while the girl revealed two pieces of brightly colored material, one over her chest and one barely covering her lower half.

Two more people came out to join them, another boy and another girl. The boy came racing over and hit into the pale boy, knocking them both into the water with a splash. The red-haired boy let out a whoop and jumped in after them.

Faunella let out a quiet chuckle at the boy's antics. It looked like so much fun. The two girls laughed as well, walking over together to sit on the edge of the pool with their feet dangling in the rippling water.

As the afternoon wore on, Faunella watched the interactions of the humans with growing fascination. They alternated between swimming in the pool of water and laying on the long pieces of fabric in the warm afternoon sun. It wasn't until the sun began to dip down, causing the sky to turn a hazy orange, that a woman came outside to where the group of young people played.

"All right you lot, it's time to get home."

The group let out a chorus of groans, their complaints overlapping even as they did as she bid. They begrudgingly gathered their clothing, and the original three waved goodbye to the two, who followed the woman into the house. They retraced their steps back along the rise and disappeared inside their own dwellings.

Faunella watched them go, a deep chasm forming in her center. She loved her life with the Fae, but something was missing. She felt a yearning to belong, to have a family that looked like her. Distracted, she shifted in place, reaching up to graze the top of her ear as her mind spun around, thoughts whirling.

When the clap of the last door closing echoed over to her concealed position, a rustle came from beneath her. Glancing down, she looked to where Huxley was backing out of the dead tree's shelter. He looked up at her and let out a quiet crackle. Faunella sighed, a weariness taking over her young body. Yes, it was time to go home.

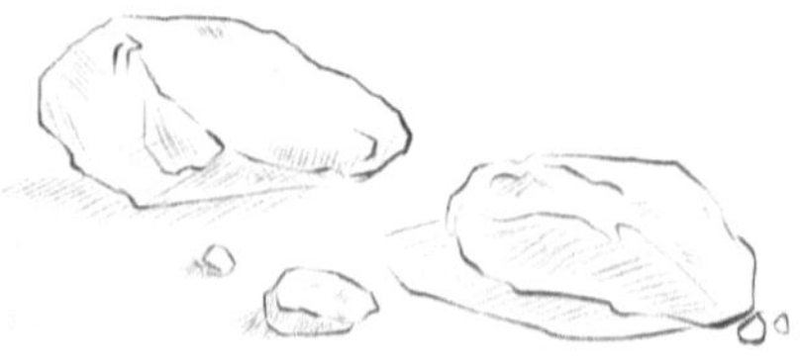

CHAPTER EIGHTEEN
HUXLEY

HUXLEY'S EYES TRACKED FAWN as she climbed down the fir tree. He frowned at the blank expression marring her usually happy face. He had never seen her anything other than bubbling with excitement after observing the humans. The two of them retreated quickly back into the forest, the afternoon sun sending long shadows shooting across the forest floor as the light turned whatever it touched a golden ember.

He snuck a look out of the corner of his eye as they began the long journey home. Her hands rubbed a strand of her light auburn hair as she stared down at the silky locks, her eyebrows lightly furrowed. Huxley's mind ran over the events of the afternoon, trying to figure out what could be causing Fawn's low mood. He couldn't think of anything out of the ordinary from what they usually saw when they came to the suburbs.

"I bet you're feeling really hungry, huh?" he asked her, bringing his hand to his mouth in an eating motion. He also rubbed his stomach for good measure.

Faunella looked at him, her blue eyes catching the golden light as she faced the direction of the setting sun. "I guess I am a little hungry." She shrugged, turning back to face forward as she continued walking along sedately. "I can wait till we get home though."

Huxley's worry grew. Fawn was passionate about many things, and one of those things was food. She could go without food when she was excited about doing something else, but as soon as her attention was drawn away, she was usually eager to indulge, generally in something sweet.

He kept his face carefully blank, not wanting Fawn to get wind of his concern. "We could make a quick stop at the berry patch if you'd like?"

"I'm not really in the mood for berries."

Huxley had to fight to stop his mouth from dropping open from the shock of her words. Something was definitely wrong.

A melodic call rang out above their heads as Beebe swept in from the treetops to circle Fawn excitedly. Fawn gave a little half smile and sent the bird an answering whistle. She raised her hand as a platform for Beebe to land on, but instead of putting the bird on her shoulder, she cupped her with both hands, holding her close to her chest.

It took almost twice as long to return home that evening. Fawn's feet seemed to drag, and Huxley struggled to figure out what he could say to draw her out of her melancholy. So, he just let her keep the pace, walking unhurriedly beside her.

Night fell rapidly as they pressed deeper into the thick forest, so Huxley kept close beside Fawn, conscious of her inability to see in the dark. He made use of the concealing darkness to watch her as they walked. His vision was as clear as day, whereas she could only see as well as a human. Despite her limitations, she didn't need much help making her way across the undulating forest floor. He only had to steady her a few times during their long trek south.

They were at the halfway point, and Fawn was giving no indication that she wanted to take a break. Seeing a moonlit patch of grass just up ahead, Huxley reached out and touched Fawn on her arm.

"Let's stop here. I've got something stuck in between my rocks," he lied, reaching down and rubbing at his stone legs when she turned to squint at him.

He took a few more steps, limping on his uninjured leg, before dropping heavily to sit in a patch of the low light. He watched as Fawn gracefully lowered herself to sit in a cross-legged position, her sadness forgotten and replaced with nothing but concern for his supposed injury.

"Are you okay, Hux?"

He brushed at his leg, allowing a few long shards to chip off and fall to the ground. "I'm alright now, not to worry." He forced himself to give Fawn a wide smile, wanting to alleviate her concerns.

Her tentative smile in return made his heart fall. She lowered her head and idly started to play with the short strands of grass in front of her. Huxley pursed his lips. It had been several hours now, and she still was in that downcast mood. He felt tongue-tied. He wanted to say or do something that would lighten her spirits. Craning his neck, he looked around the area they were in, hoping to see something that would help him get the smile back on his Fawn's face.

He scanned the brush behind Fawn, panning his head as he did, but a vibrant red color had his head snapping back around. Two black glittering eyes set in a furry face were peering out from under a fern. The black nose on the tip of its pointed snout wiggled as a red fox sniffed at the scent coming from Fawn's hunched form.

Huxley stayed still, curious as to what the animal would do. It crept forward, its large ears pricked as it placed one paw in front of another. As the fox drew closer to Fawn's body, Huxley's sharp eyes noticed another creature inching its way forward from the other side. This time, it was a small, inquisitive hedgehog. Huxley shook his head in disbelief.

His wry amusement turned into surprised astonishment when a large white owl came gliding in to perch on a low branch near Fawn's head. None of the animals seemed to be bothered by the proximity of each other. Their attention was focused solely on Fawn. Huxley stared at the scene, his eyes like saucers. The fox reached Fawn's side and sniffed at her hip, looking for all the world like it would hop up and curl in her lap. Lost in her own world, Fawn hadn't noticed any of the animals yet, but the hedgehog was inching closer and closer.

His mouth curved into a satisfied grin. He called out to get her attention. "Fawn, look." At his rumbling words, Fawn's head rose up. However, his call had an unwanted effect. The noise shattered the spell Fawn had somehow woven over the animals. The fox and the hedgehog stiffened up, turning their dark eyes to him before racing away back into the undergrowth, and the owl gave a deep hoot before it took flight. Heart sinking, he quickly lifted his arm and pointed at the retreating glow of the owl. Fawn followed his outstretched arm and just managed to catch the last glimpse of the bird's white feathers as it disappeared into the dark night sky.

"An owl!" She gave him a smile, her mouth making the motion but the smile not quite reaching her eyes.

Huxley sighed, feeling suddenly angry that he had spoiled the magical moment that unfolded around Fawn. His face fell into an unhappy frown, and he turned his head to hide the expression from her, lest she mistake his anger and think it was directed at her.

He got to his feet, ready to get back to the grotto. The inability to help Fawn preyed on his mind, and the only thing he could think of was for Fawn to have a good night's sleep. Maybe one of the other Fae would have a suggestion on how to make her feel better.

CHAPTER NINETEEN
DERICK

"**Y**EAH, WE BELONG TO the Dragons. We're actually quite high up."

Rhett elbowed him in the ribs, making him almost spill his drink. "Derick here is one of our more dangerous members. Me?" He grinned, leaning in towards the three girls at the bar. "Well, I'm more of a lover than a fighter." The girls tittered, hiding their smiles behind coy hands. Derick bit back a laugh. Rhett was always after the girls, and with his dark wavy hair, blue eyes, and dimpled smile, he was usually successful.

"Our Rhett didn't get much love as a child." Derick swiveled around on the stool, clapping the younger man on the shoulder. "Don't let his desperation put you ladies off." He winked at the trio before turning fully and striding out of the busy bar. As he stepped out into the cool night air, he sucked in a deep breath. It had been a long night, and he was desperate for some peace, something he had been unable to find among the music and the crowded, sweaty bodies that permeated the Green Locker, their gang's local watering hole.

"Where are you going?" Rhett followed him out, catching up to him with a quick poke to the side. He skipped ahead of Derick, walking backwards with a playful look in his eyes. "Bitches be in heat tonight." Lifting his face to the night sky, he closed his eyes and howled, drowning out the pulsing music inside the building. When Derick didn't join in, Rhett raised his brows quizzically. "Those girls were easy." He shoved his hands into his jacket pocket, shrugging his shoulders loosely. "We could go back in. I'll take two and leave one for you." Despite his fatigue, Derick's lips quivered upwards. He swung around, letting out a rumbling laugh, and gently threw his fist into Rhett's shoulder. "You'd leave me one, huh?" He chuckled. "Very big of you."

"I'm nothing if not big," Rhett winked, wiggling his eyebrows suggestively.

Derick smiled as he looked up and down Rhett's five-and-a-half-foot frame. "Nothing then?"

"Shut up, you dick." Now it was Rhett's turn to throw a mocking punch towards Derick. He dodged it easily, and the two men stood grinning at each other.

"So, are you coming back in?"

Derick glanced back into the lit-up bar, his stomach tightening as he surveyed the space. "Nah, I'm done for tonight." He forced a lighthearted smile to his face, not wanting to let Rhett know how tired he was of the constant drinking and partying. He had just turned twenty, but he felt so much older. It seemed like Shaun sent them out to do jobs every other day, and each time they came home successful, the gang used that as an excuse to celebrate, drinking and fucking long into the night. "You go back in. Those girls will be missing your pretty blue eyes."

Rhett surveyed him, his usually jovial face serious for a moment before breaking back into a wide smile. "Nah, bros before hoes." He swung back his fist, miming a punch to Derick's face, but then ducked down and jabbed him in the gut instead.

Derick sucked in a breath, doubling over from the sucker punch. "You ass," he wheezed between gritted teeth, then lunged towards Rhett playfully. Rhett gawked and danced away, backing off down the sidewalk.

"So, where to, Derick? The night is young, and we rule these streets. What's the plan?"

Derick shrugged. In all honesty, he wanted to go home—well, as much as the gang house could be home—and be alone. He had a half-finished novel under his mattress, and he was itching to find out how it ended. Before he could respond, Rhett stilled, a mischievous gleam in his eyes.

"How about a little joy ride?"

Derick twisted his head to see what caught Rhett's attention. It was a gunmetal Cadillac, the silver rims catching the light from a nearby street lamp. Without waiting for Derick, Rhett scurried over, peering through the slightly tinted windows. Cautiously approaching, Derick took in the scene. The car was parked further down the street. It was far enough that, likely, the owner wasn't frequenting the bar, which meant they were quite possibly in one of the surrounding homes on the street. An uneasy feeling began to grow in his stomach. He studied the car, wondering what about it had him so rattled. It wasn't as if he had never stolen a car before. In the gang, it was probably one of their most common crimes.

"I don't know Rhett. Something feels off."

Rhett glanced back at him in surprise, his quick fingers already tugging at the handle. The door swung open. Rhett's low whistle cut through the air, and his pursed lips soon broke into a wide smile.

"That's never happened to me before. An unlocked car." He climbed smoothly into the driver's seat. "It was meant to be."

The feeling in Derick's stomach spread through his chest, sending a prickle of warning up his spine. *Who leaves their car unlocked in this neighborhood?* he wondered hesitantly, reluctant to climb into the vehicle.

"Hurry up," hissed Rhett, beckoning him with a quick flick of his wrist as he messed with the wires under the dash. "Get in."

Against his better judgment, he jogged around to the passenger side and slid into the leather seat. Just as soon as he had closed the door, Rhett finished hot-wiring the car and screeched down the street, letting out a whoop of delight as they blew past the bar.

Derick settled back into the lush seat, working on tamping down his anxiety as Rhett cruised through the city. He opened the window and let the night air rush in, the cold breeze cooling his flushed face and calming him further. As the miles added up, he began to relax, his mind drifting from one thing to the next.

"You're off to see Frank tomorrow, right?" Rhett's voice broke through his thoughts, the topic sending a stab of irritation through him. He pursed his lips and looked away from his friend.

"Yeah."

"I, uh..." Rhett's words came out shaky, his usual confidence betrayed by the quiver in his voice. He coughed. "I was wondering if you could put in a word for me."

Derick swung his head back, staring at Rhett's profile, which lit up each time they passed a light.

"What the hell do you mean?" Confusion racked his body. Frank had been locked up for over seven years with Shaun now firmly the leader of the Sea Dragons. It would be at least another fourteen years before Frank had any chance of parole. Even then, Derick doubted Shaun would give up the gang easily, no matter what he had once believed.

Rhett glanced at him, letting out a sheepish chuckle. "You know. You visit him every month, and Shaun goes occasionally." He shrugged. "I figured he holds a lot of sway in the gang, and he could talk me up to Shaun."

Derick's heart sank. Even before Rhett had healed from his injuries, he had been trying to prove himself as one of the biggest, baddest members. But Derick had been around for years and knew for certain the man just didn't have that killer instinct. In fact, that was one of the reasons he liked Rhett so much. He was a breath of fresh air compared to the other men, who seemed to eat, sleep, and breathe gang life.

"Rhett," he sighed, shaking his head wearily. "Don't you ever get sick of this life, of being in a constant state of fight or flight?"

Rhett exploded with laughter, throwing back his head and slapping the steering wheel. The car swerved into the other lane, jerking back when Rhett's laughter eased.

"Good one, Derick," he chuckled deeply. "Get sick of it? Like the man who framed his own father for murder could ever convince me he wasn't made for this."

Guilt swept through his body, turning him to stone. The story that Derick had killed a man to purposely send his own father to prison was a favorite among the men. After the gang had gotten over their anger at losing Frank, Shaun spun the narrative, and Derick was given a reputation as someone cold and ruthless. He tightened his mouth, curving it into a weak grin, and forced out a hollow laugh.

"You know it," he replied, looking back out of the open window, letting his voice trail off quietly. "I'm in it for life."

By the time Rhett pulled the car up outside the chop shop on the edge of town, Derick's mood had plummeted further. Eager to be finished with the day, he shoved open the door and swung one booted foot out.

"So, you'll talk to Frank?"

There was no way in hell he would be talking to his father about Rhett. The longer he stayed off Shaun and Frank's radar, the better.

"Sure thing. I'll mention your name."

Rhett flashed his teeth, a dimple appearing on one cheek. Derick finished climbing out of the car, slamming the door firmly behind him. He leaned back through the open window and rested his forearms on the roof of the car.

"Don't get your hopes up, though. It takes something big to get their attention, and that's not always a good thing."

Rhett's grin faded, his features turning pensive. Derick shook his head, a tinge of worry running through him. His friend wore all his thoughts and emotions on his sleeve. While that was a big part of what made him popular with the ladies, it was a massive danger within the gang.

"Something big." Rhett spoke the words slowly, and Derick could almost see the wheels turning in his mind. His pulse started pounding loudly in his ears. The small amount of worry he felt grew into something more tangible. He pushed down his feelings and plastered a smile to his face, angling his head out into the night.

"Come on then. Let's get back."

Rhett jerked, blinking rapidly as if he had forgotten all about Derick's presence.

"Ah, you go back." He put the car in gear, waving away the man who had just opened the garage door for him. "I might drive for a bit more."

"Rhett—"

"I'll see you later, Derick." He winked at him, brushing off his concern. "Go and get your beauty sleep."

He revved the car, causing Derick to reluctantly step back. There was no reason that Rhett shouldn't go out and do whatever it was he wanted, but Derick couldn't shake the heavy chill coiled in his chest.

"Don't do anything stupid," he choked out, shoving his hands into his jacket pockets as Rhett tipped an imaginary hat to him, drawling out a "yes, sir."

Derick watched him pull away, following the red tail lights until the car turned the corner and disappeared from sight.

It was only when he was halfway home that he recognized the cold weight behind his ribs was dread.

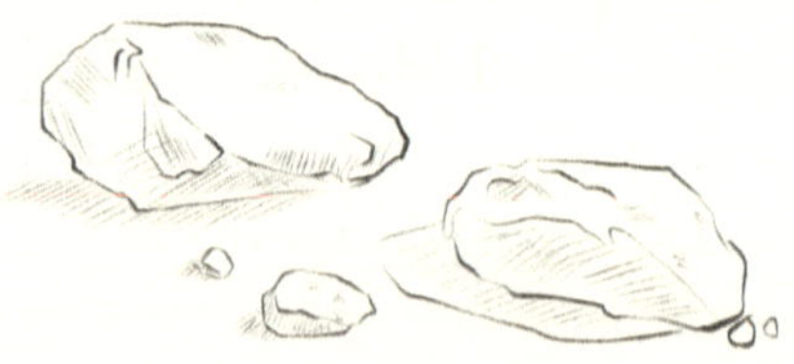

CHAPTER TWENTY
HUXLEY

THE DARK SHADOWS OF sleep were pierced by a rhythmic sensation on the side of his face. Huxley groaned in irritation. Rolling over, he swiped his hand down the contours of his cheek. His hand came away wet. Blearily, he realized the dull roar he could hear was the sheets of water coming from the sky.

He shifted out of the path of the dripping water that trickled in from one of the holes in the cave roof and settled back to sleep. Breathing deeply, a small smile crossed his lips as he brought an image of Violetta to mind. He pictured the diaphanous Fae out in the thundering rain, the clouds turning the day into shades of gray and silver. She would be dancing around the clearing, her head thrown back with abandon as she reveled in the moisture raining from the heavens. Someone cleared their throat loudly, interrupting his musings.

"What do you want?" he growled, eyes slitting open to glare at whoever disturbed his daydreams.

Erwin stood in front of him, grimacing up at his angry face. "Sorry, Hux. I didn't want to wake you, but the others sent me." He wrung his green hands. "They want to know if something happened with Fawn yesterday."

Huxley lurched up, instantly alert. "Why? What happened?"

Erwin shuffled in place, his sad excuse for a smile falling. Huxley clenched his teeth, anxious to know the information that had gotten his friend so worked up. "Fawn came out this morning and wanted to go to The Edge. Amon told her no because of the rain. He was concerned that she might get sick, especially since she didn't have much sleep last night after the two of you got home so late."

Huxley cocked his head. "Okay, what's so bad about that? She's been told no before."

"Well, that's just it. She's insisting she should be able to go and that Amon has no right to stop her or tell her what to do." Erwin's eyes welled, distress in every fiber of his springy body.

"We've never seen Fawn like this before, Hux. It's like she's a completely different person. The others are trying to reason with her, but they sent me back to check in with you." Erwin turned his earnest eyes up to meet with Huxley's own dark ones.

"Was there any indication that something might be wrong with her when you were with her yesterday? Did something happen?" Huxley felt a heavy weight sink to the bottom of his stomach.

I guess a good night's sleep didn't help.

"She did seem a bit down after we left the suburbs yesterday evening. She wasn't herself during the journey home." He got to his feet and ran a hand over the top of his head. "I thought maybe she was just tired. Nothing happened during the day that could have changed her mood so drastically."

"Well, something must have," Erwin squeaked out, leading him towards the front of the cave. "Come on. The others will want to hear it from you."

As soon as Huxley stepped from the cave mouth, the heavy sheet of rain flowed over his body, temporarily blinding his vision. He followed Erwin as they made their way across the open clearing. Once they were under the partial shelter of the trees, he wiped the moisture from his eyes and continued eastward towards the coastal town, concern pounding through him with each step.

Erwin looked back at him as they hurried along. "She keeps trying to get to the town. They've been trying to stop her, but short of grabbing her and tying her up, there is nothing they can do."

Huxley swallowed, dread pooling around the hard mass in his belly. The rain continued steadily, the high canopy of leaves combining the drops into fat ovals. Soon, he could hear raised words over the pelting sound of the rain. They hurried towards the voices, stopping abruptly when they came upon the foreign sight.

Fawn's face was a vibrant shade of red. Bent at the waist, she was shouting with all her might at the group of Fae surrounding her.

"You always try to keep me here in the forest! I never get to be with anyone who looks like me!" Her hair plastered to her body with rain tracking down her cheeks. The clear droplets hid what Huxley suspected were tears.

He stepped forwards, heart breaking as he felt the anguish coming from her slight form.

Her stormy blue eyes scanned the Fae who were trying to placate her. "Get away from me! I don't belong here with you. I belong with the humans. I'm one of them!"

Huxley's mouth fell open at Fawn's outrageous claim. The fact she believed she was a human was a dangerous idea. No wonder the others were trying desperately to stop her.

"What's going on Amon?" he asked, inching closer, careful not to incur Fawn's rage.

Amon kept his attention on Fawn, his arms outstretched in case she made a run for it. "She wanted to go to observe the humans today, but with the rain, I thought it would be better if she stayed at home where it's dry. So, I told her no. She immediately started to argue and got upset." The branches of his arms quivered slightly, the only outward sign of his anguish. "She decided she would go on her own, and when I moved to stop her, she became enraged."

Huxley wouldn't have believed it if he hadn't seen it for himself. He glanced over to where Fawn stood, her chest heaving. Beebe flittered into view, letting off frantic chirps as she circled Fawn's shaking body.

"She thinks she's a human?" he asked, looking around for confirmation from the devastated faces of the Fae.

"That's what she's been saying," said Baol from the other side of Fawn. "She's got it in her head that we've stolen her from the humans, and she wants to go back." Amon let out a choking sob, no longer able to keep his emotions in check. Huxley stepped up to comfort his friend. At the same moment, Baol shifted in place.

Fawn lost it.

"Stay away from me! You can't stop me!" She tensed to run, and Amon automatically tried to stop her, his branches shooting towards her taut body.

"I said, get away from me!" Fawn screamed the words, flinging her hand towards them in a wide arc.

A tidal wave of compressed air erupted from under the sweep of her arm. The wind pulsed from her body, first forcing Amon's branches up and then flinging his body back. On instinct, Huxley dropped low, counting on his heavy weight to keep him on the ground. All around him, the Fae were flung away, brought low by the explosion of wind blowing out from around Fawn's quaking body. The ensuing silence was broken by the harsh, jagged breaths coming from her mouth. She surveyed the fallen Fae, then stared at her outstretched hand with rising horror.

"Fawn?" Huxley came to his feet with his arm outstretched, only concerned with how she was feeling. He had no fear of anything else she might do. Never had he been so grateful for his solid nature form.

Fawn's startled gaze shot to his, her red face now bleached of all color. "I... I don't..." She cut off abruptly, unable to articulate a response to the power she had just shown. Her eyes welled up, flooding over and sending fresh tears coursing down her cheeks.

"Fawn, it's okay," he continued, steadily moving towards her. All around him, the Fae were pushing themselves upright, quietly murmuring as they marveled over the strong magic Fawn should never have been able to wield. He kept his attention fixed firmly on Fawn, knowing the pain that self-loathing could cause. He had almost reached her when a quiet tweet captured her attention from his steady gaze. Unable to stop himself, Huxley turned to follow the sound.

Cradled at the base of a knotted oak was Beebe. Unmoving, her wings spread out as she lay sprawled on the wet earth. The falling rain soaked the soft underside of her feathers, creating dark streaks among the pale down.

Fawn gave a guttural cry that pierced deep within his heart. He turned back to comfort her, but it was too late. She spun away from his embrace and fled into the forest, this time, with no one to stop her.

CHAPTER TWENTY ONE
DERICK

THE STREET OUTSIDE THE Sea Dragons' headquarters was crowded with vehicles. Every gap on the road was filled, including the sidewalk where several large bikes were parked.

Derick eased the throttle on his bike, letting the Harley slow as he swept his eyes past the unusual sight. By mid-afternoon, most, if not all, of the men should be off doing jobs for Shaun or at the pub. He frowned, thinking back over the past few days to see if he had forgotten a meeting of all their members.

Angling his bike into the end of the row, he let it idle for a moment. Surely, he would have been informed if Shaun had called everyone together? He cut the engine, pulling out his phone to check. Sure enough, there were six missed calls, four from Shaun and two from Jarred, as well as a message from Rhett. Scratching the stubble on his chin, Derick considered the messages. Shaun, he could understand, but Jarred calling him was out of the blue. Swinging a jean-clad leg over his bike, he stood and stretched out his back before opening the message from Rhett.

I fucked up.

"Shit."

Derick clenched his jaw and slid his phone back into his pocket. Striding quickly towards the building, his heart beat in time with his fast pace. Last night's dread coiled low in his belly, turning his usually warm skin cold. Suddenly, the last-minute meeting made sense, and nothing about the situation was good.

"Ah, Derick," Shaun's voice was cold as he studied him from the middle of the room. "Glad you could make time out of your busy schedule to be here."

A quiver of fear ran through him. The entire front room of their residence was packed with the owners of the vehicles outside. The members of the gang stood stiffly, fists clenched and tattooed arms folded. When Shaun gestured him forward over the sea of heads, they parted, allowing Derick to push through to the center of the group. He swallowed dryly, but he threw back his shoulders and kept his face impassive. Whatever he was about to see, he couldn't allow anything to rattle him.

That resolve was tested as soon as he stepped into the circle.

Shaun stood with his legs spread, his large form blocking out the sight of someone slouched in a chair behind him. Derick's eyes flicked to his hands, his attention caught by the smears and splatters of blood staining Shaun's skin. Dismay speared through him.

"What's going on?"

He tried to keep his eyes on Shaun's face, to stare down the formidable man and not show weakness, but, unable to stop his traitorous gaze, he found himself scanning the spaces Shaun's body couldn't hide, desperately trying to find proof that the man tied to the chair by his ankles and wrists wasn't the one person he cared about most in this world.

Shaun scowled, his narrowed eyes scanning Derick from head to toe as if he were looking for proof of some wrongdoing on his body. Seemingly satisfied, he crossed his arms in front of his chest.

"You really don't know what this is about?"

It was quick, but Derick swore he saw a flash of disappointment cross Shaun's face. Whatever this trouble was, the older man wanted him to have been a part of it.

"Know what this is about?" He unclenched his fists and relaxed his face, shrugging his shoulders like he didn't have a clue. "I've been up at the prison all morning."

"And last night?" Shaun stepped to the side, revealing the man in the chair at last. "Where were you then?"

Derick's heart dropped, his eyes taking in the picture of Rhett's beaten and bloody body slumped over in the chair. As his vision narrowed to only Rhett, a buzzing started in his ears, growing louder and louder, but not quite loud enough to drown out the nasty chuckle coming from Jarred's mouth.

No, no, no.

Rhett had done something bad enough to put him in severe danger from the gang. Guilt plagued him. He should have stopped Rhett last night, made him drop the car off and call it a night. By ignoring his inner voice, he had allowed this to happen. It was as if he had beaten his friend himself.

The ringing reached its peak, reminding him that he was being observed. Sucking in a sharp breath, he cut the noise off and turned his carefully blank face back to Shaun.

"I was at the Green Locker till late, then I came back here." He didn't know what Rhett had told them, and only one other person had seen the two of them together that night. He was hedging his bets that Shaun didn't know about his involvement. He gestured to Rhet nonchalantly. "Whatever he did, he did on his own."

Shaun peered into his eyes, deliberating over his statement. Desperately trying to calm his racing heart, Derick stood tall, keeping his gaze fixed on Shaun and away from his friend. After what felt like an eternity, Shaun gave him a small nod, then turned to a man standing to the side.

"Wake him."

"This is bullshit." All eyes turned to Jarred. He pushed himself through the circle and gripped Shaun's elbow, drawing a frown from the older man. "There's no fucking way Rhett did this by himself." He turned his red face to glare at Derick, slinging his words as if they were weapons. "The two of them are always together. The faggot—"

"Jarred!"

Shaun wrenched his arm from Jarred's grip and swung around to knock his forehead into Jarred's brow. Clutching the back of his son's neck, he held the two of them together with force. "Don't you ever try to tell me what to do," he hissed under his breath. "A little pissant like you has no clue what it takes to run this business. So until you've proved yourself, you can shut the fuck up." He flung Jarred away and faced the rest of the gang, his face severe and unyielding. "Anyone else have an opinion?" He circled the men, staring them down as if daring them to challenge him. "No? Good. Now wake him the fuck up."

A bucket of water was thrown into Rhett's face, and he lurched upwards with a gasp. The water running down his body was tinted red and pooled on the hardwood floor. One of his eyes was completely swollen and closed up, but his other eye swiveled around, frantically searching until it landed on Derick. The pain and regret shining in his blue eyes was unmistakable. He opened his mouth, winching at his split lip. "Derick."

Fuck. Don't say anything.

Derick lunged forward and kicked out his foot, sending Rhett's chair flying backward. He swallowed heavily when Rhett's head connected to the ground, the sharp crack echoing through the room. Hoping he would understand, Derick tightened his jaw and turned away from the scene.

"Whatever he's done has nothing to do with me." He forced a laugh, the noise sounding hollow to his ears. "He's just an idiot trying to prove himself. I'm sure whatever it is isn't that bad." Blood rushed to his head as he scrambled to think of a way to get Rhett out of this mess, to say or do anything that could lessen his punishment.

The men around him shifted uncomfortably, and Shaun smirked, totally unconcerned with the fact that Derick had just knocked Rhett to the ground.

"Maybe you should wait to hear what he's done before you judge his actions."

Derick stayed silent, waiting for Shaun to hurry up and inform him of Rhett's crime. The other men seemed to be enjoying delaying the moment, and Derick was trying really hard to not let Shaun see how much it was affecting him. However, as the silence dragged on, Shaun's smirk fell, and a frown returned to his face.

"A car was stolen last night. It was taken from outside a house and used in a robbery - a ram raid, to be exact." He shifted to stand beside Rhett, placing a booted foot on his shoulder and pressing down hard, eliciting a low groan from the injured man. "Rhett here left the car and turned up this morning with his score."

Nothing Shaun was saying was out of the ordinary for them. Ramming a stolen vehicle through a shop front then subsequently robbing it during the chaos was something they had all done. Derick was confused at what had gone so wrong that Rhett could be in such trouble. He shifted in place and arched a brow at the men to his left, acting like he didn't have a care in the world. Their faces slackened with mixed looks of disbelief and admiration. Derick kept his eyes high and his face cold, scanning the circle of men in the room before turning his attention back to Shaun, wondering how much longer this would go on before Rhett would be allowed to leave and he could tend to his wounds.

"But, this idiot made two big mistakes."

Derick chanced a glance down at Rhett. Regret was plastered all over his battered face, so whatever Shaun was about to say had to be true.

"There were security cameras that caught him robbing the store. My contact in the police called in the tip. He also told me that the car that was used is registered to Saul Denman."

Fuck.

Saul Denman was the head of a large generational mob family based on the East Coast. One thing that went without saying—no one messes with Saul or his operations. A hard lump formed in the back of his throat, and all Derick's thoughts of getting Rhett out of this disappeared.

"I'm sorry, Shaun. I'm sorry." Rhett's hoarse voice choked out apology after apology. His pleas for mercy went unnoticed. The only person his words affected was Derick. Each pitiful cry and sob cut right through him, sending bolts of agony stabbing through his chest.

Shaun spat a wad of spit onto Rhett, moving his foot onto his neck to cut off his cries. "I've spoken with Saul. We will be giving him everything you took and replacing his car."

Derick braced himself for the final blow. Even though he knew it was coming, he couldn't help the sharp pain that speared him through the heart and turned his mind numb.

"He also wanted Rhett." Shaun pressed down harder on Rhett's throat, making him gasp for breath, saliva flying from his mouth. "But, I convinced him we would take care of him on his behalf."

Shaun held out his hand to Derick, a large, wicked-looking knife in his palm.

An offering—a command.

He looked into Shaun's eyes, the challenge there obvious. His loyalty had to be to Shaun and the gang. That came before anything else. Derick was under no illusion that if he didn't do this, he would join Rhett's fate. Derick sucked in a breath, the motion stretching the skin over his ribs. The phantom burning in his side was like a splash of frigid water on his face, a clear reminder that his one chance to defy Shaun had been spent. Despite that, he hesitated.

"Is there a problem?" Shaun's voice was low, a warning edging his words.

Even as his mind frantically sought a solution, he found his hand wrapping around the blade. He moved on autopilot, stepping past Shaun and kneeling down beside Rhett.

He felt the men around him step back but was unable to see through the tears that pricked at his eyes. Rhett angled his head to face him, his dark hair matting against his blood-soaked head. Lips wobbling, he tried for a half-hearted smile. "I fucked up, didn't I?"

Derick didn't answer, not trusting that his voice wouldn't break. How could he kill his best friend? He wanted desperately to run away, to fight past everyone in this room and get Rhett out of here to safety. He wanted to beg for forgiveness and scream out his unwillingness to do this, but whatever Rhett saw on his face must have been enough. He swallowed, closing his one unswollen eye. "It was good while it lasted." He lifted his blue eye up to Derick's brown ones, his face turning serious. "Do it."

It took all of his willpower to stop his hands from shaking, tighten his fingers around the knife's handle, and place the blade against the thin skin on Rhett's neck, but it took no strength at all to slide the sharp point across Rhett's throat, watching with horror as scarlet blood poured through the wound and covered his hands.

Rhett gave a hollow gasp, his body jerking from the hot bite of the knife. His skin slowly leached of color, and within a few moments, the bright light left his eyes forever.

Nausea filled Derick. Rising to his feet, he threw the knife to the ground and stalked out of the room. He had to get away. Each beat of his heart pounded out those words. He should have left a long time ago. He should have forced Rhett to come with him. Why the hell did he stay?

The hot midday sun hit him as he burst through the door. Blinking against the light, he made a beeline towards his bike, pretending the tears squeezing from his eyes were from the sun's glare. Distracted, he didn't notice he was being followed. It was only after he had swung his leg over the bike that a hand reached out and clamped down on his arm.

Derick sent a cold glare to Shaun, no longer caring about deferring to the man, only concerned about getting as far away from this life as possible.

"Before you go, you might want to see this," Shaun said as he held out his phone. "In case you were thinking about leaving."

A video played on the screen. A repeat of what had just occurred a few minutes earlier. Derick's blood went cold. His jaw clenched tight, and he gripped the handlebars. He might get away from the gang, but he couldn't hide from the cops. All his thoughts and dreams of leaving the gang came crashing down around him. Shaun held his life as easily as holding him on a leash.

There was no escape. Nothing but death could free him now.

"Just going for a ride, that's all." His lip curled up into a smile, but for the life of him, he couldn't bring the smile to his eyes. "I'll be back later."

Shaun stepped back, allowing him the room to leave. His body was relaxed, a self-satisfied expression on his face.

"I'll see you then." He nodded towards Derick's hands. "And don't forget you have blood on your hands."

CHAPTER TWENTY TWO
FAUNELLA

I KILLED BEEBE. I killed my best friend. The words swirled around in Faunella's head as she ran, the trees moving past her in a dark blur. She couldn't see past the tears that pooled in her eyes, but she continued on blindly, not caring if she ran into something or hurt herself. It would be no less than she deserved after what she had done. Another choking sob burst out of her mouth.

The bird's limp form flashed in her mind.

"Beebe," she gasped, feeling a hot pressure start to rise in her stomach. Falling to her knees, she heaved the few contents of her stomach out onto the forest floor. The hot burn of acid momentarily distracted her from the pain of her emotions. Her chest felt like it had been cracked open, laid bare and raw like an uncovered nerve. The tug of the warm flutter inside of her was now still, frozen, despite the fiery pain that burned through her.

She fell to her side, curling up into a tight ball amongst the wet layer of dead leaves that covered the ground. Squeezing her eyes tightly, she let out a blood-curdling wail and dissolved into an uncontrollable release of steady tears. The feeling of being alone that led her down the path of thinking she belonged to the humans was nothing compared to the hollowness now consuming her body. Beebe had been her constant friend, always there with her in whatever she did. Faunella opened her swollen eyes and blinked blearily at her palms. Her breath came in short bursts as she tried to wrap her mind around the startling discovery. She had magic.

A sudden fear seized her. Clenching her fists tightly, she thrust them under the foliage by her chest, hiding them from sight. The power had ripped from her hands with no warning and no control. What if she did it again? She shut her eyes with a clap, her thoughts plagued by visions of the Fae getting torn apart by her uncontrollable magic. The images played out in her mind, and Faunella descended deeper into her guilt, her imagination strengthening the scenes and turning them violent. She allowed the dark thoughts to take her, believing herself unworthy of anything kind or good.

The rain eased about the same time she stopped crying. Her body was chilled, and her head felt thick and heavy. Keeping her eyes closed, she reached one hand up to wipe weakly at the mucus that was oozing from her nose.

Maybe I should just stay here and die. She curled up tighter, automatically fighting the cold despite her disparaging thoughts. *The others must hate me now, and after what I did to Beebe, I deserve to die.*

She pressed her palms against the stinging pain behind her eyes as a fresh round of tears threatened to escape. Mouth opening, she let out a series of deep, shuddering cries before her body slackened, too spent to continue crying.

I'm all alone now. No one even came after me.

Prying open her swollen eyes, she surveyed the space where she had ended up after her mad dash away from the scene of her crime. She was wrong. Her throat grew thick and her heavy heart turned over. Balanced on a fallen log, only a few steps away, sat Huxley, Erwin and Amon, their entire bodies etched with concern. Amon looked as if he had aged significantly in the short time since that morning. Faunella couldn't bear the look on their faces.

"I'm sorry," she sniffed, her chin quivering from the force of her emotions. "I didn't mean to."

Erwin came rushing forward as she began to speak. Faunella jolted, scrambling backwards to try and keep distance between them. Without hesitation, he stretched himself wide and launched over her body. Terror gripped her. Jamming her hands firmly under her body, she leaned away from his embrace and held her breath, not knowing what might trigger it. Her reaction had Huxley and Amon glancing at each other, their worry and hurt undeniable. Squeezing tightly, Erwin made firm whirring noises as he stroked small circular motions on her back.

After holding herself taut for several long moments with no explosion of power, Faunella let her body soften and took a low, shuddering breath. Erwin crooned his encouragement, and with great reluctance, she withdrew her hands, threading her fingers into his coiled moss. Relief loosened the lump in her throat, and she pressed her face into the soft recess of his neck, clutching him tight as she let the tears fall once again. She hadn't felt like a Fae, not since finding out about the humans. Her lack of magic and the way she looked had convinced her that she was a human, or maybe that was just easier to believe.

Taking a deep breath to steady herself, she looked up at Amon and Huxley.

"They look like me," she explained, her voice sounding hoarse from her prolonged crying. "Everyone has a family that's the same as them, except me." Everything that happened over the past day came flooding back to her, weighing her down with an exhaustion beyond the physical.

Huxley got up from where he was perched, taking the few steps that brought him directly in front of where she sat. His black eyes bore into her own, capturing her attention, until all she could see was him. Lifting his arm, he brought it to his chest and began to beat a firm rhythm, the loud crashing sound beating in time with her own pounding heart. Faunella kept still as he stretched his arm out and gave Erwin a nudge. The moss Fae loosened his hold on her just enough to swing his body around to settle against her back, his arms slipping around her neck to continue holding tight. Huxley returned to beating on his chest before reaching back towards her and pressing firmly onto her now uncovered heart.

Faunella swallowed thickly. The implication was clear, and she felt a wave of shame wash over her. She did have a family - not one that looked like her, but instead, a family of the heart.

"Am I Fae, then? Is that how I did what I did?"

Amon came forward to join Huxley. He lowered himself as much as he could before giving her a gentle nod. Opening his mouth, he let out a steady stream of rustles and groans. Faunella listened intently, working to understand as much as she could.

"I'm a different Fae than you? And I won't look Fae until I'm bigger?"

Amon smiled, the bark crinkling around his eyes.

"That's right, Fawn," he seemed to say.

Faunella lowered her head, sniffing wetly against the tears still dripping from her nose.

"I said such awful things." She looked up, her heart heavy in her chest. "And I did something terrible." Her hushed whisper was still heard by the gathered Fae. A leafy hand stroked down her tear-streaked face, swiping under her nose before pulling away. Huxley placed his hard finger under her chin, tipping her face back up to his. The love in his eyes was almost her undoing.

Her unsteady lips tried to curve up into a watery smile, but she couldn't quite make it. The picture of Beebe, prone and still, grew in her mind. "You should hate me for what I did."

Her skin was cold and clammy, and she fought the shiver that danced across her body. Huxley and Amon each held out an arm and raised her to her feet, but Amon was the one who scooped her in his limbs to cradle her close to his trunk.

Huxley led the way as they made their way back through the forest. Faunella cringed as she saw the trail of broken branches made by her mad dash away from the consequences of what she had done. She lifted her hands in front of her face, feeling sick again as she looked at the appendages responsible for her devastating power.

"My power killed Beebe," she choked out, throwing her arms back down to her sides and turning to press her face into the damp bark of Amon's trunk. "I get this magic, and the first thing I do is destroy." Tears escaped out of the sides of her eyes, making hot tracks down her cold cheeks.

Amon's arms tightened around her, holding her close to his body. Faunella stayed like that for the remainder of the distance, not wanting to witness the destruction. She was plagued with waves of guilt that swept over her, drowning her in sorrow. The wound in her chest ached, pulsing in time with the steady thumping of her heart.

I'll never be able to fix what I've done. The others might have forgiven me, but that doesn't change what I did to Beebe.

They stopped abruptly, the swishing sound of Amon and Huxley's steps cutting off into a still silence. Faunella took a shuddering breath and prepared herself to face the other Fae.

Suddenly, a lively twitter rang out, cutting through the quiet.

Faunella twisted in Amon's arms, her heart picking up its pace as a hopeful bubble burst through her. "Beebe?"

She blinked past her tears, focusing in on the small black and white blur that shot straight towards her. Beebe's incessant chirping increased as she fluttered around Faunella's head, plucking playfully at her wet strands of hair.

"Oh, Beebe." Faunella erupted into another round of heavy sobs, this time driven by the powerful feeling of relief. "I'm so sorry. I'm so, so sorry," she choked out, her words barely perceptible over her gasping breaths. She reached out her arms, capturing the bird gently in her cupped hands. Beebe settled down, emitting a steady stream of love through the bond.

Looking inside, Faunella examined herself, following the emotion coming from Beebe. The pulsing had disappeared, revealing the lively tether that tied the two of them together. "How?" she asked, gazing around the faces of her Fae family. "I thought she was dead?"

Violetta came forward, shaking her head.

"Just sleeping." The water Fae lifted her hands and mimed drinking some water, seemingly reluctant to say more.

"You healed her?"

Violetta nodded, reaching up to tuck a wet strand of hair behind Faunella's ear. Before she removed her hand, she cupped Faunella's cheek, tenderly stroking the skin there as she bubbled words of affection and love. Distracted, Faunella's eyebrows drew together, and she felt for the bond again. It had hurt when she thought Beebe was dead—aching, throbbing and burning in agony. She shook her head and concentrated on strengthening the connection between them. Whatever Violetta had done had reformed the tether, which made sense since the Fae's water magic had bonded them in the first place. Holding Beebe close, she gave Violetta a heartfelt smile.

"Thank you, Violetta. You saved her."

The water Fae smiled and shrugged, stepping back to rejoin the gathered Fae who milled amongst the vast trees, waiting for Faunella's return. Faunella looked shyly around at them.

"I'm sorry for what I did. I was wrong."

Nibbling at her bottom lip, she waited for their reaction, wondering if she could ever apologize enough to make things right. The Fae didn't disappoint. One by one they stepped up to her, offering her reassuring words and kind pats. Flavire plucked a bunch of his flowers and quickly wove them into a crown, which he placed on her head. Soon they had all filed past her and headed back towards the grotto.

Stroking Beebe absentmindedly, Faunella felt a thin thread of warm contentment running through the guilt in her chest. "Can I stay in the cave with you all today?"

Erwin's arms tightened imperceptibly around her neck, and Amon let out a rattling chuckle, but Huxley answered her. His loud, crashing clang was the most ferocious sound of acceptance Faunella had ever heard. She peeped down at his severe expression, and this time, she couldn't stop the smile from forming on her lips. She couldn't dare stay anywhere else now, not with that stubborn determination on his face.

Releasing one hand from where she clutched Beebe, she reached down towards Huxley, tapping her fingers together until she felt his lumpy hand slip into her own. The four of them began to walk the short distance home, but Faunella sighed, a niggling thought pressing into the nest of contentment she built. She still felt ashamed of her outburst towards the Fae, but a part of her still yearned to be with people that looked like her.

Running the thought over in her mind, she couldn't help but think that she didn't quite belong anywhere. Her appearance wasn't like the Fae either here or on Amaranth, but she obviously had powers, so she wasn't human. A heavy feeling settled deep within her stomach, churning uncomfortably.

Swallowing hard, she pushed the frightening thought away, too exhausted to delve any deeper into the new questions raised about who and what she is. Instead, she concentrated on what happened in the here and now. She would deal with the discovery of her powers when she was warm and dry. Her hands quivered, and she resisted the urge to snatch them back and tuck them away where they couldn't hurt anyone. Maybe it would be best to try and forget she had powers altogether. Beebe chirped, tilting her head to blink up at her questioningly. New guilt rushed to the surface. Her fear was worrying Beebe, who could sense the strong emotions.

"I'm okay," she whispered, lying to her friend, but trying desperately to make it true. A dull rumble began in her stomach, and Faunella honed in on that feeling, using it to distract herself from everything but that pressing need.

"Uh, Hux?" Looking down at her large friend, she gave a weak smile, hoping her words were sufficiently light hearted. "I'm ready for some berries now."

CHAPTER TWENTY THREE
AMON

A MONTH HAD GONE by swiftly, and Fawn was still refusing to try to access her magic. The cold bite of winter was just starting to make itself known, which she conveniently used as an excuse to stay indoors, hiding from the Fae who kept pressuring her to practice.

"If she won't let us teach her how to control her magic, then we need to start with something less frightening for her."

Huxley walked back and forth, his agitated steps wearing a path in the dirt. Amon sighed. Glancing through the trees, he scanned the nearby field until he caught sight of Fawn in her pink dress with her curls shining like gold in the sunlight. He had seen her fear after nearly killing Beebe. However, he had hoped that after some time had gone by, her natural excitement and curiosity would have given her the drive to start exploring her abilities.

She ducked down among the tall grass, plucking one of the last blooms of the season. Amon shook his head. Unfortunately, her reluctance had only grown. The few times she agreed to try and access her power, it had speared out of her, wild and uncontrollable, further cementing that her magic was dangerous and something to be feared in her mind. Huxley stopped his pacing and came over to where Amon stood. "Just look at her," he growled, gesturing helplessly. Venek and Baol inched closer and the four of them turned their attention to Fawn.

Unaware of her observers, Fawn walked listlessly throughout the field. Her hand held a fistful of bright goldenrod blooms, which she added to as she wandered. The westward field stretched out as far as the eye could see, only broken by the dark vista of a far-off mountain range. The picture of Fawn moving through the field was so beautiful that Amon could almost forget the challenges she would have to overcome. He wished she could stay unaware and untouched, always happy and safe in his care.

Just then, a gust of wind blew in from the south. It flew into Fawn, catching and swirling her long strands of hair. The change was instant. Uttering a sharp cry, she flinched away. Ducking her head, she released her flowers and clutched her hands to her chest.

Amon glanced to the side. The other Fae all mirrored his expression of pity, their faces lined with concern. His worry grew. The season of letting Fawn be a child was over. They were doing her no favors by coddling her and allowing her to ignore her abilities.

He pushed himself off the wide tree he was leaning on. "The longer we wait, the more her fear will grow." He looked around at Baol, Huxley, and Venek. "Give me one last chance to try to get her to cooperate, and if that doesn't work, we can go ahead with the other part of her training."

Huxley frowned, but Venek and Baol both brightened up.

"You mean—"

"The plan to return to Amaranth?"

Their excited voices blurred together, and even with the seriousness of the situation, Amon couldn't help the smile pulling at his lips.

"Yes, our mission back to Amaranth. But first," he frowned, shaking off his leaves, "we have one more attempt to help Fawn."

The other Fae had wisely continued on their way back to the grotto, leaving him alone to encourage Fawn. He stepped from the tree line and made his way towards where she sat cross-legged in the grass, her tangled red hair the only thing visible through the thick tufts. Before he got too close, a sharp whistle sounded to his right. Beebe swooped down from the sky, alerting Fawn to his presence.

"Oh, it's you."

The disappointment on her face was as clear as day, and for a moment, he felt a surge of regret that he had spoiled her solitude, but necessity made him plough forward. Plastering a smile on his face, he traversed the remaining distance between them.

"I was on my way home from The Edge when I sensed you." He allowed her a minute to translate his words before continuing on. "What are you doing all the way out here?"

She turned her head back down to her lap, her hands moving delicately over her knees and feet. Bewildered, Amon tracked her movements. A small gray mouse darted out from where it had hidden in the grass. It hopped onto Fawn's foot and scurried up her leg on the stained hem of her dress, where it stood blinking up into her face.

Fawn raised her hands, revealing half a dozen more of the small creatures. She turned her face up to his, shrugging sheepishly.

"I had a bit of a fright earlier." She flushed, flitting her eyes to the side. "When I looked around, these little guys had come to investigate." Holding her finger out, she flashed a smile when the mouse on her knee placed both of its paws on her fingertip.

Mirth bubbled up in Amon's chest. He cleared his throat, lowering himself to crouch beside her. She was so afraid of her magic, but she was totally unaware that she was using her powers right now. Ever since she was a small child, Amon had seen signs of her affinity with animals, and the day she bonded with Beebe only solidified that power in the Fae's mind.

"They sure do like you, Fawn. Most animals do."

She thoughtfully regarded the mice, or perhaps she was trying to translate his words. Jumping on this opportunity, Amon continued. "You really have a gift with animals. It's something to be celebrated, but it's not the only gift you have." Fawn's hands fluttered to a stop, her body becoming unnaturally still. Amon's leaves twitched as the air around him chilled. There was no doubt that she had understood him perfectly that time. He cleared his throat.

"Your magic is a part of you, and isn't something to be feared." A nervous energy began to churn deep within him, and he hurried to get the words out. "I know what happened frightened you, but I swear that I won't let any harm come to you or anyone around you. You'll be safe."

"Safe?"

The word was uttered so low that, even with his Fae hearing, he almost missed it. All around him, the wind began to pick up, whipping the grass from side to side. Still, Fawn hadn't looked up.

"Fawn?" He reached out his arm, gently touching her exposed cheek with his twiggy fingers. "Sweetheart, don't be afraid. Let me help you."

She wrenched her face up to meet his, her round eyes filling with tears even as she fought to stop her lower lip from quivering.

"How can you help me when my power is strong enough to send you flying through the air?" She scrambled to her feet, sending the mice running back into the grass. "How can anyone help me when no one has magic like mine?" The tears were flowing freely now, making damp tracks down her pale face.

Amon stayed where he was, making no move to stand or back away, even as the wind picked up and threatened to pull the leaves from his body.

Fawn stood within the maelstrom, her eyes flashing as the coils of her hair whipped back and forth like ribbons of lightning.

Pity tugged at his heart, but no part of him held fear. He knew what kind of person Fawn was. She was like his own child, and she would never willingly hurt anyone. She needed to know he wouldn't break easily.

"You can't hurt me, Fawn." He strengthened his roots, thrusting them deep into the earth. "You caught me by surprise that first time, but I'm not so easily pushed around." As he spoke, he drew on the life around him, feeling his own power swell. Straightening up, he towered above her, growing higher and higher until his uppermost branches reached the height of the towering forest to his back. Power rippled through his wooden trunk, splitting his bark and giving him a heady feeling of euphoria.

"Do you think you could fell a tree this size?" he boomed, flinging his limbs to the side. "Do you think I would crumble?"

To her credit, Fawn stayed standing, not once cowering away from him, even as the soil around his roots shuddered and roiled to cover her bare feet. She had her head bent back, her eyes transfixed on his body. The wind still bit at his limbs, but was it just his imagination, or was the temperature beginning to return to normal? He softened his expression, waiting to see how she would react.

Raising her arm, she tentatively placed her hand against his trunk. He saw a glint of fear flash in her eyes, just before she lowered her head to stare at where her hand rested.

"I'm not afraid," she ground out, the wind catching her quiet words and sending them swirling up for him to hear. He caught his breath - watching, waiting.

Slowly, the pressure of her hand increased. She pushed against him as if to test his strength. A second hand joined the first, shoving and hitting his bark. Amon withstood it all, her full strength nothing but an irritation.

Finally, she stopped. Dropping to her knees, she sucked in greedy gulps of air, panting heavily. Amon slowly shrunk down to his normal size, coming to a halt just as Fawn raised her face to his again.

"I am afraid," she admitted, looking away as if her whispered confession might make him love her less. His heart swelled. Reaching out, he cupped her chin with his fingers, gently turning her face back up to meet his smiling eyes.

"We can work with that."

"We can?"

"Sure." He stepped back and gestured to the open field. "We're in the best place. There's nothing to damage and no one to worry about."

She scanned the space around her, catching on something within the forest. She bit her lip. "Beebe, stay away."

Amon twisted to look behind him, glimpsing the little bird's tail as she flitted further into the safety of the forest. *Probably for the best,* he thought, his eyes softening, knowing any more damage to Fawn's little friend would surely result in her absolute refusal to ever try and access her magic again. That wouldn't do, considering their eventual return to Amaranth. He returned his attention to Fawn.

"Shall we get started?"

CHAPTER TWENTY FOUR
FAUNELLA

"*S*HALL WE GET STARTED?"

If there was ever a time when she wished she could pretend not to understand the Fae's language, it would be now. Her blood turned cold as she considered what Amon wanted her to do. The strange power lived inside her, no longer dormant, and when she closed her eyes to focus within, she could feel it roiling inside her belly like a vicious creature. It was ready to emerge, lashing out at anyone around her, hurting the forest and everyone she loved.

"*Fawn?*"

Amon stroked his leaves down her arm, drawing her back from the fear threatening to drown her. She swallowed thickly, looking again into the forest to make sure Beebe was nowhere in sight. Not trusting the bird to have gone a sufficient distance, Fawn reached inside, finding the warm tether that tied the two of them together.

Beebe, get further away. Warn the other animals to keep far from here.

Once satisfied that her feathered friend was safe from harm, she blew out a shaky breath. "What do I do?"

Amon nodded, seemingly satisfied with her resolve. His creaking, groaning voice started to rattle off instructions. "*Your power lives inside you.*" Faunella grimaced. She knew that already. She couldn't seem to get away from the tangled beast that finally made its presence known. *"You must reach inside your mind and access that part of yourself."*

Willing her heart to stop its racing, she did as she was told. With closed eyes, she imagined her hands reaching inside her belly, clutching for her power. The magic pressed against her palms, pulsing through the gaps in her fingers as she tried to hold tight. With all her strength, she willed it to settle, stay contained in her hands, and bow down to her will. "What next?" she ground out, her focus totally captured within her body.

"Use your mind and demand the magic to do your bidding." Gritting her teeth, Faunella racked her brain for something to do. She decided to do something small, something safe. In her mind's eye, she recalled the way the wind would blow through the open field, rippling its way over the long grass until it seemed as if the blades danced to an invisible melody. Settled on her course of action, she cracked open her eyes and released the power trapped inside.

The grass around her flung back, ripped from the very earth as her magic pulsed out of her in a raging torrent. Flowers tore to pieces and scattered far into the air, the vibrant colors muted by their sudden demise. Pebbles and sticks, normally hidden throughout the field, flung out around her, cracking and twanging into the forest at her back. She flinched with each sound, never more grateful that she had sent Beebe far from here. The gale raged on, leaving her body unaffected, untouched by the tidal force sweeping over the field in every direction. She clutched at her power, trying desperately to temper the onslaught, but the power continued to rip from her body despite her low cry of dismay.

With one last tug, the magic abated, leaving an unnatural stillness behind. As Faunella surveyed her destruction, her limbs grew heavy and cold with the horror of what she unleashed. Tears pooled in her eyes, blurring her vision as she turned to look at Amon, unable to stop the nausea from clawing its way up her chest.

His roots gripped the now grassless soil, only retracting once the wind had stopped. He flexed his branches with great care, sending multiple leaves crumbling to the ground.

A lump formed in the back of her throat. Despite his assurances, her power had damaged him. The pity in his eyes was her undoing. She flung herself to the ground, choking on the hot tears that flooded her face. "I can't do it." She pounded the churned dirt, sending puffs of soil flinging up with each hit. "It's out of control. I'll always be a danger."

"Fawn, stop." Amon grasped her arms, gently raising her up. *"You can't expect to be perfect straight away. Don't give up."*

That's exactly what she wanted to do. Things were so much easier when she had no power. But, she took several shuddering breaths and swiped at her cheeks, the soil on her hands leaving dirty streaks on her sun-kissed skin. This magic that inhabited her was frightening. Its presence was a very real reminder that she was something else, something dangerous to be around.

She glanced again at the damage she wrought. It had been a full moon cycle since she had gone to The Edge, and unless she got her power under control, she was unable to be near the humans. Their vulnerability would be no match for the force of her powers. She flinched as a sharp pang of loss whipped through her. Without the humans, she would forever be alone.

Steeling her nerves, she steadied her breathing and pulled her quivering lips into a determined pout. Then, at Amon's sharp nod, she readied herself to try again.

Her power flared over and over, leaving more destruction and wild chaos in the area surrounding her each time. With each failed attempt at controlling her magic, the tender ache in her chest grew, revealing her deep desire to be among the humans and belong to a group of people who looked like her one day. She wanted to sit and laugh with a friend, maybe even ride in those fast-moving cars.

This longing grew, fueling each frenzied effort even as her hope of one day not being alone faded with every frantic lashing of air produced.

After a particularly violent attempt, Faunella slumped over, breathing hard.

"I can't," she gasped. "I'm so tired." Her heart beat as fast as if she had been sprinting through the forest, and sweat beaded on her brow. She rested her hands on her knees, still able to feel the power raging inside of her, but she shook with exhaustion, her physical form unable to rally the energy needed to access it.

"You've reached your limit." Amon scooped her up with strong arms, and a heady relief coursed through her. They were done for the day. He spun them towards the forest, striding quickly into its cooling depths. Even though Faunella hadn't wanted to use her powers, she couldn't help the small spark of pride that flared from pushing past her fear and making the attempt anyway. She chanced a glance at Amon's face, wondering if he and the other Fae would leave her alone now and stop pressuring her to try to control what seemed uncontrollable. But, she was also heavy with regret. What if she would never be able to master the very thing that limited her future?

Sensing her attention, Amon flicked his eyes to hers, not quite quick enough for her to hide the disappointment that lingered there. She let out a long breath, laying her head back against Amon's branches, her tangled hair cascading down past his leafy limbs. She hated letting the Fae down.

He cleared his throat, the sound rumbling through his bark. *"We won't give up. There are other routes we can take and other things we can teach you."*

Despite her weariness, Faunella's interest peaked.

"Other things?"

"You need to learn about where you come from and things that will help you in the future."

"More of your memories of Amaranth?" She slumped down, disappointment turning her mood sour. "I've already seen so much."

Her homeworld was a touchy subject between her and the Fae. She had soaked up every last image Amon had shown her, eager for every piece of knowledge he could provide. The Fae realm was beautiful, filled with many individual kingdoms like Grecion, Madyvire, and Dursont. But, the most beautiful lands belonged to the Ancient Fae. Instead of only one territory, they had a myriad of kingdoms all ruled by one monarch who lived in a towering crystal palace—E.

Faunella desperately wanted to return. She was mesmerized by the tall, beautiful Fae, but the images had her asking questions, and it wasn't long before she demanded more.

Folding her arms across her chest, she turned her face away from Amon, sticking her bottom lip out in an over-the-top pout. "I don't know why you keep telling me about Amaranth. It's not like you'll take me there any time soon." She knew she was being petulant, but she couldn't seem to control her fluctuating emotions. "You're always keeping things from me. You'd rather lock me away in this forest instead of taking me back to be with the Fae who look like me."

"Fawn, no. It's not like that." Amon's stricken voice abruptly cut off. Whatever he was about to say was swallowed instead of sharing his reasons with her.

Hurt consumed her. Gathering her remaining energy, Fawn pushed out of his arms, landing lightly on the forest floor. "More secrets," she snarled, her eyes flashing. "Always waiting till I'm older." She raised her chin, stubbornly refusing to give in to the quiet voice telling her she might be making another mistake. "Well, I don't want anything more to do with you. I can do fine on my own." With a sob, she spun on her heel, tearing off through the forest with no thought to where she was going. She only hoped she could run fast enough to flee the confusion clouding her mind.

It felt like she had been running forever. She ignored the worried tug from Beebe, not wanting her friend to be around her when her emotions were so out of control. Everything in her life had just gone wrong. Swiping past a low-hanging branch, she launched herself off a slick rock, roaring out her frustrations even as she increased her speed.

The humans are dangerous. Stay away from them.

It's dangerous in Amaranth. You can't return till you're older.

You look human, but you are Fae.

Just stay in the Forest where it's safe.

"But I'm not safe," she whispered with labored breath. Her despair rose up and drowned out all the other voices in her head. So focused on what she was feeling, Faunella didn't register what direction she had been running in or how far she had come. Bursting through two trees, she finally gave into the grief that had chased her from Amon's side. With a scream, she erupted, sending a short burst of power blasting out like a fan.

A sharp screeching of metal cut through her turmoil, snapping her back to reality. She watched with horror-filled eyes as a black two-wheeled vehicle slid across the hard surface of the road she had unknowingly fled to. The metal sent up bright sparks as it skidded past on its side, clearly illuminating the dark-clad human clutching tightly to the crumbling frame.

The scene played out in front of her, taking eternity but also no time at all. The man skidded towards the opposite side of the road, his body angling towards a tree with knotted, jagged bark and covered in a gray film. Faunella could see the impact before it occurred and could feel the crunch as the man's back was sandwiched between the heavy metal and the great tree. Without thinking, she raised her hand, already bringing the vision of a gust to steer the man clear to her mind. Then, she paused, the fear of making things worse immobilizing her.

Time resumed, sending the man the final distance to his fate. Faunella's wide eyes took it all in, hoping with all she possessed that she was wrong. The man would be safe, and he would be protected. She closed her eyes, felt one beat of her heart, then breathed.

Please.

The screeching cut off, followed immediately by a deep thudding crunch. The forest shuddered, the sounds of breathing branches slowly fading out.

Faunella opened her eyes.

Smoke and a black liquid spilled out of the remains of the crumpled metal. Alongside the wreckage was the man. He lay sprawled at the base of the knotted tree, untouched by the frightening damage. Faunella let out a choking sob. By some miracle, the man was unharmed. She hadn't hurt anyone else. Tears of relief streamed down her face, and she stood transfixed, unable to move from her place on the roadside.

He stirred, reaching up a gloved hand to tug at the black globe covering his head. Letting out a groan, he pulled it free, revealing a younger face than Faunella had been expecting. Rolling to his knees, he surveyed the damaged two-wheeler with a stricken face. Faunella's lips parted, her eyes absorbing every detail of the young man across from her. He was tall and broader than many of the human men she observed. He raised his hands to his mouth, ripping off his hand coverings with his teeth. She angled her head slightly, trying to see more than just his profile. Curiosity burned within her. For some reason, she needed to see his full face.

The daylight dimmed, and the temperature dropped. Still, Faunella couldn't bring herself to leave. By some strange turn of fate, he hadn't noticed her standing there. So, she stayed still, waiting, even as a fine mist of rain started falling and turned the tunnel of trees murky.

Then he moved. Leaning on the tree, he pulled himself to stand, running his hand through his short brown curls as he turned his body to face her. Faunella's eyes widened as she took him in. His face was unlined except for the tiny cleft in his chin and the small furrow between his brows as he frowned down at his unharmed body. She saw the exact moment he noticed her. He lifted his face, stilling immediately as his deep brown eyes met hers. Faunella drank in his features, a fluttering warmth stirring within her chest, but it was what she saw in his eyes that held her spellbound. The moment stretched out between them, unbroken as they studied each other. He opened his mouth as if to call out to her across the hard surface that separated them, but before he could utter a sound, Beebe glided in, landing jarringly on her shoulder.

The bird's abrupt arrival broke her out of the trance she was in and brought her suddenly to her senses. Sucking in a breath, she spun on her heel and sprinted back into the safety of the forest. The warmth within her bloomed, flickering around the confines of her body like a weight that drew her back. Confusion swirled in her mind, and she searched until she found her tether to Beebe. Giving it a tug, she urged the bird to keep up with her and otherwise ignored the weight until eventually it lessened.

Beebe kept pace with her despite her speed, sending concerned messages through the bond. Faunella swiped at her damp face, only now feeling the chill of the rain covering her body.

"It's okay. He only saw me for a second."

Beebe flew around and hovered in her face, giving her no choice but to come to a stop. "Beebe, what?" The bird settled down on a nearby branch, fluffing her feathers as she sent a series of images to Faunella. "Oh." A wave of shame washed over her, tempered only by the sting of bitterness still left behind. Beebe kept the images going, showing her the worried group of Fae milling around the grotto. She hung her head, knowing she would have to return to make up with Amon but still so angry and confused about her place in life.

"I don't know what to do. Why won't they just take me back? Then, I can be with my own people."

Beebe chirped, unable to help but here for her all the same. Faunella blew at a ribbon of hair dangling in front of her face and dug her toe into the wet earth.

"I just feel so alone."

Her quiet words brought with them an image of the young man's strong, steady face hadn't been able to hide. She sighed and started walking back towards the Fae, not knowing how to fix things but needing to try. But, in her mind, she carried the look buried in the human's eyes—the same thing reflected in her own.

Loneliness.

CHAPTER TWENTY FIVE
DERICK

THE CRUSH OF PEOPLE crowding the back alley gambling den grated on Derick's nerves. His jaw tightened as he surveyed the space for the umpteenth time, wondering if he had been there long enough to keep up appearances. The sound of smashing glass sounded over the din, and he turned his head in time to see a second bottle fly over the head of a scraggly-faced man. Jeers and raucous laughter broke out as the fight picked up, turning the already deafening noise unbearable. Rubbing his temple to relieve the persistent ache, Derick pushed back from the wall. He couldn't stay there any longer. Striding through the smoky room, he headed for the doors, only slowing when several men around Shaun's age paused their card game. Despite Derick's young age, they gave him a nod of respect. Ignoring the itch to get away, he scanned the table, noticing the not-so-subtle signs that his fellow Dragons were cheating.

At the table was a very wasted middle-aged man who Derick recognized as someone currently in debt with the gang. The man was so out of it, he had no clue the other men were fleecing him dry. This game was only one of many that would increase his dependence on the gang and the drugs they could offer him.

Aware that the men's eyes were on him, Derick swallowed his grimace and angled his body towards the man's chair, where his jacket lay hanging over the back. His eyes were cold and unfeeling as he strode past, slipping his hands into the vulnerable man's pocket, swiping the car keys that lay inside, only visible by the bulge in the fabric. Forcing a cruel grin, Derick gave a nod of his own and continued out the door.

Once outside, he dropped his smile and let his face relax into a bland expression, no emotion showing for anyone to exploit. To his relief, Jarred wasn't around, but among the few men loitering in the alley was one of his sycophants—a large, heavyset man in his early twenties who hung on Jarred's every word and craved depravity almost as much. Knowing it would piss Jarred off, Derick gave a sharp whistle. "Oy, Leon." The other man swung his head up, his beady eyes squinting his way. Derick threw the keys, surprised when Leon caught them. "Take it to the chop shop. Credit's all yours." Bewilderment flashed on Leon's face as he gaped at the keys in his hands. Not waiting for a response, Derick continued to his bike and swung into the saddle, taking only enough time to slip on his gloves and helmet before roaring away to anywhere but there.

The rumbling of the bike hummed through him, grounding him even as the wind tore past his body. As he often did when needing an escape, he let the road guide him and wasn't surprised when it led him south. Entering the forest, he could feel his knot of anxiety lessen, revealing the hollowness that never seemed to go away. His fists tightened on the handlebars, and he gritted his teeth as he sped into the forest's endless quiet that stretched out beside the City of Northaven.

Coming into a sweeping corner, Derick leaned into the curve before straightening up into a long green tunnel. The towering trees to each side stretched to the sky where their great branches tangled together. The quiet settled his body but did nothing for the noises in his head. Visions flashed, piercing him with agony as he watched his hand grip the knife, felt the blood burst from the gaping slice, and saw life leave his friend's paling face.

Breathing hard, he choked back a sob, desperate to be free from the memories. He closed his eyes and opened the throttle, feeling the engine build as he tempted fate. He counted in his head until fear had his eyes popping open, swerving back into a straight line.

Fuck. He slammed his hand against the handlebars, swallowing back his nausea.

A shiver ran down his spine from the cold sweat that had broken out on his skin. What was he doing trapped in an endless cycle of hurt or be hurt, look strong or be weak, kill or be killed? All of this pretending was slowly killing him. He tightened his grip, eyeing the trunks of the massive trees that passed him in a blur.

It would be faster this way.

The next curve was approaching fast. His heart pounded loudly in his ears. *Try again.* He urged himself. Maybe this time, he wouldn't chicken out.

His eyes closed, and he increased his speed. Terror and despair tore through him, and he let out an ear-splitting battle cry. As his mind reached a fever pitch, he flung open his eyes, wanting to face his final moments head-on and have one last look at this world that let him down so bitterly.

One second was all he had to catch the glimpse of green and pink out of the corner of his eye before something hit him hard from the side.

The force sent his bike pitching to the side and his body along with it. He hit the ground hard, the impact knocking all the breath from his body. A strangled cry tore from his mouth. Despite his pain and desire to end things, Derick found himself clutching his bike for dear life, tears squeezing out of his scrunched up eyes as his too-short life flashed through his mind. In all the memories that filtered past, Derick focused on the few good things that stood out among the rest. He saw his happy moments with his mom, the feeling of riding his bike, and his friendship with Rhett. He held Rhett's image tightly, knowing this was the end.

I'll be with you soon.

The metal of his bike screeched along the asphalt, the friction burning him through the thick leather of his jacket. Within a split second, he would be gone. His body was torn and tangled between his bike and the myriad of trees bordering the road.

Then it happened. His back hit into something, ebbing his momentum even as the bike was wrenched from his grasp, flinging away from his body in an altered trajectory. Confusion overcame him as he was cushioned by something that softened around his body, not the hard and jagged impact he was expecting. The force cradled him to a full stop until he lay sprawled and breathless on the roadside.

He wasn't dead. He had crashed his bike after driving at a breakneck speed, but he was alive. Wiggling his toes and flexing his fingers, he waited wide-eyed for any indication of pain. His body responded as it should, only smarting a little where he had scraped across the ground. Sucking in a breath, he struggled to steady his racing heart. Needing fresh air to clear his head, he unclasped his helmet and yanked it off, letting it roll to the ground beside him. Derick lay still and inhaled, allowing the sweet, earthy smells of the forest to ground him. His body calmed enough for him to tentatively sit up, rolling onto his knees.

A few feet away lay his bike, the crumpled metal twisted almost beyond recognition. His mouth fell open, the sight starting an uncomfortable churning in his gut. Using his teeth, he ripped off his gloves, discarding them next to his forgotten helmet. How had he survived? He used a nearby tree to help him to his feet and ran through the events of the past few minutes, his bewilderment growing with each passing second.

"I was heading for the corner when something hit me," he murmured under his breath, turning his body as he recalled the force that had come out of nowhere and hit him from the side. Lifting his eyes, he scanned the trees on the opposite side of the road, blinking past the fine misting of rain that chose that moment to fall.

He jolted, his eyes snagging on the unmoving form of another person standing across from him. It was a tall, slender girl. She surveyed him, her fiery ginger locks tangling down over the front of a slightly dirty pale pink dress.

His thoughts whirled. What caused her to be here at that exact moment? Why this place and time? The rain landed lightly on her face, beading on long dark lashes and illuminating a fine smattering of freckles along the bridge of her nose. Despite the moisture, she remained unnaturally still, her blue eyes trained on him as if searching his face for an answer to some question. His heart began to beat again, each thud in his chest sounding loud in the silence.

Who are you?

She was younger than him, but he was unsure by how much. Her stillness seemed otherworldly, lending her an agelessness he found captivating. As the moment stretched out, he found himself forgetting his problems, drawn to the girl with an overwhelming desire to make sure she was okay.

He opened his mouth to ask her name when a motion from behind her caught his attention. He stilled, lips still parting as a chickadee flew onto the girl's shoulder. Her eyes widened, and she shot him a startled look before whipping around and fleeing back into the trees. Derick lifted his hand to call out for her to wait, but between one moment and the next, she was gone, leaving no trace that she was ever there.

Time went on, and Derick didn't know how long he stood looking after her before wiping the moisture from his face and turning back to his mangled bike.

"What the hell just happened?" He shook his head and let out a low laugh. He might be done with the world, but he guessed the world wasn't done with him yet. The rain started to fall harder, working its way down his neck. Flipping up the collar of his jacket, Derick left the wreck and turned towards Northaven. His first strides were hesitant, short and slow, as if his very being revolted at the idea of beginning the long walk back to the gang house. He gritted his teeth and ignored the insistent urge to go back, lengthening his strides to eat up the distance.

While nothing changed for him, he found himself dwelling on the encounter and the expression on the girl's face. She had seemed so lost, her blue eyes searching for something. He furrowed his brows, bringing back the image of her face. There was something deeper in her gaze, something under the surface his whole being yearned for.

CHAPTER TWENTY SIX
VIOLETTA

T HE PUNGENT STENCH OF decay had Violetta screwing up her nose.

"It's even worse than last time," she murmured, picking up her feet to skirt the oily muck oozing from the forest floor. She held her breath as she tiptoed around the putrid substance, only relaxing once the ground returned to leaf-covered soil.

A meaty thud sounded behind her, followed by a low curse. Her lips twitched. Turning around, she raised one curving brow at Venek.

"I thought it would be nice returning home, but it's awful." He rose to his feet, gingerly wiping the mud from his vivid green vines.

"Not all of Amaranth is like this," she answered, gazing around at the sickly trees above them. "Madivyre is still beautiful, fresh, and fragrant." She closed her eyes, remembering the way it felt to step out of the South Forest to the seaside kingdom. "The smell of salt in the air and the warmth of the water felt right." Venek poked her in the shoulder, breaking her out of her reverie. "That's all very well, but how about a little help?"

Violetta grinned. Placing one hand on the vine that made up the other Fae's shoulder, she let her magic fill her, rippling out from her chest until water flowed from her palm and flushed all the toxic sludge off Venek's body.

"Phew, thanks." He shook himself dry. "I sure am glad that you're with me, even though books and water don't mix." Looking her up and down, he chuckled. Violetta gave a tight-lipped smile in return and gestured that they should resume their journey. She had been as surprised as Venek when the others volunteered her for a mission again. Though, she did agree her corporeal water form was much less conspicuous than any of the other Fae in their group, especially considering where they were headed.

After several minutes, Venek broke the silence.

"You don't think the gateway will be cut off, do you?" His voice sounded strained. "I know Lothian said our people wouldn't have closed them down, but now we're here, I can't see any reason why they would keep access open."

Violetta considered the sorry state of the South Forest, mourning the loss of what was once a vibrant paradise for the ancient Fae to come and connect with their nature forms. Venek made a good point. Unlike the other kingdoms in Amaranth, the Ancient Fae had multiple territories all spread throughout the realm. They used gateways to travel to different parts of their kingdom without encroaching on the High Fae's lands.

"I don't think anyone would have bothered to close the gates," Violetta mused. "Even though our people haven't come here in so long." She ducked under a low-lying branch. "Anyways, it's not like any other Fae can use them." Brandishing her hand with a flourish, she grinned back at Venek. "They are keyed into our very life-blood."

"True, true." Raising his head, he quickened his pace. "I guess we'll see soon enough."

A short distance ahead through small gaps between the rough-hewn trees was the unmistakable sight of the gateway. The pale blush of apricot stone contrasted sharply with the foliage around it. As they approached, Violetta bit her lip. Just like the forest, she could feel no life coming from the stone, but the color was still present.

"It has to be active," spoke Venek excitedly. "See, it's still pink."

Kneeling before the stone, she placed her hand reverently upon the surface, careful not to bring to mind the place she wanted to travel. All ancient Fae had the ability to realm jump, but jumping within each realm was impossible. Because of that, the gateways were created. Life is a sacred thing among the Fae, so by taking the placenta of an Ancient Fae female and using the magic embedded in the life-giving organ, her people were able to form the gates, hence the faded scarlet marking each gateway.

She got to her feet, body warming with pleasure. The gateway was open.

Her cheeks flushed hotly as Huxley's brooding face crossed her mind. "Uh, it's open," she stuttered, swishing her long hair over her shoulder to cover up her embarrassment. "Shall we?"

Venek stepped up beside her and reached out a long green tendril. Pulling the image of E to mind, Violetta closed her eyes, and they touched the stone.

Their capital city's gateway was a blush-coloured archway of quartz. They appeared under it and stepped forward, blinking past the bright glare of the sun. Violetta sucked in a sharp breath. She was home.

Unlike the other Fae on Earth, she had actually grown up in the Eu-hedral, spending her youth exploring the glistening domes and passages that stretched up from the bottom of a great valley. She gazed around the square courtyard, picturing her years as a child. The bustling city once provided ample entertainment for her and her friends. They would observe the Fae come and go, morphing from their nature states at will. She had eagerly watched them, desperate for the day when she would be old enough to transform.

A pang of sadness ran through her. Who would have guessed they would lose their ability to change between states with the loss of their monarch? Suddenly angry with herself, she brushed off her reminiscing and focused on the mission at hand.

"Quick," she hissed, pulling Venek away from the arch and into an alley. "I don't want anyone questioning where we've come from." Glancing behind them, she dragged the willing Fae in the direction of the great library. "Even though Petrov is in charge now, our royal orders are still to remain on Earth. Technically, we're breaking the law." Her heart beat fast as they made their way past rows of homes and businesses. The seriousness only just occurred to her.

"Slow down," Venek tugged at her arm. "Haven't you noticed? This isn't exactly a lively metropolis anymore."

Keeping up the pace, she cleared her head and actually studied the buildings around her. It was true. Nearly every third shop was closed, their doors and windows boarded with cobweb-covered wood.

On the other side of the cobbled road, a male ambled past. His gaunt face was trained on the ground, the angle doing nothing to disguise the hopelessness in his gaze. Violetta's eyes widened. She whipped her head around to take in another Fae. Their worn shirt was so threadbare that she could see several hollow ribs. Just looking at them had her stomach bottoming out, a sympathetic hunger gnawing at her well-fed belly. Turning back to the road in front of her, she pushed herself faster, taking the bend at almost a run.

Skidding to a stop, she vaguely felt Venek reach out to steady her from behind, but her focus was trained on a child in front of her. One of her legs was smaller than the other, a birth defect that their Fae health should have made impossible. She couldn't have been more than eight years old, not even a blink into what should be a long life. With great care, she limped along the street, holding heavily to the brittle branches of the Fae helping her.

"How can he let things stay like this?" snarled Venek from under his breath. "Our people deserve better." The catch in his voice had her own throat thickening. "Petrov will pay for this," he fumed. "When we return, we'll kick his pretender ass off the throne and make things right."

Still shaken, Violetta could only nod her agreement, not trusting herself to speak. She resumed walking, feeling Venek step up beside her. The mention of returning had her thoughts flying back to just before they left for Amaranth and the young fae who had changed everything.

"What do you mean you didn't go after her?" She bit her lip, unable to keep the hint of concern from her voice. Amon reached out to her, hurt shining in his eyes when she sidestepped his touch. He sighed. "She needed space. We've been expecting a lot from her." Swinging around abruptly, he called out to where Huxley was slowly disappearing into the treeline. "She needs space from all of us."

Despite her worry, Violetta hid a smile as she watched Huxley's retreating back stiffen up. He swung around, a stone brow raised high in surprise.

"What? I wasn't going anywhere. Can't a Fae take a walk?"

She watched the two Fae argue, her own mind on where Fawn was and how she must be feeling. Jaw tightening, she threw up a blast of water, catching the attention of not only Amon and Hux, but also the other Fae scattered around the cave entrance. "That's enough out of you two. You should have let me help Fawn." She glared at the males, hoping Laurel knew her ire was not directed at her. "My magic isn't just for healing. It's elemental, just like Fawn's. I should be able to help her understand her power better than anyone."

Amon stepped forward, a stricken expression on his face. "We all want to help her control her power and help her wield it."

"That's just it," she cut in, frustration making her water ripple. "It's not always about control. Sometimes you just need to settle into your power, to embrace it." She had watched as the others tiptoed around Fawn, trying unsuccessfully to help her tame the untapped power that had been freshly awakened. Lifting her hand, she allowed a ribbon of water to weave through her translucent fingers, swirling over her knuckles as she berated herself for waiting so long to interfere. A delicate cough had her looking up.

"A gentle touch," Laurel added. "A female's experience." Violetta smiled at the small bushy Fae, giving her a slight nod. "Exactly!" Swinging around, she placed her hand on her cocked hip and stared around at the

eight males in the group. "From now on, Laurel and I will be the ones to guide Fawn through her magical awakening." She arched one brow. "Any questions? No? Good."

She came back to herself just in time to see the ivy-covered walls of the library looming in front of them.

"Do you think Fawn made it back to the grotto alright?"

Violetta sucked in a breath, her face drawing upwards in surprise. Venek's words almost mirrored her thoughts. He studied the library thoughtfully, his earlier vehemence replaced with a quiet concern. "I wonder if the others have told her yet." Placing her hand on his arm, she gave it a light squeeze. The time had come to reveal their truth, but Violetta had no idea how Fawn would react. Her brow furrowed lightly, and she let her hand fall away. She disagreed with the Fae's decision to withhold the whole story from Fawn, but in the end, she had been outvoted.

"I'm almost certain she knows by now," she said, glancing to the side where several Fae stood surreptitiously watching the two of them. Her heart beat faster. "That's why it's even more imperative for us to get these books. Fawn will need every advantage we can give her."

Violetta pressed back her shoulders as she stared down at the library, a renewed vigor fueling her blood. She tugged Venek forward, ducking her head to avoid detection.

What am I doing? She straightened up and pushed open the wooden door. *Anyone who ever knew me is long dead.*

As they stepped past the foyer, she grinned up at Venek's stunned face. "It's pretty impressive, huh?"

"I had no idea," he breathed, gaping at the mammoth domed window that encompassed rows of leather-bound tomes. The pattern of the stained glass cast colored light onto the pale stone walkways that spread out from the center of the room like a star. "I wasn't into reading before Earth, so I never had a reason to visit." A smile toyed at the corner of his mouth. "It sure is pretty."

As his gaze fell from the roof to the stacks, the smile slipped from his lips. "Why was there such a big deal about coming?" Violetta looked at where he was gesturing. "There's barely anyone in here."

"Oh, this isn't where we're going," she said, taking the two steps down to the library floor, slipping into an aisle before the graying librarian stacking shelves could spot her and demand she transform. Librarians on Amaranth hated having elements like water and fire inside the library since they threatened to damage the fragile books. She braced herself, knowing this was the part of their mission that mattered the most.

"We need to break into the royal archives." A nervous giggle bubbled up inside of her, which she tampered down quickly. "And by we, I mean you."

"Me?" He snaked out a vine and caught her arm, spinning her around to face him. "What about you? I thought we were doing this together."

"Cool your jets, Venek." She peeled off the green tendril. "I'll be distracting the guard so you can slip in and get what we need."

"By the fates, shouldn't we have discussed this before?" He threw up his arms, frustration lacing every word. "We had the whole journey, and now we're here. What's the plan?"

Violetta's water molecules vibrated with nervous anticipation of what was about to happen. She hadn't wanted to discuss the plan that formed in the back of her mind, preferring to let instinct guide her. It was easier to adjust to any unknown changes this way.

"You see that door down the end there?" Venek leaned his head around the end of the bookcase, nodding when he saw the copper door. "Through that door is an antechamber, and there should be a guard inside."

"Should?"

She ignored his raised brow. "Past that is another door. It'll be locked, so you'll need to break it down." Pausing, she took a breath. "Do you have the list Amon gave you?"

He tapped his side, his vines sliding open to reveal a hint of paper. "Yes, of course, but—"

"Good. Once the guard leaves, then make your move."

"Violetta, I don't think—"

She didn't wait any longer. Stepping back, she exploded.

The still silence of the library was broken by the panicked yells of librarians and the few patrons scattered through the aisles. Violetta's matter flung out, pelting books and toppling shelves. Harnessing her power, she recalled each element, bringing each droplet of water swirling back into a large mass. Keeping her form fluid, she rushed forward, smashing into a shelf with the force of a tidal wave. The sound of panicked feet vibrated towards her, and she quickly streamed through a crack in the floor. Following the crevices in the stone, she rolled away from the archives, satisfaction pulsing through her when she heard someone call for the guard. On the other side of the room, she let herself explode upwards, shooting almost to the stained glass before showering down onto the thousands of books kept safe in the building.

Regret flooded her. Each bit of damage she caused felt like a knife in the gut. She continued saturating the paper, moving easily from aisle to aisle, evading the Fae trying to contain her.

Eventually, she began to tire. Her water took longer to recall, and the force of her assaults weakened. To buy herself some time, she shot back into the crack in the ground, making her way back to a quiet spot by the exit. After returning to her humanoid water form, she leaned against a shelf and caught her breath.

She absent-mindedly scanned the titles, cocking her head when one jumped out at her.

Elemental Powers Through the Ages

Her fingers itched to pull the book from its place and flip through the pages to see what information it contained. "Blast!" Punching the shelf at her stomach level, she turned away, grinding her teeth in frustration.

"A little bit of notice would have been nice."

Venek skidded to a stop beside her, blowing out a breath as he shifted his vines, securing the mass of books plastered to his body. He looked around sharply, scanning the space around them. "Are we ready to go?" Patting the lumps dotting his body, he gave her a cocky grin. "I got them all."

Heart leaping, Violetta grabbed him closer, hurriedly pointing at the book on elemental magic. "Quick, grab that one as well. The book on magic."

Feet pounded. "Over there," someone called out. "I heard something coming from section G."

Venek slid the book from its place, shoving it within his body just as several Fae rounded the end of the aisle. "Time to go," she chirped, bolting for the doors as cries of outrage rose up from behind them. They burst into the sunshine at a run, skillfully evading their pursuers through the winding city streets. Only when she was sure they were undetected did she lead Venek back to the gateway.

He touched it first, disappearing instantly. But before she reached out to join him in the South Forest, she took one last look around. The sun glinted off glass peaks, hiding the poverty that touched every part of the Euhedral. She blew out a breath. The next time she would step foot within her city would be when they had the strength to deal with Petrov.

Reaching out behind her, Violetta felt for the cool quartz, keeping her eyes on what once was her home, even as she brought to mind the South Forest. The world shifted, and she found herself facing Venek, the dark trees blocking out the light of the day.

"Ready to get home?" he asked.

Pulling Fawn's sweet face to her mind, Violetta pursed her lips into a smile. The young Fae was her present and her future. Even though she had a long way to go, Violetta was proud to be one of the people tasked with watching and shaping her as she grew. Tucking her hair behind her pointed ear, she stepped forward, taking Venek's proffered hand. "I'm ready."

As they stepped through the trees, she took one last look at the gateway. Then, turning away, she kept her eyes fixed ahead where Fawn and her Fae family were waiting.

Fawn was her home now.

CHAPTER TWENTY SEVEN
ERWIN

"**S**HE'S COMING," CRIED BAOL, darting into the clearing, his usually carefree face pinched with concern. Erwin rubbed his hands together and moved closer to Huxley, anything to quell the anxiety growing in his belly.

His staunch friend let out a rumbling breath. "Violetta only just left. We should have waited longer before letting her go."

"Them go," murmured Amon, glancing down and locking eyes with Erwin. "We should have waited longer before letting them go."

Even Huxley's obvious obsession with the water Fae couldn't make Erwin muster more than a weak smile. His mind was caught up with worry. It had been like that ever since Amon had returned and told them what happened with Fawn.

"Yes, them," bit out Huxley. "That's what I meant."

Flavire sidled up beside them, toying absentmindedly with one of his fuchsia flowers. His position blocked Erwin's view of the forest where Baol had appeared. Brow furrowing, Erwin scrambled up Huxley's side, desperate not to miss the moment Fawn arrived.

"It wouldn't have made a difference if they stayed behind," Flavire drawled. "We can handle what needs to be done."

Huxley tensed underneath him.

"It's not about making a difference, Flavire. It's about being a part of something important—something life-changing."

Amon's quick words saved Flavire from Huxley's sharp tongue. The floral Fae ruffled his foliage and gave the three of them a wry smile, but didn't reply. Erwin narrowed his eyes and studied Flavire more closely. The Fae adjusted his foliage again, his carefully bored eyes marred with strain.

Erwin glanced back into the forest. "Who's going to tell her?" he asked no one in particular as he slid off Huxley, needing to see for himself where Fawn was.

"I will."

"Lothian."

Amon and Flavire glared at each other, then promptly broke into a tense debate.

Ignoring their heated words and Huxley's rumbling chuckle, Erwin lay down on the earth and closed his eyes, accessing his magic.

The low hum of every living thing filled his senses, rolling over him like a blanket. Erwin settled in deeper, pushing his power out in a wide arc with quiet confidence. His friends in the clearing fell away as he lost himself in his search, hunting for the light tread of Faunella's feet.

Movement drew his attention, a body weaving through the trees.

Fawn.

His body relaxed, a smile pulling at his lips. She was almost here, closer than he thought, but she was coming from the wrong direction. Erwin frowned and concentrated harder. The footsteps were heavy, their slow thudding contrary to Fawn's usually light gait. A second body joined the first, and Erwin's heart stopped. The dense trees masked their presence.

It wasn't Fawn.

He came back to himself with a snap, his mossy body recoiling so hard that he lifted slightly off the ground. Amon and Flavire were still bickering, their argument drawing the attention of all the Fae and ensuring no one could hear the approaching humans.

"Stop!" Erwin cried, fear making him brave. "Humans are coming!"

Every Fae in the clearing froze. Then, almost in unison, their heads swiveled in the direction of the now unmistakable sound of boot-clad feet only moments from the tree line.

Amon was the first one to react.

"Fawn," he breathed, twisting to look in horror at the opposite side of the clearing where her soft footfalls could now be heard steadily approaching. He lurched forward, fear etched in every aspect of his being. Huxley's arm shot out. "There's no time." He gripped Amon's branch, regret in his eyes, then transformed, keeping Amon in place.

Erwin slunk back to the ground, his heart beating fast. In all of their years on Earth, they never came so close to being seen. One by one, the Fae around him transformed, becoming no more than inanimate objects, just as two humans stepped into the clearing.

Erwin was the only one left, but his small body went unnoticed among the grass. His ears pricked up. Fawn was so close now. She would be stepping into the clearing with no clue what awaited her. The humans took off the large backpacks they were wearing and settled down near the cave. Erwin felt a moment of relief. Baol and Baeroot had intertwined their branches and formed a barrier over the mouth of their home, effectively hiding it from sight.

However, his relief was short-lived. Blood pulsed loudly in his ears. He had to do something. His eyes roved frantically around the clearing. He had to get to Fawn, but the humans would see him move. As his gaze brushed past, he locked eyes with Laurel's panicked face. She hadn't transformed either.

With painful slowness, she nodded at him, then reached inside of herself and snapped off one of her main branches. Erwin flinched, but the loud crack drew the attention of both humans, and they turned towards the sound. Using the distraction, Erwin bolted towards the treeline, staying low and praying he would be fast enough.

Launching himself past the first tree, he let out a gasp and kept moving. He didn't stop until he latched eyes on Fawn and hurtled into her legs, wrapping around her with a shuddering cry.

"Don't go any further," he choked out. "It's not safe in the grotto. Please, Fawn, don't move."

Faunella wobbled, reaching out her hand to a tree to keep from falling.

"Erwin, what's wrong? Is everyone okay?"

Indecision warred within him. He wanted to tell Fawn about the humans, but only to keep her away from them. She had scared him when she tried leaving the forest—when she had tried leaving him. What if she tried leaving again? He looked up into her sweet face, watching as concern grew in her eyes.

"Where are the others?" She pried at his arms, her jaw tight with that familiar stubbornness. "Let me go, Erwin."

"You can't. There are humans in the grotto."

"Humans?"

Her eyes brightened, and her hands stilled. Erwin's heart sank. As quick as a whippet, Fawn slipped free of his embrace. She'd obviously been waiting for him to be distracted.

"No, don't."

She ignored him and crept towards the clearing, shooing Beebe away when the bird tried to land on her shoulder. Erwin followed, wringing his hands. She needed to stay with them. She needed to learn from them. If she abandoned her life as a Fae, she would ruin everything.

Panic filled him. She was creeping closer and closer, her fascination growing with every step.

She had to stop. He had to make her see that they needed her. A light went off in his brain. He had to tell her the reason they had been gathered today.

"Fawn, wait!" He darted out in front of her, stopping her just as she reached the clearing, her focused face peering through the foliage. "You can't leave us." Leaping up, he gripped her hand, finally getting her attention. "You can't leave. You're our missing heir."

CHAPTER TWENTY EIGHT
FAUNELLA

ERWIN CLUTCHED HER ARM and tugged her down, the distress in his eyes doing more to keep her in place than the tenuous grip he had on her body.

"I'm the missing what?" She kept her voice low, conscious of the humans nearby. His feather-light voice spoke again, repeating the same sounds as before. Faunella frowned, frustration tightening her jaw. "Erwin, I don't know what that means. You've never said that word before."

"Just wait here with me," he pleaded. *"Let the humans leave, and Amon will explain."*

Lifting her face, Faunella peered into the bright clearing. The two humans were relaxing on the grass, eating some sort of food removed from their packs. Their deep voices carried across to where she hid, clearly identifying them as males. Curiosity burned within her, making her inch closer.

The thought barely formed in her mind before she squashed it, the now familiar self-doubt taking its place. She chewed on her lip, her mind conjuring images of the two men getting flung back and their bodies blown apart. Flinching, she swallowed hard, fighting to tamp down her rising fear. Instead, she turned back to Erwin, needing the distraction.

"Come on," she ground out, retreating deeper into the forest and tugging Erwin behind her. "You have some explaining to do."

By the time Amon and the other Fae congregated around her treehouse, Faunella was undeniably confused.

"Ground. Danger. Dying." She scratched her head, trying to find the connection. "Missing. In charge. Life."

Erwin paced the floor, getting more noticeably upset with each explanation. Faunella couldn't tell if it was her just not understanding or Erwin's distress making him lose his faculties.

"Is everything okay up there?" called Amon.

Faunella scrambled to her feet and popped her head over the windowsill, a smile lighting her face when she saw all the Fae gathered, except Venek and Violetta.

Huxley leaned close to Amon. *"Get her to come down,"* he failed to whisper, the words coming out urgent and loud. *"I can't get up there, and there's no way I'm missing this conversation."*

Faunella ducked back, her interest peaked. Her eyes flicked towards the still-pacing Fae, his muttered words indecipherable. It was something important, from the look of it.

"Erwin?" she called gently, breaking his concentration. He glanced up with wide eyes filled with feeling. Faunella's heart softened, her curiosity coming second to the Fae in front of her.

"The others have come to get us. You don't have to do this on your own anymore."

Instead of the relief she expected to see, Erwin drew back, guilt and worry working across his face.

Grasping his tiny hand, Faunella smiled reassuringly. Whatever this news was, it couldn't be that bad.

Faunella landed lightly at the base of her tree, Erwin a second behind. She barely rose to her full height before the Fae surged around her, their bodies thrumming with unrestrained energy.

"Woah," she stumbled back, arms outstretched. "What brought this on?" Her eyes lifted to Amon's face before darting away, heat rising to her cheeks as she remembered the harsh words she spat in his direction earlier that day. Laurel inched her way past Bael and Baeroot, clearing her throat shyly as she approached.

"Are you okay, dear?"

Faunella grimaced. Amon must have told them all about her latest disastrous attempt at controlling her magic. She sighed and accepted Laurel's outstretched hand, her fingers closing around the flexible, twiggy limb.

"I'm sorry, everyone. I didn't mean to worry you." Squaring her shoulders, she met Amon's eyes again. "I shouldn't have talked to you that way."

Amon's mouth curved up into a gentle smile. *"It's forgotten."*

A weight lifted off her shoulders. The hurt she caused with her thoughtless anger was erased with a few heartfelt words. Faunella squeezed Laurel's hand, happiness coursing under her skin. She let out a short laugh, remembering the real reason for the Fae being gathered.

"So, what is this big news Erwin's been trying to tell me?"

"Erwin!"

Huxley dove for the younger Fae, his face contorted with outrage. Erwin let out an alarmed squeal and dove behind her legs, gripping them with tight fingers amongst the varied cries of the other Fae.

"Oh, Erwin," groaned Amon, slapping his hand to his face. *"Please tell me you didn't?"*

"I didn't know what else to do," he babbled, peeking out from behind her legs. *"She wanted to leave with the humans. I had to stop her somehow."*

Faunella's mouth dropped open. Erwin stepped around her, his dark eyes pleading.

"She didn't understand me, Amon." His cheeks flushed a dark green. *"I couldn't make her understand."*

"I wasn't going to leave with them," Faunella blurted out. "I know I'm dangerous to be around. I just wanted a closer look."

"Oh, Fawn," Amons voice dripped with sorrow, and the Fae murmured quietly, their faces laced with pity. Faunella squirmed under their attention, digging a toe into the ground to avoid the weight of their stares. She already felt bad enough about her power; she didn't need them making it worse.

"Can we just get to the point?" she said in a small voice. "You tell me this important thing, then we can get back to normal?"

At her words, Erwin's guilty expression from earlier appeared on every face surrounding her. Faunella's confusion grew. She scanned the group, brows furrowing with each Fae's refusal to meet her eye.

"Amon?" she pleaded, her chest tight.

Amon sighed. *"This was meant to be a happy moment."* Erwin and Laurel left her side as Amon stepped forward. *"After all these years, we have decided you are old enough to know the truth about why you live on Earth with us instead of Amaranth."*

Faunella translated his words automatically, filling in the unknown sounds to the best of her ability. Her eyes widened. She would finally get some real answers and fill in the strange blanks that surrounded her life. She pressed closer to Amon, her heart pounding.

"Tell me." She reached out her hand. "Show me."

Amon placed his wooden hand on hers, his face carefully devoid of feeling. Fighting her impatience, Faunella danced in place, waiting for the moment she would be whisked away into his memories. As she studied his face so intently, she caught the brief moment of indecision that flashed behind his eyes, but before she could question it, her mind went black.

A land sapped of life, slowly decaying with each passing season.

Dark soil leached in toxins, unable to provide adequate harvest for our many people.

His hand brushed over the grass at his feet, crumbling at his touch.

"Our lands are dying."

Faunella wrinkled her nose, fighting against the vision. This memory felt different than the others - deeper, more important.

Despair choked him, filling him up until a fair-haired male flicked into his mind.

Then came the hate, a rising fury towards this amber- eyed Fae.

The sole reason for the decline of the Ancient Fae.

Petrov.

The false king. The usurper.

A shudder ran down her spine at his name. *Petrov.* Faunella braced herself as the memories and thoughts came faster. It felt so different from Amon's usual style.

Ancient Fae are sick and injured, not healing as they should.

Children are born sleeping, even their innocence touched by Petrov's rule.

Decay.

Death—so much death.

Their lands need a ruler, their kingdom a true king...

The images slowed to a stop, making Faunella's mind whirl and causing her palms to sweat. Then, in the stillness, a new memory began to play. It started slowly, filling her up with the importance of what Amon was revealing. He strode through a dying forest that tickled the edges of Faunella's memory. Among all the rot, he felt a flicker of a light that was impossible not to follow, a light that could only be an Ancient spark. Holding her breath, she watched the moment he peered through the trees. His eyes found a tiny girl, her nightgown torn and dirty, feet bare, and her hair a tangled mess of red curls.

Faunella gasped, her eyes flying open as Amon's thoughts echoed in her mind.

...a queen.

PART THREE

Counselors,

My tireless research has begun to yield results. I believe I am right on the cusp of creating a treatment that rivals the abilities of the Ancient Fae healers. However, I would be remiss not to admit it is those very Fae who are the reason for my tentative success.

Before they ostracized themselves from civilization, two Ancient Fae, whom I had considered friends, donated specimens to aid in the healing of our people. One of them, a rather fetching female, gave me several waterlogged willow branches from her nature form. These have proved to be the key.

As you know, the High Fae with healing abilities are able to heal all but the most critical injuries. The only downside is the potency of our magic. We just can't seem to heal fast enough.

So, I am ecstatic to announce that will soon be a thing of the past. My power has isolated the properties of the Ancient magic, and with my own healing magic, I can combine them to create a more fast-moving treatment. This will save many more precious lives in the future—whether High Fae, low fae, or Ancient, if they ever deign to return.

I will write again soon.
Yours respectfully,
Veriad

—Correspondence from Physician Veriad to the Council of Healers

THREE YEARS LATER

CHAPTER TWENTY NINE
FAUNELLA

CLIMBING TREES HAD NEVER been easier. Faunella reached for the next branch, her long gangly limbs grasping it effortlessly. She grinned up at Beebe, who sat preening herself on the uppermost branches. "If you were a little bigger, you could help me carry this up." Adjusting the thick book strapped to her hip, she pulled herself higher, the desire to reach the sky pushing her further than the narrow limbs allowed. A crack from the branch had her stilling, her heart beating heavily as she clung to the smooth wood. She worried her lip, studying the sun glinting through the leaves only seconds away. She was so close to the top.

Swallowing past the lump in her throat, she willed away her nerves. Stubbornness filled her with an icy determination.

Breathing deeply, she closed her eyes, focusing on the way her breath felt as it escaped from her nose. She did it again, appreciating the tangible feel of it caressing down her face before it joined the breeze swirling through the treetops. Her eyes flashed open.

"Here we go."

She pushed up, reaching for each branch while remaining centered in the feel of the air around her. With each exhale, the air quivered before solidifying around her and supporting her weight.

Gentle does it. She calmed herself. *The air wants to work with you, not against you.* Violetta's words came easily, so often repeated that by now they were second nature.

As she broke through the final layer of leaves, a gust of wind broke away from the air supporting her, sweeping along the side of her face before twisting through a fiery curl. Faunella blinked back her surprise. That never happened before. She balanced on the narrow branch, tracing the path the wind had made on her cheek. Her nerves stilled, replaced by a cautious hope.

"Maybe I'm finally getting it, Beebe."

Closing her eyes, she felt inside of herself for the pale swirl of constantly moving ether. It danced through her mind, gentle like a summer breeze.Focusing, she willed the air to form a cocoon around the thin branch she was sitting on. She tensed, ready for the explosion of power that usually occurred when she actively tried to force the air to her will, but it didn't come. Instead, the air solidified. Her mouth fell open.

"I can't believe that just happened."

Violetta had been working with her to overcome her fear and embrace her magic. Both she and Laurel advised Faunella to avoid trying to will and dominate her magic. Instead, she had been focusing on just enjoying the air around her, learning to embrace it as it was with no control and no restrictions.

Relaxing her body, she nestled into the makeshift seat. Beebe flitted closer, settling down on the branch next to her.

"How was that, Beebe?" She grinned at her little friend. Pursing her lips, she wriggled around as she let out a little happy humming tune. Something was changing for her; she could feel it. She gazed around the wide vista, untouched by the world and marveling in the peace she found up in the air. She closed her eyes and let the warm summer breeze sweep over her face, feeling a tug at her lips when she felt the tickling wind tear up through her hair. It was as if all of a sudden, the air had a mind of its own.

"None of that." She chuckled nervously, swatting at the invisible sensation and unsure how to feel about the change. The air swirled playfully, this time pushing and pulling at the thin cotton of her lemon and white checkered dress. Faunella threw back her head, unable to help the laughter that burst from her mouth. She smoothed down the fabric, happiness flooding her. The garment was a gift from Huxley. She found it at the base of her tree with a distinctive gray stone perched on top. It had appeared the morning after she had been admiring the pretty dresses that the human girls her age wore.

Faunella smiled broadly as she traced the small yellow squares, remembering the way Huxley had looked down, trying to hide his pleased smile when she had worn it for the first time.

Ah, my sweet Hux, always so embarrassed when he does something nice.

Stretching out her legs, she leaned back and untied the book from her hip.

Agriculture and Horticulture: *Considering Geological Magic use.*

Learning to read had been a trial, but her enthusiasm had carried her through. The knowledge that there was a concrete plan for her life, the Ancient Kingdoms to rule, and a people to save gave her a renewed drive to learn. However, that was three years ago, and her childish innocence was beginning to wane. She screwed up her nose, sighing heavily. Why did her royal studies have to be so darn boring? Flipping open to the marked page, she scanned the inky text and settled into her study session.

Although she tried to focus, it didn't take long for her mind to wander. As the words blurred together, her dream from last night crawled from the back of her mind.

The dark shadows snapped at her heels, pushing her further from safety. *"Mama!"* she cried, her words choking off as an oily pressure wrapped around her throat.

Faunella took a shuddering breath. It was the same dream she had been having since the Fae informed her that she wasn't just lost on Earth, but rather the Heir to the Ancient Kingdoms.

I hope my family is doing okay.

The thoughts about her family pushed her when things got hard. Somewhere out there, her parents were suffering under the rule of Petrov. Her stomach churned. She wanted to help, to take her place and heal the lands. But sometimes that pressure seemed too much and too frightening for her to face alone.

Beebe chirped at her, sensing the unease.

"I'm okay." She stroked the bird's downy plume, reassuring the both of them. "It was just the dream again. It's always that dream." Shutting the book, she rested her chin on her hand, staring out at the mountains beyond the forest. Last night's dream was different though. The images and sounds were much more vivid, leaving her soaked and gasping when she finally woke. It had almost felt like a memory. Unbidden, the venomous words from the nightmare came to her. *"Dirty halfbreed!"* Flinching, she looked down her long legs and wriggled her toes. A thin layer of dirt seemed to perpetually cover the skin on her feet. She tried wearing shoes this past year but didn't enjoy the feeling of having her feet confined. She shook her head, curls bouncing in front of her face. How could anyone have so much hate and animosity in their heart?

She was pulled from her thoughts when she felt something on her leg.

She pushed her dress to the side and held one of her legs to her chest, angling her knee so that she could have a closer inspection of her thighs. Craning her neck, she pressed her face forward until her nose was inches from her skin.

The insides of both legs were streaked with blood. Nibbling at her lower lip, she studied the skin, looking for a cut or a scrape that would explain where the bleeding originated. As her gaze traveled upwards, her neck twinged from the impossible angle. Straightening up with a sigh, she pulled back her shoulders and stretched out her cramped muscles.

Dream forgotten, her only thought was finding one of the Fae to take a look. She swung off the branch, dissolving the cocoon she had formed. In her haste, she forgot to draw on her burgeoning power to take some of her weight. As soon as she landed on the next branch down, it gave a sickening crack and fell out from under her. Faunella flew through the now-empty space, letting out an ear-splitting scream. Clutching wildly at the thin branches of the tree, she only managed to break them as her weight plunged her further toward the forest floor. A large branch caught her in the chest, knocking the wind out of her. Wincing past the dull ache in her ribs, she sucked in a pained breath. Her fall had been stopped just above midway down the large tree, the rounded branches finally thick enough to support her weight.

Faunella felt a slight breeze on her cheek, followed by a light tug on her hair from Beebe hovering around her head.

"Oof," she muttered, gingerly pushing herself to a seated position. "Not fun." Easing to her feet, she used the tree as support. "That was a close one. I guess I just forgot about my powers for a second." Beebe's concern pulsed through their connection. "No, really. I'm okay." She reassured her friend, stretching her body to prove her point.

Shaken, Faunella took her time returning to the ground, only breathing easy once her feet touched the forest floor.

I haven't had a fall like that in a long time.

Looking back up in the tree, she searched for Beebe, but couldn't see her. She tugged on the bond inside that connected them. She felt the thread of hunger and smiled.

Deciding to wait a few moments, Faunella scanned the dense forest surrounding her. As her eyes passed a large leafy bush, a warmth flickered under her breast.

Faunella focused intently on the greenery, opening herself up to the tentative feeling from before. A moment later, a twitching black nose emerged from under the lower layer of leaves, revealing a fox.

Pleased to see the usually wary animal, she lowered herself onto her knees, careful not to spook it. "Why are you here, little one?"

Willing the fox to sense that she meant it no harm, she stretched out her hand and smiled into its dark eyes.

The moment she acknowledged it, the warmth bloomed. The heat increased until the hot pressure burst in her stomach. Gasping, she clutched at her abdomen, letting out a small cry when the tingling heat pressed out from underneath her skin and into the small creature.

Faunella pulled at her dress and fell backwards, staring wide-eyed at the fox now walking towards her. She felt curiosity and deep concern coming from the animal. It let out a low whine, cocking its head as a flood of worry filled her senses. She heard the echoed remnants of her yell, and somehow, she knew her terrified scream was the reason the fox had come to investigate. It all suddenly clicked.

She had somehow formed a bond with another animal. She had—not Violetta, not the magic in her water—but her. Faunella. It had been her magic all along.

Beebe chose that moment to come darting back down. She circled Faunella before coming to land on her shoulder. The fox dropped low to the ground, the instinct to hunt firing through the fresh bond.

"Oh no, you can't eat Beebe!"

Swiping the bird off her shoulder, she clutched her to her chest. Finding the tangy tether to the predator, Faunella attempted to convince it to leave Beebe alone. Unsure if it understood, she kept hold of Beebe, ignoring the bird's outrage at being restrained.

Now having two reasons to go find the Fae, Faunella stood up, intent on getting some answers. The fox moved to follow her, its large ears twitching. Amused, she hesitated.

"I'm alright, little fox. You can go back to your life now."

She smiled at the beautiful creature, honored to have been worthy of its concern. Turning, she took off in a sweeping run towards the grotto, a slight breeze carrying her along.

Faunella burst into the clearing, her hair flinging wildly around her as she skidded to a halt. Standing in the center of the grassy space stood two tree Fae, their brown limbs intertwined. Letting out harsh grunts, they strained to pin the other's branches down. One of them stuck out his thick leg, barking out a triumphant cry, hooking it out and behind the other's trunk. With a loud crash, the Fae came slamming down, one on top of the other. At the creaking cry of delight, Faunella recognized Baeroot as the winner and Baol the unfortunate loser.

"Baol? Baeroot?" she called out, not wanting them to suddenly start a second round of their wrestling game.

The two Fae turned to her, wooden faces lighting up as they smiled their greetings.

Baeroot rolled away, drawing himself up until he was standing once again. He reached out a limb and offered it to Baol, letting out a rustling burst of laughter when Baol knocked it away, choosing to roll onto his side and get up unaided. Once they were both standing, Baeroot wrapped his arm around Baol's trunk, and they both turned to face her, grinning broadly.

Faunella felt herself smiling back, enjoying their playful antics. Any other day she would have joined in, but today she had more pressing matters on her mind.

"I was climbing one of the tallest trees not too far away," she began, starting to feel her cheeks heat, not wanting to mention she had almost fallen and broken her neck. "When I climbed down, I connected with a fox."

She closely watched their faces, expecting to see shock, amazement, or maybe even surprise. Instead, much to her frustration they only gave her amused placating smiles, making sounds like *"Nice."* and *"That's good."* Her smile fell.

"No you don't understand. I connected with a fox like I did with Beebe." She gestured wildly up at the Fae, annunciating the word, needing them to know exactly what she was saying. "I saw it, and I felt power inside. Then, all of a sudden I could feel what it felt, and I could share my thoughts as well."

The Fae turned to face each other, their thoughtful expressions slightly mollifying Faunella.

"Her powers are starting to grow," croaked out Baol, ignoring her completely.

"What was that?" she asked, not content to be left out of the conversation. "You know I don't speak tree as well as you two, but it sounded like you said my powers are growing."

She threw up her hands, letting out a dramatic huff. "I didn't even know I had these powers! I thought I connected with Beebe because of Violetta's magic."

Baeroot shook his head and pointed at her. *"It was always your magic,"* he told her, *"But now it's growing."*

"My air powers are growing as well," Faunella added.

The two Fae didn't seem as interested in her discovery as she had hoped. Deciding to put that to the side for now, she lifted her dress halfway up her thighs to get their help figuring out where her injury was.

"Before I fell — I mean, climbed down, I noticed I was bleeding."

Lifting one leg as high as she could, she angled it to the side for Baeroot and Baol's inspection. Wobbling wildly, she quickly closed her eyes and concentrated on thickening the air on either side of her to help keep her upright. She was pleasantly surprised when the magic proved as easy as it was earlier.

The two Fae brought their faces down low, studying Faunella's leg as she held it out. Baol extended a smaller limb from the side of his body, winding it around her ankle to try and get a better idea of what she was showing them.

"Ugh, here," said Faunella, reaching out a hand and pulling the dress up higher. "It's covering both my legs, but I can't get low enough to see where the cut is."

Baol quickly placed her foot back onto the ground and took a small half-step backward. He fired a panicked look at Baeroot, the other tree's face mirroring his panic. Faunella's heart began to quicken.

"What is it? What's wrong with me?"

Looking back and forth between the two of them, she didn't miss the way their cheeks seemed to darken or the fact that neither of them looked like they were going to answer her questions. "It's just a cut isn't it?" She cut herself off as both Fae backed further away. "What's wrong?" Her stomach began to tighten painfully, an ache pulling at her lower abdomen.

Dropping into a crouch, she brought her face close to her legs and began frantically wiping at the red liquid. "Where is it coming from? Why is this happening? How do I get it to stop bleeding?"

Faunella's thoughts spiraled. Not knowing frightened her more than anything. She was just about to blurt out another round of questions when a bubbling voice spoke out. Her head shot up. Violetta sashayed over, coming to a stop between Baol and Baeroot. Relief washed over her.

"Violetta, I'm bleeding. It won't stop, and I can't find the cut!" The words came out quickly and breathlessly. She gestured between her legs, then stared earnestly at her friend, waiting for the female to tell her what terrible thing was wrong with her.

Violetta's mouth fell open. Turning around, she let out a hissing whistle as she reached out her arms and flung two icy orbs of water into both the male's faces. Faunella stiffened up in surprise.

Flinging an arm to the side, Violetta gave a gurgling command to the now sheepish-looking Fae. They ducked their heads and ambled off, shooting Faunella small smiles as they left. Turning back around to face her, Violetta shook her head from side to side. *"Males!"*

She lowered herself to the ground in front of Faunella, easing her out of her crouch and into a seated position.

"What's happening to me?" Faunella asked in a quiet voice, some of her earlier panic easing in the water Fae's calming presence.

Violetta smiled. *"Why don't you tell me when this all started."*

Faunella quickly ran through everything that happened that morning, sniffing a little bit when she recalled Baol and Baeroot's reaction to her injury. "You see, it must be pretty bad if they reacted like that." She pressed her hand to her abdomen, rubbing at the tender ache. "And now my stomach hurts."

Throughout her whole story, Violetta had sat patiently and calmly, not showing any reaction besides the occasional nod or encouraging word. She reached forward and clasped Faunella's hands within her own.

"You're not injured," she said with a small laugh. *"You are a Fae female."*

Faunella frowned, her relief replaced with confusion. Violetta's smile grew wider. She stroked one of her hands down the side of Faunella's face, leaving a light misting of tingling water behind. Trying again, Violetta used her hands to gesture as she used simple water sounds to communicate her meaning.

"Once each season, you will bleed from between your legs." She carefully lifted her dress and washed the blood from Faunella's thighs, showing her the blood staining her underwear. Faunella listened in awe, translating the sounds as she listened to Violetta's explanation on how to care for herself during her bleeding times. *"As you get older, your body will continue changing."* She touched the golden hair on Faunella's legs and smiled, also pointing between her legs and lifting an arm to point to her armpit. Squinting her eyes, Faunella craned her neck and peered into the pale skin under her arm.

"There's hair growing already!" She pressed her armpit forward and pointed at the two tiny hairs that sprouted from the delicate skin. Violetta let out a twinkling giggle and nodded her head. Faunella smiled back up at the older Fae.

"It's not only hair that will grow. Your body will start to shift into its grown female form." Violetta traced her hands over her own rounded curves, starting at her chest and tracing the flow of her body until she reached the rounded swell of her hips. *"Like me."*

Giving her another large smile, she stood, pulling Faunella up to join her. *"Soon, you will grow into such a beautiful Fae."* She let out a delighted peal of laughter, swinging Faunella around the clearing as they danced to an unheard beat.

Faunella flushed slightly, embarrassed for not realizing that the recent changes were from her growing up. However, Violetta's happiness was contagious, and soon Faunella forgot her wrong assumptions. Instead, she lost herself celebrating the start of her journey to becoming an adult.

CHAPTER THIRTY
DERICK

THE SHARP STACCATO HIS foot made on the floor soothed his ragged nerves. Derick hated being inside the concrete compound. The stark gray walls pressed in, suffocating him. It was always the same when he visited the prison where Frank was kept. The knot grew in his stomach, knowing his father had spent the past ten years in this place and still had four more years before the possibility of getting parole.

Movement through the glass drew his attention as Frank was brought into the small room across from him. Straightening up, he shifted his leg to stop the compulsive tapping and scratched the underside of his jaw.

"Dad."

He nodded his greeting through the glass, face carefully expressionless. Frank placed his cuffed hands on the table in front of him, chains rattling as he leaned forward to talk.

"I haven't seen you in a while." He furrowed his brow, crinkles distorting the tattoo inked around one eye. "You missed last month's visit. I hope business is going well?" Derick's fists clenched under the table as he took note of his father's furtive glances around the room. "I haven't heard otherwise," he continued, "but when you didn't show up last time, I was worried."

Derick inwardly scoffed, chafing at the unspoken message Frank was asking.

If you can't make your regular visit, I'll find someone else to be my informant.

Tell me what the gang is getting up to. My connections in the prison haven't said anything, but that doesn't mean something hasn't happened.

I'm not worried about you. I'm worried about my standing in the gang.

Keeping his feelings to himself, Derick answered. "Things were getting a bit hot last month, and I had a lot of heat on me." He lowered his voice, leaning forward to get closer to the glass. "We took on a fair bit of new business, so I was just trying to keep any unwanted attention away from us." He sat back up, his body rod straight.

"Ah, good. More business is good." The satisfied smile on Frank's face made Derick's stomach clench. He stared at the man in front of him, barely able to recognise what he had become. The orange of his jumpsuit turned his skin a sickly yellow, highlighting its now dull pallor. The years in prison hadn't been kind to Frank. Any piece of kindness or softness that Derick remembered of his father had long since disappeared. His monthly visits to the prison were now only out of obligation for his decade's worth of guilt. Clearing his throat, he braced himself to deliver some news that he knew Frank wouldn't take well. "So, Shaun has decided to move the headquarters, and he's also changing the group's moniker."

Frank's response was instantaneous. Slamming his fist down onto the metal table, he swore violently.

"He's cutting me out. The fucking ingrate is cutting me out after all I've done for him." He swung his dark eyes to Derick. "How long have you known about it? Did the two of you plan this?"

Derick swallowed and pushed past the cold sweat that erupted on his skin. There was no right answer here. This had been a long time coming. "I don't think there was ever a plan to let you come back." He pushed out of his chair, standing in one smooth motion. "It's Shaun's gang now. You're done."

The jaundiced skin on Frank's face darkened to a deep red, the vivid shade creeping up from behind his collar. His jaw tightened as he ground his teeth and let out a hollow growl.

Derick crossed his arms, keeping up the strong front that his father always demanded from him. He tightened his thighs, banishing the weakness threatening to turn him to jelly. *Don't let him see your fear,* he told himself, reminding the young Derick within that the quaking in his legs was reminiscent of his childhood, back when he was weak and helpless. He wasn't that child any more.

Launching himself out of his chair, Frank beat his bound hands onto the glass between them, spit flying out of his mouth as he roared in rage. The guards sprung into action, one pressing an alarm while the other raced over to try and subdue him. In what felt like years, Frank was pressed down onto the concrete floor, several knees in his back as they redid his cuffs, this time latching his arms behind his body.

Derick stilled his shuddering breath and ran his eyes over Frank's prone form. He was sure this was the last time he would ever see his father. Looking down at him now, he couldn't help but feel a rush of pity for the man.

He turned his back and walked away, not sparing one more look at the man who used to be his father.

"Is it done?"

Shaun sat on the hood of his 69 Dodge Charger, a cigarette hanging out of the corner of his mouth as Derick exited the prison.

"It's done. I told him everything you wanted me to."

"Good boy. Stabbing your old man in the back couldn't have been easy." He laughed and slid off the car, sauntering over to clap him on the shoulder.

Not needing to say anything, Derick nodded once, still bristling at being called a boy. He was twenty-two years old and very much a man. Shaun inhaled deeply before opening his mouth to let the billowing white smoke ooze out of his mouth. He walked Derick back to his car, Shaun's arm still wrapped around his broad shoulders.

It was testimony to Derick's effort over the past three years that Shaun would be so relaxed with him. He had scrubbed any softness from himself, doing whatever it took to please Shaun and serve the gang. Shaun had absolutely no idea of the resentment that still remained just simmering under the surface.

Resisting the urge to pull away from Shaun's embrace, Derick asked a question that had been bothering him.

"What are you planning to do once he's out? Four years isn't a long time, and he'll be out for blood."

The cold sneer on Shaun's face had a heavy weight settling in his stomach.

"He won't be getting out." He let his arm drop. "You don't think I'd plan all this with Frank potentially getting out and ruining everything? Nah." Stepping back to the door of his car, he flicked the bud of his cigarette away with two stained fingers. "I've arranged for some evidence of past crimes to be sent in to the police. He's not going anywhere."

Derick could only stare at Shaun as the man got back into his car and started the engine, fighting to keep the surprise off his face.

He swallowed hard. He had proven himself time after time to Shaun. There was no double meaning in what he had said. The evidence was all his father's - nothing else to it.

Mixed parts of grief and relief swirled around Derick's mind. Pushing the emotions down, he put his hand out on the roof of the car, stopping Shaun from driving straight off.

"You're not worried about him sending people after you?"

"That's the best part," Shaun chuckled. "I've paid off all his connections, inside and out. He's got no one left now."

Derick stepped back as Shaun sped off, watching the retreating vehicle without really seeing it. Shaun's parting words repeated in his head. *"He's got no one left now."* Stretching out his back, he shook off the interaction and strode over to his bike, zipping up his leather jacket as he went.

The Harley Softail Slim was his prized possession and the only thing he gave a damn about. He ran his hand over the shiny metal, frowning when he recalled the circumstances that led him to its purchase.

Starting the long ride home, he left the prison and Frank far behind. He found himself taking the road through the forest, retracing the path he took all those years ago when his pain had proven too much. Slowing, he reached that unforgettable stretch of road. Frustration burned within him. Was it all in his mind? Was the girl even real? He shook his head, unable to find a satisfactory explanation. All he knew was that girl was the reason he was still alive. He spun his bike around, finding no answers here. For months after the incident, Derick had driven the stretch of road, searching the treeline for a glimpse of the girl's red hair to no avail. She remained elusive, and he began to question his sanity.

He shot out of the forest and turned left, preferring to ride through the small town of Mull Crest and up the eastern road along the coast. The sound of the sea crashing into the shore coupled with the stillness of the forest reached him in a way not much else did. He pushed open the visor on his helmet, breathing in the salty air. When he rode at breakneck speeds along the windy road, he almost felt like he was flying. Derick smiled. He could almost feel like he was free.

He strode into The Green Locker a few hours later, his heavy black boots echoing loudly against the wood of the well worn floor. The pub was blaring some old 90s rock, and the dingy space smelt of cigarettes and motor oil. Despite this, Derick held a certain fondness for the place, and sometimes when the night was late but not quite morning, he could sit and pretend he was someone else. Today, he wasn't that lucky.

As soon as he slid into a vacant seat at the bar, he heard the click clack of heels tottering over towards him. He lifted his hand to signal the barman, Jack. He needed a drink to get through the encounter with Crystal that he knew was coming.

Jack came down the bar, flipping his customary cloth over his shoulder, and placed a beer in front of him. Derick shot him a nod, and as the stool beside him was scraped back, he raised two fingers and mouthed *two*. The barman, worth his weight in gold, darted his eyes to Derick's right, then gave him an understanding nod before he bustled off to get him his second beverage.

A hand snaked up over his shoulder, long nails scraping the side of his neck.

"Haven't seen you in a few days, hon. What have you been up to?"

Derick sat still, ignoring the urge to pull away from the roving hands that claimed ownership over his body and the scratchy voice screaming desperation. He took a long draw of his drink instead, focusing on the cool, bitter liquid sliding down his throat. Only after finishing half the bottle did he let out a loud sigh, place his drink back down in front of him, and finally speak.

"Been busy," he muttered. "And out of town. I only just got back."

Despite the gruff tone of his voice, Crystal continued scraping her overly long nails over the shaved skin at the back of his head.

"Oh honey, you must be exhausted." She slid off her stool and pressed her body hard against his, bringing her bright red lips close to his ear. "Why don't you come home with me, and I'll make sure you spend a good long time laying on your back?"

Derick's stomach roiled. The woman had about as much subtlety as a bull in a china shop. He clenched his teeth and admitted a low growl.

"Never gonna happen, Crystal."

"Still recovering from last time, huh Ricky?"

That name took him back to the past, and Derick grimaced, taking another long drink as he tried to banish the memories of all the interactions he had with the woman beside him. It felt like years ago, but there had been a time when Crystal, along with several other women like her, had been his escape from the pressure and expectations of the gang. As he had aged, he realized that the women who were available to a man like him were only another form of prison. They had expectations of him and needed him to constantly keep up the facade. Before long, he found that the only chance he had to breathe deeply and step outside of that expectation was to forgo women entirely.

Well, maybe not entirely. The occasional woman from out of town would come through, allowing him to escape reality for a moment and spend a few hours enjoying the pleasure of another's flesh. Despite the physical release, he always seemed to walk away feeling hollow and bereft.

Jack plonked his second beer down on the bar. Derick took it, pushed his empty bottle away, and stepped down off his stool away from Crystal's clawed grasp and cloying perfume.

"It's been years. Take the hint."

He made to step away, but a pinching grip on his arm stopped him in his tracks.

"When are you gonna stop pretending you're so much better than the rest of us, huh?"

Her hissing voice cut through the music and muffled voices of the few people in the bar.

"What's all this?"

Derick inwardly groaned, turning his head to take in the wiry form of Jarred, flanked by three of his pals from the gang. They swaggered into the room, instantly causing the atmosphere in the pub to turn rife with tension.

Crystal abruptly released his arm, letting out a high-pitched squeal as she tottered over toward Jarred.

"Jarred baby, I've been waiting for you." She shot a sultry look back in Derick's direction. "Derick was just keeping me company." Her lips puckered up into a bright red pout as she batted her eyelashes up at Jarred's face. "You know how much I hate being on my own."

Derick stifled his wry grin of amusement. At least she was right about that. Crystal always had a man on the go, sometimes more than one, and Jarred was currently her number one plaything—a match made in heaven, so to speak.

Jarred slung his leather-clad arm over Crystal's bare shoulders, crushing her close to his body as he sauntered up to Derick.

"That right, Derick? You've been keeping an eye on my girl?"

Derick straightened himself up and pushed out his chest. He looked down at Jarred, knowing the other man hated that Derick was over six feet with the body to match.

"I wouldn't keep an eye, or any other part of my body, on 'your girl.' I suggest you keep your cat at home where you can keep an eye on her."

"How dare you!"

Crystal raised her hand, fingers splayed, and made to swipe her nails over the side of his face. He snatched her wrist mid-swipe and threw her arm back to her side.

"Keep your claws to yourself."

Crystal gasped and spluttered, lifting her stilettoed foot and stomping it to the ground.

"Jarred, you're not gonna let him talk to me like that, are you?"

"Shut it, Cris," he said, not taking his eyes from Derick's. "Go get me a drink, and let the adults talk." Removing his arm, he gave her a light shove, ignoring her indignant muttering as she flipped her hair and stalked away to the other side of the bar where Jack hovered.

Derick was wound tight and in no mood to deal with Jarred's petty, self-indulgent conversation. The two of them had never gotten along, but ever since last year when Shaun picked Derick to be his second rather than his own son, Jarred held a burning hatred for him that had only grown with each passing day.

Leon, Craig, and Becket spread out, claiming the stools he and Crystal had just vacated, effectively boxing him in.

He tightened his muscles and squared his jaw, all while maintaining eye contact with Jarred, not wanting to give him the satisfaction of backing down.

"What's there to talk about? If it's anything related to the gang, I'm sure I already know." He gave a little smile to the shorter man. "I'm Shaun's second, after all."

Jarred's gaze narrowed, the unrestrained fury swirling around in his eyes evident. He cocked his head, a muscle jumping in his cheek as he tried to control his anger. Swallowing back his frustration, he gave Derick a sly grin and stepped forward to straighten the front of Derick's jacket.

"How was your visit to dear old dad today? Did you enjoy telling him the new direction the gang is taking?"

Derick breathed through his nose, not letting Jarred's barbed comments get to him. One thing he had learned about keeping safe in this type of life is staying calm and not responding was a must. So many times he had seen someone react to a snide comment or a shove, sometimes even a sidelong look, and the next moment, that person would be flat on their back, needing stitches.

When Shaun had approached Derick about becoming his second, one of the reasons he gave was Derick's ability to stay calm and think things through rather than reacting, unlike Jarred. That man had one of the hottest heads in the gang and was personally responsible for three of their fellow members being behind bars.

"Frank is no longer any of our concern, especially not yours."

He looked down his nose, easy to do due to Jarred's shorter height.

"I suggest you stick with what you know - running your mouth and not using your head."

Brushing past Jarred, he made to leave the bar with his drink in hand when a heavy hand pushed out and latched on to his bent elbow. Jarred pulled back roughly, spilling Derick's beer as he tried to spin him around.

Looking down at the drink coating his arm and puddling on the floor, Derick simply listened as Jarred's voice cut under his breath.

"One day you won't be so cocky. You won't have anyone on your side, and on that day, you'll need to watch your back." He released Derick just as roughly, flinging his arm down to the ground.

Jarred turned on his heel and walked back to his cronies, a swagger in his step as if he had done something impressive.

Derick scoffed and shook his head, abandoning his beer at a nearby table as he made his way back outside to his bike. He mounted up and turned back toward their new headquarters, the looming edge of the forest outside of the city clearly showing him the way.

CHAPTER THIRTY ONE
LUCY

MOM AND DAD WERE fighting again. They seemed to always be doing that these days. Lucy shifted on her bed, staring at her closed door. Sighing, she slipped off the large mattress with a wince and carefully walked over to the desk where she kept her headphones. Retreating back to her bed, she curled up by the large double windows that ran the full length of the wall.

Her mum had been against the idea of her sleeping so close to the glass. She was worried Lucy might catch a cold, which could cause complications. Thankfully, her dad sided with her, agreeing that Lucy needed to live a little, though no one had mentioned that nothing would change her diagnosis.

Lucy put on her headphones and started the playlist one of the nurses at the hospital made for her right before they left. The music blocked out the sounds of her parents' strained words, and she sighed in relief, pressing her forehead against the cool glass.

As the sweet country tunes swirled around her head, she huffed a breath onto the clear glass. Using her finger, she drew a heart in the patch of fog. She was beyond bored. Her family had uprooted from their home in Pittsburgh and moved to Mull Crest, a small coastal town on the East Coast, just last week. They claimed it was because her dad had gotten a great new job opportunity, but Lucy was there when they made the decision. She knew it had nothing to do with him and everything to do with her.

She let out another sigh, rubbing at the tightness in her chest that never seemed to go away. She hadn't wanted to leave. At least back in Pittsburgh, she had her doctor and nurses to talk to. Ever since they arrived here, she hadn't spoken to a single soul other than her parents, and the loneliness weighed on her.

A movement outside caught her attention. Her parents had gone into the backyard, Dad first, followed by her mom. Lucy scooted herself back, not wanting her parents to look up and know she was witnessing their fight. Dad threw up his hands, yelling something at her mom. She shook her head, dark braids bouncing, and reached out pleadingly to catch hold of his sleeve. Lucy's heart sank. Pulling away roughly, he strode off towards the garage, leaving her mom standing alone in her robe wiping at her eyes. A moment later, their car reversed from the garage and disappeared down the side of the house.

Lucy felt a sick feeling settle low in her stomach. She knew she was the reason for their fight. She seemed to be the reason for all of their fights lately. Her mom turned around to head back into the house, glancing up to Lucy's second-story windows. Jerking back, Lucy hopped out of sight and hoped her mom didn't see her watching.

Quickly scrambling to the other side of her bed, she threw back the covers and scooted herself down. Closing her eyes, she tried to settle her breathing and focused on relaxing her body. A few minutes later, she heard a faint knock over the sounds of the music playing in her ears. She tried to look sleepy as she opened her eyes and watched her mom come into the room.

"Morning," she smiled faintly, blinking her eyes in what she hoped was a convincing manner.

"Hey there, Luce. How are you feeling this morning?"

Her voice was quiet as she came over to perch on the side of Lucy's bed. The mattress dipped down, and Lucy slid towards her mom. Shifting away from the contact, Lucy removed her headphones, knowing her mother needed this daily contact.

"I'm fine, Mom," she lied. "I had a really great night."

Her mom leaned forward, placing her hand on Lucy's forehead. Her face drew into a frown, the tight lines on either side of her face making her look older than she was.

"Are you sure? You feel a bit flushed."

Lucy pulled the hand off her face, giving it a squeeze as she placed it back on the bed between them.

"No, I'm totally sure. Maybe it's from coming here and being beside the forest. I feel better. I guess I'm on the mend." She gave her mom a bright smile, willing her eyes not to give her lies away.

Her mom nodded, not looking quite convinced, but letting it go anyway.

"Has Dad left for work yet?"

The skin around her mom's mouth tightened before she gave a thin-lipped smile.

"Yes dear, your father had to leave early this morning. You can see him tonight."

Getting up from where she sat, she tightened the tie on her robe and walked back to the door.

"So, what would you like for breakfast this morning?"

The false happiness had Lucy turning away towards the window, not wanting her mom to see her disappointment. If only her parents could be real and honest with her, then maybe she could be honest back. Then, none of them would feel so alone.

"Anything would be great, Mom. Thanks."

She turned, gave her mom the smile she needed to see, and then replaced her headphones before curling up on her side and closing her eyes until she was alone again.

The door clicked shut.

With a groan, Lucy flopped back onto her back, ripping off the headphones and tossing them beside her. She pressed her fists to her eyes, fighting back the tears that threatened to spill. Ever since that day in the hospital, she promised herself that she would be strong and keep it together, wanting to make things easier for her parents.

It was less than a month ago, just after her eighth birthday, that her illness had taken a turn for the worse. In the middle of blowing out the candles on her cake, she erupted into a series of great hacking coughs. Unable to catch her breath, her parents rushed her to the hospital to see Dr. Travis. She spent the next several days going through yet another round of painful testing, and by the end of it, she was just so tired. She had been in and out of hospitals for years. She was never in school long enough to make friends, never allowed to spend too much time outdoors. She let out a shaky breath, remembering the conversation that changed everything for her.

After a particularly invasive test, Lucy had been resting in the hospital bed. Her parents must have thought she was asleep because when Dr. Travis came to talk to them, they only stepped out the door. They were close enough that Lucy could hear every word from Dr. T's mouth.

"Bailey and Jim, I'm sorry. I'm afraid there is nothing more we can do for Lucy."

Her mother burst into muffled tears, the sound so heart-wrenching that it overtook Lucy's own feelings for a moment.

"How long do we have?" came the strained voice of her dad, his soft voice thick with emotion.

"It's hard to say, but from the looks of things, I can't see Lucy making it halfway to her next birthday. Worst case is maybe a month, and best case is six."

There was a heavy pause, and Lucy's emotions churned as she strained to hear what the doctor might say next.

"I'm really very sorry. Would you like me to be there when you tell Lucy?"

"No, no." Bailey sniffed, immediately cutting the doctor off. *"I don't want Lucy to know. I want her to have hope."* Her words dissolved into another round of heavy sobs.

"I strongly recommend against that. Lucy is an intelligent young lady, and she's only going to be in more pain."

"Can't you give us something to ease her pain, doctor?" argued Jim. *"We could take her away, somewhere new. It would be good for her to see a different place before the end."*

Her mother's wail cut through the doctor's reply, only enabling Lucy to hear the second half of his sentence. *"—somewhere by the sea. The salt air won't help, but it won't do any harm either."*

Lucy chanced opening her eyes a crack, taking in the sight of her mom wrapped in her dad's arms, their dark skin ashen as they wept. Dr. Travis patted Dad on the shoulder before walking off and leaving them to their grief. Lucy closed her eyes again and pretended to sleep, willing herself to anywhere but there as her father's and mother's sobs washed over her, cementing themselves in her memory forever. She pushed back the blankets covering her body and crawled over to her spot by the window.

They packed up and moved out to Mull Crest two weeks later.

Lucy rolled her eyes at all of the lies her parents had told her over the past few weeks, wondering if she would have believed them if she hadn't heard the conversation between her parents and the doctor.

Taking a few breaths, she pulled the air as deep into her lungs as she could, wincing at the sharp pain under her ribs. Even if she never heard the prognosis regarding her diagnosis, she would never have believed it when her parents told her that she was over the worst of it. The ache in her body had grown steadily worse. She wasn't sleeping. The pain never left her, and her appetite was almost nonexistent. Lucy looked down at her body. Her ebony skin was gaunt and dull. She had never been a very big child, but the last few months had stripped all the remaining fat from her body, causing her skin to stretch tight over her small muscles and highlighting the sharpness of her bones.

Lucy pressed her forehead and nose against the glass again, staring beyond the backyard into the large forest that stretched out far to the north and south.

She could feel it deep inside. Dr. Travis' worst-case-timeline of one month was feeling more and more likely by the day.

Despite her situation, a small smile spread on her lips as she surveyed the mysterious green forest. What would it be like to go outside? Perhaps she could find a fairy ring and step inside, instantly being transported to a magical land where she could be rid of all of the trappings of her weak mortal body. Huffing out a croaky chuckle, she laughed at her fanciful thoughts, glancing behind her at the shelf overflowing with stacks of books.

But wouldn't it be wonderful? She turned back to the window to continue her daydream. *Maybe Mom will let me go out into the yard if the weather stays nice. I could read outside.*

Her mom chose that moment to come back into her room. She carried a full tray.

"Ah, Lucy, you're up. Good. I've made you some toast, eggs, and a nice hot chocolate to warm up your chest."

Placing it down on top of the duvet, she stood back with her hands on her hips.

"Now make sure you eat it all up, young lady. You need to put some meat on those bones."

Lucy scooted over to the tray, picking up the hot drink and taking a sip. She smiled up at her mother, animating her face as much as possible.

"I'm feeling good today. I thought I could spend some time outside later."

A flash of panic ran across her mother's face before it was quickly concealed behind a bland smile.

"Let's see how you feel today, then perhaps tomorrow if the weather stays nice."

Her hopes dwindled.

"Good, then. Oh, don't forget your medicine." Reaching into her pocket, she removed a brown pill bottle, removing two large white tablets.

"Thanks, Mom," Lucy said, holding out her hand to take the pills. She popped them into her mouth, taking another swallow of the warm drink.

Her mother smiled and leaned over to place a kiss on top of Lucy's head. As she drew away, Lucy caught a whiff of the sour wine her parents sometimes had with dinner.

"Right then, don't let your breakfast get cold. I'll just be downstairs if you need me." She turned and left the room, closing the door with a soft click behind her.

As soon as the door closed, Lucy screwed up her face and bent over, spitting the soggy pills out into her hand.

"Yuck."

She had taken them at first, eager for relief from the ever present ache. But, with the lessening pain came the dulling of her mind. The pills warped her thoughts, leaving her unable to move and unable to think, giving her no time to do anything but lie in bed, too sluggish to move around or even read her beloved books. Lucy had started to keep them in the corner of her cheek until she was able to spit them out and dispose of them somewhere her parents couldn't see.

She placed her drink down and slid off the bed, walking across to her attached bathroom. Throwing the medicine down the toilet, she pushed the lever and watched them wash away. Making her way back to her bed, Lucy picked at the eggs, eating as much as she could before her energy plummeted and made it too hard for her to continue chewing.

Tomorrow, I'll go outside, she promised herself, pushing open the window to let the crisp smells and the buzzing cries of cicadas in. *But this will have to do for now.*

Scanning the dark leafy trees lit up by the rising sun, she was surprised to see a flash of bright auburn peeking out between two branches. She leaned forward, her hands pressing on the window ledge. It went again.

The bright color shone gold, catching the light as it bobbed between the swaying leaves. Lucy squinted her eyes, her focus solely on that one tree in the forest. The branches quivered imperceptibly as the vibrant flicker descended to the lowermost branches. Lucy's mouth popped open, and she let out a quiet gasp when the object of her focus dropped out of the tree, landing lightly on the ground. It disappeared quickly into the forest, but not before Lucy saw that the auburn glint she had seen was the red hair of a teenage girl.

CHAPTER THIRTY TWO
FAUNELLA

FAUNELLA WOKE UP BEFORE the birds that morning. She couldn't get the man and woman from yesterday out of her head. The interaction she witnessed had been short, but the emotion in their voices had struck something deep inside of her.

That night she dreamed about their house, the warm brown paneling with large glistening windows facing the forest. The woman's earnest voice echoed in her mind as a jumbled-up blur of the day swirled by.

She sat up, plagued with a strong instinct to go back. She didn't understand why, but following the urge, she got up and got dressed for the day. Slipping out of her treehouse, Faunella left Beebe sleeping in her small nest by her bed. She climbed down the tree and tiptoed quietly past where Rafi was sleeping curled up in a fluffy ball among the roots of the great tree. Her eyes softened. Although she told the fox to go back to its life, he had refused to leave her side. He followed her around so much that she had finally caved and given him a name, but she still hasn't figured out a way to get him in and out of the treehouse.

Leaving her friends to sleep, she headed towards the coastal town, reaching the house with plenty of time to spare. The sun was only just starting to light up the sky, and the houses up and down the forest's edge were all quiet and still. Peeping out from behind a tree, Faunella surveyed the space, noticing an overgrown garden near the house's boundary. A glint of deep purple caught her eye.

She perked up, scanning the tangled mass of plants more carefully. Now that she was looking, she could see several large juicy berries scattered throughout the garden. Mouth watering, Faunella tried to resist the alluring pull of the delicious fruit.

She remembered Amon's rules. *Faunella, you are not to leave The Edge. It's important that you aren't seen.*

She bit her lip, looking around at the dark and silent house. No one was awake yet. Maybe if she was quick, she could grab some.

Before she could second guess the wisdom of her decision, Faunella darted out from behind the tree, making a beeline towards the garden. Her heart pounded with the fear and excitement from being out of the forest and in one of the human places. A rush of air pushed up behind her, and she stifled her laughter as it vaulted her over the fence. Ducking down beside the patch of plants, Faunella picked the berries as fast as she could, not even pausing to put one in her mouth. Once she had gathered as many as she could hold, she swiveled her head to check for movement before speeding back to her hiding spot behind the tree.

The first taste of the berry had her closing her eyes in delight. The fruit tasted all the more sweeter with the knowledge that she had gotten it from the forbidden place. With a cheeky grin, she launched a berry into the air and arched her eyebrow, willing the fruit to stay hovering just above her head. Happiness bubbled up in her chest when it obeyed, spinning slowly in place as her magic moved as an extension of her. Laughing, she let it drop down into her mouth and sat back against the tree, savoring the treat.

Faunella was only halfway through her berry pile when the whining creak of a door rang out through the stillness. She froze, her mouth pausing mid-chew. Dropping the last of the purple fruit, she pulled herself up into the tree, making sure she stayed hidden behind it as she climbed.

Halfway up the tree, she chanced a look at the house, expecting to see the man leaving the house again. To her surprise, it wasn't the man. It was a small dark-skinned girl. The girl made a beeline to the back of the section where Faunella had crouched and liberated the berries. Faunella watched with mounting horror as she walked straight past the garden and started to climb over the small fence.

Faunella's heart started to pound, and a cold sweat began to form on her skin.

The girl grunted and gave a little cry as she finally managed to flop herself over the barrier. Faunella winced as the child collapsed in a heap on this side of the fence. This human seemed particularly weak compared to all of the other children she had seen.

Pushing her mass of black curls out of her face, the girl rose unsteadily, using the fence to help push herself back to standing. Taking small steps, she made her way over to the tree Faunella perched in. Faunella sucked in a breath, holding it so she wouldn't make any sound that could give her away.

"Hello? Are you still here?"

Faunella's whole world came crashing down around her.

She'd been seen.

The first time she broke the Fae's rules and left the safety of the forest, she was seen. She clutched the branch she was sitting on, frantically trying to think of a way to get out of this situation.

"I saw you from my window," continued the girl, breathing heavily as she pointed back to the large panes of glass on the upper floor. "I wanted to meet you."

Faunella stared down at the top of the girl's head. The words touched a quiet place in her heart, and her breaths came more evenly. She studied the girl closely. The wild mass of curly hair on top of her head made her look larger than she was. This close up, Faunella could see that the arms and legs hanging out of her sleeping clothes were thin and frail. She frowned. Everything about this girl seemed fragile, except her hair.

The girl glanced down, zeroing in on the scattered berries. She leaned over, extending her hand to the ground even as she glanced around the shadowed trees.

"Hello?"

She broke off, dissolving into a fit of steady coughing. She reached out an arm to lean on the tree, sliding down it to brace on her hands and knees. The coughing continued, interspersed with shallow gasps of air. Faunella's pulse quickened, instinct telling her that something was seriously wrong.

She's sick, she realized with a start. *She shouldn't be out here.*

The coughing eased but was replaced with a wet crackling wheezing.

"Mama," the girl choked out, falling onto her side on the damp forest floor. The discarded berries crushed under her weight.

Faunella was torn. She knew she shouldn't let herself be seen again, but she couldn't just leave this girl without helping her. *What if her parents don't find her?*

Mind made up, Faunella squared her shoulders and swung herself down out of the tree, landing lightly beside where the child lay curled up. With clammy hands and a pounding heart, Faunella crouched down, reaching out both her hands to grip the girl's frail arms. She pulled her upright, noticing two dark spots on her cheeks and deep gray circles under each eye. What was more concerning was the purple starting to infuse the girl's once-russett lips. Her mouth hung open as she gasped for air, too weak to even open her eyes.

Faunella took in all the information, instantly knowing that the child needed help immediately. Closing her own eyes, she tightened her hands around the girl's upper arms. Faunella breathed in deeply, feeling the way the air swirled in from around her, easing down the back of her throat and stretching her chest with its light essence.

Don't mess up. Don't mess up.

Gripping the warm power coiled within her body, she breathed outwards, focusing the air into the girl's rasping mouth. Holding tight to her power, she followed it as it pressed down the tight tube that led behind the chest. Once there she let go, filling the girl with lifesaving air.

The girl jerked away, letting out a gasping inhale. Her eyes shot open as the color returned to her face with the easing of her breath.

Faunella stood up, backing away from the girl's hazel stare.

"Wait," she called out, her voice cracking slightly. "Please don't go."

Faunella paused, warring with her need to flee and her desire to stay.

"Who are you, and how did you do that?" She pressed her hand to her chest, staring with wonder up at Faunella. "You stopped the attack. It's never stopped on its own before. Please stay." A stray tear escaped from the corner of her eye, glistening as it tracked down her cheek. She swiped it away, her lips wobbling up into a tentative smile. "My name's Lucy."

Lucy tried to get up, using her shaky arms to press off the ground. Faunella leapt forward, her hand reaching out to help steady the frail girl. Lucy beamed up at her, gripping her arm tightly.

"Thanks."

Faunella just stared. Having someone talking directly to her in words she could perfectly understand was such a foreign feeling, especially because this girl was a human.

She swallowed thickly, still torn on what she should do. She knew she should leave. The Fae had been as clear as they could about her staying in the forest and away from the humans. So why was it so hard to walk away?

Biting her lip, she backed away but hesitated when Lucy's expression fell. The thin child looked so lost and alone standing under the great tree, and Faunella felt a connection to her that she couldn't explain.

"Before you go," said Lucy, clasping her hands in front of her. "Will you at least tell me your name?"

Faunella's heart pounded loudly in her ears, picking up its pace as she steeled herself to do something she had only ever dreamt of. She ran her tongue over the smooth skin of her upper lip before opening her mouth and taking a shallow breath.

"My name is Faunella." She took two steps backward. "But you can call me Fawn."

Then she turned, sprinting away as fast as the wind could carry her.

Why did I say that? she berated herself as she paced her home. *"You can call me Fawn." When is she going to call you Fawn? Never, that's when!*

Throwing herself on her bed, she pressed her face into her pillow, opening her mouth and forcing out a low cry. Beebe hovered nearby and gave a confused chirp. From outside came a rasping bark from Rafi, not content to be left out.

"Oh, Beebe," she wailed, rolling over to look up at her friend. "So much has already happened today, and I don't know how to feel about it."

Beebe flew over and landed on Faunella's chest, puffing out her feathers and settling down to sit. Faunella flung her arm across her brow and stared up at the leafy roof, letting out a loud breathy sigh.

"There was this girl."

She closed her eyes, pulling the girl's appearance to mind.

"She had the most beautiful brown skin." Her lips twitched up at the corners. "It glowed in the sunlight. Her body was skinny, but she had thick curly hair. It was so curly that it stood up around her head like a black cloud. I've never seen a human like her." She paused, considering. "I think she's really sick. Sick in here."

Placing her hand on her chest next to Beebe, Faunella tapped above the slight curve of her newly changing body.

"She saw me, Beebe, but she didn't do anything bad. Even though she's sick, she still put herself at risk and came out of her house to try to meet me."

Her heart fluttered, and without meaning to, the corners of her mouth lifted.

"Her name is Lucy."

The name felt right rolling off her tongue, and her smile grew impossibly wide.

Stop it, she chided herself. *This isn't a good thing. What is Amon going to say when he finds out?*

The thought of having to tell the Fae she had been seen chased away all the good feelings meeting Lucy generated. A cold shiver ran down her back. Faunella sat up, dislodging Beebe, who flew off, giving her an indignant squawk. Crossing her legs in front of her, she chewed nervously on the corner of her thumb. She could just picture how riled up Amon would get, ruffling his branches as he creaked and groaned his displeasure.

Maybe I don't need to tell him. She stilled, considering the thought. *If I don't tell him, then he can't get upset. Lucy didn't look dangerous.*

"That's it. I just won't say anything. I'll pretend it never happened."

Feeling happy with her decision, Faunella stood and walked past the curve of her wall into the other partition of her home. She idly started to sort through her belongings, throwing her clothes into piles and rearranging several shelves full of trinkets. She polished the beautiful glass bottles that she had found scattered around the forest close to The Edge. She loved the way the sun glinted off their edges, sending green and brown lights bouncing around her room.

Picking up several woven wreaths, she studied them objectively. She had made plenty of flower crowns over the years, only keeping the ones she was most proud of. Turning one of the larger wreaths over in her hands, she admired the blue and purple flowers knotted into the green foliage. The flowers had retained their shape and color as they dried, creating an alluring effect dotted throughout the intricate circle. It would look pretty in Lucy's hair, and it was about the right size.

Faunella shook herself, remembering the decision to pretend the situation with Lucy had never happened. Throwing the flower crowns down onto a bench, she went to walk away. After taking only two steps, Faunella paused.She turned around, chewing on her bottom lip.

"I could leave it on The Edge for her."

No that won't work, it didn't look like she came outside at all.

She thought back to Lucy, curled up and gasping on the ground. She's too sick for that.

Suddenly, her head shot up, and her mouth dropped open with an audible pop.

"I could help her get better."

Her mind raced with the possibilities of her plan.

Night would be best. She could leave the crown and some of Violetta's water on Lucy's doorstep. Shaking her head, Faunella furrowed her brows. That wouldn't work. Her parents could see. Racking her brain, Faunella thought back to her interaction with Lucy, sure that Lucy had unknowingly given her another option .

"I saw you from my window."

"I'll leave them outside her window," Faunella decided, nodding her head to cement her decision.

Full of energy, she spun around on the ball of her foot, her long hair whipping around to tangle in her face. Laughing, she pushed it back, weaving the fiery strands together in a loose braid as she danced across her floor. She'd wait until the moon was high, then take the crown and some water from Violetta to Lucy's window.

Faunella paused. She hadn't thought about how to get the water to Lucy. Gazing around her room thoughtfully, her eyes snagged on the pretty glass bottles she had just been admiring on her shelf.

"The bottles. I'll carry it in a bottle."

She skipped back over to her things and gathered them up, all ready for her evening adventure. Then, with a satisfied sigh, she settled in for the long wait until dusk.

"I just came to say good night." Faunella announced to the Fae later that evening.

At her words, Erwin who had stood up, arms outstretched with a huge smile on his face, eased himself back to the ground. His smile faded to an embarrassed grin. Faunella laughed, running over to the little green Fae and throwing herself into his loving embrace.

"I'll still take a cuddle before I go."

She smiled into Erwin's soft body, breathing in the sweet earthy scent that always clung to him. A sharp bark at the entrance of the cave had her pulling away.

"Rafi still won't come into the cave," she explained. "He doesn't feel comfortable around you all." Glancing around the cave, she shrugged apologetically.

Spotting Violetta across the rapidly darkening cave, Faunella got up and made her way over to where she sat. Clearing her throat, she tried to keep her voice even as she approached the Fae.

"Violetta, it's quite warm tonight, and I was wondering if I could have some water."

Her heart pounded, and her mouth suddenly felt dry. Faunella had never purposely tried to deceive her family before, and she didn't like it. Glancing over at Amon, she swallowed thickly, convinced the tree Fae could see right through her.

A chiming bubble brought her attention back to Violetta. The Fae was smiling, holding her hands out in front of Faunella's face.

"Oh," she exclaimed, feeling her cheeks heat. " I was hoping you could put it in here for me so I could have it later." She reached towards her hip, pulling the bottle free from where she had strapped it to her body.

The back of her neck began to prickle. Faunella was sure everyone was staring at her, seconds away from accusing her of meeting with a human. When nothing happened, she completed her mission on autopilot, accepting the water from Violetta and giving the Fae a final farewell. It wasn't until she was out of the cave that she began to breathe easier. Rafi weaved around her ankles, sending out little huffs of pleasure to be with her again. Faunella smiled, enjoying the breeze of air that cooled her flushed face. Turning away from the path that would lead her to the treehouse, she took a few steps in the direction of the coastal town when a crunching rumble sent her heart leaping up into her throat.

"Huxley, I didn't see you there." She turned to face the rock Fae, only able to see him as a darker shadow against the dark night.

He rumbled again, and Faunella thought she saw his arm swing up to point towards her tree.

"You wanted to walk me home?" she guessed, heart pounding so loud that she couldn't decipher his words. His grinding reply confirmed her question.

"That's so sweet, Hux," she tried, trying to find a way out of the situation. "But I thought I'd go for a little walk around the grotto before heading to bed. You can stay in the cave, though." She hurriedly added when Huxley took a step towards her. "Could you thank Violetta for me? I forgot to thank her for the water, and I'd hate to be rude."

That seemed to do the trick. Huxley paused, looking back towards the cave. Faunella darted forward, giving him one last hug before releasing him and watching as he disappeared from sight.

With no more barriers to her plan except for the darkness, Faunella started forward. Counting on her air powers to guide the way past any obstacles, she let out a breath and began her journey.

242

CHAPTER THIRTY THREE
LUCY

HER MOM CAUGHT HER trying to sneak back inside that morning.

After Faunella's abrupt departure, Lucy stared after her for a while, enhanced by the lilting echo of the forest girl's voice. Before long, she was forced to go back inside by the pebbling skin on her arms and the cold shiver up her spine. She opened the door to the kitchen and was hunting around the unfamiliar drawers for a tea towel to dry off her damp shoes when her mom walked past the open door on the way to the bathroom.

All at once, her eyes, still bleary with sleep, sharpened with concern. She came inside the kitchen, taking in the scene with one swoop of her head. Her eyes narrowed.

"Have you been outside?" she screeched, her voice cracking with the last dregs of sleep.

Lucy had to think fast. She didn't want to tell her about Faunella. She knew that her parents wouldn't understand. Spinning a made up tale about feeling too hot and overheated, she successfully convinced her mom she had only stepped outside for a few minutes to cool off. As Lucy retreated back to her bedroom, her mom had moved to the cupboard, removing a half-full bottle of wine.

The day dragged on. The sun seemed to stay high in the sky forever before it slowly creeped back down behind the dark layers of trees across from her windows. She spent the whole day with her face pressed against the thin glass, hoping against hope for Faunella to come back.

She never came.

Nighttime was always the worst. The burning ache in her chest grew more intense, consuming her so much that she couldn't escape it. It made it nearly impossible for her to go to sleep. She almost caved and took the pain medication that her mom gave her, but, not wanting to waste the last of her time spaced out, she chose to flush them like normal.

Lucy lay curled up on her side with her eyes squeezed shut, listening to the subtle night sounds that grew in volume the more she concentrated. The distant roar of the sea mingled with the chirping cries from the endless crickets that made their home in the trees and bushes around her house. Her mind turned back to Faunella, like it often had over the course of the day, and Lucy wondered what she was doing right then.

Tap, tap, tap.

The rhythmic sound cut through the noises of the night. Lucy stiffened, opening her eyes as if it would make her hear better. Her head twitched.

Tap, tap, tap.

The sound was coming from outside. Sitting up, she shuffled over to the edge of the closest window, carefully pulling back the curtain to peek out into the darkness. As her eyes adjusted to the light, the sound came again. Using the soft glow of light from the moon, Lucy's eyes followed the sound, landing on a small black and white bird sitting just outside on her window ledge.

Upon seeing her, the bird gave a short chirp and flew off towards the bottom of the garden. Lucy tracked its movement, ducking under the closed curtain to get a better view. The heat from her breath fogged the glass, turning it a cloudy white. She hurriedly swiped it away, pressing her nose to the glass to try and catch a glimpse of the bird again, trying not to breathe so the window stayed clear. It was no use. She lost sight of the bird, the night swallowing it whole. Lucy squinted her eyes, scanning the still forest for any movement. A glint of white flittered past.

She drew her knees to her chest, hugging them tightly as she watched the little chickadee make small circles in front of her bedroom window. She was so enchanted by the bird, she didn't notice another figure moving quickly across her lawn until the pale face popped up from over the edge of the first story roof. A soft squeal of surprise forced its way out of Lucy's mouth. Clutching her hand to her chest, she tried to still her racing heart.

"You gave me a fright." Pushing open the window, she whispered the words to Faunella as the tall girl nimbly climbed over the roof to perch easily on the open window ledge.

"You came back?"

She gave the girl a big smile, feeling her cheeks stretch with the force of her pleasure.

"I hoped you would come back," Lucy whispered shyly. "Faunella."

Faunella had only stared at her nervously until then, but at the sound of her name, her eyes lit up, and her pink lips began to curl at the corners.

"Lucy?"

"Yes, that's right. My name's Lucy."

"Lucy," Faunella tried again, seeming to enjoy saying her name.

"Why did you decide to come back?" Undeniably curious, Lucy asked the first question she could think of while trying not to blurt out the hundreds of questions she had for the strange girl.

"I took your food. I wanted to say thank you." Faunella's voice was low and light. It had a musicality to it that made it pleasing to the ear. Once

Lucy got over the sweetness of the sound, she had to double take, finally registering what Faunella had said.

"You took my food? Oh, the berries. You ate some of the berries in the garden." She couldn't help but laugh. "That's okay. They were there before we moved in. None of us would have eaten them."

"You don't like berries?" The look of shock that appeared on Faunella's face made Lucy laugh even more.

"Of course I like berries, but we usually just buy them at the store if we want some."

"The store?"

Lucy stopped laughing, taking a better look at Faunella. The girl had clothing made of leaves pieced together with some sort of green vines. The top wrapped across her chest and up over one shoulder. She had two bands of leaves encircling her upper arms, and it looked like she was wearing some old green sweatpants two sizes too small. The pants had a band of matching leaves around the top of them, and they supported a wrapped wooden belt of some sort, which hung an assortment of items.

"You don't know what a store is?"

Faunella shook her head, biting her lip and looking worried.

"It's okay," Lucy reassured her. "I guess you don't get out much, huh?"

"I've never met a human before. I'm not supposed to leave the safety of The Edge."

Lucy wrinkled her nose. Faunella's word choice was strange, not to mention that she had never met another person before. She decided to ignore that for now and just focus on the second, slightly less outrageous thing.

"Do you mean the forest? You've never left the forest before?"

"Yes. It's not safe for me out here. Only the forest can keep me safe."

Lucy sat back on her bed, pushing open the curtain wrapped behind her shoulders. Every time Faunella talked just gave her more questions and no real answers.

The night air came in through the open window, and Lucy could feel the burning starting deep in her lungs again. She rubbed her palm against her chest.

"Did you want to come in? It's really cold out."

Faunella peered past her, taking in the shadowy silhouettes of the furniture in the room.

"Your parents?" she asked, her dark eyebrows drawing low over her eyes.

"It's alright. They're asleep downstairs, but I can lock the door if you want." Easing from the bed, she gingerly walked over to the door and flipped the latch. When she turned back to the window, she let out a breath. Some part of her thought that when she looked back she would find Faunella gone, the interaction nothing more than a figment of her imagination.

But Faunella was still squatting, crouched down in the window opening. The moon illuminated her, turning her dark wavy hair a red sheen.

"I'll turn the light on." Making her way over to her bedside table, she went to reach for her lamp.

"No, don't."

Lucy paused, her hand inches from the switch.

"You don't want the light on?"

Faunella looked around warily. "Someone might see me. I'm not meant to be seen." She looked down, her long hair coming forward to cover her face.

"That's okay. I'll keep it off if you'd like. But come inside. You can sit on my bed and keep warm." Lucy pulled back her bedding and sat against her pillows, gathering her blankets up around her waist to keep the chill away and make room for Faunella. Carefully, Faunella raised up from her crouch, easing slowly forward until she settled down at the end of the bed. She folded her legs underneath her, sitting cross legged on the soft blankets.

"Can you close the window?" Lucy gestured to the open window, nodding encouragingly when Faunella leaned forward to snap it shut. Before it could shut all the way, a black and white blur shot through the gap and into her bedroom.

"Oh, it's that bird again. The little chickadee."

"She's not a chickadee. She's Beebe."

The bird, Beebe, flew around in a large circle before coming to rest on Faunella's shoulder. Lucy stared at it, delighted with the close proximity of the creature.

"She's your bird? Beebe?"

Faunella nodded, placing her finger at the black strip of the bird's glossy breast. Beebe gave a little jump, coming to land on Faunella's finger.

"She's not mine," Faunella began thoughtfully, holding Beebe out towards Lucy. "She belongs to the trees and the sky, but she is my friend." Her eyes softened. "She's my best friend."

"She's beautiful." Lucy stretched out her hand, carefully touching one finger to the back of Beebe's head. Her feathers were so soft to touch, and when she didn't show any signs of flying away, Lucy stroked her more purposefully. A giggle bubbled out of her mouth.

I'm sitting here in my bed, across from a strange forest girl and patting a wild animal.

Her giggle grew into a chesty laugh. The situation was just so bizarre. Lucy drew her arm back, not wanting to accidentally knock Beebe over from the force of her laughter. Faunella lowered Beebe, staring at her curiously before the edges of her own mouth began to tilt upwards. Lucy's laughter was infectious, and soon the two girls were leaning over laughing together, their hands pressed tight to their mouths to muffle the sound.

"Shh," Lucy giggled out, wiping the tears from her eyes. "My parents could hear us."

She grinned widely at Faunella, still buzzing with the pure joy of no longer being alone.

Faunella's smile fell slightly, and her gaze dropped to Lucy's chest. Lucy looked down at herself. She had been absentmindedly rubbing her chest, trying to ease the ever present ache.

"You're sick," Faunella said, but it wasn't a question.

Lucy dropped her hand quickly. Smiling sadly, she shrugged one shoulder.

"I have been for a while. My parents moved me here because I'm getting worse." For some reason, she didn't want the older girl to know she was dying. Lucy felt bad that the conversation was focused on something so sad.

"Don't feel bad," she added, seeing Faunella's expression fall. "I only wish we had met sooner."

Faunella reached around behind her, fiddling with something on her belt before presenting Lucy with an open beer bottle. Lucy drew back in disgust, not sure why Faunella would have something like that.

"This is for you. You need to drink it. It will help." Faunella offered the bottle more insistently, almost pushing it into Lucy's reluctant hands.

Not wanting to offend her new friend, Lucy sniffed at the open top of the bottle, relieved to find that it didn't smell of alcohol. Instead it had a fresh, almost sweet smell that invaded the nostrils.

Faunella smiled, nodding encouragingly as she eyed the liquid dubiously. "Drink."

Closing her eyes and grimacing, Lucy put the rim against her lips and tipped back the bottle, allowing the liquid to slide into her mouth. All at once, her mouth felt alive. The liquid was water, but it was like no water she had ever tasted before. It seemed to tingle as it coated the inside of her mouth. It tasted of sunshine and had the crisp flavor of the air on an early spring morning. Her eyes popped open, and she stared at Faunella, who was grinning smugly at her surprised expression.

"You like it?"

"Do I like it? It's like nothing I've ever had before. Where did you get it?"

Faunella looked out the window, not meeting her eye. "It's from the forest, but it's not something everyone can get."

Lucy took another drink from the bottle, finishing the water easily.

"That's okay. I'm not meant to leave my house anyway. Mom keeps me in bed most of the time so I don't get sicker. But thank you for the water. It tasted really good."

She handed back the bottle, relishing the last of the water's taste. Faunella tied it back onto her belt. When she withdrew her hands, she held a circular object.

"What's this?" Taking the offered item, Lucy held it up to her face, trying to see what it was in the dimness of the room. It looked like a small wreath made of flowers and vines woven together into an intricate pattern.

"It's a crown. I make them and thought you might like this one." Her lips twisted. "But you're already wearing that thing."

A giggle bubbled up from Lucy's belly, and she touched the silk wrapped around her head. "It's a bonnet. We wear them at night to protect our hair."

"We?" Faunella's brow creased and she lay her head to the side. "Does everyone wear one to bed?"

"No, silly." She untied the bonnet and pulled it off, letting her hair spring free. "Only black people. We have different hair, see?" Grasping a tight curl, she rubbed it between her fingers. Faunella tentatively reached out and gently touched the top of her head. Her eyes widened. "It feels so springy." Her lips split into a wide grin, evidently delighted by the texture. She lowered her voice to a whisper. "It's so beautiful."

Lucy blushed, a warm pressure growing in her chest that had nothing to do with her illness. No one aside from her parents had ever called her beautiful before. Faunella still hadn't looked away, her focus entirely settled on Lucy. "You wear it on your head. Look." Faunella took the crown and placed it over Lucy's curly locks. Smiling shyly, she sat back and clasped her hands in her lap.

"I hope you like it. I thought the colors would look nice against your dark hair."

Lucy reached up and lightly touched the fragile flowers. "I'm sure the colors will be lovely. I'll have to turn on the light to see them though."

Faunella nodded, looking back out the window. She got to her knees and undid the latch.

"I should go now. I'm not supposed to be here, but I wanted to bring you those things."

Lucy couldn't hide her disappointment. It had only been such a short time, and she had so many questions. She hadn't even had a chance to ask Faunella any of them yet.

"But you'll come back?" she asked, leaning forward and placing her hand on Faunella's arm.

Stopping what she was doing, Faunella sunk back down in front of her, turning her large eyes to face her.

"I want to come back, but I'm not meant to. No one is supposed to know about me."

"What if we're really careful?"

Desperate not to lose her new friend, Lucy clutched her tighter. An ache built behind her eyes.

"I promise not to tell my parents about you, and the neighbors are at work every day. No one would see you."

Faunella looked into the darkness, the moon illuminating the slight lift of her nose and the cupid's bow above her top lip. "I have things I need to do at the beginning of the day. It's something to prepare for."

"Well, that's perfect then," she chirped, "My mom has a nap nearly every afternoon, so you could come then."

Faunella tilted her head, looking at Lucy thoughtfully.

"We can keep you safe," Lucy pressed, still not sure what Faunella needed to be kept safe from but willing to do anything to keep her one chance at a friend. "I could put something in my window when it's safe for you to come and visit."

"What would you put in your window?"

Lucy caught her breath, trying not to grin too broadly in case Faunella hadn't quite made up her mind. The question did give her more hope than before. Hopping out of her bed, she walked over to her desk, sliding open the second drawer down.Spotting the correct artwork, Lucy took it out of the drawer, bringing it over to show Faunella.

"I made this last year in the hospital. It's meant to look like stained glass. Dr. T said it was the prettiest one out of all of his patients."

Faunella looked at it curiously, picking it up and turning it over in her hands.

"It doesn't look very good in the dark," apologized Lucy. "But during the day, it has really bright colors that catch the light. Here, I'll put it in the window now so you can see where it'll be." Scooting around

Faunella, she took the picture back and placed it on the upper pane of glass that didn't open.

"Okay, I'll try to come back after the sun starts to descend from its peak."

Deciphering the strange terms, Lucy gave a little laugh.

"Yes, in the afternoon when my mom is asleep. I'll put the picture up when it's safe for you to come up."

Faunella gave her a quick smile, glancing at the window, then back at her.

"I really have to go." She looked so uncertain that Lucy leaned in and wrapped her arms around the older girl's firm body. She held her tentatively, only tightening her grip when she felt Faunella's arms slide around her back.

"Thanks, Faunella, for being my friend," she mumbled into the leafy fabric of her top. Faunella jolted, stilling for a moment, before her arms held on tighter. Lucy held on, needing the closeness as much as Faunella seemed to enjoy the connection.

They stayed locked together for several minutes. Lucy relished the silence of the night and the joy of having a budding friendship until a yawn pulled at her jaw. She drew back, breaking the hug and opening her mouth wide, letting out the deep exhalation.

"I probably should go to bed as well." Her brow furrowed, pondering the heavy feeling sweeping over her body. "I feel sleepy all of a sudden."

Faunella grinned, her teeth sparkling in the moonlight. "Yes, you sleep and heal. I will go." She reached out her slender hand and picked up Lucy's small one, giving it a quick squeeze. "Sleep well, friend."

Pushing open the window, she slipped off the ledge, quietly disappearing over the edge of the roof. Lucy watched her vibrant hair catch the light of the moon as she raced across the lawn and jumped the fence, vanishing from sight into the black forest. She closed her window and took the crown off before crawling back into bed, letting out another yawn as she went.

Snuggling down under her warm covers, she eased the blankets up and tucked them under her chin. As her eyes fluttered closed, she briefly thought of Faunella, thanking her lucky stars that the girl came into her life.

She briefly thought of her bonnet, but then there was nothing. She drifted off into a deep, dreamless sleep.

CHAPTER THIRTY FOUR
FAUNELLA

COLOR HAD COME BACK to Lucy's cheeks. The early afternoon sun shone down on her, giving her a healthy glow. Sitting further inside the forest boundary, Faunella studied her friend as she animatedly threw her arms around, telling her a story about a boy called Jack and a magic beanstalk.

"That sounds like Venek," she interrupted, drawing Lucy's attention and gaining a stunning smile.

"Who's Venek?"

Faunella flushed. She had done it again. Lucy was too easy to talk to, and it was becoming increasingly difficult to keep the Fae a secret from her. Smoothing out an errant leaf on her handmade tunic, she kept her gaze averted, shrugging nonchalantly.

"Oh, just someone I know. It's not important," she hedged. "What did Jack do after the vines grew up to the clouds?"

Lucy pulled her blanket up over her arms and gave her a knowing look, letting Faunella off the hook again. She tucked her black curls behind her ears and leaned back against the tree in view of her house. Returning to her tale, she wove Faunella a story about a golden goose and people as tall as the tallest tree in the forest.

Faunella's mind filled with images. Each word spoken created a story so rich and vivid that she could see the character just as Lucy described. A sigh escaped her.

"How do you come up with these ideas?"

"Oh," Lucy laughed. "I read them in books."

Faunella thought of the dusty old tomes she had to read. She wrinkled her nose, then smiled wryly at Lucy.

"I wish I had books like yours."

Lucy studied her thoughtfully, then got up and made to walk back towards the house, her blanket discarded behind her. Faunella's heart sank. Lunging forward, she reached out to grab the edge of Lucy's top, pulling her to a halt.

"Wait, don't go yet."

Lucy's small white teeth flashed as the sunlight caught her grin. She gently pried Faunella's fingers off her clothes.

"I'm only going into the house for a second. I've got something you can have."

Undeniably intrigued, Faunella didn't try to stop her again and nibbled on her lower lip.

Even though Lucy felt well enough to spend her afternoons sitting on the outer edge of the forest, her mom still fretted and checked on her often.

"Your mom might see you and stop you from coming outside again today."

"It's okay. When I came out, Mom was in the middle of her second bottle of wine." She rolled her eyes. "She'll be asleep for hours. I'll be quick."

She flashed Faunella a toothy smile and trotted off to the house, her breathing clear and even. Faunella sat back to wait, still worried despite Lucy's assurances that she wouldn't be seen.

She had been coming to see Lucy every day since that first visit. Observing humans from The Edge no longer held any enjoyment for her, not when she had her very own friend to talk with and learn things from. The first few days had been nerve-wracking. Coming up to the house when the sun was high was something she thought she'd never get used to, but after several visits of not being spotted, the girls had fallen into a comfortable rhythm.

Lucy had been teaching her so many new names for things and explaining how they worked. When the sun was high, it meant 'noon' or 'lunch time.' Faunella was incorporating these types of words and more into her vocabulary every day and simply soaked up the new information. Lucy seemed equally pleased to be imparting this knowledge to Faunella. Each visit, she had a new object or idea she wanted to share. Faunella fingered the pink watch tucked on a cord around her neck. Lucy had given it to her on the second day, showing her what the numbers and the little moving lines meant. With the exception of bathing, she hadn't taken it off.

The crunching of grass underfoot caught her attention. Peering around the tree, she watched Lucy scramble over the low fence, a bundle tucked under one arm. She skipped the last few steps over to where Faunella waited, her cloud of hair bouncing with each step.

"Whew!" she exclaimed, collapsing in a heap on her discarded blanket. "Got them."

She held up the bundle of books for Faunella's inspection before placing them down on the ground between them. Rafi gave a short bark, drawing both of their attention to where he lay tucked under a nearby bush. Faunella snorted, shaking her head at the animal. Lucy swung her head between the two of them.

"What's so funny?"

"He wants to know if you brought food," Faunella explained, pointing to the books.

"Oh." Lucy's full lips started to turn up at the corners, then suddenly stilled, her brows creasing instead. "How do you know that?"

Faunella froze.

"I mean, I like your animals and all. But usually, people don't have foxes or wild birds as pets." She looked up in the currently empty trees.

Glancing at Rafi out of the corner of her eye, Faunella silently urged the fox to leave, hopefully taking the evidence of her otherness away. She tugged at her hair, staying close-mouthed as Lucy waited for her to answer. When the silence stretched out, Lucy's open face shuttered, crumbling in disappointment.

"It's okay," she forced out. "You don't have to tell me anything you don't want to."

But it wasn't okay. Her stomach clenched tightly. Faunella wanted to tell Lucy everything. To share her whole world with her newfound friend and the weight that lay heavy on her shoulders, the constant pressure to learn and grow so that she would one day be capable of ruling the Ancient Fae's Kingdoms.

"So, come on." Lucy plastered a smile on her face and patted her stack of books. "Take your pick. You can have any you'd like."

Faunella blew out a breath, the moment gone. She reached out her hand and tentatively ran her fingers over the glossy covers. An excitement started inside her as she looked at the bright pictures.

Lucy whipped the first book out from under her revering touch.

"Okay, this one's my favorite." She clutched it to her chest, hugging it tightly for a moment. "It's called *Alice in Wonderland*, and it's the best book ever written."

"Her hair is so bright."

Lucy turned the book around to face her, looking at the picture of the girl on the cover.

"I guess it is. It's pretty different from mine." She laughed, lifting her hand to press down on her wild curls. "I wish I had long hair like hers."

"I think your hair is much nicer."

Lucy's face heated. "I changed my mind. I wish my hair looked like yours. It's such a pretty color."

Faunella pulled the long strands over her shoulder, working through the tangles with her fingers. The sun caught the auburn waves, turning them a burning, brilliant red.

"It's the same color as the leaves before the cold season," she mused, studying the loose curls with a critical eye. "I do like the color, but it gets so tangled."

"Don't you have a hairbrush?" Lucy asked in surprise. "I guess not." She added after seeing Faunella's blank look. "Don't worry. I'll give you mine when you come back tomorrow. Mom can get me another one when she goes shopping." She tucked her own hair behind her ear and lowered the book to her lap. "And by the way, the season before the cold season is Autumn. It goes Spring, Summer, Autumn, and Winter, then it starts all over again. Didn't your parents teach you?" Faunella's eyes hit the ground again, and Lucy cut off. She swallowed hard.

She's not going to want to be my friend if I can't tell her anything about my life. She raised her head and glanced further into the forest. *Maybe I should just leave.*

A small hand slipped over hers. Faunella's heart jumped.

"I know you aren't like normal girls," Lucy's hazel eyes were earnest. "I don't mind. I like you for who you are." She gave a small smile and squeezed Faunella's hand before withdrawing it. "It's just nice to have a friend."

Faunella's chin wobbled, and she smiled brightly at Lucy, grateful for everything the younger girl did for her. She hadn't felt so right in such a long time. The Fae loved her, and she loved them, but having a friend who looked and sounded like her was something new that she cherished beyond belief.

"Anyways, here. Take this."

Taking the offered book, Faunella turned it over in her hands, studying the design on the front and letting it fall open to reveal the words within.

"Are you sure?"

Lucy just laughed. Overcome, Faunella released the book and flung her arms around Lucy's thin frame, squeezing tightly. She buried her face into the crook of Lucy's neck, enjoying the warmth and connection. Lucy held her back, gently stroking her knotted strands of hair.

"I'd do anything for you, Faunella," Lucy murmured against her shoulder. "You're my best friend."

Faunella squeezed her eyes shut, trying to ease the burn of the happy tears threatening to spill.

"You're my best friend, too."

CHAPTER THIRTY FIVE
AMON

"D o any of you know where Fawn has been going these past few weeks?"

Amon looked at each Fae, taking note of their unsure expressions. He sighed. The heavy mid-afternoon sun shone down on the seven of them gathered by the stream. Lothian was back at the grotto, once again sleeping during the day. Laurel had joined Flavire in the large meadow by the nature reserve.

Violetta shrugged and ducked under the water, completely disappearing before shooting upwards and firing water at any Fae who had the misfortune of getting too close. Huxley was sitting on the bank, his rock legs dangling in the cool liquid. He had been splashed several times now, and though he grumbled every time, he still hadn't moved further away.

"I see her nearly every morning," called out Erwin from where he was leaning against Huxley's broad back. "But it's only for her study session. She's gone by lunch."

"You don't think she's venturing out past The Edge, do you?"

Amon stiffened and turned to face Venek. A thread of worry tugged at his chest at the thought. It had been years since Fawn had started observing the humans, and since her outburst four years ago, she hadn't given them any reason to think she might try and cross The Edge again.

"So what if she does?" called out Baol, knocking his silvery branches against Venek's dark wood. "She's not a little girl anymore, so the danger of a human 'rescuing her' from the forest is gone."

Amon's leaves curled, and he shot a sharp glare at Baol. Baeroot opened his mouth, presumably to agree with his friend. When Amon turned his stare to him, he clapped it shut with a snap.

"Baol's right, Amon." Violetta arched out of the water, her hair sparkling in the sunlight as she bobbed back down to float on her back. She gave him a knowing smile. "Fawn knows what's expected of her. If she does break your rules and ventures out, she's not going to suddenly run away and abandon her duty."

Amon, shuffled in place, his irritation cooling. "They're not my rules," he mumbled. "We all agreed that staying in the forest and away from humans was the best way forward."

"She isn't a kid anymore," added Venek, glancing at him for approval. "But she's only just starting to control her powers. What if she slips up in front of someone? They would think she's a freak."

He began to agree but was cut off when Violetta threw an orb of water into Venek's face, defending Fawn's control over her magic. Venek retaliated, crying in outrage at the assault. Amon shook his head when Baol and Baeroot joined in, their voices rising in pitch and intensity as they each argued their point of view.

"How did a simple question turn into this?" he murmured, walking over and easing himself down beside Huxley and Erwin.

"I'm sure Fawn's staying safe." Erwin stretched out on the grass. "Yes, she's not spending as much time with us these days." His mournful tone had Amon stifling a smile. He looked over at Huxley and had to cover his mouth with his hand when he saw the rock Fae doing the same "But, that's part of growing up, I guess."

"I still wish I knew where she was going." He tipped back his head and stared at the ring of sky visible through the high-up tree tops.

Huxley cleared his throat, recapturing his attention.

"I might have unintentionally followed her a few days ago."

His words effectively cut off the fighting, bringing all eyes to his sheepish face.

"Unintentionally?" Violetta raised her eyebrow, gliding closer to rest with her arms on the bank beside Huxley.

His cheeks darkened, and he looked away from her, throwing his arms up into the air.

"Fine, it was intentional. I was missing her. Amon was right. She has been gone a lot these days, and I wanted to know where she was going."

"And?" Amon prompted, anticipation thrumming under his bark.

"And nothing. She's just been going to the eastern edge of the coastal town. I watched her for an hour, but she just sat in a tree and watched a house. Nothing exciting happened. She just sat and stared." He shrugged. "I left her to it and came back here. Obviously, something's caught her attention, but I can't guess what."

Amon thought it over, not finding anything in Huxley's statement to be concerned about.

"She comes to me every morning as well," Violetta chimed in. "She gets me to fill up one of the beer bottles she collects. I'm assuming there isn't a water source wherever she's going." She grinned wickedly. "Maybe there's a boy she's been watching? Perhaps our little Fawn has a crush on a human."

Amon recoiled back, joining the other males as they cried out, vehemently rejecting Violetta's outrageous statement.

"Don't be ridiculous," he spat. "Fawn's too young for that. She's still a child in many ways. There's no way she has any notion about males, especially not a human male."

"She's not as young as you all think. Especially you, Amon." Violetta gave him a pointed look before gazing around all of the other males in the clearing. "Fawn is starting to change into a young female Fae, and Fae mature much sooner than humans." She lifted herself out of the water and placed her hands on her hips. Huxley's eyes shot to the ground, pointedly avoiding looking at the curves of Violetta's body. "If it hasn't happened already," she continued, "then it won't be long before she'll start being interested in the opposite sex."

"No, no, no," spat out Huxley, his brows narrowing into a frown as he stared daggers. "It's not safe for Fawn to have feelings for humans. You've all seen how some of these 'men' treat their women." He pulled his legs out of the water and stood up beside her. "I'll not have Fawn falling for one of their men. Our Faunella deserves someone who will cherish her and treat her like the special princess she is."

Pride filled Amon as Huxley finished speaking. The Fae stood glaring at the rest of them, as if daring someone to disagree with his passionate speech.

"I agree with Hux." He grew out a limb and clapped Huxley on the shoulder. "As much as it pains me to admit it, Fawn is growing up and will be having—" He shuddered. "—interests. But we need to make sure she doesn't form any attachments to any of the human males she might see on The Edge. What if she got infatuated and decided to follow one out into the human world?" He shook his head. "No, Huxley is right. It's too dangerous."

Violetta swished her hair over one shoulder, and Huxley's eyes trailed down her body before he quickly turned his head away.

Speaking of infatuations.

Walking past the group of them, Violetta gave a heavy sigh.

"All you males are too protective. It's good for a female to admire the male form sometimes. Some of these human men aren't that bad to look at. Fawn is a smart girl. A little sheltered maybe, but she's not going to chase after the first human boy she thinks has a nice smile. Give her some credit. Now, I'm going to go and see what Flavire and Laurel are up to. I'm being smothered in all this testosterone."

She flounced off, leaving damp patches on the warm grass and the rest of them trading looks.

"Do you think she's right?" asked Baol, motioning after Violetta's retreating form. "Are we being too overprotective?

"Nah, don't listen to her," voiced Huxley, rolling his shoulders. "We've got to do whatever we can to keep Fawn safe." He looked in the direction Violetta had taken. "But maybe we shouldn't bring it up around Violetta again, yea?"

The gathered Fae murmured their agreements, breaking out into light chuckles as the tension broke.

"Let's keep an eye on Fawn though. Something has changed for her recently. I've noticed she's been looking happier and more excited to go to The Edge. I would like to know what's causing it." He turned to Erwin. "Erwin, you're the smallest out of us. Maybe you could follow along behind her in the next day or two, just to see what's capturing her attention. As Huxley mentioned, it can't be just a random house."

"You can count on me. I'll keep an eye on her." Erwin puffed up, bristling excitedly. "I'll go right now."

Amon laughed, stopping the male from running off. "Tomorrow's soon enough, Erwin. Just simmer down."

He continued chuckling to himself as the remaining Fae settled, quietly enjoying the last of the afternoon sun before it descended behind the tall trees to the west. Though his body relaxed, Amon's mind still ran, always worrying about the logistics of keeping Fawn safe.

Getting up, he stretched out his limbs, creaking and groaning as his leaves rattled vigorously from the movement.

"I'm going to jump back to Amaranth." Five sets of eyes rushed to him. "It's time we checked the status of what's happening in our territories. I also want to see if Fawn's family are still waiting for her return."

"Be careful, Amon." Huxley scratched the side of his face, looking worried. "Don't let yourself be seen. Fawn is growing in her powers, but she's still not strong enough to protect herself from her aunt and Petrov. We can't have them suspecting we have her."

"I know, Hux. I just want to keep an eye on the situation. I'll be careful and meet you all back at the grotto later tonight."

Making his way eastward, Amon passed through the lichen-covered trees that lined this part of the forest, striding under the thick canopy of leaves and plant growth that blocked much of the sun. As he drew closer to the area that contained the Earth side portal tree, Amon stopped walking, not wanting to get too close to his destination before he jumped.

I'll just take a quick peek.

Closing his eyes, he drew on his power. It felt as familiar to him as breathing. In an instant, he felt himself shift, the world picking up and swirling around as he stayed in place.

Once the world settled, he opened his eyes, finding himself back in Amaranth. It was darker here than back on Earth. The fading magic drew life out of the very heart of his land. Amon dug his roots deep, hoping against hope that there was some improvement from the last time he had visited.

He shook his head, disappointed but not surprised. Petrov still ruled, and no other Heir had been found. Fawn was still their only chance to return their lands and people back to health, and she was still in danger if Petrov found out. Retracting his roots, he shook off the crumbling soil, watching the way the once luxurious dirt scattered lifelessly along the forest floor. It was getting worse.

Concerned but unable to do anything about it, Amon carefully crossed the remaining distance to the portal tree. As he approached, he heard low voices.

"It's about time you got here. Six months with no one to keep you company and this forest making you jump out of your skin every five seconds is too much." Stilling, Amon transformed fully into a tree and settled in to listen to the interaction.

"It's not my fault," came the second voice. "I left when they told me to. At least your time is over. Mine's just beginning."

"That's true," the first male chuckled. "Now that it's over, I'll never have to come back to the South Forest ever again." He shuddered audibly. "It's not even our kingdom. We're lucky Queen Nyssa decreed each guard only had to do one six-month shift in their lifetime."

A harsh laugh rang out from the second male.

"You'd think she'd get the hint that her great-granddaughter isn't coming back. It's been over ten years now. The girl is long dead."

"I have to agree with you. I've been here six months, and other than some creepy sounds at night, I haven't seen or heard a peep from anyone."

The second male lowered his voice. Even with his Fae hearing, Amon had to strain his ears to hear the hushed words.

"I heard that the Queen has started training Princess Solanine to take over ruling Madivyre. Maybe she does realize that the girl is gone."

"Now that's one Fae I wouldn't want to cross." He spat, the unmistakable sound making Amon grimace in disgust. "She's pleasing to look at," he added. "But I've never met a Fae that cold before."

"Nah, Queen Nyssa knows what she's doing. Other than placing us on guard here for no reason, I mean." He gave a wry laugh.

The first male shuffled around for a moment, the clinking of items getting louder as he moved closer to where Amon hid.

"Well, that's me," he puffed out, straining as though he picked something up. "I'm out of here. Don't want to stay any longer than I have to. Good luck, soldier."

Amon listened to the male's retreating footsteps, coming out of his full tree state when he was sure there was only one male remaining. As quietly as he could, he slunk away, jumping back to Earth when he could no longer hear the grumbles of the male left behind.

So they are still watching for Faunella.

He walked sedately back towards the grotto, needing the time to absorb all that he had heard.

Feeling proud, he couldn't help but smile when he thought of how magic had already come to Fawn. Her powers impossibly appeared when she was a child, despite her lower fae body.

Once she reaches second puberty and transforms into her High Fae body, Solanine and Petrov won't know what hit them.

He gave a light chuckle, reminding himself that they really needed to do more to train Fawn to purposely use her powers. She was doing well under Violetta's instruction, but she would soon be coming up against two formidable forces. Amon wanted to give her all the help he could.

CHAPTER THIRTY SIX
DERICK

"GET UP, YOU DOGS. We have a job tonight."

Shaun's voice called from the ground floor of the warehouse, easily reaching through the thin walls of the loft where Derick slept.

Grimacing, he glanced up from his book and checked the time. 11:30 in the morning. The day was almost half done. With great care, he replaced the dollar bill he was using as a bookmark and rolled off his mattress. Staying low in a crouch, he reached into the dust-covered cavity under his bed and pulled free an old crate. Unlike the others, Derick had been up for hours, which gave him the time alone to try and carve out an inch of peace and quiet. Stashing his novel back in the crate, he wished he could ignore Shaun's summons and escape for the whole day. He stood up, stretching his arms high up into the air until he felt the bones in his back pop.

Feeling more refreshed, he walked across to the large rectangular window set under the apex of the roof. Not only did Shaun rename the Sea Dragons to the Shadow Vipers, but he also moved their central location to a more remote spot on the other side of town. They were now in an abandoned industrial area on the edge of the forest, making it easier to stay under the radar of the local police. The rebranding also more easily hid them from the prying eyes of society.

Derick peered out the grime encrusted window of his new abode, craning his neck to find a less filthy part of glass to see through. The view was the only nice thing about the place.

A sudden gust of coolness blew in from a gap in the wall, causing him to flinch, his abdomen tightening uncomfortably. The naked skin on his chest and back pebbled with goosebumps.

Throwing on a light colored t-shirt and his leather jacket, he sat back down on his bed to pull his boots on. The items were like a layer of armor, giving him the illusion of safety. They cemented his well-crafted position as someone not to be messed with.

He lingered in his room, reluctant to leave and join the other members of the gang. But, taking a deep breath and forming the stern mask back over his features, he opened his door and strode through.

The night was dark, lit only by the light of the moon when the clouds parted to reveal its shine. The rhythmic crashing of waves colliding with the cliff face far below dwarfed any other sounds that might try to permeate the stillness of the night.

The newly named Vipers had abandoned their vehicles further down the lane and were in the process of stalking up to a lone beach house. It was perched in the open space between the forest and the ocean, halfway down the coastal road. Its isolation gave them the perfect ability to break in undetected.

Derick moved with a lightness that didn't match his size, his steps hurried as he ducked around the open gate, keeping close to the stone pillar it attached to. For once, Shaun managed to stumble upon a plan that seemed to harm no one. It turned out that one of the more wealthy families on the East Coast were going away for an undetermined amount of time, leaving their beach house relatively unattended. *"Easy pickings. It's like they're begging to be robbed."* Shaun's cocky words sounded in Derick's head, sending the slightest prickle of warning up his back. The gate had been left open. He studied the wrought iron, frowning when the lock was intact. Another figure joined them through the darkness, striding confidently through the shadows to clasp hands with Shaun.

Derick stiffened, not knowing about this part of the plan. Shaun beckoned him forward, his whistle sharp in the quiet. Moving through the other men, he ignored the jab in the ribs Jarred gave him as he passed. Instead, he focused on getting to Shaun and finding out the unknown element to the night's plans.

"Derick, this is Pete. He works for the family." Shaun locked eyes with him, conveying some sort of message other than the one his thin lips were giving. "He's the one who gave us the tip off and left the gate open. All he wants is a share of the take."

Derick stepped closer, pleased when Pete had to step back to look him in the face. He matched stares with the much shorter man, taking in the greasy sheen on his forehead and the thin line of hair sprinkled across his upper lip. The man reminded him of something he couldn't quite put his finger on. A tugging in his gut had his eyebrows drawing together. "Why are you doing this?" He took another step forward. "I'm sure the family pays you well. If you've got steady employment, why betray them for such a small payday?"

Pete licked his lips, the moonlight glinting off the wetness that formed around his mouth.

"I'm not the best worker." His hands rubbed together, twisting and itching like he was one big hit away from an overdose. "I've heard I'll be let go as soon as they're back."

Despite his distasteful appearance, his words rang true. Derick stepped back in disgust, unable to quiet the niggly feeling in the back of his mind that something wasn't right.

"Come on, Derick. I've vouched for Pete. The job is simple for God's sake. Don't go and complicate things now with that brain of yours."

Shaun's voice was stern, leaving no room for argument. Lowering his head in submission, he let the men file past him before taking a spot in the rear.

It was an easy matter to break in. The front door was kicked in, loudly swinging open to reveal a large foyer. Pete disarmed the alarm, and they spread out, taking in the grand architecture through the beams of their flashlights. Derick strode cautiously through the double doors to the left of the entrance, entering a sitting room of sorts. The furniture placed around the room was large and well-made, exuding the family's wealth. He stepped closer to a small coffee table in front of the stuffed couch, a glint catching his eye. His stomach bottomed out.

Straightening up, he glanced quickly around the room, a sick feeling tightening and churning its way into his chest. Then his eyes came back to what sat on the table. It was a mostly finished bowl of food, the spoon catching the light of his flashlight.

The house wasn't empty.

Stumbling back, he opened his mouth to call a hurried warning to the other men, fear making his heart race. A light flashed on, blinding him momentarily.

"What's the meaning of this?"

A sickening thud rang out, and Derick's vision returned just in time to see an older man wearing a black robe fall to the ground.

"He went down like a stack of wood," Jarred laughed loudly, totally relaxed, and drew back his leg, sending a vicious kick into the unconscious man's stomach.

Derick turned his piercing gaze on Pete, furious that the man lied and put them all at risk. He kept his voice calm but stepped forward and gripped the edge of the man's coat.

"Why didn't you tell us the family was home? What's your game?"

Pete's lips drew back into a sly grin, exposing his yellowed teeth.

That's what he reminded me of. He's a rat.

Throwing Pete away from him in disgust, he looked at Shaun, wiping his hands on his jeans to get off the slimy sensation he imagined coated Pete's body.

"We need to go. The family is home, and that changes things."

A cackling laugh sounded from behind him, and Pete's weedy voice spoke about the same time as the stairs above them creaked.

"Not the whole family. Just one."

Derick's body went cold as his head shot to the top of the stairs, landing on the pale face and wide-eyed gaze of a pretty young woman.

"Oh, boy."

Jarred bolted up the stairs, giving a loud whoop when the girl turned to run. Not able to help her escape Jarred's clutches, he turned back to Shaun, hoping the leader would be able to stop this madness. Shaun stood over Pete, a frown marring the skin on his forehead.

"Tell me what you know." Shaun drew back his fist and knocked him to the ground. "The truth this time." He placed his booted foot over Pete's hand and pressed down slowly, eliciting a pained whimper from the prone man.

"What I told you was true," he gasped. "The family is getting rid of me when they get back, and they have gone away for a few weeks." He nodded at the elderly man, unconscious in the doorway. "He's not in the family. He works here. It's only him and Sandra still at home. I was going to have her as my portion of the take." The pained expression on his face turned into an angry sneer. "That bitch has been teasing me all summer. She's the one who got me fired, so I'm going to take what I'm owed before I go."

Shaun stiffened his jaw, his eyes unseeing as he contemplated Pete's words. Derick's body hummed with pent-up energy. He felt trapped. Eyeing the top of the stairs, he hoped Shaun would call the whole thing off and let both the girl and the older man go without any further injury.

"The job's still on." Shaun stepped off Pete's hand, giving him a swift kick instead. "Jonny, Devan, I want you to take our 'friend' here and show him why you don't mess with the Shadow Vipers."

The two men jumped to do as they were told, dragging the now pleading Pete back out the door. His pleading turned into wails, and after a particularly high-pitched scream, a meaty thud silenced him.

The remaining men gathered around Shaun, eagerness coating their faces. Derick stood back from the group, his arms folded and a carefully crafted expression of boredom masking his thundering heart. He resisted a second glance up the stairs where Jarred was hunting down the woman, but he couldn't help listening intently for any sign of the two of them.

"The job continues like planned. We take their stuff, we rob the safe, and we get out." He nodded to the old man. "Someone, tie him up and put him somewhere. We don't want him waking up and getting in the way again." He looked up the stairs. "Jarred! Get down here and bring the girl."

The thumping of Jarred's heavy footsteps quickly became apparent, the sound not masking the soft whimpering of the girl he dragged with him. He stopped at the top of the stairs, looking down on them from over the railing.

"Come on, Dad. I think I'll take Pete's tasty treat for myself." He reached over and gripped her throat hard enough to bruise. Licking his lips, he trailed his hand down under her nightgown, ripping it aside to grasp roughly at her breast. The girl blanched and let out a low cry, struggling more vigorously to get away from Jarred's roving hands.

Derick gritted his teeth, sickened by the act going on in front of him. He needed to figure out how to get her out of there. Shaun opened his mouth, but before he could give Jarred permission to rape the girl, Derick stepped forward, cutting him off.

"I want her."

Shaun stopped, surprise coloring his face.

"I want her," he repeated. "Give her to me."

Jeers and laughter rang out from around the group. Several men came up and clapped him on the back. Through it all, Derick kept his eyes on Shaun, knowing it was up to him.

After a moment, his surprised face brightened into a large toothy smile, and he threw back his head to join in on the raucous laughter.

"All right then, boy. If you want her so bad, then she's all yours. But don't take too long. I want to be out of here in an hour."

Jarred swore, withdrawing his hand from the girl's body and throwing her roughly to the ground. She lay there, stunned from the impact. But when Derick crested the top of the stairs and reached for her, she exploded into a fiery ball of fury, kicking and swiping at him desperately. Despite her protests, Derick scooped her up easily, throwing her over his shoulder to keep her contained.

Wanting to get as far away from the others, he stalked down the wide hallway, brushing past a furious Jarred as he went.

"That's the last thing you'll take from me," he hissed, the words barely loud enough for Derick to hear.

Ignoring the threat, Derick made his way to the end of the hall, moving through two large rooms until he was at the far corner of the house. He shrugged his shoulders and hefted her onto the wide bed in the middle of the room. She landed with a small cry, immediately scrambling backwards to get as far away from him as possible. The fear on her face made him sick. He ran his hand through his hair, letting out a breath as he scratched at the stubble on the back of his head.

Turning, he studied what he could see of the room. It was a decent size, with a door on the wall to the left of the main entrance. The opposite corners both had large windows currently covered in drapes he could barely see.

"Turn the light on."

When there was no response, he looked back at the girl, her silhouette still curled up at the head of the bed. He softened his tone.

"It's okay. Sandra, wasn't it? Sandra, I just want you to turn on one of those lamps beside the bed. Can you do that for me, please?"

She didn't move. However, when Derick started to come around the side of the bed to flick one of them on himself, she gave a small cry of alarm and shuffled over to flick the switch.

"That's better."

He moved away and returned to the open door. As soon as he pushed it shut, locking it with a quiet click, Sandra started weeping more openly, her great shuddering sobs relaying her despair. He ignored her, instead striding to one of the windows and flinging open the heavy caramel drapes. The window pushed up from the bottom, allowing the lower half to fully open. Derrick pushed it up and poked his head out, judging the distance from the second floor to the ground.

Straightening up, he swiveled around, taking in the room in a new light. Sandra still lay weeping on the bed, and the side tables only contained a few useless knick-knacks. He crossed to the other side of the room and opened the other door, which revealed a full-sized bathroom.

Perfect.

As he was unhooking the thick, clear plastic that made up the shower curtain, he registered that the weeping in the other room had stopped. He turned just in time to see Sandra dash across the room and launch herself at the locked door.

Derick cursed, dropping the curtain and rushing after her, the sounds of the lock rattling spurring him on. Reaching her just in time, he clutched her to his chest, his arms coming around to pry her cold hands off the door handle.

"No, no, no. Please, please don't. Just let me go." Sandra dissolved into another round of tears, the warm drops falling and making soft plonks onto the arms of his jacket.

"That's what I'm trying to do," he ground out. "Would you just stop struggling?"

She gasped, her movements stilling. Derick could feel her trembling beneath his hands.

"I'm going to move you away from the door now. I'd appreciate it if you didn't fight me."

Picking her up under her arms, he rotated his body and walked her over to the open window. Thankfully, she didn't struggle, and her tears had all but dried up.

Placing her down, he gently turned her stiff body around to face him. Wincing at her red, splotchy face, he reached into his pocket and withdrew an old napkin left over from whenever he wore his jeans last.

"Here."

Thrusting the napkin forward, he waited for her to take it, only divulging his plan when she finished blowing her nose and was dabbing at the tears covering her cheeks.

"I'm going to help you get away, okay? I won't touch you or hurt you in any way, but I can't say the same for the rest of them downstairs. So, can you keep calm and give me a hand?"

Sandra stared at him with wide bloodshot eyes. Her lower lip trembled, but she gave a tremulous nod.

"Good." He quickly moved back to the bathroom, retrieving the shower curtain from where it had fallen to the floor. "I'm going to lower you to the ground with this. It looks strong enough to hold your weight, and it's our best bet for getting you out of here safely."

She didn't say anything, just watched him move with her mouth slightly open.

"Sandra, are you with me? Do you understand?"

"Yes."

"Good. Now, after you get to the ground floor, you need to hide away from the house. Don't go to the road, or you might be seen as we leave." He looked at his watch, seeing that it had been twenty minutes already. "We should be leaving about half an hour after you get out, so if you can stay hidden until then, then I think that will be safe."

"Can't I just stay here?"

Her voice, although quiet, had started to gain some confidence.

"I'm sorry, but it's not safe for you. I wouldn't put it past some of the men to come back up here to find you after I leave."

Sandra shuddered, crossing her arms in front of her chest as if to banish the memory and feel of Jarred's hands.

"Are you ready?" He held up the twisted shower curtain, attempting an encouraging smile, although his own nerves were stretched tight.

Face pale, Sandra allowed him to guide her to sit on the window ledge. He handed her the plastic, suddenly doubting she could hold onto it long enough.

Too late now.

"Hold on tightly and use your feet to push yourself away from the side of the house. Then, when you reach the bottom, stay low and run."

He stepped one leg back, bracing himself against the wall. When he was in position, he nodded to Sandra, who carefully slid off the window sill. The sudden increase of pressure on his arms almost made him lose his hold on the slippery fabric. Gritting his teeth, he leaned back, the muscles on his back and arms straining. Inch by inch, he released the shower curtain, watching as Sandra's head slowly disappeared beyond the window frame. To get her as far to the ground as possible, Derick had to lean his body out of the window, extending his arms down while still holding tight to the plastic. Sweat began to run down the side of his neck, his shoulders burning from the strain of holding Sandra's weight and lowering her slowly.

Before she reached the ground, she looked up at him, the glow from the moon illuminating her pinched face.

Her mouth moved. It was only after her hands lost their grip that Derick registered the shape of her words. *"I can't."* He cursed under his breath, flinching when she hit the ground hard, going down like a sack of potatoes. She lay there, stunned.

"Get up," he hissed. "Get out of here."

He looked at his watch again. They were running out of time. Gingerly, she sat up, touching the side of her head with a wince. He hoped that she would disappear into the extensive gardens to the side of the house. Derick pulled the shower curtain back inside and stretched out his strained muscles, enjoying the pleasant burn as he flexed and shook out his arms. Carefully replacing the shower curtain back on its rails, he mussed up the covers, then ducked back over to the window to make sure Sandra had gone.

Horror filled him. Obviously confused, she was limping down the side of the house towards the wide gate, oblivious to the fact that, with the light of the moon, she would be spotted any second.

"Shit. Shit. Shit!"

He ducked inside and rushed for the door, unlocking it and wrenching it open. As he raced down the hallway, he untucked his T-shirt and unbuttoned the top of his jeans, revealing the band of his gray briefs. Then, as he approached the stairs leading back to the front door, he slowed right down. Taking a deep breath, he squared his shoulders, formed an expression of sly satisfaction, and stalked down the stairs.

He arrived downstairs just in time. The safe had been opened and the house trashed. He received the winks and elbows to the ribs with good humor, not wanting to do anything that might tip them off about what really happened in that room. He absolutely wanted to keep their attention from the injured girl currently limping her way down the driveway.

He caught sight of Jarred staring at him from his seat on the small bench beside the front door. His eyes were narrowed, assessing him as if he looked deep enough he might uncover all of Derick's secrets.

Derick smirked at him, his smile growing when Jarred's eyes narrowed with fury. Leon shifted beside him, momentarily taking his attention off of Derick. Grateful for the distraction, he ducked into the next room, looking for a way out of the house without anyone seeing him.

He took two steps, then stumbled over a large form lying on the floor. A weak groan met his ears. Concern flashed across his face. Ducking down, he ran his hands over the trussed-up man, sympathy flooding him. "I'm so sorry," he whispered, reaching for his torch while racking his brain to find some way of helping the old man.

A loud holler rang out, sending his head shooting up with a snap.

"Yee-hoo boys," cried Jarred from the other room. "Looks like we'll get some sport after all!" The door crashed open, and the voices faded away. Derick rushed from the room, heart sinking as he watched Jarred lead several men down the drive. Their attention was captured by the pale glow of Sandra's white nightgown as she slipped across the road and disappeared into the pitch black forest.

Knowing he could be seen and it would place him under suspicion. Derick didn't even think twice. He sprinted after the men, veering to the right, and aimed to enter the forest away from where Jarred was. He hoped his chosen direction would lead him to Sandra first. As his body left the moonlit road, he flicked on his flashlight, illuminating the wide trees that stretched out endlessly. Then, with a pounding heart and a sweat-soaked back, he started forward.

CHAPTER THIRTY SEVEN
FAUNELLA

IRONICALLY, IT WAS THE quiet that drove her from her bed. Faunella sunk into a crouch, heart pounding as the jeering voices got closer. The night pressed in around her, all dark except for the small patches of dappled moonlight filtering in through the thinner trees by the coast.

Rafi pressed his wet nose into her leg, whining softly.

"I know, Rafi. I know." She glanced back the way she had come, hoping that the male voices would cover the sound of her retreat. Staying low, she eased through the damp undergrowth, holding her breath with each hint of sound her feet produced. The crunching of heavy feet sounded loudly, and she bit her lip, eyes wide, frustrated at the events of the day that led her to this place in time.

On her way to visit Lucy again, she caught Erwin not-so-subtly following her. Unable to cross The Edge and interact with a human with the Fae trailing her, she detoured and found another spot.

Faunella moved more surely now, Rafi trailing silently in her wake, as the voices echoed behind her. She blew out a quiet breath. After interacting with another person, simply watching the humans from afar did nothing for her. So she gave up, trudging grumpily back to her treehouse.

"I should never have come out here," she hissed. "We should have stayed home with Beebe."

But the night had been so still, so quiet. She had lain in her bed, unable to quiet her mind, until she couldn't take it anymore, threw back her covers, covered her body with a white woolen wrap, and disappeared into the night.

She glanced down at herself, wrinkling her nose at the bright garment. In the darkness, the color stood out starkly. Rafi whined again, weaving between her feet and stopping her from continuing. "This is all your fault." She scratched behind his pricked-up ears. "All I wanted was to see if Lucy was awake, and now look at the mess we're in."

A noise had her whipping her head to the right, her hand stilling on top of Rafi's head. Concern bloomed in her core - Rafi's or her own, she couldn't tell. It sounded again. A soft scuffling, followed by a stifled sob. Just like earlier, the fox slunk towards it, tugging on the bond to get her to follow.

Indecision warred within her. She felt drawn to investigate the sound, worry filling her at the thought of something injured or hurt. Glancing back towards the deep voices and flashing lights, she tugged nervously at her unbound hair. But, she had followed the fox here, detouring from Lucy's house, only to find herself surrounded by loud, harsh-sounding men. Their presence sent shivers of fear running up her back.

The cry came again, making the decision for her. With great care, Faunella pushed through the ferns and skirted the large trees. Straining her eyes, she searched the ground for the sound, only giving up when the forest became denser. Another tug pulled on her bond.

Closing her eyes, she reached inside of herself, wrapping around Rafi's tether. She yanked it, smiling at the returning tug. Leaning into the feeling, she let it guide her forward, not stopping until she came upon a small gap in the trees. Lit up by the moonlight, Rafi stood with a lowered head, staring at a fungi-covered log. Faunella cocked her head, taking in the sight quickly. The tree must have fallen many years ago. It had deep hollows in its side, the cavity large enough to fit her body. Movement caught her eye, a flash of white peeping out from within the tree. She craned her head, stepping closer.

A woman's face appeared, her dark eyes wide with fright. Faunella jerked back, her mouth popping open with a slight gasp of surprise. The woman turned towards the sound, blinking rapidly when she caught sight of Faunella.

"Please," she whimpered, her eyes darting from side to side. "Please help me."

Behind Faunella, the sounds of calling grew louder. She looked over her shoulder, pulse pounding when the distant flickers of light grew closer. Confusion grew. Ducking down, she wrapped her arm around Rafi's back, drawing comfort from his warm body. The woman let out another hoarse sob. "Please don't let them find me."

Faunella's breathing began to come quicker. Her mind ran over the situation, putting all the pieces together until a picture began to form.

The men were hunting her.

She studied the woman with renewed interest. There was dark blood dried on the side of her face and a tear in her clothes. She reached through the hole, letting out a pained groan when she dragged herself free. The sound tore through Faunella. She lunged forward, wrapping her arms around the injured woman's shoulders.

"They hurt you?"

The woman's eyes flashed, her face so close that Faunella could see the tear marks down her face.

"They're men," the woman hissed, disgust dripping from every syllable.

Faunella flinched at the sharp change in the woman's tone. So, it was true. The Fae's warnings that the humans could be dangerous were right.

But what about Lucy? She loosened her hold, drawing back from the woman's vehemence. *What about her?*

"No, wait. Please don't go." She clutched at Faunella, her voice getting higher and more frantic.

Faunella shook her head, tightening her arms back up. It couldn't be all humans. She had seen it for herself. The humans were good, full of life, love, and oozing energy and passion as they went around their daily lives, totally unaware that they were being watched from the shadows. She flicked wide eyes towards the approaching men, remembering her earlier fear when she first came upon them. It was only a few of them. A few of them had rot buried beneath their skin.

"I'll help you," she whispered, helping the woman all the way free. "I'll get you somewhere safe."

Her relief was palpable. She stood up and took a step, crying out sharply as her leg buckled. Faunella stumbled under the woman's weight, almost falling to the ground. She gritted her teeth, bracing her body as the woman leaned heavily against her.

"I heard something that way!"

She froze, the world narrowing in on the delighted cries that were so close she could almost feel them. Rafi whined, urging her to flee. She couldn't move, frozen with indecision. She could get away. She wanted to get away, to flee to safety with none of the men aware of her involvement. The woman began crying. Lucy's house flashed in her mind.

Breath coming faster now, she closed her eyes, concentrating on the power swirling harmlessly in her center to take some of the weight off her leg.

So focused on attempting to harness her power, she didn't hear the crashing coming from behind. The woman gave a cry of alarm and clung to her, pressing her face into the crook of her neck. Rafi barked, his hackles rising as he put himself between Faunella and the imposing man bursting into the clearing.

The man drew up short, the darkness doing nothing to hide the surprise on his face.

Faunella felt a terrified whimper work its way up her throat. She kept her eyes locked on the man, even as her senses warned her the others were closing in.

He shook himself out of his stupor and took a step forward, an arm outstretched. Faunella shrunk back, gripping tightly to the woman.

"I'm not going to hurt you." His voice was deep, the words smooth despite his panting. He ran his hands over the short hair on top of his head, cursing softly.

Faunella felt a prickle of recognition. The man flicked a light on, covering the beam with his hands. "Sandra, it's me, remember?" He flashed the light in his face, illuminating a strong wide jaw and warm chocolate eyes. "See. Just me." Faunella sucked in a breath, her terror lessening.

It was the human from the road.

Sandra peeked around her neck, her body relaxing when she took in the tall man's face. "I tried to get away," she sobbed. "But they saw me." She clung back to Faunella, her tears soaking the white wool of her wrap.

The man flicked the light onto the two of them. Faunella flinched away, blinking back stars. He flicked it off, and she let out a breath of relief.

As her eyes adjusted back to the darkness, she could feel him studying her. Suddenly frightened he might recognise her, she ducked her head, letting a thick sheet of hair cover her face. He cleared his throat. "I can hold them off," he said softly. "But I can't get her away by myself."

He took another step towards them, jolting back when he bumped into Rafi. "Holy mother."

Faunella tugged on the bond, sending Rafi jumping out of sight.

The man rubbed his eyes and scanned the ground again. Faunella worried her lip, rhythmically patting the weeping woman's shoulder. A loud call rang out only a few trees away, and a light flashed over her back. The man flicked his head up, his brows sliding down to shadow his eyes. He strode in a circle, placing his back to her, and faced the oncoming onslaught.

"Can you help me?" he whispered between his teeth, turning his head to the side to look at her. His eyes widened when he registered how close they were standing, and he shifted slightly to give her some more room. "You need to go."

Faunella's pulse jumped. He was helping them. He was prepared to fight his own people to help her and the woman get away. Swallowing thickly, she pushed away her fear and wrapped the woman's body with a thin layer of air. Her power wobbled, struggling to follow her command. Not having any more time, she began dragging the woman away, slowly and painstakingly, inch by inch. Before they disappeared into the trees, she glanced back at the man. He stood with his legs planted and fist clenched as he faced the lights bobbing more frequently on his body.

A rush of gratitude filled her, and she cleared her throat softly, not knowing if he would hear her gentle words.

"Thank you."

She pulled Sandra behind the tree, yanking her forcefully to keep her moving.

"It's just Derick," groaned a voice from the clearing a moment later. "It wasn't the girl."

Faunella's brows shot up. They knew each other. A second later the man, Derick, replied, and Faunella had to stifle her mouth to stop herself from crying out.

"Of course it's me." He swore loudly, his voice now devoid of any kindness. "If that bitch could still walk after I was through with her, then she obviously needed more." He laughed coldly. Faunella felt sick. She clutched her stomach with her free hand, wondering how she could have trusted him.

"He's just pretending."

Faunella turned to look at the women beside her. "He's only pretending," she repeated. This time, she was the one to pull Faunella forward.

"Pretending?"

"Yeah." Her eyes fluttered shut and she blanched from the pain. "He never touched me. Not once." Her voice trailed off. "He's the one who helped me escape."

Faunella's mind was a blur as she traveled the distance to Lucy's house. She left Sandra knocking on the door with a promise not to tell anyone about Faunella's involvement. The night's stress and exertion must have taken its toll, and she had readily agreed, not once questioning who Faunella was and why she was out in the forest in the middle of the night.

It was only after climbing back into bed that she realized what was unsettling her. She couldn't understand why Derick would pretend to be someone he wasn't, cover up his goodness and choose to join with men who only wished to hurt others.

She rolled over, burying her face in her blankets. Her heart hurt, and she couldn't figure out why.

CHAPTER THIRTY EIGHT
LUCY

"**H**AVE YOU NOTICED THAT Lucy seems to be doing a lot better lately?"

Lucy crouched outside her parents' bedroom door while they got ready for bed. Her mom gave her a strange look that night after tucking her in, which had led to Lucy's late-night snooping.

"Oh, I don't know. I haven't noticed much improvement."

Her mom scoffed, speaking almost too low for Lucy to hear. "Well, maybe if you didn't work so much..."

"What was that?"

"I said, she's been breathing a lot better than before we moved here and hasn't had an attack in well over two weeks. Maybe the sea air really is making a difference?"

"That could be wishful thinking, Barb. The doctor said nothing would make a difference now."

Lucy shifted her weight, adjusting her legs to avoid cramping in the uncomfortable position. She pressed her ear to the door, wondering if her parents would get close to the real reason for her improving health. She wasn't even sure if she believed it herself.

"I don't know, Jim. You haven't seen her. It used to be a struggle to get her to eat anything, but lately she's been eating everything I've given her." The bed let out a quiet creak, signaling that her mom had gotten into bed. "And tonight, guess what she asked me? Go on, guess."

Blankets rustled and her dad gave a tired sigh.

"I wouldn't have a clue."

"She asked for two rolls and a whole pizza for lunch tomorrow." She let out a stunned laugh. "Can you believe it? I asked her why she wanted so much food, and she just said she's been getting hungrier, and she wants to have a picnic in the forest tomorrow. But two rolls and a whole pizza? I'd like to see you get through that by yourself."

Lucy grimaced. Perhaps she hadn't been as subtle as she thought. No wonder her mom had looked at her strangely that evening. Easing herself up, she tiptoed back along the hall and slowly climbed the stairs.

Faunella had come to visit earlier and was still eating her lunch when Lucy signaled it was safe to come up to her room. Always generous, Faunella had opened her small pack made out of ferns and offered to share her meager lunch. To her shock, all of the food laid out was totally raw and unprocessed. There were several pale mushrooms, their white and tan skin still covered in a layer of dirt, and a second type of mustard yellow fungi that Lucy wasn't quite sure was edible, but Faunella ate it with no hesitation. Lucy had reached out to pick up what she thought was a berry, but when she looked at it closely, she saw that, while bright red, it looked more like a grape. All this food was laid out on a bed of what looked like grass, but Faunella ate every last strand of that as well.

Lucy climbed into bed. The two girls had been friends for several weeks now, and she never once wondered what the older girl ate. In fact, there were a lot of unanswered questions that surrounded Faunella, questions that Fawn seemed to want to keep unanswered, but the food issue was something that Lucy could solve - which is what brought her to ask her mom for an exceptionally large amount of food for lunch. To be honest, the only reason she thought she could get away with it was because she was dying. Her parents couldn't seem to say no to any request lately, no matter how outlandish, and if she admitted it to herself, she might have been milking it a bit.

Snuggling back under her blankets, she closed her eyes, letting the past few days swirl around in her mind.

Faunella loved the books, the older girl's joy apparent with each exchanged story. Lucy even 'borrowed' a few of her mom's novels and gave them to Faunella to take to wherever her home was.

Where does she live? I know she lives with someone. She made that clear enough. But what kind of people live out in the middle of nowhere and don't teach their kid anything?

Making up her mind, Lucy decided to ask Faunella some pointed questions tomorrow. She would soften her up with a delicious lunch of rolls and pizza. The corners of her mouth lifted.

She's going to love the pizza.

Lunchtime came and went with no sign of Faunella.

The next day was the same.

By the third day, Lucy was beginning to worry. What if something had happened? Faunella could be lying out there in the middle of the forest with a broken leg. She spent the morning frantically pacing her room, peering out the window every few turns. Finally, shortly after lunch, she spotted the familiar swath of bright hair glinting through the trees.

Her stomach jumped into her chest. Twirling around so fast it made her dizzy, she bolted down the stairs and through the kitchen, calling out a hurried "I'm going outside for a while," to her startled mom.

As she zoomed through her yard, she felt a familiar burn start to make its way up from behind her ribs. Ignoring the ache, she scrambled over the fence and flew through the first line of trees, flinging herself on the very surprised Faunella.

"I thought something happened to you!" she sobbed, tears of fear and relief flowing freely down her face. "When you didn't show up, I thought you had hurt yourself. I was so scared."

Faunella stood rigid, loosely holding Lucy's shaking body.

"You were worried about me?"

"Of course." She pulled back, sniffing loudly as she used the edge of her sleeve to wipe the moisture from her face. "You're my best friend, and you live in the forest. Anything could happen in there." Gesturing wildly in the direction that Faunella came from, Lucy let out a quivery sigh. "I don't really know anything about you, Fawn. How could I help you if you needed help?"

"Lucy? What are you doing out there?"

Her mom's voice startled the two of them, causing their heads to swing around in the direction of the house. Even though they couldn't be seen from where they were standing, Faunella still released Lucy and drew back further into the concealing forest.

"Don't go anywhere, okay?" said Lucy, hurriedly wiping her eyes.

Quickly walking back out into the bright midday sun, Lucy blinked past the glare as her mom came into focus.

"There you are, Lucy. Why did you rush off so suddenly?" Bailey's voice was raised to travel the distance to where Lucy stood.

"I just wanted to explore the forest a bit," Lucy called back. "I'm feeling really good today. I won't go far."

"Well, okay then. Please be careful."

Lucy watched her disappear into the house before making her way back to where Faunella waited.

"Oh good, you're still here."

Faunella stepped forward to clasp one of her hands.

"I'm sorry I wasn't here until now. One of the F... one of the people I live with followed me, so I had to go somewhere else for the day."

"I don't understand. Why aren't you allowed to be my friend? What's so wrong with me?"

Lucy could feel her lip start to quiver again. She had finally found a friend, and now there were people trying to take her away.

"Oh, Lucy."

Faunella looked stricken, her smooth skin stretched tight and pinched around her mouth. Her own eyes were glossy with unshed tears.

"There is nothing wrong with you. It's just—" She cut off, eyes darting around the area they were in before finally landing at her feet. "I'm not meant to say."

Lucy swallowed, determined to take away the worry that plagued her friend. Tugging at their clasped hands, she started off away from the house, pulling Faunella deeper into the forest.

"Come on. Let's find a place that's just for us."

The two girls walked for a few minutes, not so far that she couldn't hear if her mom came looking, but far enough that they knew they were alone. When they stumbled across a big oak, Faunella turned to her, the sparkle back in her eye.

"Let's go up."

"Up?" Lucy gulped, her head slowly traveling up the enormous height of the tree. "Are you sure it's safe?"

Faunella gave a short laugh, drawing her closer to the base.

"You'll be fine, Lucy. I'll keep you safe."

Lucy felt awkward at first, not knowing where to put her feet. Her body was still weak and not strong enough to pull her higher. But with Faunella's guidance and encouragement, she eventually managed to get into the tree, wedging herself firmly into the Y of a sturdy branch. To her surprise, it almost felt like she was getting held in the tree, like even if she tilted to the side and pitched herself forward she wouldn't be able to fall.

Don't be silly, Lucy, she said to herself, shaking her head lightly in amusement.

Now that Faunella wasn't helping her, she simply flew up the remaining height of the tree. Lucy watched her with awe, admiring the way she looked at home in the wild oak.

"Come down and talk with me," she called, awkwardly patting the limb beside her.

In an instant, Faunella had scaled down the tree and was smiling happily at her from the next branch. Lucy licked her lips, ready to start probing Faunella for answers.

"I want to know all about you, Fawn." Seeing Faunella opening her mouth, she hurried on. "I know you have rules and things you feel like you can't tell me, but I'm your best friend. You can tell me anything. I would never tell anyone anything you told me. I promise."

Placing her finger to her chest, she drew two crossing lines over her heart. She held her breath as she watched the indecision flit across Faunella's face. The older girl chewed at her lip while staring into Lucy's earnest eyes. The change was instant. Flickering worry dissipated, the softness hardening into a mask of determination.

"Okay." She gave a short nod. "You're my best friend, and I can tell you anything?"

Not daring to say more lest she change Faunella's mind, Lucy jerked her head up and down, her hair falling into her face. When she brushed it out of her eyes and could see once more, she watched Faunella take an audible swallow, then she opened her mouth.

Out of it came the most outlandish and fantastic tale Lucy ever heard.

As Faunella told her story filled with shifting creatures, other worlds, and magic, Lucy could only stare open-mouthed at her friend. She didn't interrupt, apart from the occasional gasp or uttered 'wow.' When the story reached the point when Faunella had met her, she couldn't help but smile.

"No wonder you were so happy to have a friend. I really am your first friend, aren't I?"

Faunella reached out her hands again, taking both of Lucy's in a firm grasp.

"You're the best friend I could ever ask for, and I don't know what I would do if I ever lost you."

Lucy's heart stuttered. Faunella's earnest words gave her a rush of pleasure, but they left a sticky feeling of dread coiled deep in her belly. The water—the magic water—she was drinking seemed to be working for now. It's been giving her back her energy and appetite, making it easier to breathe and move around. But Lucy could feel deep inside of herself that her illness hadn't really gone away. It had only been put on hold for a little bit.

She gave a slight smile back to Fawn.

"I feel the same way, but I know you'd be okay if something happened to me."

Shaking off her melancholy, she withdrew her hands and forced a wider smile.

"Never mind all that. I want to hear more about your powers. Can you really control the air?" She did a double take. "Is that why I haven't fallen out of this tree yet?"

Faunella shook from the force of her laughter.

"No, silly. You haven't fallen out because you're safe where you are." She suddenly looked a bit sheepish. "Though I might have a light layer of air around you just in case."

The girls laughed together.

"Will you show me some of your magic? We don't have magic here on Earth, but I bet everyone has magic back on—what was it called again?"

"It's called Amaranth. I don't remember it at all. I came here when I was really little, and the Fae here in the forest have been looking after me ever since."

Lucy thought that was strange. Why would a little girl be sent to a different world to live with strange creatures?

"But what about your parents? Are they the ones who sent you here? Why would they do that?"

Faunella's face fell. Feeling empathy for her friend, Lucy placed her hand over Faunella's knee, hoping the simple touch was enough to let her know she wasn't alone.

"All I know is it's dangerous for me back in Amaranth."

Lucy pondered that for a moment. Something sounded off about the whole situation.

"Hmm, I guess it's hard for them to tell you anything, right? Since they're not able to talk."

"I can actually understand them pretty well now. Not at first, but as the seasons have passed." She blushed, giving her head a small shake. "I mean, as the years have passed, I've learned what a lot of their sounds mean. It's not perfect, but it works for us."

Lucy thought it was amazing to understand the speech of trees, rocks, and all manner of wonderful otherworldly creatures.

"I wish I could hear them talking."

"I could say a little something if you want?"

"Really? That would be so cool!"

Faunella cleared her throat, coughing and grinding to clear the moisture in her mouth. When she didn't stop, Lucy became concerned.

"Faunella, are you okay? What's wrong?"

The sounds stopped immediately, and Faunella looked at her, blue eyes bemused.

"Of course I'm okay. I was just telling you how happy you make me and how I love to climb trees."

Lucy's jaw dropped. "You mean, that was it?"

Faunella laughed, the musical sound so at odds with the grinding, grating nose she just uttered.

"That's how Huxley talks. He's a big rock—a big grumpy rock, I mean. But he loves me to bits."

"I can't believe that means anything. It's amazing." She shifted around on her branch, excited to be learning something so new. "Tell me more. What do the trees sound like? What about the water lady, the one whose water makes me feel better?"

They spent the next few hours learning more about each other, hidden safely up inside the old oak. As the sun grew dimmer, Lucy heard her mom's faint voice calling from the direction of her house.

"I've got to go home now, but I want to know more about everything tomorrow."

As she said the word "everything," she flung her arms wide, the vigorous motion throwing her off balance. She tipped slightly, feeling her thighs shift back off the slippery limb. Before she even registered that she would fall, she was pushed firmly back onto the safety of the branch.

Her heart stuttered erratically, her body still gearing up for the terrifying anxiety of falling. However, she hadn't fallen. As her pulse settled back into its natural rhythm, she stared wide-eyed at Faunella, whose expression of surprise matched her own.

A moment passed with no words spoken, which then stretched into several more.

The surprised silence coupled with her near-miss started to cause a tickling amusement that bubbled up from behind her ribs. Her lips began to quiver and shake as she tried to hold in the burgeoning laughter. Finally, after noticing Faunella's lips perking up at the sides and her large eyes glittering with mirth, the tension broke, and a loud gasping laugh erupted from Lucy's mouth.

The two girls howled with laughter, the relief evident in their voices.

"I thought I was going to fall," Lucy gasped, clutching at her side.

"The look on your face," replied Faunella. "I was so scared for a second."

"You saved me, though. You didn't let me fall."

"I'm glad. It would have been hard to explain to your mom."

That caused them to dissolve into another round of giggles. Once they had calmed down enough, Lucy started to make her way down the tree. Faunella supported her the whole time, using her hands and her powers.

"Now that I know about your magic, I can feel it easily. You're so lucky, Faunella. I'd love to have magic and powers. It would be so fun."

Faunella shrugged. "It is pretty great, but I would much rather be a normal girl like you. Then maybe I could have a home, a family, and be around other people."

Lucy stopped, turning around to face her.

"You're not sad, are you?"

A broad smile lit up Faunella's face, making the blue of her eyes shine brighter and the colors around her seem more vivid.

"Not now that I have you as my friend. I'm not lonely anymore." She tilted her head thoughtfully. "I wish we could be together all the time, though. I miss you when we're not together."

Lucy's heart grew warm and full. Her illness had taken so much from her, including the ability to make and keep friends. If only Faunella knew just how grateful she was to have her.

"I miss you, too. I would love to see your treetop home and meet your Fae family. I know we can't, but it's nice to dream."

Her mother's voice broke through the trees, sounding more strained than before.

"I'd better go. Mom's not going to wait for much longer."

She reached in and wrapped her arms back around Faunella's waist, holding her tightly. Faunella held her just as tight, fusing their bodies together until it felt as if they were one.

"I'll see you tomorrow, right? You won't be followed by one of your tree friends, will you?"

Faunella giggled into her hair, the warmth from her breath brushing past the ebony curls.

"No, they shouldn't check on me for a while. Tomorrow should be fine." She drew back and looked into her face with a small smile. "But if I don't come one day, please don't worry. I'll be fine. I hardly ever get hurt, and if I do, then I have the Fae to look after me."

"But how will I know?" Lucy asked as she pulled away, remembering her anxiety from the past few days. "I don't think I can stop being worried."

Faunella gave her a little push in the direction of home. Reluctantly, she started walking, still looking back at the figure of her friend.

"I'll send Beebe," Faunella called. "I'll send Beebe with a message for you. Red leaf for danger, green leaf for if I'm ok."

Lucy nodded her agreement from across the space, throwing out her hand in a thumbs up gesture. It was only when she was back out under the late afternoon sun that she realized with a laugh that Faunella probably had no idea what the gesture meant.

PART FOUR

Since the dilution of Fae blood leading to an insurgence of Fae known as High Fae, we have noted a stark change in magic abilities.

Unlike the original Fae, these High Fae do not seem to be able to transform, whether into nature form or beast. This power seems to be solely reserved for the pure blooded Ancient Fae. Only seldom do we see this latent ability manifest in one of their kind.

The High Fae have retained the Fae gift of enhanced senses, maintaining their heightened sight, strength, smell and hearing. But, in all but a few rare cases, the High Fae are left with nothing more than what we consider simple enchantments.

Though, once in a blue moon we have heard whispers of a magic that harks back to our origins, a magic beyond that of a regular High Fae. But as these reports are few and far between, we have dismissed them as nothing more than the High Fae's desire to return to our own level of power.

—Addendum to the *Histories of Amaranth*, Vol. 1

THREE YEARS LATER

CHAPTER THIRTY NINE
LUCY

I T HAD BEEN THREE years. Three glorious years since Lucy's doctor had given his devastating diagnosis, leading her to the most amazing opportunity of her life: becoming friends with a real life fairy, or 'Fae' as they preferred to be called. Three years of improved health and incredible experiences, exploring the forest and doing things she never dreamt she could do. Three years of no doctors, no tests, no prodding and poking. Nothing until now.

"I'm amazed, my dear," the wizened doctor said, peering at her scans through small, circular glasses. "Your tests show that your illness has not progressed much further than what it was three years ago. You are a medical miracle indeed."

"She seemed to improve almost as soon as we arrived in Mull Crest, getting steadily better until we—" Her mom paused, gesturing to her dad sitting quietly beside her. "We thought that she had been cured, perhaps by something in the air." She gave a small chuckle, the sound almost immediately cutting off as she shot a guilty look at Lucy.

"Well I don't know about that, but whatever it was seems to have stopped working." He cleared his throat, taking the time to rub at the white stubble lining his jaw. "I'm afraid, young lady, your disease has almost run its course. There is nothing more we can do."

"But surely medicine has improved in the past few years. There must be new treatments, even experimental treatments."

"I'm so sorry, but this is a rare disease, and unfortunately doesn't get as much attention as it should in the medical world."

"But—"

"Mom, that's enough."

Lucy coughed, clearing her throat as her mom looked at her with tear-filled eyes.

"It's okay. I've known for a long time." She clasped her mom's trembling hands, keeping her own face calm. "It's going to be okay."

She comforted her weeping mother, feeling strangely detached when her dad joined, wrapping them all in a shuddering embrace. Lucy had suspected for a while now that her illness had finally proven too much for Violetta's water. After waking up three mornings in a row coughing up blood and struggling to breathe, her mom insisted on seeing a doctor. The confirmation of what she already knew was almost a relief. But, as she sat sandwiched between her weeping parents, the only thing on her mind was how she was going to tell Faunella.

CHAPTER FORTY
FAUNELLA

LUCY TOLD HER SHE would be spending the day in the city. Well, she hadn't *told* her, but when Faunella had arrived at Lucy's house that morning, it had been shut up tight, no one home at all. A piece of white paper in her window had caught her eye. Intrigued, she had sent Beebe up to retrieve it.

Pulling it out from the slit woven into her shirt, she opened it up, eyeing the hurried letters for the fifth time that day.

Fawn, I want you to know that I'm okay.My parents just decided to take me to Northaven, and I couldn't say no.I should be back later on this afternoon, socome up to my room tonight. I want to see you.Don't be worried. Why don't you take the day to spendtime with the Fae? I know you've been missing them.Lots of love,Lucy

Closing the letter, Faunella peered up through the trees where the sun was shining brightly. She huffed; it was still only a little after midday. The sun had barely moved since the last time she checked.

Maybe I should go and see what the Fae are up to.

Rafi barked from down below. She glanced down, leaning over the branch she was perched on. Beebe was flying around above Rafi, swooping in from behind and yanking tufts of red fur from his coat.

"Beebe! Cut that out."

She sent her displeasure down the bond, chastising her feathered friend. Swinging lightly down from the tree, she scooped up Rafi, stroking at the roughened fur on his back.

"It's okay, Rafi. She's just teasing you."

He snuggled into her chest, swiping his tongue over the underside of her chin. Giggling, Faunella squeezed him tight before releasing him back to the ground to trot beside her.

"Beebe?" she called up to the bird flitting from branch to branch. "You need to leave Rafi alone. He's part of our family, and I won't have you teasing him."

Satisfied that her message had been understood, she continued through the forest, enjoying the way the sun dappled over the rough bark on the trees, causing interesting shadows when they hit the ruffled lichen. Lucy had been right, as she often was. Faunella had been missing her Fae family. Gone were the days when she would spend all of her time with one or all of them. She instead found herself drawing away from their company, preferring the comfort of having a friend, a *kindred spirit.* Faunella had read the term in one of Lucy's books, instantly knowing that was what she and Lucy were.

But Lucy wasn't here today, and the Fae were. Based on the humidity in the air, Faunella would bet she knew where some of them were. She grinned, changing her course and zipping through the dense brush, her magic creating a path through the tangled foliage.

Erupting in a rush of air and leaves, Faunella emerged into the large clearing, startling the usually unflappable Fae cooling off in the stream.

"Fawn," sighed Violetta, placing her hand on her watery chest as she shook her head. *"Where did you come from? We didn't even hear you coming."*

Faunella laughed, enjoying the fact that she could surprise the Fae, even with their advanced hearing.

"I thought you all had this super good hearing. Shouldn't you have heard me coming from way off?"

Huxley crunched to his feet, a dark scowl on his gray face.

"Not when you use your powers to fly through the forest like that. Tell me, how many times did your feet even touch the ground?"

A warm bubble of happiness filled her chest, the gruff sarcasm from the moody rock making her giggle. She sauntered forward to join Violetta in the stream, leaving Rafi hidden in the bushes on the edge of the clearing.

"Where are the others? It's such a hot day. I thought everyone would be enjoying the water." She removed her outer clothes, slipping into the water in nothing but her underwear. The coolness of the silky water made Faunella sigh in contentment. Huxley sat back down on the edge of the stream, placing just his legs in the water.

"Oh, they were here." Violetta grinned at Huxley, placing her hands on the surface of the water and sending a wave of water washing over his entire body. *"But they left after I started to 'play' with the water."*

Huxley gritted his teeth, the motion making a loud grinding noise ring out around the clearing. The water that covered his body evaporated quickly on his hot stone, sending up tendrils of steam that perfectly portrayed his mood. Faunella kicked herself around the water, diving and giggling with Violetta.

I wish Lucy could be here, she thought in a moment of calm. It wasn't the first time she'd had that wish, and she suspected it wouldn't be the last. But as she enjoyed the warmth of the afternoon with the two Fae, she held onto the little hope that one day, being friends with a human wouldn't be something she had to hide.

CHAPTER FORTY ONE
LUCY

THAT NIGHT, LUCY FELT butterflies bouncing off her stomach—and not the good kind. They were bad. They were the kind of butterflies that churned and ate at her stomach, causing a sick feeling of nausea. It mixed with the burning feeling that flared up each time she breathed, making each moment that she waited filled with pain and discomfort.

I'll take the medication as soon as I've spoken to Fawn.

The doctor had sent them back home with more inhalers and a script for heavy-duty pain killers. The finality of the situation sent a glimmer of fear through her if she thought about it too long, which she tried not to do. Sitting up in bed, she leaned forward to check that the picture was still in her window, hoping Fawn wouldn't be too much longer.

A white grinning face appeared from the darkness. Lucy jumped back in fright, her weakened lungs trying unsuccessfully to get enough air with her startled gasp. She coughed and spluttered, drawing rattling breaths as she tried to get her breathing under control. This was not the way she wanted Fawn to find out.

"Lucy, are you okay? I'm sorry, I didn't mean to frighten you."

Fawn's cool hand, smooth despite years of rough living, gripped her arms, and a light rush of air caressed her face. Instantly, she felt her chest expand, relief filling her as fresh, abundant oxygen flooded her lungs.

"Thanks," she choked out, wiping the tears from her eyes. "I just got a fright and choked, nothing to be worried about."

Now, why did I say that? There is something to worry about.

"I'm just glad you're okay." Faunella settled down on the thick comforter, glancing over to the door to make sure it was locked. "I missed you today. Did you have fun in Northaven?"

"Well, ah, it's always nice going into the city. We had New York Pizza for lunch."

She chewed on her bottom lip, stretching out a curly strand of hair and letting it bounce back into shape. Her diagnosis sat in the forefront of her mind, begging to be shared, but she was beyond nervous. How could she do this to Faunella? How could she tell her that her only friend was going away, and she could never see her again?

"That sounds so good."

Faunella wrapped her arms around her middle, closing her eyes in rapture as she dramatically collapsed onto the bed beside her. Lucy felt her heart sink. Faunella was so happy, so relaxed, and with two little words, Lucy would shatter that. She forced a weak smile, reaching out to stroke Faunella's auburn locks.

"Your hair is really soft today. Did you wash it?"

"I did! It was such a hot day, so I took your suggestion and hung out with the Fae. Violetta and Huxley were at the stream, so I went swimming with Violetta."

"No swimming for Huxley?"

The blue of Faunella's eyes sparkled at her question. She rolled onto her side and smirked at her, a mischievous expression on her face.

"No swimming for Huxley, but he somehow always finds himself around the stream when a certain water Fae is there." She looked expectantly at Lucy, who felt her own eyes start to crinkle.

"Does Huxley have a crush on Violetta?"

Faunella exploded with laughter, pressing her face into the bed to smother the sound.

"He totally does. He follows her everywhere. It's so cute."

Lucy sat back and enjoyed Fawn's mirth, joining in half-heartedly as she relished what could be one of her final times with her friend.

I don't want to ruin the moment. I'll tell her tomorrow.

CHAPTER FORTY TWO
FAUNELLA

L UCY HADN'T BEEN THE same since she'd gone to the city. She didn't want to go exploring in the forest anymore, instead preferring to hang out in her room and talk. Faunella didn't mind, not really, but the change did have her worried.

She left Rafi behind today, the fox not able to come into the house. Strangely enough, Beebe also decided to remain, giving Faunella a slight hope that the two of them were finally developing a tentative trust.

Being alone for once, Faunella raced through the forest, putting on a burst of speed since she didn't have to worry about her animal friends keeping up. She held a water bottle in each hand, careful not to drop any as she nimbly dodged each tree. She had decided to bring two today, hoping that Lucy would return to her normal self with just a bit more of the healing liquid. As she neared The Edge, she slowed, brows furrowing as a strange red light came pulsing through the thinner trees.

What's going on?

Carefully staying concealed, she peered around the final tree, stomach tightening as she saw the out of place truck sitting outside Lucy's house. Its white sides cut through with stripes of red, and the flashing lights caused the red glow she had seen through the trees.

"Ambulance," she mouthed, reading the word splayed out on the side.

The car was also at home. Lucy's dad was never here this time of day. Something was wrong. A thick sense of urgency laced the scene, the flashing lights and open back door giving an air of panic to the otherwise peaceful home. Clutching the bottles so hard her knuckles ached, Faunella had to restrain herself from dashing into the house. Ignoring all good sense, she almost did several times, only the fear of being discovered stopping her from taking more than one step past the tree line.

Movement from Lucy's window had her gaze shooting upwards, straining her eyes for a glimpse of her friend. There was no picture in the glass, but she could see blurry movement in the shadowed bedroom. Heart pounding, Faunella watched and waited, counting down the minutes until two uniformed men came out of the house, taking the ominous vehicle and leaving. But still, she had to wait. She let out a strangled groan, pressing her forehead into the roughened bark of a tree.

When can I see her?

It felt like forever, but one of the hundreds of times she looked up, the bright picture appeared in the lower corner of Lucy's window.

Eagerness overwhelmed her, filling her up with a burning energy. Sending out a burst of air, she propelled her body quickly over the fence and through the yard. She barely felt the sides of the house as her magic fired her up to the second story, landing lightly beside the window. Suddenly she paused, a thin thread of dread unfurling from the back of her mind. Shaking away the thought, she tapped on the window, opened it, and climbed through without waiting for an answer.

The sight that greeted her had her recoiling in shock.

Lucy lay flat on her bed, propped up slightly by two fluffy pillows. Her skin, while usually a rich chocolate, had dulled to an ashy gray. She was connected to a large canister beside the bed by a thin tube that ran to each nostril. Faunella felt the air, pushing and pulling, shocked to discover that the canister seemed to be delivering pure oxygen to Lucy.

"What happened?" she whispered, her voice not able to sustain the energy for more volume. Crawling forward on her knees, she glanced at the door, heart jumping when she saw that not only was it unlocked, it was wide open.

"Lucy, the door!"

Leaping off the bed in one swift jump, she raced across the bedroom and pressed the door closed, firmly sliding the lock into place.

"I'm so sorry."

The rasping voice came from behind her, so unfamiliar that Faunella briefly thought someone was in the room with them. Turning, she stared wide-eyed at Lucy, barely recognizing the girl in front of her. She swallowed thickly, coming back to kneel at the side of her bed.

"You were fine." Her voice caught, a hot burning starting to press from behind her eyes. She blinked quickly, clearing her throat to hide her emotion.

"I should have told you."

Faunella winced at the roughness of Lucy's words, her usually sweet, energetic voice flattened into a shell of itself.

"Told me what?"

The pity in Lucy's eyes was almost her undoing. Faunella looked away, not wanting to see the answers that lay in their shining depths.

"I'm dying."

Faunella's heart stopped, gave a jolt, and then started again, its rhythm picking up pace as Lucy's words echoed again and again in her frozen mind.

"No. No, you can't. You're not."

Her mind caught up with her heart, scrambling madly for a reason why this wasn't happening—a way to stop this from happening. Her skin felt hot, and her clothes were suddenly too tight. She leaned over and grasped Lucy's hand, squeezing tightly as if her hands were the only thing that could keep her from slipping away right in front of her eyes.

The water.

Breathing in sharply, Faunella felt a bloom of hope blossom behind her chest. Her head whipped up to where she had left the bottles sitting on the windowsill.

"The water, Lucy. I've got the water."

Without waiting, she got to her feet and climbed over the side of the bed to grasp hold of the life-saving liquid. She turned back to Lucy, a broad smile on her face, holding the two bottles out for her friend to see. Instead of the returning smile she hoped to see, Lucy had her eyes closed, a single tear tracking down the side of her hollow face.

"Lucy, please." She shuffled closer, holding the bottles out desperately. "I've got Violetta's water, the magic water, remember? It's always helped before."

Lucy opened her eyes, her dry lips inching up into a halfhearted smile. "It stopped working, Fawn. It hasn't worked for a while now." Her breathing was labored, breaking up her words in a halting whisper. Dread crept up Faunella's spine. She stiffened, choking down her helplessness before it overwhelmed her.

"No, you're wrong. It always works. Please, just please drink some."

Lucy nodded slightly, her curls bouncing with the motion. Faunella helped support her head, placing the mouth of the bottle against Lucy's lips.

"That's it; that's right."

After a few small swallows, Lucy weakly shook her head, pulling away to lay her head back down. Faunella let her, watching with burgeoning hope as color started to bloom on Lucy's face.

"It's working!"

She cut off, watching with lead in her stomach as the fresh color rapidly faded back to the same anemic tint as before.

She didn't know what to say, the water was her last hope at saving the only friend she had ever known.

"I know. It's okay."

Patting the bed beside her, Lucy motioned for Faunella to lie down. Lips trembling, she did as she was told, placing her head onto the pillow next to Lucy, their heads pressing together.

Lucy took a deep breath, the sound short and shallow. Without having to think about it, Faunella strengthened the breath, using her magic to ease the burden of Lucy's lungs.

"Thanks."

She could hear the smile in her voice. Faunella turned to lay on her side, curling her body around Lucy's much smaller form.

"You don't have to thank me for that. I'll stay with you forever and help you breathe."

Lucy gave a weak chuckle. Her hand made its way down the bed, reaching blindly for Faunella's. Grasping it tightly, Faunella brought it up to her face, pressing the back of Lucy's hand against her lips.

"You always make me laugh, Fawn, but that wouldn't be a good life for you." Her words were coming slower now. Lucy's voice trembled with effort. "I'd never let you sacrifice your life for me. I love you too much."

Faunella squeezed her eyes shut, sniffing loudly as she pressed Lucy's hand even closer.

"I love you too much to let you go."

The words were muffled, but Lucy seemed to hear them. She shifted slightly, bringing her other hand over to lightly stroke over Faunella's long hair.

"When we first met," she whispered, "I was already dying. My parents refused to tell me, but I knew," she took a rattling breath. "I was relieved. My life was so bland, filled with limitations and pain. I was happy that it would soon be over." She sniffed, her voice thickening.

Faunella opened her blurry eyes, and stared into the soul of the most important person in her life, her chest feeling as if it were getting crushed under a heavy weight.

"But then I met you."

Faunella gasped, her voice breaking as more tears filled her eyes, spilling over to dampen the hair pressing on the pillow.

"You saved me, Fawn. And not just with the water. You made me want to live again. You were my first real friend." Faunella's pulse thundered through her veins. Lucy was growing more and more pale. The effort from talking was taking all her strength. "Lucy stop," she ran her fingers over Lucy's lips, begging her with her eyes to stop, to conserve what energy she had left and to live. But Lucy's head shook, tilting minutely to the side. Even in this, she was so strong.

"You showed me a whole world that I never dreamed I would get to see. Meeting you was the best thing that has ever happened in my life." She paused to catch her breath, her eyes closing in pain. "If dying is the price I have to pay, then I will gladly pay it."

"No, Lucy. No."

Faunella wept openly, her mouth gaping and shoulders heaving with the force of her sobs. She flung her arms around Lucy, burying her face in the crook of her neck as she cried her pain and anguish into the loving embrace of her best, most loved friend.

Lucy patted her back, rubbing soothing circles as she poured her despair out, only stopping when her tears stopped flowing and her sobs turned to shuddering breaths.

"I'm sorry I didn't tell you sooner. I wanted to, but I couldn't bring myself to say the words. Will you forgive me?"

Raising her head, Faunella wiped at her wet face, nodding her head lest she break out in tears again. Lucy smiled, her face serene. She reached out and smoothed back the hair plastered against Faunella's face.

"I've always loved your hair. It was how we met, you know." Her face took on a wistful look as she stared off into nothing. "I was staring out the window, and I saw your hair flashing from a tree. I wanted to meet you so badly, but I didn't know how." She smiled broadly, her lips quivering slightly. "Then you came back."

Relaxing back into the pillows, she closed her eyes again, exhausted from the talking.

"It was meant to be. I'll never forget you, Fawn. Never."

Her breathing became more strained, making a nasty rattling sound in her chest. Faunella's eyes welled up again, the tears seemingly endless.

"Don't talk anymore, Luce. Save your strength. We still have time, right?"

Lucy's small, sad smile was answer enough, and the tears spilled over again, sending hot rivulets streaking down her cheeks.

"You've given me three more years of time. I'm afraid I can't stay any longer."

The creaking of steps had Faunella ripping her devastated eyes to the locked door. A moment later, the door handle rattled.

"Lucy?" came Bailey's voice, worry giving the word a certain urgency. "Lucy, are you okay? Why is the door locked?"

Faunella's heart clenched. It was too soon. She couldn't leave now.

"Lucy."

"You have to go. My parents can't see you."

Jim's voice joined Bailey's, their panic now evident. The door shuddered as a loud crash sounded on the other side.

"I love you, Fawn. I'll always love you."

Lucy clenched her hand one more time, her eyes shining with feeling as she thrust Faunella away with what little strength she possessed. "Go!"

Faunella sped to the window, sending one more tear-filled glance at Lucy.

"I'll come back tomorrow. I'll come back tomorrow, and we will have more time."

Lucy's eyes filled, silent sobs now shaking her slender frame.

"Go." she choked out.

"I love you. Always."

With a crash, the door burst open, but Faunella was gone, the wind carrying her away as her heart shattered into a thousand pieces.

CHAPTER FORTY THREE
LUCY

THE NIGHT WAS QUIET and still. Lucy woke up with a start, her breath coming a bit easier. She looked around, not knowing what had woken her, but certain that someone was in the room.

"Fawn?" she breathed, peering around the darkness as a sweet breath of air rushed across her face, filling her with sweet memories of times spent high in trees, and afternoons sharing laughter, tangled in the warm grass. She sighed, her body relaxing as a weight left her chest. A smile pulled at her lips, and she closed her eyes softly.

Her last thought was of her best friend, the shine of her hair and the sparkle in her eyes as she beckoned Lucy to keep up, laughing as they ran through sunlit fields.

And then she was gone.

CHAPTER FORTY FOUR
FAUNELLA

F AUNELLA SLEPT FITFULLY, TOSSING and turning all night, unable to still her tumultuous mind. Rafi crawled up to curl up by her head, licking gently at the salty tears that wouldn't seem to cease. Blindly reaching out, she gripped his coarse fur and held on tightly, desperate for the connection.

The night passed slowly, the darkness seemingly endless as it covered the sky. Before the whistle from the first morning bird had faded, Faunella was up, dressing haphazardly and eager to get back to Lucy. Sensing her distress, both Beebe and Rafi followed as she traveled across the well-worn route toward the house. Even though she was itching to see Lucy, her steps were sluggish, dragging behind her as she traipsed the distance.

Dawn was well and truly here by the time she passed the old oak the two girls had climbed that first time many years ago when Faunella had saved Lucy from falling after sharing who she really was and where she came from. Her throat caught, tightening painfully. Hurrying on, she approached The Edge, relieved to see no flashing red lights like yesterday. Her heart picked up, hoping a good night's sleep helped Lucy regain a bit more energy. She still had so much to tell her, so many things to share.

The sight that greeted her from between two trees had her stopping in her tracks. The ambulance from yesterday had returned, carefully positioned at the side of the house, the large double doors at the rear wide open. Unlike yesterday, there were no flashing lights, no sense of urgency or panic at all. Faunella worried her lip, biting at the tender flesh as she waited with bated breath.

No lights. That's got to be a good thing.

Her heart thudded down to her toes, mixed parts of hope and dread battling for dominance inside her chest. She rubbed at her sore eyes, trying to remove the gritty, dry feeling that hadn't gone away since she left last night. She would wait as long as it took until it was safe to go up and see Lucy.

"Beebe, she might not be strong enough to tell me it's safe, so you'll need to fly up and check it out once the ambulance leaves."

Beebe chirped and flitted up to the tree, ready to fly straight up to the room that instant if needed.

"Wait till it's clear. I'm sure they won't be much longer."

The back door pushed open and Faunella stiffened, expecting to see the uniformed men from yesterday emerge. To her confusion, it was Bailey and Jim who made their way outside.

What are Lucy's parents doing out here?

Jim had his arms around Bailey, supporting her weight as they shuffled out towards the yard. Bailey had her head pressed into Jim's chest, a white tissue clutched in her hand.

A uniformed man was backing out of the door, carefully supporting something hidden by his body. Another man emerged, swiveling to the side to reveal what they both carried. All the blood drained from Faunella's face, her skin becoming cold and clammy.

They carried a stretcher between them. A stretcher with a small form resting on top, her delicate features still visible even with the white sheet that covered her from head to toe.

"Lucy."

Faunella's world narrowed to a pinprick - all the things she never got to show Lucy, all the things she should have said. She would never hear her voice again or be able to laugh with her. All of that was over, never to be done again.

She fell to her knees, a keening wail starting to rise in pitch and volume from the depth of her soul. A screaming howl joined her as Rafi, feeling her anguish, shared in her pain. As Faunella poured out her despair, she cried out Lucy's name over and over, holding on to her friend whose presence she would never enjoy again. Unable to stay a minute longer and with nothing to keep her here, Faunella turned, sprinting away as fast as the wind could carry her, leaving a small piece of her heart in the back of the ambulance with Lucy.

CHAPTER FORTY FIVE
AMON

"I DON'T KNOW WHAT'S wrong with Fawn. She hasn't been the same for well over a week now. She never goes to The Edge and barely leaves her tree."

"Not to mention she's worn the same clothes for all of that time as well."

Amon and Huxley walked along the forest path, making their daily visit to see Fawn. Since she had suddenly had a major change in personality, the Fae had made it their mission to check in on her each day, sometimes twice a day.

Amon was at a loss. He felt personally responsible for Fawn, and up until last week, he had no reason to worry about her state of being. But all of a sudden, that changed. He peered down at the jumble of berries he had collected for her, hoping the tasty morsels would be enough to entice her to eat. He was almost ready to allow Huxley to go past The Edge and find her some chocolate - anything to put the life back into her eyes.

"I can't get up into her tree, but if she doesn't want to leave again, then I think you should forcibly get her. It's not right for her to never leave her room. And, well...I miss her."

"We all miss her, Hux, even those of us who can see her. We haven't seen our Fawn, not really—only the shell of who she is." He shook his leafy head, feeling a tightness prick behind his wooden eyes. "I'm beginning to think something really bad happened to her, but she won't talk about it. The most any of us have been able to get out of her is that she wants to be alone...that she *is* alone."

Huxley cleared his throat, his gruff voice sounding even more thick as they discussed the girl who meant so much to them.

"I'm not afraid to admit that I'm worried, real worried. Can't you—" He mimed placing his hands on his forehead. "—you know, use your powers and pull her memories?"

Amon walked along in silence, not wanting to admit that he had considered that very thing many times. But every time he reached forward to do so, Fawn had looked up at him with red-rimmed eyes, their hollowness tearing his heart in two, and said, *"Don't do that."* The way she curled up afterward, as if to safeguard her memories, was the only reason Amon hadn't broken her trust and peered inside her past.

"I won't do that to her. She's been through something, and I don't want to do anything that could make her retreat even further from us."

Huxley huffed, not even trying to argue with him.

At the base of Fawn's tree, Amon looked up at the structure that was almost fully hidden by the thick branches.

"Has Violetta already been here today?" He glanced down at Huxley, sure that the Fae would know this information.

"Yes, she came earlier. She told me that the water she had left yesterday hadn't been touched."

Amon shook his head, his body filling with a restless energy. If only he could change things. If only he could make Fawn eat and drink.

"Okay, I'm going up."

A hand on his trunk stopped him. He looked down into Huxley's earnest face.

"Please, bring her down. I can't help her if I can't see her."

Huxley's feelings mirrored his own, and he nodded grimly. Stretching his limbs up high, he concentrated on thickening his trunk, gaining height with each second that passed. Within a few minutes, he was high above the forest floor, his branches brushing the outside of Fawn's home. He latched onto the structure and retracted his legs, letting his roots come up to meet the rest of his body. While he could get up to the treetop home, he was too big to fit into the dwelling, so he was only able to interact with Fawn through the multiple windows dotted throughout the walls.

A chirping call broke his attention from the structure. Beebe came flying out from a gap in the woven wood, circling around in front of his face, demanding his attention.

"I know. I know," he spoke to the bird. "We're all worried about her."

He pulled back the floral curtain and peered into the murky room. There was only silence coming from inside. A musty smell wafted out, making him wrinkle his nose against the offensive odor. His heart sank within his wide trunk. Fawn was facing away, lying curled up on her bed, unchanged since he saw her yesterday.

"Fawn?"

A pair of black eyes popped up from the hollow of Fawn's body. Rafi let out a whine, resting his muzzle back down on top of her hip. Fawn didn't answer, only curling in tighter, her back and tangled red hair the only things he could see. Instead of getting better, she seemed to be getting worse. Huxley was right; they needed to intervene. Just supporting her low mood wasn't enough anymore. Stealing his resolve, Amon hardened his heart, determined not to let Fawn sway him from his decision.

"Fawn," he said in a stronger voice, putting a firmness in his tone that he didn't feel. "It's time to get up. You need to get outside, bathe, and have something to eat and drink."

No motion from the bed.

"Right, that's it!"

He snaked several branches through the window, the smooth limbs stretching out towards Fawn's still form. Rafi leaped up in alarm, jumping off the bed to avoid the animated branches. However, instead of running away like he usually would when the Fae got too close, he stayed beside the bed, sinking low onto his stomach.

Amon prepared himself for resistance when his limbs reached Fawn, scooping her up, blankets and all in one quick motion. To his dismay, her limp form stayed curled up, not even caring that her body was being pulled back out into the fresh air of the forest.

"I've got you, sweetheart. It's going to be alright."

The situation was worse than he thought. The girl in his arms seemed to be slipping away as if life no longer held any pull. Tears pricked at the back of his eyes, his throat catching as he murmured soothing words to her while climbing carefully down the tree.

Huxley cursed under his breath when Amon reached the ground, his gray face paling as he took in Fawn's despondent form.

"You never told me she was this bad."

Amon hugged Fawn tighter to his chest, Huxley's words making the situation even more real.

"She's gotten worse since yesterday. I don't know what to do."

His voice caught, drawing a compassionate look from his friend as he tried to regain his composure. He began to walk away, taking several long steps towards the grotto when a sharp bark stopped him in his tracks.

The fox.

"I've got him."

Huxley strode over to the pulley system Fawn had built and quickly lowered the basket, bringing Rafi safely to the ground. With growing alarm, Amon watched as Rafi made a beeline for him, coming as close as possible to where he stood holding Fawn, his concern for her overriding all his usual trepidation of the otherworldly Fae.

"That's worrying," said Huxley, echoing his thoughts.

"Let's just get to the others. Maybe one of them will know what to do."

The two of them, followed by Rafi and Beebe, made their way quickly to the grotto. Amon glanced down at Fawn often, feeling sick at the vacant look in her eyes. They walked into the clearing, and Huxley broke away from Amon, disappearing into the cave.

"She's out of her tree. Amon's got her, but she's not looking good."

Huxley's low voice came back to him, as well as the distressed murmurs from the Fae residing inside. He lowered himself to the ground, not willing to release his hold on Fawn as Huxley led the Fae out into the daylight. Gently stroking the hair off her pale face, he couldn't help but think back to when she had first come into their lives as the small stumbling toddler who had so quickly wrapped them all around her little finger. Staying focused on Fawn, he felt more than saw the Fae gather around them both. Their silent comradery gave Amon a warm sense of peace. He wasn't alone, and he didn't have to come up with a solution by himself.

"It feels as if she has given up on living." Lothian's deep gravelly voice cut through the silence. "If you will not take her memories, Amon, then we must only assume what has caused this depression."

"She had been taking my water nearly every day for years now, but now it seems as if she will not drink. I don't imagine that she's ill."

Soft voices of agreement spread throughout the group, but Violetta's words had triggered something in Amon—something long repressed within his mind.

"Not an illness of the body," he whispered, turning Fawn's head gently in his wooden hands, needing to see into her bleak face. "But an illness of the mind, an injury caused only by the deepest of losses."

He looked into her blue eyes, allowing himself to feel the deep-cutting pain of his past, letting the shuddering anguish wash over him.

"Have you lost someone, my Fawn? Have you lost a piece of your heart?"

She flinched, her eyes glossing over with the bright sheen of tears. Audible gasps rang out among the gathered Fae.

"It's true."

"How can this be?

"Who could it have been?"

The Fae drew back, talking quietly amongst themselves as they tried to unravel what they now knew to be true. Fawn tried to turn her head away, clenching her eyes shut and uttering one breathless sob. A matching whimper from his side caught his attention. Rafi was inching closer, trying to get to a place where he could touch Fawn.

"It's okay."

The words were meant to reassure the animal and the young woman in his arms.

"That's enough," barked Huxley, the venom in his voice had the surprised Fae all quieting down, looking at Fawn's pained face in realization.

"Amon?"

He looked up into the sympathetic face of Lothian, knowing what the Fae was going to say before he said it.

"She needs to know she's not alone. One can learn to grow with pain, time eventually lessening the sting." Lothian paused, taking a steady breath. "I think you can show her that—if you are willing."

Amon's chest tightened uncomfortably, the painful past relegated to a small quiet part of him suddenly bursting at his time wrought confines. The long years had been crucial to his recovery, the journey to Earth an escape from the constant reminder of what he had lost. His burning eyes looked down at Fawn, taking in the face of the young female that he had helped raise.

I can feel the pain for her.

Steeling his resolve and drawing comfort from the presence of the nine Fae who had become something of a family, he reached out, softly placing his hand above Fawn's pale brow, and made the connection.

He arrived home, eagerness coating his steps. The day had been long, and he knew Sabine, his new wife, would be waiting for him. Pushing open the freshly painted blue door to his home, he called out a light greeting.

"Sabine, I'm home."

Striding through the dwelling, he headed into the kitchen where the soft lilting voice of the most beautiful Fae in the world could be heard. Pausing to lean against the door frame, he watched her for a moment, a heady rush of love and longing burning through him as her slender hips swayed in time with her melody.

"I know you're there, Amon," she laughed. "Are you going to stare at me all day, or are you going to come over here and give me the kiss I've been dreaming of since you left this morning?"

She turned around, her blue eyes twinkling with mischief.

His heart jolted in his chest, straining to escape from the confines of his ribs. Launching himself forward with breathtaking speed, he scooped her up, twirling her around the room as peals of laughter rang out, making him grin with warm pleasure.

He loved her laugh.

"Amon! Amon, put me down," she giggled out, her smooth hands resting lightly on his forearms. "I'm too dizzy."

He stopped spinning but didn't release her, relishing the feel of her warm body in his arms. She stared up at him expectantly, her tongue running over the soft swell of her upper lip. Giving in to what they both wanted, he lowered his head to hers, kissing her soundly until all he could feel was her.

Moving along, Amon skipped through the multitude of happy moments that he had with Sabine. The longing for those times almost overwhelmed him. Throat tight, he chose another of his most precious memories, a time he had kept close to his heart, not wanting to share the private moment with anyone else.

Sabine giggled, nuzzling into his ribs from under the blanket. He couldn't help the broad smile that pulled at his mouth. Forcing a playful sternness into his voice, he tickled at the shape of her body wriggling under the soft draping sheet.

"Get out of there, you wild thing. Come back up here so I can see your beautiful face."

She wriggled down further, her sharp little teeth nipping at the skin covering his ribs.

"Ahh," he yelped, throwing up the sheet and scooting down to rescue himself from any more of her playful teasing. The sheet settled back down, covering both of their heads and highlighting the rosy glow on Sabine's face. They lay face to face, Sabine running the tip of her nose against his, her breath hot against his mouth. Not daring to blink lest he break the enchantment they were under, he kept his eyes locked onto hers, gazing deep within their shining depths. The fluttering of a thousand butterflies teased at his stomach, making their way throughout his chest and into his throat. His love was unbearable, turning his body into a burning ember that set each nerve in his body alight. Only one person could ease the fire, and that was the very Fae who cultivated the first spark every day.

"I have something to tell you."

Her voice shook with excitement, lips pursing together as if to stop herself from saying more.

Amon wrapped his arms around her lower back, drawing her even closer to his body.

"And what's this little secret you have?" he asked, playing along with her teasing mood.

"We're going to have a baby."

Her whispered words washed over him, blanketing his mind with stunned disbelief.

"What?"

He drew back slightly, scanning her face for any sign that she might be lying, but all traces of teasing were gone. The smile on her face lit her up from the inside out, her joy contagious, sending his pulse skyrocketing as he processed her words.

"A baby? We're going to have a baby?

"Yes! I couldn't believe it when I found out. It happened so soon, we've only been married for a few months." She closed her eyes, snuggling back

against his face. "The fates have been kind. Can you imagine?" She sighed. "A sweet little baby, all of our own."

Her voice tapered off into quiet contentment, her pleasure making her hum with feeling. Amon's mind wasn't so still; he couldn't get the picture of a small pink child out of his head. His love swelled, stretching out to cover the unnamed child. He hoped it would be a girl, a sweet beautiful girl with eyes as blue as a summer sky.

Amon groaned, pulling his hand away from Fawn's head, the visions too painful to relive.

"Clara," he choked out, a wail of misery spewing forth from his mouth.

A firm hand clasped his shoulder, squeezing tightly as he wept. Another hand joined it, and then another. The Fae bunched closer, lending their support as he battled with the waves of grief that wracked his body.

The soft warmth of skin touched his face, sending his eyes flying open. Fawn was gazing up at him, her wide eyes shining—her eyes so much like Sabine's. The pain in her face mirrored his own, and her lips quivered as she took a shuddering breath.

"They died?"

Her voice was croaky with disuse. But, to Amon, it was the most beautiful voice in the world.

"Yes, my Fawn. I lost them both."

The words were strained, but easier to say rather than to delve into the most painful memory of all. The worst day of his life. He could still feel the heat of the fire, hear the cracking and popping of wood as his home burned down, taking the two loves of his life away from him forever. His beautiful Sabine and his most precious Clara, her sweet life snuffed out before she was even two months old.

"This pain is the worst pain you will ever experience, but you can't let it turn you away from the living. You are not alone, little one. We are all here with you. Let us take your pain and help you shoulder the burden."

She reached up, wrapping her arms around his trunk and holding on tight. Her body shook with sobs as she released the anguish that had been so painful she would rather have slipped away than face. Erwin pulled himself up to wrap around her from behind, cocooning her in a layer of warmth and love. As Fawn let her grief play out, Amon felt his own pain ease its sting. The trauma from that time retracted back to its rightful place, no longer pushed away never to think of again. In some small way, the death of his wife and daughter was perhaps the very thing that had saved Fawn from letting her own grief wash her away.

He stroked the back of her head, whispering words of love as she started on her path to healing, but Amon knew this loss would forever leave its mark.

CHAPTER FORTY SIX
FAUNELLA

WINTER WAS BEGINNING TO make its presence known, darkening the forest with its early chill. The cold suited Faunella just fine. Her heart was still raw with the agony of loss, and she relished every hint of the biting cold as it took her attention from the greater wound in her soul.

She let out a sigh. The Fae had been beyond supportive, lavishing her with kindness and care for weeks. Even after Faunella had revealed that she had been leaving the forest for years now, they had done nothing more than scoop her into their arms and murmur with concern, loving her—smothering her.

Today, the sun was unusually warm, one last-ditch effort at warming the land before winter had it firmly in its grasp. The high heat spilled out over the field, unhampered by the stillness in the air. Faunella hugged her knees to her chest and raised her face to the light, eyes closed as she enjoyed the quiet.

Like always, a niggling thought wormed its way into her mind, plaguing her with the question of 'What if?'

What if she had met Lucy sooner? Could she have helped banish the illness before it garnered roots? Or, what if she had shared her secret with the Fae? Maybe they could have done something. Too afraid that the answers might have been yes, Faunella kept her questions to herself, blaming herself for the loss of her only friend.

She flashed open her eyes and thrust her fist into the ground with a huff.

"If only I had been stronger, tried harder to wield my magic."

Rafi's ears pricked up, and he let out a chittering bark, scooching forward on his belly to rub up against her legs.

"Oh, Rafi," she stroked her hand over his thickening coat. "I'm not upset with you." Her gaze lifted, and she focused on the distant mountains while trying to stop the hot burn of tears. "I'm upset with myself."

Raising her other hand, Faunella harnessed her energy and flicked her fingers, willing the air to snake a path through the long grass. Power flowed from her easily, blowing the stalks to the side. She sighed and let her hand fall. The elemental magic finally felt like a part of her, which should have made her happy. But although it had helped Lucy, it hadn't saved her.

Rafi jumped to his feet and turned his nose to the forest behind Faunella. A tug on the fluttering tether in her chest a moment later made her understand why.

Beebe.

Despite herself, she smiled. Lucy was gone, but she still had her two animal friends with her. Rafi disappeared into the undergrowth, presumably to meet up with the small bird. Faunella shook her curls and let out a groan. Even after all this time, the sly fox still delighted in toying with Beebe.

"Rafi," she hissed, turning to follow. "Leave Beebe alone. She'll come to us."

The delighted sparkle that pulsed behind her rips, followed by an indignant burst, stopped Faunella in her tracks.

My air couldn't save Lucy, but it's not the only power I have.

She sank back to the ground, the animals forgotten. Over the years, she had focused so much on mastering her explosive elemental power that she hadn't ever considered what else her affinity with animals could do. It was too late for Lucy, but what if someone else needed her in the future? What if there was something she could do next time? Excitement burned through her. After all their smothering, where were the Fae when she needed them?

Faunella leapt to her feet, feeling more alive than she had in weeks. She needed to find Violetta and ask her. In her haste, she tripped over Rafi, who had just trotted back into the clearing. Faunella shrieked and pinwheeled her arms, trying to stay upright. She swiveled on one foot for half a second before pitching headfirst into Violetta's watery arms.

"Violetta," she gasped, blinking the water from her eyes. "I was just coming to look for you."

"For me?" Violetta beamed, the smile transforming her from beautiful to radiant. *"Well, aren't I the lucky one."*

"You're not the only lucky one," huffed Huxley, his eyes moving from Faunella's wet face to Violetta's chest where it had been pressed moments before.

Faunella followed his gaze, her confusion melting away when she deciphered his words. She was lucky to have fallen face first into Violetta's body. If Huxley had emerged through the trees first, she could have ended up with a split lip.

Violetta carried on with no more than a sidelong glance at Huxley, a translucent brow arched high. She gently tucked an errant curl behind Faunella's ear. *"So, why were you looking for me?"* Her eyes softened. *"I've missed seeing that excitement in your face."*

Faunella brightened, her enthusiasm renewed.

"I want to know if you can teach me more about my magic."

"Of course!" Violetta clasped her hands in front of her, practically brimming with joy. *"There are some defensive maneuvers I thought we could try. After that, we could work on your offense."* Her brow shot down and her eyes turned inwards. *"Actually, Huxley, maybe I should start with offense. What do you think?"* She turned to him, ignoring Faunella entirely. *"I mean, I feel like defense is the best way to protect yourself."*

"No."

They both turned to look at her, familiar worry on their faces. Faunella gave them both a small smile, letting them know that for once they didn't have to.

"You misunderstood me. I wasn't asking about my air magic. I want to know what else I can do with the powers I have with animals." She lowered her head and looked at them through her lashes. "I want to see if I can help people."

Huxley looked to Violetta, but the water Fae just smiled sadly. *"There was nothing you could do for your little human, Fawn. Sometimes, these things just happen."*

Unwilling to be dissuaded, Faunella pressed on. Convinced that if she could just explain herself, Violetta would be willing to help her.

"But I've been able to connect with animals for far longer, and we've never explored that." She tugged on her tether with Beebe and asked the bird to come and sit on her outstretched finger. "Surely, there is more that I could learn." An idea scratched the corner of her mind. The power connected her to animals, drawing them to her, so why not humans as well? "What if instead of just animals, this power could work with all creatures, including humans?"

"Let me stop you there. I love your heart and the way you want to help others. But..." She looked at Huxley, her face pinched with concern. *"This animal power is nothing compared to your gift with air."* Placing her hands on Faunella's shoulders, she turned her and marched the two of them back into the field. *"The best way you can help our people is to master your power and protect yourself."*

Faunella let herself be guided, despite the sense that Violetta was wrong. She nibbled on her lower lip, debating whether she should push this train of thought.

But Violetta seems so sure.

Huxley ambled up beside her and arched his brow, grinning to put her at ease. *"Come on, Fawn. Let's see what you've got. We've got a kingdom to take back."*

Faunella's mouth twisted. Maybe they were right. Her elemental power was the thing that would help take back the throne from Petrov, the Fae they all seemed so worried about. Resigned, she sent Beebe back to wait in the tree line beside Rafi and readied herself for another lesson.

"So what are we working on?"

Violetta pursed her lips, then nodded sharply.

"Yes, defense."

She placed her hand in the center of Faunella's chest, directly above the curve of her breasts. Faunella breathed in deeply, then closed her eyes, centering herself in the swirling vortex that was her air power. The lightness filled her, now soothing rather than something to fear. It was a part of who she was.

Before she gave her attention back to Violetta, she took a moment to delve deeper, to search for the thing that gave her the ability to relate to animals, the magic that had moved beyond her control and bonded her to both Beebe and Rafi.

The familiar ether parted, shifting around while she searched. There was her bright tether to Beebe, and right next to it shone the warm earthy tie to the fox. But where was her other magic?

Faunella felt her brow furrow, but she pushed further, determined to find that elusive power.

"Faunella, what are you doing? Just center yourself, and we can begin."
Just a second more.

The strain was real. She could feel it all around her; only when she tried to look, to grasp it, it wasn't there. With one final effort, she scanned the house of her power, and as her attention passed the two animal connections, she could almost swear she felt the shadow of a third.

"Darn." She withdrew in a rush and came back to the present, disappointed with herself and breathing heavily.

"Are you okay?" Violetta looked on with concern. *"We don't have to train today if you're not up to it. You already have an impressive grasp on*

your magic, especially considering the fact that as a low fae, you shouldn't have any."

"No," she took a breath and forced a smile. "No, I'm ready."

"Good." Violetta shook out her hair and backed away, shooting a toothy smile to Huxley. *"Now I want you to work on stopping objects in place. Huxley, can you?"*

Huxley tore his eyes off her and zeroed in on Faunella. With a flick of his fingers, he launched a stone from his hand, flinging it directly at her face.

Faunella ducked down and threw up her hands instinctively. Power rushed from her body and flung the stone back. Huxley dodged to the side, narrowly avoiding getting hit.

He grinned, rolling several new stones over his palm as he readied himself to launch more projectiles.

"Wait. Huxley, hold it a moment."

Faunella straightened up and gave Violetta a questioning look. She thought she had deflected that well and had been preparing to protect herself from the dozens that were sure to come.

"Stop the rocks in place," she emphasized the last word, in case her meaning got lost in translation. *"Flinging them away works to protect yourself, but what if there are people around that could be hurt? No. You need to stop the rocks and hold them in one place. That way you can be sure to keep yourself and anyone around you safe."*

Heart sinking, Faunella turned her head and found the animals behind her. She understood Violetta's meaning perfectly. It wasn't enough to protect herself. She needed to think of others.

"Okay, let's try again."

Blowing out a breath and squaring her shoulders, Faunella concentrated on the air around her, feeling the way it moved between her and Huxley. When she thought she was ready, she gave him a nod.

The rock flew from his hand, pushing through the air between them. Faunella tried desperately to stop it, to thicken the air around it and hold it in place. Like she had once before—with Lucy.

Her concentration broke, either because of the speed of the rock or the pang of memories. Regardless, the sharp stab of pain under her left eye had her recoiling in shock.

"Fawn, are you alright?"

Huxley rushed forward, anxiety written in both his words and his actions. Faunella held out her hand to still him, gingerly dabbing at the cut on her cheekbone.

"I'm fine. It just got away from me that time."

Violetta glided forward and pulled her hand from the wound. *"It's deep,"* she murmured. *"We can stop and try again another day."*

"No, I want to keep going. I know I can do this."

Concern pulled on the two strings behind her ribs, and Faunella looked back to where Beebe and Rafi stood, both looking ready to rush to her side.

I'm really okay, she told them. If this skill could help keep them and others safe, then she would master it, no matter any injuries she had to suffer along the way.

"Violetta, please." Faunella gestured to her face, then sighed in relief when the healing tingle of water smoothed over her cheek. "Thank you."

Faunella stepped away and widened her stance, beckoning Huxley to continue with a wriggle of her fingers. "Come on, Hux. I can take it."

Huxley's severe face frowned at her, but he obliged, tossing a stone weakly towards her at hip height.

"Is that all you've got?" she teased, attempting to lighten the rock's mood.

"That's all you're going to get," he replied, eyes falling to the still healing cut on her face. Faunella let a sigh escape her, and she readied her magic. That would have to be enough—for now.

It took several more weeks of being carefully coddled by the Fae before Faunella felt ready to venture to The Edge again. She had thrown herself into growing her magic, but the yearning for human connection was a siren call she couldn't ignore. She managed to push aside the sensation for the next few days, but all that did was grow that feeling of missing something, leaving her dissatisfied with her simple life—never able to interact with the people who lived just out of reach.

"Don't you ever miss the friends and family you had in Amaranth?"

She directed the question to Erwin as they lay on the floor of her treehouse, the day too cold to go outside.

"I miss my Fae body." He ran his small hands over the springy moss that made up his form. *"This one just isn't the same. But as for my friends and family? Well, I didn't leave any family behind. They died long before I left to come to Earth."*

"Oh." Faunella's face heated with embarrassment. She had known Erwin her whole life and had never once asked him about his life. "I'm really sorry. I had no idea."

"It's okay. It was a long time ago." His lips curved. *"And I had my friends. Huxley found me when I was just a child. He looked out for me and pretty much raised me, so I didn't leave any friends behind either. I came here to Earth with them."*

Faunella grasped his hand, not knowing what to say in response. Erwin's life followed a similar path to her own. Though she had no real memories of how she came to be on Earth, she thought her parents were alive. But even if they were, they might as well be dead.

"I don't know how much longer I can stay here," she said instead, her voice small.

Erwin propped himself up on his arm to look down at her, his kind face betraying his worry. Faunella bit her lip, feeling guilty for putting that on her sweet friend.

"I know you've been feeling stuck lately, stuck and alone. But, I promise you that it won't be forever. Soon enough, everything will change. You just need to be patient."

Later that night when she was alone, curled up under her warm blankets, she ran his words over in her mind.

I've been as patient as I can. If I can't go back to Amaranth till I'm older, then I'll have to make my place in this world.

Decision made, Faunella rolled over, her mouth sporting a sleepy smile.

Tomorrow, she would go out and find herself a friend.

CHAPTER FORTY SEVEN
DERICK

THE ITCHING ON HIS arm was getting worse. Derick growled deep within his throat, his fingers twitching as he resisted scratching at the fresh tattoo inked on his skin.

I'd rather take a stab to the gut than deal with this goddamn itching!

He leapt to his feet and strode across his small room, snatching his jacket from where he flung it the night before. An icy breeze blew against the back of his neck, sending a shiver down his spine. He still hadn't fixed the wall. He opened his drawers and pulled on a hoodie while glancing between the obvious hole and the crate peeking out from under his bed. The weather was only going to get colder, and he knew from previous winters just how frigid the nights could get. The smart thing would be to fix the wall. He shrugged his leather jacket over the hoodie, immediately relaxing into the warmth.

Tomorrow. I'll fix it tomorrow.

He snatched up his novel from its hiding place in the crate and stuffed it in the hoodie pocket, conveniently forgetting that he had been promising himself that he would fix up his room for the past three years. He had discovered a small coffee shop in one of the nicer suburbs circling Northaven. So, rather than hide away in his drafty room with his ears pricked for intrusion, Derick found himself retreating to the soothing clink and whir of the cafe.

Locking his door behind him, he thundered down the stairs, stomach tight. It was always a risk, leaving the warehouse. He kept his eyes locked on the front door as he counted down each step to freedom.

Six. Five. Four. Three.

A smile started to pull at his lips. The book burned a hole in his pocket, just begging to be read. He could feel the taste of the coffee on his tongue, and nobody interrupted him when he had his nose stuck in the pages.

Two. On—

"Ah, Derick, there you are."

He skidded to a halt, his hand tightening on the cold handle.

Motherfu—

He glanced over his shoulder, nodding respectfully at Shaun. "Shaun." He pointedly avoided looking at Jarred, but Derick couldn't help but register the almost frenzied excitement on his washed-out face.

"I'm glad I caught you." The older man came up behind him, clapping his arm paternally over his shoulder. "I have another little job for you. And for this one, I want you to take your time on it."

Derick's blood ran cold. He swallowed back the rush of saliva that filled his mouth, forcing his body to relax.

"No problem. Just tell me where and when."

Shaun filled him in, his voice low. All the while, Jarred fidgeted beside them, his usually sour expression nowhere to be seen. Something didn't sit well with the situation. A thin thread of worry tugged at the back of his mind, momentarily taking his attention from the dread of Shaun's task.

"When you're done, meet me at The Locker. I want to discuss some of these ideas you had regarding the trajectory The Vipers are taking."

His eyebrows raised up. He had talked to Shaun weeks ago and was under the impression that his suggestions had all been ignored. His carefully formulated plans were all centered around ways they could make money while minimizing the men's risks. There had been no need to mention that his ideas were spawned by the desire to avoid hurting the innocent people usually destroyed by their actions.

He cleared his throat and zipped up his jacket. "Sounds good."

Jarred leaned against the wall, anticipation glinting in his eyes. His lips peeled open, teeth flashing. "Did you hear—" Shaun's arm shot out and hit the front of Jarred's chest, effectively cutting off what he was about to say. He drilled the younger man with his stare, a warning of some sort. Derick frowned at the display. Something was definitely going on. Not wanting to get involved and eager to get his dirty business over with, he nodded again at Shaun and slipped quickly out into the frigid day.

All the pleasure had been sucked from the day. Derick pulled up in front of The Green Locker, the neon sign flickering intermittently in the dimming light. He removed his helmet, rubbing at the pulsing pain behind his eyes. He didn't want to be here in the slightest.

Shaun's job had been bad—beyond bad. He could still feel bones crack under the force of his hands and taste the terror that spread through the room. One man had fought back, pulling out a wicked looking knife to protect himself, so Derick had no choice but to take it from him. A shaking began in his hands, highlighting his weakness. Derick clenched them into fists, trying to expel the feel of the cold steel on his palm.

Stop thinking about it!

Shaking off the thoughts, he blew out a breath and strode through the door, ignoring the weight pressing heavily on his shoulders.

He spotted Shaun easily. The man lounged in a booth near the back, certain of his place in the world.

Just get this over with, and then you can leave.

He gave Jarred and his friends a wide berth, not able to deal with their shit after the day he just had. They sprawled out at the bar, their slurred voices loud and obnoxious. Derick screwed up his nose. They were all idiots.

"It's done?" Shaun had several empty bottles and glasses around him, but the look he gave Derick was clear and direct.

"It's done," he replied, sliding into the faded seat across from him.

"Good, good." Shaun's face broke out into a wide grin, and he lifted his hand to signal the barman. "Let's celebrate."

Derick's chest tightened, his body deflating. He was really hoping this meeting would be short and sweet, but no one said no to Shaun.

Jack brought over two beers, quickly scooping up the empties and disappearing back behind the bar. Shaun sculled back his brew, not seeming to mind Derick's silence.

Derick sat ramrod straight, his head pounding from the loud base. He counted down the seconds until Shaun slouched back in his seat, studying him with a thoughtful expression.

This was it. Shaun was finally going to take one of his suggestions. Hope bloomed under his skin. Maybe this day wouldn't be a total waste.

"So, these ideas..." Shaun leaned forward, eyes narrowing. "I don't know what to tell you, Derick."

Derick leaned his forearms onto the table, matching Shaun's position. The small thread of hope he had been fortifying withered away to nothing, leaving him all out of sorts with nothing but a rising anger and a tenuous grip on his control.

"I think you should just go ahead and say it."

"Watch your tone, boy." Shaun jerked back, the surprise in his eyes, followed almost instantly by anger. "Don't you go around forgetting who owns you." He took another swig of his drink, and Derick took the opportunity to compose himself, pushing down the rush of true feelings that had risen to the surface. He clenched his fists under the table but bowed his head deferentially to Shaun.

"I'm sorry. I forgot myself."

Mollified by his apology, Shaun gave a little grunt, then slid out of the booth and towered over Derick's seated position.

"Your ideas were fine. They just lacked balls." He gave a snorting laugh. "You're good with the men, but any more of your pussy suggestions, and I'll start to question if you're man enough to be here." He adjusted his pants. "Now, I've got to piss. Maybe think up a job that doesn't make you look like a faggot while I'm gone."

Derick forced a dry chuckle, grinding his teeth together to stop himself from screaming out loud. He didn't even get a minute to himself before Jarred appeared, blocking him in his seat.

"How does it feel to be an orphan?"

"What the fuck are you talking about?" He kept his eyes on the empty seat in front of him. His patience was just about at its limit, and he knew if he took one look at Jarred's smarmy face, he would start throwing punches. He grasped his drink to give him something to do with his hands and lifted it to his lips.

"Dad didn't tell you?" He chuckled. "Frank's dead. Got shanked by his cellmate."

Derick froze, his body swallowing the beer on autopilot even as it turned sour on his tongue.

Dad's dead?

He couldn't move, couldn't think. He had considered Frank dead to him for years now, but now that it was reality, he didn't know how to feel.

"Oh, whoops, that's right." Jarred playfully smacked his hand to his head and smirked. "He told me not to tell you."

Derick's drink thudded back to the table, his ears ringing with Jarred's laughter as he walked back to his friends. Why wouldn't Shaun want him to know? When did this even happen? Energy began to build up in his core. His hands clenched open and shut as he tried, unsuccessfully, to still the pressure.

Why did he tell Jarred?

He turned to face the bar, considering walking over there and pummeling the information out of the wiry man, but Jarred's attention was taken. His face sported a lavish grin as he stared through the smoke-filled room. Derick twisted to see what he was looking at, catching a brief glimpse of bright auburn hair.

The young woman peeked in past the door. Pink lips popped open, and, even across the room, Derick could see her eyes widen. She pulled back, the door swinging shut behind her and hiding her from view. It was only a second, but it had the cogs in his mind whirring. He sat back against his seat, rolling his drink from hand to hand as a warm pressure built up under his skin.

It had been years since he had seen the girl with the red hair. His brows furrowed, the pain from this shit storm of a day forgotten.

It probably isn't even the same girl. He scratched his head, thinking hard. *I don't even know if the girl who helped Sandra get away was the same as the one from the crash.*

"Fuck." Chugging back his drink, he glanced back across the room just in time to see Jarred and the three other men exit the bar. Derick's heart rate picked up.

"It's probably three different people."

"What was that?"

Shaun slid back opposite him, one eyebrow cocked as he waited for an answer.

"Nothing. It's nothing." He forced himself to relax, but couldn't stop glancing at the door. He didn't know how, but he had this feeling, this certainty. The girl—the young woman who kept appearing in his life— just made her third appearance.

And Jarred had gone after her.

Panic seized him. Lunging out of the booth, he dropped some money on the table, ignoring Shaun's scowl. "I've got to go!" He shoved past men and women with no care for their muttered oaths or nasty looks.

All he cared about was getting outside and stopping Jarred from doing whatever had formed in his mind when he laid eyes on the girl from the forest.

CHAPTER FORTY EIGHT
FAUNELLA

IT WAS A CHALLENGE to convince Beebe and Rafi to let her go alone. They could sense the thick excitement that churned around her stomach, and both of them were anxious.

"I have to do this on my own," she told them while putting on the finishing touches of her outfit for the day. "I'll be back as soon as I've made a friend. I've done it once, so I can do it again." She stepped back, smoothing her hands down her front. "There, all done."

She had chosen an outfit Lucy complimented her on many times. She wore a warm green pair of tight fitting pants with a good amount of stretch and her favorite leaf dress over top, the autumn colors a striking contrast against the green.

She hadn't been too sure about the dress initially, but after spending the morning going through all of her clothes, she decided it was her best option. While it wasn't what the humans would wear, it was Lucy's favorite, and she wouldn't have lied about that, so it must be good.

"I'll be back by sundown."

She held out her hands for Beebe to land in, pressing her lips to the soft feathers on the bird's head. She released her with a smile, turning around to scoop up Rafi in a squeezing embrace.

"Be good," she whispered into his fur, her mouth stretching into a wide smile as a nervous excitement prickled under her skin. Lowering

346

the fox, she swung out of the treehouse and headed through the forest to Northaven.

"I spent too much time getting ready."

She glanced up at the deepening sky, hesitating at the forest's edge.

Maybe I should start fresh tomorrow.

Biting her lip, she considered her options, eyeing the barren street stretching out in front of her. Then, deciding not to waste the trip, she squared her shoulders and took a deep breath, stepping out from beyond The Edge and walking along the asphalt street.

I'll just go a little way, and if I can't find anyone, I'll turn back.

The road felt rough under her bare feet, the texture cold and strange. Unable to stand the jarring sensation for long, she veered her steps, coming to walk along the grassy verge lining the street. The houses looked different from this perspective, and Faunella studied the structures with wide eyes as she passed them by. Each house was the same as the next one, and after a considerable distance, she stopped looking at them, the similar buildings holding no more wonder.

A car passed her, slowing slightly before speeding off. Faunella felt her heart jump. She had been seen, but they had done nothing at all. Feeling emboldened, she quickened her pace, arms swinging with each bouncing step.

Where are all the people?

Aside from the occasional car, Faunella hadn't seen a single person. Feeling a rising frustration pulling at her skin, she pushed herself further, determined to meet at least one person today.

As she turned the next corner, her efforts were rewarded. On the pavement, in front of a long metal bench, were five teenage girls.

Faunella stopped still at the sight of them, her mouth growing dry as her heart leapt into her throat. She swallowed, her tongue darting out to moisten her lips.

The girls glanced over, their eyes looking her up and down. Faunella took a step towards them, anxiousness battling with her excitement. Before she could take another step, a high-pitched giggle rang out. One of the group, a narrow-faced girl with hair like the warm bark of an oak, covered her mouth, the motion doing nothing to stop the sound from reaching where Faunella stood.

The other girls joined in, their snickering sounding out of place in the quiet street.

"Look at what she's wearing," the first girl sneered loudly, pointing a finger in Faunella's direction. "I wouldn't be caught dead wearing something as hideous as that."

Faunella's brow wrinkled in confusion. Surely, they couldn't be talking about her. She glanced over her shoulder, briefly wondering if there was someone behind her.

"Ew, and where are her shoes? Maybe she can't afford them."

The laughter picked up, but the sound didn't give her the usual feeling of happiness. Instead, it made her stomach hurt.

They're talking about me.

"What about her hair? I mean, have you ever heard of a hairbrush?"

"Maybe she's homeless?"

"She probably lives under a bridge."

Their voices got louder, the words more venomous. Faunella didn't understand some of what they said, but their tones left a cutting wound in her heart. The back of her eyes prickled, their actions so contrary to what she was expecting. She crossed the road, walking quickly to get as far away from the girls' churlish laughter.

As their laughter faded, Faunella's steps became heavier, her confusion over the girl's reactions making her slow.

Why would they say those things? I didn't even get the chance to say hello.

A car drove past, sending a gust of air blowing past her nose. She looked up as a delicious aroma invaded her senses. Following the scent, she turned another corner, coming parallel to a wide spread of buildings on the opposite side of the road.

Craig's Hardware.

Laundromat.

The Green Locker.

The names were written in large bold letters in front of each building, Faunella could read the words, but she wasn't sure what they signified.

She lifted her nose and sniffed, manipulating the air to blow in at her so she could pinpoint where the mouth-watering smell was coming from.

There.

It was coming from the last door before the building abruptly cut off. She found her feet taking her along the sidewalk, past all the other doors until she was standing outside a wide glass window. The window allowed her to see inside the building where a gray-haired woman was standing behind a low counter. Behind her were several large racks of trays, scattered through with an assortment of large and small items.

With a flick of her fingers, Faunella drew the air towards her from the open door, her lips twitching upwards as the warm sweet smell invaded her nostrils once more. Then, with a few more easy steps, she walked through the door and into the room.

"How can I help you?"

The woman pursed her lips as she waited for an answer. She had deep grooves in her skin that puckered in around her mouth as her lips got thinner and thinner.

Flashing her a hesitant smile, Faunella scanned the shelves, mesmerized by the items they contained. There were large brown rolls and brightly decorated domes that were wrapped in some sort of paper. Large thin disks, that oozed deep red juices that smelt like the berries she loved so much. However, there was one scent that brought back a long-ago memory of a sweet treat that melted in her mouth. Several dark brown wedges sat on a plate on the bench, drawing her in with their rich colors.

Faunella took a step forward and reached out her hand to point at them while flicking her eyes up at the woman.

"What are those?"

The woman's brows drew down together, and she let out a breathy scoff, looking Faunella up and down.

"It's cake. Chocolate cake. Now are you going to buy any or not?"

"Buy?"

Faunella's hands began to feel clammy. She did want some of the cake, but the woman was looking at her strangely, and her body language was not friendly.

"Yes, buy," the woman snapped back, crossing her arms in front of her chest. "We don't do charity here. So, if you have no money, then you need to leave."

Faunella jolted back at the vehemence in the woman's words. She didn't understand what she meant but was afraid to ask any further questions. Heart pounding, she turned to leave, stepping back out into the cold air outside. From behind her, she heard footsteps and glanced back to see what was happening. With a rush of hot air, the door clanged shut behind her, making her flinch at the abrupt sound. The woman glared at her from behind the glass, and with a sinking heart, Faunella lowered her eyes and shuffled back down the pavement.

When her eyes raised back up, she was shocked to see that the sky had begun to turn a burnished gold, the deep blue streaks of night stretching out ominously from overhead. She let out a weary breath, turning to make her way back to the forest, the chill from the impending night making her skin pebble. As she passed the corner of the building, an air-pulsing sound emerged from within the large door. Unable to resist, Faunella pushed open the door, peeking her head into the dimly lit room. She wrinkled her nose in disgust. While the music was interesting, the smell emanating from the room made her eyes water and her nose burn. Scattered within the room were a small handful of people, but when a thin-faced man with dirty yellow hair met her eyes, she recoiled back, allowing the door to swing shut and obscure her from sight. A shudder made its way up her back as she walked quickly away. There was something in the man's eyes that, in that brief moment of contact, had sent a prickle of warning in the back of her mind.

The world around her continued to darken, and more cars drove past her, lighting the way as she journeyed home. She shivered, wrapping her arms around herself to try to keep as much remaining body heat as the plummeting temperatures robbed her of her warmth.

I should never have come out here. What was I thinking?

A light above her flicked on, causing her to look up in alarm.

"Oh."

She chuckled, a blush heating her cheeks briefly. The street lights spread out down the street, lighting the area underneath but making the space between even darker. She looked behind her to see the lights lining the way she had come. Her breath caught in her throat.

Walking through the fluorescent light about two street lights away was a burly man wearing dark clothing. His hands were in his pockets, and he walked slowly along the street behind her.

Something inside Faunella tightened, her eyes widening in alarm. She continued walking, picking up her pace with each turn of her head. Passing the now empty bench, she wished she wasn't alone. The memory of the mocking girls seemed much more preferable than the rising fear she felt each time she looked back and saw the steadily approaching figure of the man.

She took one last look as she turned the final corner that took her on the long stretching road that led to the forest. The man was closer now, but he was no longer walking.

The corner obscured her from view, so she took the opportunity to run. Her heart thumped painfully. Faunella knew she was breaking the rules being out in the human world, but she reasoned that no one would know she was anything other than human since she looked just like them. But if she drew on her powers, making her run like the wind, someone would immediately know she wasn't one of them if they saw her. So, she ran, not using any of her abilities. She just ran steadily, even as something within her cried out for her to reach the safety of the forest as fast as possible.

The darkness of the forest loomed up in front of her, the blackness of the trees warming her heart as she felt safety exuding from the rising forest .

I'm almost there.

Her mouth curved into a smile as she ran towards the final street light placed on the corner of a side street.

A flash of black caught her eye, stepping out from the opposite corner of the street. She skidded to a halt, hands flying up to press against her chest. This man was smaller than the man following her. She glanced behind her, taking note that the burly man was gone, before quickly returning her attention to the man between her and the beckoning forest. It was only a short distance away, the road already growing rougher against her icy feet. Only ten more steps and she would be safe.

She took another step, keeping her eyes pinned on the man. He was just to the side. She could get past him and be on her way. She kept moving forward, coming level with him where he stood. He just watched her with a dark look in his eyes, making no move to talk with her or to come closer.

Faunella passed him, finally drawing her eyes away from his unreadable face. She was safe. She let out a shaky breath, laughing at herself softly. The negative experiences of the day had made her assume the worst, seeing danger behind every tree.

Stepping off the road, her feet sunk into the soft, welcoming grass at the base of the forest. Suddenly, a scuffle had her turning to look back.

"Where are you off to?"

The reedy voice belonged to the man on the corner. He was sauntering towards her, half of his face lit up by the glow of the light.

Faunella's pulse began to pound in time with her frantic breathing. He had a smile on his face, but it wasn't a pleasant grin. It filled her with a cold feeling of dread. She backed away, trying to put as much distance between herself and the man.

So hyper focused on the danger in front of her, she didn't hear it when she was approached from behind. She only realized two more men had crept up on her when a rough hand clamped over her mouth, cutting off any ability to scream.

CHAPTER FORTY NINE
FAUNELLA

"**P**RETTY LITTLE THING LIKE you shouldn't be out here all by herself."

His hot, putrid breath whispered into her ear, the stubble on his jaw scratching the side of her face.

Her vision narrowed, turning her sight to pinpricks as the danger registered in her panicked mind. She wriggled her body, trying to pull away from the man who held her pressed against his body, her eyes flooding with tears even as he muffled her sobs.

"Now, now, none of that. The boys and I are going to take you somewhere where we can get to know one another."

He dragged her backward, giving her the first glimpse of the three men who stood beside him. One of them was the burly man who had been following her. Her wide eyes scanned the night, searching frantically for someone to come along and get her away from the frightening humans. She felt a tight pulse inside of her stomach, a strong thread of concern. She choked against the man's hand.

Rafi, Beebe.

They could feel her. They could feel her fear.

Help! she screamed through the bond, desperate for rescue. *Come find me!*

The man grunted as she struggled against him, tightening his other hand in the delicate leaves of her dress. Faunella flailed her legs, desperately trying to rip herself out of his embrace.

"Hurry up, and get her down."

The terse voice came from one of the other men. She latched her eyes on him, silently pleading with him to stop whatever this was.

"Don't take too long, Jarred. I want a turn with her."

The man holding her, Jarred, spun her around, briefly taking his hand off her mouth. She gulped in a breath, preparing to shout for help, but before she could release the scream building in her throat, his hand clamped back over her mouth.

"None of that. We don't want to spoil the fun before it's begun."

The distant light from the street illuminated him, revealing the gaunt face of the man from the strange-smelling building. She choked back a gasp. He had followed her all this way. Why? He didn't even know her.

He pushed her to the ground, dropping down, his much larger body straddling hers.

"Please let me go," she forced out. "Please—"

His hand clamped down over her mouth again, effectively cutting her off. She reached her hands up, pushing at his arm. Her heart pounded loudly in her ears, her skin cold and clammy.

"Come hold her."

Faunella whimpered against his hand as two of the men came and ripped her arms away, pinning them to the grassy earth, one of them replacing Jarred's hand with his own.

Now that his hands were free, Jarred leaned down over her, trailing them through the leaves that began at her neck. She felt sick, the man's touch leaving her numb and trembling.

"I've never seen anything like this. Hmm, I wonder what's underneath."

He licked his lips, a bright gleam in his eye. Before she could process his words, he gripped the thin garment and ripped it open. Faunella felt the sting of the cold air brush against her exposed breasts. She sobbed, kicking her legs in the dirt to try and dislodge him, pulling frantically against the hold the other men had on her.

Instead of dislodging the man, it only seemed to excite him. His teeth shone white in the moonlight, and his breathing came heavier. He placed his rough hands inside the tear in her dress, pawing at her breasts roughly. Faunella squeezed her eyes shut, tears leaking from the corners.

Please stop, please stop, please stop.

The words repeated inside her mind, desperately pleading for this to all go away.

"Yeah, you like that baby?" He gripped her breast, twisting her nipple between his fingers.

She let out a scream, the sound muffled against the other man's hand. "You want more? I'll give you more." He pulled his knee back, thrusting it between her thighs, spreading them in one powerful push. She felt his hands creep up under her dress, the leaves rustling as he pushed it up. The button of her pants popped, and the zipper tore. Before she knew it, her pants were down, and his hands...she bucked against him, wide-eyed and frantic as his fingers wormed in under her underwear, poking and probing against her most tender parts.

"Yeah, this is going to be good." He ripped her underwear away and then fiddled with his pants, his gaze not leaving her exposed body.

Her body fought and her mind screamed.

No! No! Please no.

She retreated inside of herself, drawing on the power buried deep inside of her. She latched onto it with everything she had, pouring all of her fear and desperation into the warm, swirling ether that until this moment proved to be intangible.

Help.

She sent the plea out, the force of her feelings giving her a physical pulse from the slight hollow at the base of her ribs.

She felt the air shift.

"Uh, Jer?"

Jarred paused his fumblings, looking up in irritation to his companions. Faunella looked up too, her terror lessening as she gazed into the eyes of a large tawny owl.

"What?" he spat out, placing his hands back on Faunella's bare thighs.

The burly man shifted uneasily. "Look up."

Jarred sat back, rotating his head to take in the sight around them. Faunella also took in the scene, her heart nearly bursting with gratitude and relief. Her call had worked. Surrounding them, scattered among the trees, perched dozens of birds. They stood, intently focused on the men, their round eyes never blinking.

Faunella's mouth curved slightly under the perspiring hands of the man, her power completely her own and as pliable as clay.

Now.

The birds attacked. All as one, they launched themselves out of the trees, plummeting down with beaks and talons gleaming like knives. They clawed at the men who attacked her, letting out caws, hoots, and whistling cries as each creature from big to small collided with the men, drawing out a series of pained screams.

Faunella's arms were the first to be released, the men holding her flinging their hands up to protect their faces from the onslaught. Eyes flashing, she grunted, taking the opportunity to harness the air, frustrated with herself that she hadn't thought to do so before. Her other power swelled, and she sent a heavy gust at Jarred, who remained over her, ducking down and swiping at each bird who attacked.

The wind caught him in the stomach, flinging him back and freeing her at last. His frightened scream rose above the calls of the birds, and with his distance from her, the birds doubled down their attack. With a quiet sob, Faunella pulled up her ruined pants and scooted back until she felt rough bark pressing behind her. She had been all but forgotten as the men held up their black jackets, their sole attention on beating off the birds as they tried to get away, all except the one called Jarred. He lay curled up on the ground, ear-splitting screams of terror escaping from his blood-soaked face. The birds continued their assault.

Faunella readied herself to run away, not able to bring herself to care about the pain she had inflicted on the men. She shuddered, pulling her clothes tighter.

They didn't care about my pain.

She eased to her feet, a numbness pulling at her body. Her head continued to ring, and it took a while before she realized that the rumbling wasn't coming from her. A moment after she registered the sound, she and the frantic men were lit up in an arching yellow glow.

She froze, heart beating faster. The sound abruptly cut off, leaving only Jarred's screams behind. Another leather-clad man stepped into the light.

"What in the world?"

It was as if his presence unlocked something. The birds scattered, leaving nothing but a few feathers to indicate they were ever there. The three other men took off running, disappearing into the darkness, leaving her and her abuser alone with the newcomer.

He stepped closer, his focus entirely on her.

Faunella choked back a cry of alarm. This man was even bigger than the others. Silhouetted by the light, he seemed to dwarf her. His height was only tempered by the broad width of his shoulders. Nausea churned hot inside her belly. She took a shaky step behind the tree, trying to calm herself enough to rally her air power again, but instead of continuing on his path to her, he paused. Faunella's breath came in short bursts as the air grew thick with tension. His head tilted away from her, towards where Jarred lay curled up on the earth, then back to her.

He swore violently, leaping forward with his arm raised, but not towards her.

"You filthy prick! What did you do to her?"

He rained down blow after blow, each punch drawing out an unhinged sob from the cowering man.

Faunella's mouth fell open, the tight band suffocating her lessening slightly.

He was defending her.

The light shone on his new position, highlighting the brown curls tumbling down his forehead with each of his vigorous punches. Her eyes narrowed.

Is that...?

Jarred's cries cut off, his body slackening. Her defender glanced up, his blood-flecked face finding hers. The concern in his soft chocolate eyes was her undoing.

Rallying her strength, she fled.

She had only managed to run a short distance before a crashing through the undergrowth sounded behind her.

"Wait," he pleaded. "I'm not going to hurt you."

There was a dull thud followed by his low curse.

Faunella slowed, her mouth dry. Fear still had her in its clutches, but within that burned a quiet curiosity. Although she had only seen him twice before, both times had stuck with her, his face often coming to the forefront of her mind. Who was he, and why did their paths keep crossing?

"Please. I just want to make sure you're okay."

His whispered words were earnest, drawing an empathy from her that shouldn't have been possible so soon after her own attack.

She took a deep breath, nerves quivering, and stepped out from behind a tree.

His back was to her, one arm raised as it rubbed the back of his neck. Faunella nibbled on her lip, clutching at her ruined clothes even tighter. The light from his vehicle shone through to where they stood, creating a feeling of twilight.

"I'm not okay," she breathed, forcing herself not to flinch when he spun around in surprise.

"You're not?" He looked her up and down, face darkening as he took in her torn clothes.

"Jarred." He growled, clenching his jaw as both hands formed tight fists.

His vehemence had her eyes widening. Why should a human man care so much about what happens to her? Sensing her surprise, his face softened, and he took a step towards her, freezing when she backed away.

"I'm sorry." He ran his hand over the top of his head, eyes glancing to the ground before shooting back up to lock onto her face. "I'm sorry I couldn't stop it."

He looked devastated, wholly upset that he couldn't stop what his fellow humans had done. Much to her dismay, her chin began to quiver.

Don't cry. She dug her toes into the frigid ground, using the sharp bite of pain to stop her tears. *I stopped it. I was strong then, and I can be strong now.*

She tried to open her mouth to say as much, but couldn't speak past her thickening throat.

"Please. Tell me what I can do?" His Adam's apple bobbed up and down, and even in the dim light, Faunella could see the sincerity in his eyes. Compassion welled up in her, easing her jumbled mind and lending her a quiet determination.

"Forget about me."

His jaw dropped, forehead creasing. He wouldn't understand. He thought she was human. She swallowed, backing away further.

I need to go.

"Wait." He reached out his hand. "I can't forget. Just tell me who you are. Why do we keep meeting?"

Faunella shook her head, unable to give him the answers to his questions. His eyebrow shuttered down, then shot up as if something had occurred to him.

"At least take this." He reached into his pocket, pulling out a well-worn book. He held it out to her, shrugging lightly. "Something to remember me by."

Her fingers itched to take it, to study the cover and explore the words hidden inside. Swallowing thickly, she loosened her grip and tentatively reached out to take it only to have her top fall open, revealing her freshly bruised chest. She let out a small cry of dismay and snatched her arm back to her breasts, covering her naked skin quickly.

His face fell. "I'm sorry. I didn't think."

Despite the kindness on his face, Faunella wanted to get away. He was a man, a human man, and it was too soon, and she was too raw to leave herself vulnerable like this. His gaze dropped to her arms, slowly taking in every inch of her. She whimpered, fear taking over again. His jaw tightened. Dropping to a crouch, he placed the book on the damp earth, then looked up at her from his lowered position, eyes dark and full of violence. She couldn't move, couldn't breathe, until his face smoothed out into a gentle smile, eyes lightening once more.

"It's yours. Okay?"

He unfolded himself, swiveling around until his back was to her. Then, for good measure, he took several steps away.

Faunella didn't even need to think. She darted forwards on shaky legs and snatched up the treasure, then retreated, quiet as a whisper.

Guilt pulled at her as she made her way through the darkness. She felt guilty for leaving him with not even one word of thanks and probably as many questions as she had. She brushed a piece of hair out of her face, frowning. She couldn't answer his question because she had no idea why their paths continued to cross. This was the third time now, and obviously, he was just as aware of that as she was. Pursing her lips, she pushed him from her mind and broke into a careful jog. It was no good thinking about him. She should never have spoken to him again.

She was only halfway home when two tugs on the bond broke her out of her run. Rafi launched himself at her, jumping up at her legs as he licked any part of her he could reach. She dropped to her knees, letting out a light laugh and buried her face in his bushy fur. Two light feet landed on her shoulder, and Beebe's warm body pressed up into her neck as she twittered softly.

Faunella bowed her head, breathing deeply. Surrounded by her animal friends, she let the tears come, her heart feeling like it was breaking in two as the fear from what had just happened finally sunk in.

They hated me. Those men only wanted to hurt me.

She continued to sob, shuddering in relief to be away from them and back in the safety of the forest. When her tears had run their course and her breathing returned to normal, she pulled back, leaving one hand on Rafi as she reached up to stroke Beebe's soft crest.

"It's not safe for me out there." She sniffed, letting out a shaky breath. "The Fae were right. I need to stay in the forest."

She stood up, holding the front of her dress together, longing for warmth so she could bathe and scrub the feel of the men's hands from her body. Squaring her shoulders, she willed her lips to stop quivering.

"I'll be safe here. As long as I remain in the forest, I'll be away from danger." The curly-headed man flashed into her mind, and she felt a brief moment of regret. Pursing her lips, she shook away his sensitive eyes and strode onwards towards her home. "I'll never go near humans again."

PART FIVE

Bringing the humans into our society, while at first was a mere curiosity, has proven to be a boon to Fae civilisation.

Unbeknownst to us, our long lasting lives have hardened us to the magic and delights of living. In comparison to the humans, we appear almost cold, stilted in such a way that is now a concern. Most of us find little joy in the life around us.

The humans, on the other hand, are a bright spark in an otherwise endless existence. Their fleeting lives burn bright with shared experiences and the beauty of everyday occurrences.

With humans now in Amaranth, we can share our magic and knowledge, giving them something that is lacking in their own world.

In return, we can learn their warmth and gain their propensity to love. I, for one, do not see any problems arising from this step forward in our civilization's advancement.

—Recommendation to the council of Elders from Lothian Birchamp

THREE YEARS LATER

CHAPTER FIFTY
FAUNELLA

F AUNELLA'S CRITICAL EYE SCOURED her home. She tapped a long slender finger against her pursed lips. Something was missing.

Walking along the original length of her dwelling, she climbed the single step that led into another chamber. The last three years had brought her into her second decade, and although she was now fully grown, she found herself spending much more time in her tree-top home, leading her to ask the Fae to make some modifications so she could have more space to spread out.

Yes, something was missing here as well. Raising her arms, she made a square out of her thumbs and first fingers, using the shape to look through from a different angle.

"Ah-ha. That's it. I need more color."

Walking back into the other room, she hunted through her supplies for something that would fit her purpose. Coming up with a handful of autumn leaves, she sat up on her heels and wrinkled her nose in disappointment.

"Rats."

A nudge came through the bond, followed by a cold wet nose on her leg.

"It's ok, Rafi," she said through the bond. *"I'll just need to think of something else."*

Her mind traveled back to a time when she had access to tools and supplies she could have used to decorate the blank spaces on her walls—a time when she had a friend. Pushing away the memory and the hint of pain that accompanied it, she stood and decided to see if the Fae could borrow some supplies from the nearby town for her.

Rafi bounded after her, staying close to her feet as she walked. With the ease of years of habit, Rafi descended to the forest floor. Before she joined him on the ground, she tugged on the warm fluttering feeling inside, calling on her bond with Beebe. She had sent her friend out scouting to see if the season's berries had ripened yet. Sending out a message, she let Beebe know she was headed in search of the Fae.

Satisfied that she had everything in order, she swung down from her tree, easily using her power to support her descent.

It almost feels like I don't need the tree to support me anymore.

Deciding to test her theory, Faunella waited until she was about one full body length off the ground before she thickened the air under her and prepared to step out into the open air. Uncertainty of the success of the plan made her grit her teeth, steeling herself to trust in her magic to catch her.

Come on, Fawn. You're not a child anymore. Just do it.

The first step off the safety of the branch sent her stomach lurching wildly. She tried to ignore her nerves and instead focus on strengthening the power to hold her weight. To her delight, she didn't go plummeting to the ground, and instead drifted down like a leaf falling from its tree. Giving a throaty laugh, she landed lightly, spinning on the ball of one foot to celebrate her success.

"Well, it's not flying, but it sure will come in handy."

Rafi barked in response, trotting over to join her as she headed towards the grotto.

Beebe arrived at the grotto at the same time as Faunella, flitting out from between the trees.

"No luck with the berries?"

Beebe's answering disappointment was clear through the bond. Faunella shrugged, knowing it would be soon enough that they would have more berries than they could ever expect to eat.

As Beebe came in to land, she gave a flurry of chirps, flying around Faunella's head in greeting before landing lightly, but not on Faunella's shoulder. Instead, she perched on the thick red fur on Rafi's back. Faunella shot a maternal smile at the two of them, pleased with the bond that had developed over the years.

While the fox and the chickadee were natural enemies, their bond to Faunella had brokered a tentative trust with an eventual friendship blooming between them. Rafi, though, was still wary of the Fae, not wanting to be too close to them. He sat on the edge of the clearing with Beebe keeping him company as Faunella entered the cave to see who was around.

"Hello, is anyone in here?" she called as her eyes adjusted to the dark. Unable to see anyone, she walked further into the cavernous space. Blinking several times, she focused on looking where she was going. To her surprise, the more she blinked, the clearer she was able to see. Stopping abruptly, she circled her head around, looking for new holes in the ceiling that might explain the sudden extra light in the cave. Her heart began to pick up its pace. Walking more quickly, Faunella headed deeper inside, moving to where Lothian usually slept. With every step she took, the cave became brighter until at last she reached Lothian and could see him as if they were outside in the bright midday sun.

"Lothian?" She gaped, needing answers and hoping the elderly Fae could provide them. "Lothian, wake up." She stepped in close and gave him a vigorous shake, causing a few old dry leaves to dislodge from various nooks and hollows.

Lothian creaked and groaned as the pale wood of his eyes peeled open. *"Fawn? Is everything okay?"*

"Lothian, I can see!" Her heart was beating faster now, uncertain as to why her vision had suddenly improved so drastically.

"Of course you can see, child. You have eyes, do you not?"

Faunella inwardly rolled her eyes, not sure if she wasn't being clear enough, or if Lothian was being purposely obtuse.

"Lothian, I can see you now as clear as day. It's not dark for me anymore."

Understanding lit up Lothian's glassy eyes, followed by the edges of his mouth creeping upwards until he had a broad smile plastered on his wooden face. He gave a raspy chuckle.

"Why, this is wonderful news. You are entering your second puberty. The time has come for you to start growing into your High Fae body."

Even though Faunella couldn't understand all of Lothian's words, she could understand enough to be shocked into awed silence, but only for a moment. Soon enough, her mind was overflowing with questions that demanded to be answered.

"High Fae? I'm going to grow to be a real Fae?"

She instantly felt silly for not realizing straight away what was happening. She had known for years that her Fae family could all see better and hear better than her and the humans.

Her heart continued to beat faster than normal, but instead of uncertainty fueling the rhythm, it was now excitement.

Lothian stretched out his petrified limbs, coming to stand more fully. *"I believe this calls for a meeting."*

He brushed gently past her and traveled up the length of the cave. Faunella followed him, the way now lit up easily to her rapidly evolving eyes.

Thankfully, when she stepped back out into the sunshine, her sight didn't amplify the already bright day. Instead, they adjusted instantaneously, causing there to be no change from the cave's light to the light in the clearing. Upon seeing her, Beebe and Rafi made to move towards her. Beebe launched off of Rafi and came flitting over to her shoulder, but Rafi, wary of Lothian, held back.

"The others are scattered around The Edge. We can wait for them here, or we can go and collect them."

Faunella's skin went cold, her chest constricting painfully. The Edge was not somewhere that she went anymore. She wrapped her arms tightly around her body, willing the hard lump in her chest to ease.

"I'll stay here, Lothian. You can go, and I can send Rafi and Beebe to get some of the others."

Lothian nodded, disappearing quickly into the thick trees. For such an old Fae, he could still move fast when he wanted to. Taking a few deep breaths to calm her racing heart, Faunella connected with her two animal friends and sent them instructions to go find the Fae and bring them back here. Then, as soon as she was alone, she slid down to the ground and tried to sort through her tangled mess of emotions.

By the time the Fae started arriving, Faunella had collected herself and was now back to bubbling with excitement over her changing abilities. It was obvious which Fae Lothian had sent, because those Fae gathered around her excitedly, touching her bare arms and pulling back her hair to touch the rounded shell of her ears. Faunella laughed, enjoying seeing and hearing the happiness on the faces and in the voices of some of the usually more reserved Fae. Who knew this would be such a celebration for them all?

"Okay, that's enough." She chuckled. "I'm still me. Nothing's changed that much."

She gently drew back from their probing hands after they began to get a bit too vigorous in their searching. They allowed her to disengage, their myriad of voices starting to settle down, but their delighted smiles did not. At the arrival of Lothian and Amon, they all drifted into the large circle used for meetings. Faunella stayed where she was, roughly in the middle of the group.

"It is finally happening." Lothian announced. *"Faunella has begun her second puberty, and, like we all suspected, it looks as if she is transforming into her High Fae body."*

A loud cheer broke out around the group. Faunella scanned the circle, her lips slightly parted. This definitely seemed like a bit of an overreaction.

"So what else can I expect to happen, other than my improved vision?" She raised her voice to be heard over the din. "Better hearing? Super strength?"

At her words, the Fae's smiles grew impossibly wide, nodding their heads in response to each of her queries.

"All of that?"

One side of her mouth curved up. This was going to be better than she thought. Amon stepped out of his place in the circle and moved over to stand opposite her. He called Lothian over to join him, and the wizened tree immediately came to stand at his side. Offering her one of his branches, he gave her an encouraging nod, his eyes positively sparkling with pride.

"Let us show you."

"Us?"

Amon grinned, placing his other branched hand on Lothian's arm. *"Yes. It won't be my memory this time."*

Intrigued at the thought of seeing Lothian's history, Faunella took his extended limb, closed her eyes, and waited for the familiar sensation of being shown another's memories.

They were on a field just outside a small thatched village. The air smelt fresh, and the grass crunched under his leather-clad feet. He and a few other Fae had interacted with the humans several times, and word had soon spread among them of the strange new people who would come and go through the nearby forest.

"Lothian? Lothian?" came a feminine voice from across the field.

Although he and his fellow Fae were a fair distance away, he could still hear and see the small group of humans emerging from the village towards them. Leading the group was the one who had called for him, a bright-eyed woman. Her light brown hair was pulled back in a well-worn cloth that matched the state of her homespun tunic. From the dirt staining her hands, Lothian could tell she had come straight from the garden. He waited until they were closer before returning her call.

"Greetings, Henrietta. I hope you and your people are well."

He gave a short bow, still towering over the humans, even in his lowered state. The Fae with him spread out, mingling with the awed humans who had come out to see them.

"Greetings, Lothian. You are most welcome here." Henrietta's voice was breathless, showing her exertion from rushing to be among them. "We have been eagerly awaiting your return. Some of us even began to doubt that you would come back since so much time has passed."

Lothian studied her more closely; he hadn't realized that it had been that long. To his surprise, the full plump skin of her face present during his last visit had transformed into a thinner, more gaunt, mature face. Henrietta had aged.

"Forgive me, I had not realized. Such a time is but a blink of the eye in the life of a Fae."

"It is no matter. You are here now." She beamed up at him, revealing two dark gaps where there used to be teeth. "Come, teach me more of the Fae." Grasping his arm, she led him a small distance from the others, coming to sit on a slight grassy rise in the field.

Lothian was amused. This human had no fear of them and had successfully convinced a large portion of her village that the Fae were a good thing for their world, something to embrace, not something to fear.

"How are the Fae so different from us? Is there something different in your world that causes you to grow like that?"

She gestured up and down his large body, her awe-filled eyes displaying her attraction to his well-muscled physique. He gave a hearty laugh, delighted by her question.

"Only the fates know why Amaranth has magic and Earth doesn't. I am no philosopher, so I cannot answer your question. I can advise you on all of

the differences between the human and the Fae, though. Would you like that?"

Henrietta gave an eager 'yes' and settled back on the grass, fluffing her skirts around her in preparation for his lesson.

Using one of his fellow Fae as an example, Lothian scooched closer to Henrietta, ignoring her soft gasp as his arm brushed hers. He ducked down and raised his arm to point at where a Fae and a human stood conversing.

"The first thing that is obvious to see is that the Fae are much taller than humans. We grow about a foot on average higher than you. Our females are lovely. They have graceful, slender bodies that seem to float as they move. Our males are more muscular than your human men and almost three times as strong."

"What about your women? I mean, females. Are they just as strong?"

"Ah yes, our females are much stronger than human men and women but not as strong as Fae males. But, since all things must be in balance, many Fae females have stronger magic."

Henrietta gave a self-satisfied little smirk at his explanation. Lothian grinned and continued.

"We treat our females well in Amaranth. There are even some who have expressed the desire to only allow females to rule and have a purely matriarchal royal line, but I digress." He straightened up. "Along with our height and strength, we also have advanced sight and hearing. Our skin has a slight luminosity to it, and our ears draw up into points."

Reaching out, Henrietta stroked a finger over the pearlescent sheen on his forearm. "I noticed all of that," she said shyly. "But what are the differences I can't see?"

"Our age. How old do you believe I am?"

He moved away slightly, allowing the woman to get a better look at him. Her gaze ran the length of his body, a faint blush staining her weather worn cheeks. He knew what she was seeing. Straight golden hair hung to his chin, catching the light of the sun with each of his movements. His light blue eyes were set in a strong face with high cheekbones and a sharp jawline.

The smoothness of his pale skin shone compared to the dull skin that she was used to seeing - a young, muscular body in full health that glowed with life and vitality.

"You look to be in your twentieth year," she finally said, nervously brushing at the dirt still staining her fingers, as if his magnificence had highlighted her inferiority.

He reached out and placed his large hand over her much smaller ones, squeezing gently until she brought her eyes back up to meet his. He gave her a tender smile.

"I am eighty-seven years old, Henrietta, and I'm still young."
Her mouth fell open.

"The Fae age as humans do until age eighteen or even as long as twenty-one, but then our aging slows down. We can live several thousand years, and my kind of Fae can sometimes live much much longer if we pass the years in a certain state."

Henrietta still hadn't responded to him, and he began to think he had given her too many answers. But, he needn't have worried. After a moment of absorbing the information, she shook her head and blinked her wide eyes.

"And the magic?"

"We have limited magic as we age, but when we reach the time when our aging slows, our powers grow in ability and intensity."

"Wow, your people sound wondrous. One could wonder why such beings would choose to come here."

She didn't phrase it as a question, but Lothian answered anyway, reaching out to run his finger down her aging cheek.

"We come because the strength and fragility of the fleeting human life holds an unattainable beauty that we cannot help but admire."

The memory faded to black, its job of informing Faunella of the changes her body would make now done—but it had shown her so much more than that. She looked at Lothian, trying to reconcile the Fae from the vision with the Fae in front of her now.

"You once interacted with the humans?"

Amon stepped back, allowing Lothian to answer.

"Once, child. Once, a very long time ago, I was one of the first Fae to bridge the barrier between our two peoples. But no more, for our king forbids it."

CHAPTER FIFTY ONE
DERICK

"**J**ARRED'S BACK!"

The words echoed around Derick's room, fading even as his dismay grew. He let his head drop back and emitted a low groan. It would have been too much to expect that Jarred would stay away forever. The man was like a bad smell—impossible to get rid of.

Despite his disappointment, he found himself curious about how Jarred had fared in the years apart. His lips twitched. The nervous breakdown he suffered that night was a bright spot in Derick's otherwise bleak life. He frowned, the strange memories coming back to him—Jarred's terror, his injuries, and his friends' reluctance to talk about what had happened before he had arrived. Letting out a sigh, he pushed to his feet.

I need to see this for myself.

No one noticed him as he slid into the back of the large warehouse. The other members of the gang littered the room. Some lounged on worn couches, but others crowded around and blocked who he presumed was the man in question. His hands fisted. Anger burned within him, hot and heavy. He hadn't seen the girl since that night. However, the memory of her fearful eyes and torn clothing had him wishing he could rip into Jarred all over again.

"He's telling everyone about his time in prison."

Derick stiffened, his heart nearly leaping out of his chest. He glanced to the side, taking in Leon's frowning profile as he fitted in against the wall beside him.

How the fuck is he so quiet?

He took a half step away, his lips pursing, annoyed at being caught unawares. It was dangerous in this line of business to not be fully focused on his surroundings.

"What do you want, Leon?" He turned his attention back to the gaggle of men. "I thought you'd be pleased to have him back, nasty as he is."

To his surprise, Leon didn't respond right away. As the silence drew out, Derick turned more fully towards the other man.

Leon shrugged and avoided looking into his eyes.

"It's different now," he mumbled, tugging at the fabric strained tight across his midsection. "I don't know. It's been kind of nice with him gone."

Derick's brows shot up. Now this was something he hadn't been expecting.

"So, what's changed?" He crossed his arms, his muscles bunching up and making him appear bigger. "Happy to keep doing the same old thing, singing his praises while he's not here? But now that he's back, you what? Don't feel like kissing his ass?"

"I, uh—"

"What's all this?"

Without either of them noticing, Jarred had made his way over to where they stood. Leon blanched, his face slackening for a moment before breaking out into a wide, shit-eating grin.

"Jarred. Good to see you, man."

Derick rolled his eyes. Some things never changed.

Pathetic.

He lifted his chin slightly and stared down his nose at Jarred, getting his first good look at the man since the night Shaun had bundled him off. He remembered it like it was yesterday. After emerging from the forest to find Jarred wide-eyed and frantic, he called Shaun. The two of them managed to keep things quiet, smuggling Jared's bloodied and whimpering form away from the city—and the forest that lay beside it.

Snapping back to the present, he tamped down his anger and smirked, which grew into a wide, toothy grin when Jarred's face tightened into a scowl, the pale scars around his eyes standing out starkly, a harsh reminder of what had transpired that night. Jarred knew exactly what was running through his mind. Derick scratched idly at his forehead, running his finger over his skin in a mockery of Jarred's wounds.

"So, how was prison? Make any new friends?"

Out of the corner of his eye, he saw Leon glance between the two of them. Jarred ground his teeth, not able to call him out with everyone around.

"I bet those years on the inside felt like forever," he continued, pushing away from the wall and bringing his face nose-to-nose with Jarred. "I bet it drove you crazy."

All the blood drained from Jarred's face, his fury giving way to shock. Derick leaned back and angled his head.

Interesting. He didn't know that I knew.

Only a few of them were privy to the details. Jarred hadn't been caught doing a job and sent to prison. He suffered a mental breakdown and needed to be sent to a different kind of jail.

Sherward's Cross. The closest psychiatric hospital in the state.

Leon jumped between them, practically shoving him out of the way in his haste to lessen the tension. "Let's hit the pub to celebrate," he choked out. "I'm buying."

Derick let out a huffing chuckle. Jarred probably didn't realize that his three cronies knew as well. Jarred bared his teeth and opened his mouth, but before he could snarl out the words building up behind his eyes, Derick clapped Leon on the shoulder and sidestepped the two friends.

"I'm sure you've got a lot to catch up on and lots of ass kissing to do." He winked at Leon. "I'll leave you to it."

Nodding at the few men openly watching the exchange, he headed back up the stairs, curbing the urge to look back at the eyes he felt staring daggers at his back.

When he pressed his door firmly closed behind him, he let the bravado slip off his face. Slumping against the battered wood, he sighed heavily and slid down to sit with his arms resting on bent knees.

"What the hell am I going to do?"

The breathed words faded into nothing, leaving him with no answer other than to carry on as he had been.

Jarred's return had changed everything, and at the same time, changed nothing.

The rest of his day was spent in solitude. The illusion of peace was preferable to the roaring party that had been carrying on downstairs ever since night had fallen. A heavy thud crashed against his door.

What the hell?

A second later, the door flew open. "Derick, baby," Crystal crooned as she half fell, half clung to the curved handle.

For the love of god. "Crystal, what the hell are you doing?"

He jumped up from the bed and hurried over to shrug on his jacket. The material was a layer of protection against the roving hands that were sure to come. Crystal straightened up with a pout and sashayed towards him. At the last minute, she tripped and fell against his chest. "Whoops." She smiled up at him coyly, her red painted nails slipping under his still undone jacket.

It took everything in him not to roll his eyes at her obvious seduction.

"Why don't you take this back off?" Her hands ran up his stomach, sliding over the soft material of his t-shirt. Irritation pricked at the back of his neck. He backed up quickly, coming to a stop when his back hit the window. Crystal clutched at him, stumbling after him with a sloppy laugh. "Don't be like that." She blinked up at him, her eyes cloudy.

His upper lip curled. "Jesus, Crystal, how much have you had to drink?"

Her face twisted into a frown and she reached up to wrap her arms around his neck. "Don't be so high and mighty. Stop acting like you're better than the rest of us." She tried to tug his head down, her face angling up to meet his. But even with the extra height from her heels, she couldn't get her lips higher than his collarbone.

"That's enough." He gripped her wrists and gently pried her hands from his body. "You need to leave. Now."

Pressing her arms down, he gave a little shove, strong enough that she took two unsteady steps back. Her heavy-lidded eyes flashed, and she glared up at him. Then, with a flick of her hair, she turned and sprawled herself over his bed. Derick let out a groan.

She stretched her arms up, the short sparkly fabric of her dress riding up to reveal more than he cared to see. "I only came to tell you something," she whined, rolling onto her side, all traces of her early annoyance gone.

Derick brushed down the front of his shirt, then securely fastened his jacket. He might have to physically remove her from his room. The last thing he needed was more tension with Jarred, especially since he didn't know how his time in the mental institute changed him.

"Are you listening to me?"

He ran his hand over the back of his head. His patience waning. "No, I'm not. Because you shouldn't be here."

She ran her hand over her hip, idly playing with her hemline.

"Well, you should be listening to me, because I have a message for you."

He scoffed. "Who would trust you with a message?"

She hissed, her eyes shooting daggers. "You fuckin' prick. Don't know what I ever saw in you." She collapsed onto her back and let out a grunt. "Shaun wants you."

Derick's jaw dropped. Crystal was the last person he would ever have though Shaun would have trusted with a message. Suspicion flared.

"Why didn't he tell me himself?"

"Ask him yourself." She began cleaning under her fingernails, pointedly not looking at him.

He strode to the door, his stomach clenching at the thought of what job he might be told to do.

"I haven't told you where he is yet."

Stopping short, he twisted his head back to his bed and raised one eyebrow quizzically.

Letting out a short breath, Crystal pursed her lips, but when Derick stayed silent, she finally relented.

"Mile marker nine on the coastal road."

Surprise shot through him. Why would Shaun be out there this late at night? He frowned. Maybe he wanted to discuss Jarred's return without anyone overhearing. Whatever it was, Derick needed to hurry. Crystal had wasted enough time, and Shaun didn't like to be left waiting.

Leaving Crystal to have her way with his bed, he pushed down the stairs and through the crowded room. No one noticed him leaving, too absorbed in their own enjoyment.

The tranquility he usually felt while riding his motorbike was overshadowed by the insistent jumble of his mind. His thoughts were trying, unsuccessfully, to figure out Shaun's reasons for meeting him in such a strange place. Before long, his headlights highlighted the number he was searching for. He pulled over, a thread of worry pulling at his stomach. No one was there .

"Shaun?" he called, dismounting slowly.

With no sounds from his engine, the night was eerily quiet. Derick left his helmet with his bike and walked the tree line. The forest at his side was darker than the road, its towering trees allowing no light to penetrate the thick canopy. He peered into the forest, looking for any trace of Shaun. His worry grew.

Why would Crystal tell me to come all the way out here?

The answer hit him hard and fast.

"Jarred."

The undergrowth moved. A tall, lanky figure launched out of the blackness and swung something heavy into the vulnerable expanse of his stomach.

Winded, he hunched over, craning his head up to stave off the next swing. His heart pounded when he saw the three other men materializing out of the tree line. Their faces were obscure, but Derick would have to be dead to not know who the four men were.

He drew in a painful breath, straightening up and clenching his fists as he readied himself to fight.

"You're not going to get away with this, Jarred. You'll be out of the gang this time. Not even Daddy will want to save you."

Even in the darkness, Derick could see the lank form of Jarred stiffen up, but instead of the verbal sparring he expected, Jarred swung out again, this time aiming for his head.

Derick reached up in surprise, grasping the thick branch mid-swing. He clenched it so hard that Jarred couldn't pull it from his grasp.

"Don't just stand there. Get him!" Jarred demanded.

Derick tried to fight, swinging wildly at the men who surrounded him, but it was no use. They darted in from all sides, striking him with heavy objects, and when he felt a sharp sting in the back of his thigh, he couldn't help but fall to the ground. A branch whistled around and caught him in the side of the head with a sickening thwack, sending a burst of light flashing behind his eyes.

Another burning pain registered, this time in his chest. As his vision swam, he heard distorted laughter coming from above him. Swinging out an arm, he managed to sweep out someone's leg as he braced himself on one arm on the side of the road. He heard a violent curse and smiled.

Ah, Jarred then.

The beating continued, and before long, Derick could do nothing more than curl up and take it. As his mind muddled and the pain began to take him, he had a fleeting thought that maybe letting go wouldn't be the worst thing. There was nothing left for him in this life except pain and suffering. He was trapped, so perhaps this would be his only escape.

Just as he had decided it was finally time to give up his hold on life, the beating stopped, and a hot breath blew in his face. Even this close to passing out, he recognised Jarred's voice, his words jumbled around, not making any sense. Derick grappled for reality until a heavy thud connected with his face, and he slipped out of consciousness.

CHAPTER FIFTY TWO
FAUNELLA

THE NIGHT WAS STILL, frozen in such a way that it felt like the darkness would never end. Faunella lurched out of bed, a tight pressure wrapped around her body, constricting her until she couldn't breathe.

She sucked in short gulps of air, dimly aware that Rafi and Beebe surrounded her. Heedless of their worry, she threw off her blankets and shot to the window, needing the night breeze to temper the cold sweat pouring from her skin. The moonlight shone down, its silver glow highlighting the seemingly endless forest. Faunella's pulse skyrocketed, her lips parting in a choked-off cry. Not able to bear the confinement, she left her home without bothering to change out of her nightgown. Her mind swirled erratically, so jumbled that the cool feeling of dirt and moist leaves beneath her feet did little to rouse her. Taking several deep breaths, Faunella placed her hand against the base of her tree, bracing her body as the constricting force pressed harder over her chest, giving her an almost frantic buzzing along her skin that she was desperate to expel.

She didn't give Beebe and Rafi another thought, knowing that they were both nearby and capable of looking after themselves. She only focused on herself, suddenly incapable of thinking about anyone else. Faunella gave a little groan and braced her body, feeling like the only thing that might help her escape this feeling would be to run away from it—run so fast it couldn't follow.

Taking off at a loping jog, she soon increased her speed, running through the familiar trees and leaping over obstacles easily. Her pace increased, leaving her alone with her thoughts as the wind blew through her hair, its tender touch clearing her mind and giving voice to the maddening thought that had given root to her frantic flight.

You are trapped and alone.

She fled, the wind now at her back, pressing her body forward at a dizzying speed, her feet flying over the ground as she raced onwards.

Soon, she could smell the warm hints of salt in the air, her improved hearing enabling her to hear the rolling pull and ebb of the ocean as it teased the sandy shore. Putting on another burst of speed, she raced for the coast, her heart about to burst if she spent one more minute within the confines of the forest.

With a ragged cry, she broke through the last layers of trees, throwing her arms out in time to catch her body on the final tree as she hurtled her way towards the road that separated her from the sea.

Miraculously, the road was empty, and by the orange and pink glow rising from the distant horizon, Faunella could see why. It was barely morning.

She stayed where she was, relishing the openness after so many years of hiding herself away.

Why now?

Her breathing settled, the anxiety abating the longer she breathed in the fragrant air and felt the warm rays of the new day upon her face. As her heart returned to normal and her skin lost the maddening tickle, she rubbed at her arms, beginning to feel the chill of the morning.

Not willing to return home just yet, she crouched down, wrapping her arms around her legs to conserve her body heat, suddenly glad she had a nice warm home to sleep in and keep her comfortable.

I'd hate to spend a night out in the open.

Closing her eyes, Faunella focused on the sounds around her, enjoying the soothing crash of the sea coupled with the wide array of warbling calls from the surrounding birds. One call soon stood out from the others, and it was getting louder. A smile graced her lips, and she opened her eyes. Beebe had caught up, which meant Rafi wouldn't be far behind.

She stood, taking one more look at the open ocean, the tangy air still beckoning her towards the swaying depths. Then, a sigh escaping her, she turned back towards the forest and reentered the place that was both her protection and her prison.

She had only walked a few steps when a black and white flurry collided softly with her chest, landing with a small thump in her outstretched hands. Faunella laughed, cradling her friend's warm body up to her chin.

"I'm sorry." She nuzzled Beebe's soft feathers. "I just needed to get away, Beebe, but I'm okay now."

Continuing to walk, Faunella studied this part of the forest, enjoying the brightness that the smaller trees allowed. Her improved vision gave her a new appreciation for the coastal foliage, and she dipped down to run her fingers through some brightly colored grasses. *I should come here more. It seems safe. Maybe I'd be okay.* Beebe hopped down to join her, pulling tufts out with her beak. Faunella smiled down at her little friend, and, taking the pieces, she began to weave them into her hair.

After a few minutes, her peace was interrupted by a cold thread of worry that snaked down her back. Rafi should have joined them by now, or at least be close enough to hear.

"Was Rafi close behind you when you reached me?"

Beebe angled her head and gave a chirp, concern thrumming through their connection. She launched herself into the sky and streaked away to find Rafi.

"I can just find him through the bond!" Faunella called to the retreating bird.

Shaking her head, she chuckled. Now Beebe was the worried one.

The bond inside her had become all the more easy to access now that she started her change. The threads that connected her to both Beebe and Rafi were tangible now, more than just the warm feeling she previously had. Drawing on the warm, brown connection, she sent her intention through to wherever Rafi was, asking him to lead her to him.

The answering pull had Faunella's worry abating, but replacing it was a concerning confusion.

Hurrying northward, she followed the pull, moving faster when Beebe's uneasiness came through her bond.

She was almost there when her ears picked up a low groaning, the faint sound laced with pain. Her stomach clenched, certain that what Rafi had found was a wounded animal. Her heart went out to the creature, and she braced herself for the sight of the injuries that could produce a gut-wrenching sound. As she rounded the last copse of trees, her body froze, her heart leaping into her throat, cutting off any ability she had to speak.

It was not an animal that needed help. It was a large human man.

Faunella's muscles tensed, ready to flee, when another pained moan cut through the air. Her heart pounded violently, remnants of terror long since passed fighting for dominance in her unconscious mind. But, the weak sounds the man emitted stopped her from retreating, his need for help superseding any other urge she might have.

Keeping slightly hidden behind a tree, she studied the man on the ground, still prepared to bolt if she needed to. The prone man was much larger than the men in her memory, his splayed form taking up a large space on the forest floor. He wore blue pants, but that was the last piece of color on his body. His boots, shirt, and jacket were all made from different inky black materials, the colors lending him a frightening air. She shuddered; the men from that night wore similar clothing, the smell and the texture of their cold jackets seared into her memory.

But something was different here; something about this man, other than his damaged state, made her pause. His size reminded her of the man with the kind face and curly brown hair. She sucked in a breath and zeroed in on the man's head. Relief swept through her. From what she could tell through the grime and the blood, his hair looked dark, almost black, and there was only the slightest wave in the disheveled strands. Rafi gave a little whine, coming close and sniffing the man.

"Rafi, get away from him," she hissed, motioning the fox back towards her. "He's dangerous. You should know that."

He should know that.

Faunella studied the scene more closely. Rafi was sitting close to the man's shoulder, his wet black nose sniffing and bopping into the thick black material of his jacket. Her eyes shot up. Beebe was perched slightly above the man, waves of concern radiating from her. Faunella's heart unclenched slightly. Their concern wasn't for the danger that the man presented; it was for the man himself. Both Beebe and Rafi, it seemed, were worried about the human.

What makes him so special?

Steeling her nerves, Faunella came around the tree and crouched down, creeping closer to the unconscious man. Up close, he was even worse than she had thought. His face was a bloodied mess of swollen tissue, the contours of his face completely erased. Inching even closer, she drew in a ragged breath before reaching out her hand to touch one finger to the dark material plastered to his chest. Her finger came away covered in fresh blood.

He's still bleeding.

A battle waged inside of her, the fear making her want to run away and never come back, but an even stronger feeling urged her to make sure this man would be okay. A flash of memory suddenly came to her, the situations like night and day, but perhaps, at further thought, not so different at their core.

The memory was of one of Lucy's final days. Her friend had known she was dying at the end and had spared Faunella from the truth as long as she could. But something she had said had never made sense until now.

"The day you chose to ignore your fear and let your heart drive you was the day you saved my life. I thought it would be better to die, but you

showed me that everyone deserves an extra chance at living. You gave me that chance, and my life with you has been the brightest it's ever been."

She had died a few days later, leaving Faunella in a world suddenly devoid of color. But the heartfelt words came back to her now, echoing in her mind as she contemplated the human in front of her.

Does he even deserve another chance?

Wrestling with the thought of this man being in any way as deserving as her precious Lucy, Faunella sat back on her heels, letting out a huffing breath.

Twin eyes of black stared at her. Her friends both sat, expectantly waiting for her to spring into action.

"But he's a human. He's like one of those..." She couldn't even finish the sentence, her mouth drying out with the mention of her abusers.

The man stirred again, causing Faunella to hop back in fright. A dark hole appeared in the center of the mess that made his face.

"Please."

The word was nearly indistinguishable, his misshapen lips garbling the whispered sound, but it touched something deep inside of her body, taking her fear and wrapping it in the sweet weight of compassion Lucy once credited her with.

Faunella didn't know if his whispered plea was to ask for help or to beg for death, but she stiffened her resolve, suddenly determined to save this man, no matter the cost.

She pushed the remnants of her fear aside, jumping to her feet in an explosion of energy.

"I can't care for him here. It's too close to the edge." Biting her lip, she looked around. "I'll have to take him home."

Moving around to the top of his head, she gingerly reached down and slid her hands under his broad shoulders. Pulling with all of her growing strength, she heaved, sliding him back a pathetically small distance. Faunella's heart sank. She released his shoulders and straightened up. The man was too heavy for her to move. Pacing the ground, she nibbled on her lip, considering all her options. Finally, she closed her eyes and sent a thin layer of compressed air to flow under his body. It raised him just off the ground enough so she could pull his body behind her. The corners of her mouth tugged upwards. She reached for him again, but he let out a hollow cry, blood dripping from his body to the ground. Her smile fell. Even with her strength and powers, he might not survive the journey halfway across the forest.

Slapping her hands to her thighs in frustration, she racked her brain for a solution, desperate to avoid the obvious answer tucked in the back of her mind. As she lifted her hands from their place on her legs, her mouth dropped open in dismay. There was a perfect handprint plastered onto the pale material, the bright red shape standing out starkly. She raised her hand, much more blood covering it than what had been transferred onto the cloth.

His back is bleeding, too.

The situation was a lot more dire than Faunella had thought. Left with no choice, she turned to Beebe, her serious frown making the bird ruffle her feathers in anticipation.

"Go and get Amon." She held out her hand as Beebe made to launch into the sky. "Wait." Bending over, she used her hands to rip the material of her nightgown, tearing off a strip that contained the man's blood. She knew this would make the Fae frantic with worry, but could think of nothing else that would get the Fae to come to her aid faster than the thought of her in danger. Handing the strip to Beebe, she stepped back, giving the bird room. "Go now, Beebe, and hurry."

Beebe stretched her wings and took off into the treetops, the bond emitting her pride in the task Faunella had set.

Faunella sat back down by the man, confident that Beebe would get help. Rafi whined, weaving around and climbing into her lap, and the two of them set out to wait until help arrived.

Before long, the telltale sounds of something big rushing through the forest registered in Faunella's ears. Since Beebe left, the man had not stirred or made any further sounds, and Faunella had spent the last little while fighting off unwanted pangs of worry. So, as the Fae drew near, her relief at having help outweighed her fear of their reaction to her discovery.

She looked up as Amon crashed through the final trees that separated them, a frantic look of panic etched on his face. To her surprise, he was not alone. Huxley, Erwin, and Baeroot emerged seconds later from behind his trunk. Beebe glided down from where she had been sheltering in Amon's branches, landing with a soft chirp on Faunella's shoulder.

"You were just supposed to bring Amon," she whispered out of the corner of her mouth, knowing full well that the Fae could hear every word. Beebe ruffled her feathers and looked away, leaving Faunella with no choice but to face her family.

"What is going on?"

Faunella flinched at the harshness in Amon's creaking shout, his words sending his branches bending wildly. But instead of cowering under his displeasure and shock, she shook off her initial reaction and gritted her teeth, curving her body around as if to shield the man from her family's eyes.

"I just found him. Rafi led me here." She gestured to the man's pathetic state, tears pricking at the corner of her eyes. "Just look at him. He'll die if he doesn't get help."

Amon steeled his face, making Faunella's heart sink, sure that he was going to refuse to help her. Abruptly, his face softened, and he glanced down to where Erwin had come forward, placing his mossy hand upon Amon's trunk. Faunella waited with bated breath, insanely curious as to what Erwin was showing Amon. After a few minutes, Erwin stepped away, coming to stand between the Fae and Faunella.

"We shouldn't penalize Fawn for her tender heart. She has always been drawn to sick injured creatures, and this man is no different."

"But he's a danger to her and us," Huxley added as an afterthought. *"No one wants the human to die, but after he is healed, he could come back with more men. Fawn would be vulnerable."*

Translating as many of the quickly spoken words as possible, Fawn wrinkled her nose, displeased with their under-appreciation for her abilities.

"I can look after myself now. I'm just as much a Fae as all of you."

She turned back to the man, reaching out a finger to brush a blood-soaked lock of hair off his swollen brow.

"He can't even see. His face is all puffed up."

Baeroot pushed past Amon, coming over to look at the man closely, his advance caused a chain reaction, bringing the other Fae crowding around as well.

"She's right. He won't be able to see for at least several days, maybe even a week."

"That's if he survives," mumbled Amon under his breath.

Faunella swung her head up to glare at him, determination fueling her body.

"He will survive, even if none of you help me. I'll stay with him here and care for him myself!"

Huxley chuckled, causing them all to stare at him.

"She sure told you, Amon."

"We need to vote." Amon rustled, ignoring Huxley completely. *"The four of us should vote now on whether we help this human."*

"The five of us."

Now it was Faunella's turn to have all eyes on her.

"I said, the five of us. I'm an adult now, and I deserve the right to an opinion."

Mixed expressions of pride and surprise flashed in the Faes' eyes.

"My vote is that we save him. I just need your help to get him back home."

Erwin smiled, coming over to place a small arm around her shoulders.

"I'm with Fawn."

"As am I."

"I'd hate to disappoint her, so I vote yes as well."

Faunella sent a watery smile up to Erwin, Huxley, and Baeroot, touched by their willingness to help her. Amon's voice was the last to sound, his reluctance obvious in each creak of his voice.

"Fine, I vote yes. But only until he can survive on his own. As soon as he can see, he's gone."

"Thank you."

Now that the hard part was over with, there was nothing else to do except get the man across the forest where she could care for him. Faunella moved out of the way, grateful for the way Amon took charge. He sent Baeroot ahead to prepare the others and got Erwin to perch on the man's bleeding torso, his mossy arms perfect for stanching the blood still flowing from his wounds. He easily stretched out his own arms, picking up the man, careful to keep him flat and not hurt him further. But the human was beyond the point of caring and didn't so much as utter a single groan. The silence worried Faunella, and she followed behind Amon as he made his way home, Huxley staying reassuringly at her side.

CHAPTER FIFTY THREE
DERICK

H IS BODY JERKED, ROUSING him from the haze of pain. He couldn't see, only able to feel his battered body as it swayed rhythmically. A groan worked its way up past the dryness of his throat, not making it past his cracked lips.

"Careful, watch his head."

The woman's voice came from somewhere close by, but before he could think about it any further, his mind faded back to blackness.

The next time he woke, he was lying on something soft. He tried to move but found himself somewhat disconnected from his body. He tried to open his eyes instead, wincing when they remained closed, feeling as if someone had scooped them out and replaced them with bowling balls.

Where am I?

He listened to the sounds around him, hoping for a clue to where he was. The stillness was his first clue that he wasn't in the city. Even on the outskirts of town, it had never been this silent. He swallowed, trying to open his mouth far enough to moisten his lips. A pain in his jaw had him easing his mouth back shut, a moan bursting from the back of his throat. His head swam, and a heavy wave of exhaustion flooded over him, pulling him back down. Just as he lost his grip on reality, he heard light footsteps, then felt a cool hand brush along his brow.

This time, it was a sweet voice that pulled him from unconsciousness.

"Hush, Beebe. He needed our help. I couldn't just leave him."

There was a pause, and Derick listened for the answer, but nothing came.

"I know, but you've seen him. Even with the water, he's healing slowly. He was close to death." Another pause, and then she spoke again, her lilting voice threaded with a touch of maternal fondness. "Besides, you and Rafi were determined to save him, remember?"

He stayed still, not wanting the woman to know he was awake. He could feel his injuries more acutely now, an aching behind his leg and in his shoulder, and a tight feeling wrapped around his ribs. A surge of anger came over him so swiftly that it left his head reeling.

Jarred.

Jarred had done this to him, beaten him nearly to the point of death then left him alone on the forest floor. A hand on his arm made him jump. He hadn't even heard her approach. The woman gave a startled squeal, removing her hand instantly.

Derick gritted his teeth, his injuries sending out a shooting pain from his jolt.

"I know he's awake," the woman whispered, her voice sounding more strained than when he heard her speak last.

Who is she talking to?

He hadn't heard another voice yet, but it was obvious that she was responding to someone else. He opened his mouth, surprised to feel that the pain in his jaw had lessened.

"Water?"

She gasped, a soft sound that managed to merge almost musically with the silence. A moment later, the sharp clinking of glass came from beside him, followed by the warmth of a body as it leaned over his chest. The instant he felt the cool touch of moisture on his lips, he forgot everything else, only feeling the thirst-quenching liquid as it slid down his throat. After a few eager swallows, he paused, rolling the water over his tongue. It had the most amazing flavor he had ever tasted. He couldn't even pinpoint what it tasted like, only that it felt alive in his mouth. He could swear the flavor was pure starlight.

She pulled the bottle away, leaving him feeling more refreshed and rested than before.

"Thank you."

He reached out with his uninjured arm to grasp her hand, grateful to be alive despite his despairing thoughts during the attack. Instead of the hand he was hoping to hold, he brushed against long, thick hair. Unable to resist, he rubbed the strands between his fingers, admiring the silky texture.

"Oh."

The hair pulled through his hands like water from a bucket, leaving him feeling like a fool. His face heated, making the tight swollen skin burn.

"I'm sorry. I didn't mean to scare you."

She didn't answer, but he could hear the rapidness of her breathing and feel the tension in the air between them. Not having his vision seemed to be enhancing his other senses.

"Can you tell me where I am?"

She didn't answer.

"What about who you are?"

Silence.

A tight ball of frustration began to build up in his chest. He let out a steady breath, wanting answers but not wanting to scare the woman who had obviously saved him.

"Look, I know you can talk." He kept his voice even, giving no hint to his emotion. "I just want to know where I am and who you are." He sighed, sure he would get no answer from his mysterious savior. "Why'd you even save me if you won't talk to me?"

"You were hurt."

Her voice was quiet, but rich like honey, curling like a warm drink deep in his stomach. She said the three words with such conviction that

Derick couldn't help but believe them. He was hurt and needed help, so she helped him. He swallowed thickly, touched beyond belief that a perfect stranger, one who seemed to be wary of him, cared enough to bring him to safety and care for him.

"You're the one who found me?"

She didn't respond. He couldn't understand why she didn't answer such simple questions. He pulled his arm back, beginning to feel heaviness return to his limbs and a fog to his mind.

"I guess it doesn't matter. But thank you."

He tried to move his body, stiffening when his injuries flared up again and letting out a grunt of pain. A small hand touched his shoulder, pressing down lightly.

"Just lie still," she said, her voice only an arm's length away.

"So you will talk to me." His lips curled upwards in amusement, the movement causing him to wince again when the smile pulled at the swollen skin around his eyes. Hoping to make her talk more, he tried to reach for her hand, but she withdrew it before he could touch her. "But only sometimes, huh?"

Derick felt her retreat and couldn't stay awake any longer. He let himself drift off, feeling the safest he'd ever been since his mother had died many years before.

The next time he woke up, it was to an uncomfortable pressure in his bladder. Shifting uncomfortably, he ignored the ache from his leg and ribs. He still couldn't see. The swelling still obscured his vision, so he didn't know what he could do to relieve himself.

Letting out a gentle cough, he hoped there was a man around who could help him to the bathroom, or at least give him a bowl or something.

"Uh, is someone there?" Waiting a moment he tried again. "I need some help."

Light footsteps padded towards him.

Please be a man. Please, be a man.

"What's wrong?"

Derick's heart sank. While he was looking forward to coaxing more answers from the woman, she was the last person he wanted to help him right now.

"Is there a man around? I need to go to the bathroom."

Her sharp intake of breath made his cheeks heat. He felt embarrassed. Here he was, a grown man of thirty-one needing to ask for help urinating—and from a young woman, too.

"There are no men here."

His heart sank further. The woman would have to help him then. He tried to move his right arm, gritting his teeth as it sent a flare of pain through his shoulder.

"Wait." He felt her hands fluttering against his arm, stopping him from moving any further. "I'll get help."

She stepped away from him, leaving him squirming in pain.

"Beebe, get Erwin."

At that moment, he didn't even think to ask who this Erwin was. If he wasn't a man, then what kind of woman had a name like Erwin? But his discomfort made it impossible for him to talk anymore. His only focus was on not wetting himself like a child as he lay in this bed.

It felt like an eternity until the girl let out a relieved sigh, indicating that this 'Erwin' had arrived.

"He needs to relieve himself." Her whispered words were strained. "I can't. I'm sorry, I couldn't—"

"Please," he gritted out between clenched teeth. "I can't wait any longer."

He didn't hear anyone approach, but he felt the bed sink down slightly and something small move to his bad side.

Was Erwin a child?

Erwin put pressure on his wound, bracing him and helping to roll him onto his side. Derick cried out as his body moved, sinking back against the small body behind him. With great relief, he felt a large plastic bottle pressed into his good hand. Releasing the bottle for a moment, he fumbled at his jeans, unbuttoning them and pulling himself free. Less than a second later, he had the bottle in place and was having the greatest pee of his life. He let out a moaning sigh of satisfaction and relaxed even further into the body of the person behind him. Child or not, he was beyond grateful.

"Thank you."

The bottle was taken from his hand, and he hurriedly covered himself up. Erwin lowered him back down carefully, then moved around him and hopped off the bed.

"Maybe you can answer some questions for me?" he called out, hoping for answers at last.

A quiet murmuring, like two pieces of fabric rubbing together, started up. Derick's jaw dropped, and a chill ran its way up his back.

What in the world?

"Thanks, Erwin." The woman was back, appearing out of nowhere. The strange noise continued, the gentle thrumming sounding concerned. Derrick gently shook his head, shaking away the ridiculous thought.

Jarred and the boys must have beaten me harder than I thought.

"Alright, I'll tell him. But tell Amon that I'm fine. You know how he worries."

What was going on? Derick had more questions now than he did when he first woke up. Erwin? Amon? Who were these people, and why was the girl looking after him when it sounded like there were other men around?

Her steps came closer, breaking Derick out of his confused internal rambling.

"Erwin said not to wait too long next time." She sounded embarrassed, her sweet voice hesitant. "Just tell me, and I'll send for him."

His mouth pulled up on one side. "I will, thanks." Clearing his throat, he used the moment to quickly rack his brain for another question that she might answer. Something, anything. Just one little question to keep her talking and hopefully give him something tangible to latch onto in this strange and dizzying reality. He heard her step away, the fabric of her clothes rustling slightly.

"Wait," he called out, the deepness of his voice making it sound like a command. "I mean, please wait. What do I call you? Will you at least tell me your name?"

The silence stretched out for so long that he thought she had gone, but then he heard a quiet sob and she spoke, her voice thick with tears.

"My name is Faunella." Her voice shook. "But you can call me Fawn."

CHAPTER FIFTY FOUR
FAUNELLA

FAUNELLA SCRATCHED THE TOPS of her ears, pulling at the irritated skin to relieve some of the itching.

"I've been looking forward to getting my Fae body for a while now, but no one told me it would itch this bad."

"Sorry love, but beauty is pain."

Faunella rolled her eyes at Flavire, who doubled the amount of flowers dotted over his body, stroking his hands down his front and preening as they walked.

"You didn't have to walk me back, you know. It only takes a few minutes for me now."

"I just wanted to ask you about the human in your bed. How's he healing? Can you tell if he's handsome underneath all of that mangled flesh yet?"

He winked at her, making her draw back in surprise. Handsome, why would he be handsome to her?

"He's getting better," she said, her brows furrowed slightly. "Violetta's water is healing him fast, so it shouldn't be long before he's well enough to leave."

Flavire sighed. *"That's probably for the best. There's no use getting attached."*

Faunella was still musing over Flavire's words when Rafi sent a warning down the bond.

"I've got to run. He's waking up."

She dashed off, leaving the Fae behind, and closed in quickly to her home. As she approached, she picked up the faint traces of a voice. She paused at the base of her tree, looking up curiously.

"Is anyone there?"

Her mouth grew into a wide smile, and she let out a breathy laugh. She could hear the human. She could hear him as clearly as if he were standing right beside her. She rubbed at her eartips again, not minding the itch so much now. Rafi sent another pulse down the bond, followed by a tug from Beebe. It wouldn't be long before they came down to get her, so she closed her eyes, danced her hands over the air, and gathered it up to boost her into the tree, lightly using the branches to push herself higher.

Faunella walked through her rooms, coming into the original chamber where the man lay. If it hadn't been for Rafi's warnings or her own improved hearing, she might have thought he was asleep. He lay unmoving, his eyes still swollen closed, the skin an angry shade of blue and purple. She walked closer, the pungent tang of old blood making her nose wrinkle.

He needs to bathe. Soon.

When she was still four strides away, he tilted his head in her direction, his lips pressing together in a little smirk.

"Fawn, is that you?"

She stepped back, her hand coming up to cover her heart. How did he know it was her? Was he getting his vision back?

He turned back, letting out a deep chuckle.

"Now I know it's you. You never answer my questions."

She let out a breath, her pulse returning to its normal rhythm. He was just guessing. Shaking her head, she laughed inwardly at herself. Of course he knew it was her; she was the one caring for him.

"I appreciate all the care you've given me, and as much as I love drinking that liquid—" he paused, letting out a rumbling hum. "—that delicious liquid. Well, I'm getting hungry. I don't suppose I could have something to eat?"

Faunella felt her face turn red with mortification. Why hadn't she thought to feed him? She had been focusing so much on giving him the water and getting him healed that she hadn't even considered he might need to eat.

"Yes," she choked out, turning to rummage through her supplies. "Of course you can."

She made him an assortment of dried fruit and several filling nuts. Glancing back at where he lay, she tried to gauge how much someone of his size could eat. As far as humans went, he was exceptionally tall but filled out in such a way that he looked proportionate. She blushed, turning away from her careful study of his body. What was wrong with her? Ever since he had asked for her name last night, his deep voice echoing the long-ago words of her dear Lucy, she struggled to see him as something to fear. Instead, her lonely heart had been lit with the tiniest spark, the smallest ember of hope that she might have found a friend.

"Do you feel like you can sit up?" she asked, bringing the platter over to his prone body.

"I'm not sure."

He gritted his teeth and tested out his right arm, his jaw tightening when he moved it too much. Under the dirt and blood on his face, the skin paled, but he kept moving his arm, trying to get it under him to prop himself up.

Faunella dropped to her knees, placing the platter on the ground and reaching without thought to brace under his shoulders. She helped push him up, struggling under his weight despite her growing strength. He let out a loud growl, swinging his legs off the bed in one great motion. Faunella gasped, leaning his back against the ropy wall. Her hands fluttered over his chest and neck, biting her lip as she took in his bloodless face.

"Ow," he murmured, his full lips curving into a weak smile. "I guess that could have gone a bit better?"

"It's too soon. You pushed yourself too far."

He reached out his left hand, swinging it towards her, and it blindly landed on her knee. She scrambled back, heart in her throat. Helping him was one thing, but having his hands touch her was another. To cover her fear, she reached for another bottle of water, knowing that the healing liquid would do more to help him than she ever could. She pressed it into his hand and watched as he tilted back his head and drank deeply, his neck pulsing with each swallow.

"Ah, I don't know what's in that stuff, but it makes me feel ten times better."

A smile pulled at her lips. If only he knew how right he was. After finishing the bottle, the color had come back to his face, and the swelling had begun to recede. At this rate, he might be able to see in just two or three more days.

"I bet I look a sight. Is that why you don't talk to me?" He pressed his jacket out of the way and felt the front of his t-shirt. He grimaced. "It's covered in blood, isn't it?"

Faunella crept forward and placed the food onto his lap, backing away to sit in the middle of the room while he ate. He did need to wash.

"You should bathe."

He would heal faster and feel better with all of that grime removed. She sniffed. He would also smell a lot better.

"I'd like that." He chewed around the fruit in his mouth. "Did you have someone to help me to the bath? Or the shower," he said hurriedly, coughing as he swallowed the food too quickly.

Faunella thought hard. Bathing in the stream was the best option, but the man probably shouldn't be moved again until he was more healed. If she did move him, the Fae would have to help, and Amon was adamant that the man not find out who or what they were. Erwin helping the man relieve himself these first few days was one thing, but even someone as blind as the human would be able to feel the limbs of a tree dragging him through a window. She pursed her lips. He would have to stay here, but she had nothing to bathe him in. Letting out a sigh, she stood up and began to pace, frustrated at her lack of options.

"Even just some water and a cloth would be good. And perhaps a clean shirt if you've got one?"

His voice stopped her in her tracks, solving the issue with one sentence. He could get clean a bit at a time; no bathing needed. She dashed over to the shelf, scooping all of the water-tight containers she had into a large woven bag.

"I'll be back soon," she called back as she swept out of the treehouse. *He'll need some clean clothes as well.*

"Beebe, can you get one of the Fae, please? I need to ask them for a favor."

Beebe flew off with a chirp, leaving Rafi to watch the man and Faunella to collect as much water as possible.

Faunella arrived back at the tree at the same time as Amon and Huxley. The two of them were accompanied by Beebe, who promptly flew up to join Rafi in the treehouse.

"What's all this?" asked Amon, motioning at the bulging bag.

"He needs to bathe but is still unable to get to the stream. I got him some water to wash with."

She thrust her chin out, sure that Amon would have something to say about her decision. To her surprise, he merely nodded, glancing up towards her home.

"Don't get too close to him. These humans can be dangerous."

Her eyes flashed. "I'm being careful, Amon. I won't let him hurt me."

She felt the hard cold ground against her back, the heavy weight pawing at her chest. Shaking away the memory and the feelings that accompanied it, she locked her eyes with Amon.

"I won't let anyone hurt me."

Huxley gave a growl. *"He'll be long gone before he ever gets the chance to lay a hand on you."*

"He needs to go soon, Fawn. Him being here puts us all in danger."

She felt a tight feeling in her chest at the thought of him leaving and being alone once again.

"He's still barely able to move, and he can't see. Just a few more days. He's no danger until then." She sucked in a breath, surprised at how panicked her voice sounded. Forcing herself to breathe evenly, she reached out to touch Amon's trunk. "Just give him three more days. Then we never have to see him again."

"Three days, and then we'll be back to take him away."

Amon turned to leave, but Huxley stuck out his hand to stop him.

"Wait a minute. Why did you get Beebe to come and get us? What was it you wanted?"

"Oh, that's right." She brightened up, flashing them a toothy smile. "I have a request for you. Can one of you go to The Edge and see if you can find some fresh clothes for the human?"

A sly smile grew on Huxley's face, and he nodded once, turning away from both her and Amon.

"Not a problem, Fawn. I'll get something suitable for the human."

Bewildered by Huxley's tone of voice, Faunella could only offer her thanks and let him go. Hoping that he would hurry back with something clean and large enough to fit. Giving Amon a brief hug goodbye, she shot back up the tree, intent on her task.

"You're back." The man sighed, gingerly touching his swollen eyes. "It's so strange not being able to see and be so helpless."

Faunella opened her mouth to respond, and then shut it with a snap. She had to keep her distance. This man couldn't be a new friend for her. She had to heal him and then send him on his way. That was it. He sighed, dropping his hand into his lap.

"You know, back home, I was the quiet one." He chuckled, the sound drawing a smile from Faunella's lips. "But here with you, I don't think

I've talked so much in years." He cocked his head. "Are you always so quiet, or is it only around me?"

She smacked her lips together, making a point with her silence.

His smile grew, revealing slightly crooked white teeth. She covered her mouth, trying to stop the giggle that bubbled up her throat.

"Only around me then." He laughed, the deep rumbling noise vibrating through Faunella's chest. "So, how's that bath coming along? I don't know about you, but I think I'm beginning to smell."

Giggling silently, Faunella hurried over, bottles sloshing and clinking in her bag. She had an old blanket that she had torn up that he could use to wipe himself clean. The man was in a good mood. The food had obviously done the trick and made him a lot happier. She couldn't help but think it was a good thing. He needed to be in a good headspace because cleaning over his wounds was going to be painful.

"I have some water and a cloth. You'll need to take your clothes off to wash away all the blood." A blush heated her cheeks. The man would need help, that was obvious, but the thought of caring for him in that way made her stomach clench uncomfortably.

He cleared his throat, smile faltering.

"I might need some help." His voice was quiet, apologetic, as if needing help was something to be ashamed of. Faunella's heart went out to him, her embarrassment lessening.

"I'm here," she swallowed, placing her pale hand on top of his much larger one.

He flung his head up, bringing it abruptly to face hers.

"I wish I could see you."

His gentle voice made her heart pick up its pace and sent butterflies flying through her stomach. She withdrew her hand, confused at her reaction.

"Jacket first," she said, needing a task to keep her hands and her mind busy.

"Okay."

Between the two of them, they managed to pull his good arm out of the thick black jacket, only causing him to wince once when Fawn had to peel it off from where it had fused to his shoulder wound with dried blood. From there, it slid off his other arm easily, revealing an assortment of scrawling black images. Faunella studied the markings with interest, enjoying the way the shapes enhanced the sweeping curves of his tanned skin.

"Now the shirt?" he asked, looking slightly pale from the movement.

She flushed, glad he wasn't able to see her staring and focused on how she could get the tight-fitting shirt off his body without hurting him more.

"Hold still."

She jumped off the bed and rummaged around her things, coming back with a small knife. Carefully peeling the neck of the shirt down, she cut a small slit in the fabric. Then, gripping either side, she pulled firmly, tearing the shirt clean down the middle.

"Oh!"

Her mouth fell open. The man's body was so different from hers. The markings tapered over his shoulders and stopped just above a wide chest which tapered downwards to a well muscled abdomen. Even covered in a light smearing of blood and mottled with bruises, it made Faunella's mouth go dry. The feeling caused her to wring her hands in confusion. Throughout the years, she hadn't seen many undressed humans, but the ones that she remembered did not look like this. She couldn't look away, fascinated by the light dusting of hair that covered his chest and trailed down his stomach to disappear into his pants.

"Is everything okay?"

His words broke her out of her stupor, and she shook her head, blushing furiously. With an almost frenzied pace, she cut away the sleeves, ignoring the strong rounded muscles of his arms that had to be at least three times as thick as her own. When her hands tugged at his pants, he reached out to stop her.

"I think we can leave them on till last."

She removed her hands, sitting back on her heels, feeling grateful to him, but not knowing why.

"If you could wet a cloth and pass it to me, then I can get started."

Faunella did as he asked, placing the moist fabric into his good hand. He gingerly wiped the cloth down the side of his face, changing the color of the blood but not removing any of it at all.

"I think we should get your body wet first," she explained. "The blood isn't coming off."

He smiled in her direction. "I like hearing your voice. I wish you'd talk more often." He splayed his arms out to his sides, careful not to jostle his shoulder. "Okay, Fawn, you're in charge. You tell me what to do."

Faunella pursed her lips together, fighting the smile that threatened to bloom on her face. The cheek of this man, playing games with her to make her talk. Well, if he wanted her to be in charge, then she would be in charge.

"Water first then," she said sternly, ignoring his look of delight.

Her lips drew back into a sly smile as she had a wicked idea. Lifting up two of the full bottles, she climbed slowly up to stand beside the man on the bed. Then, at the same time, she tipped the bottles upside down, dumping all of the water onto his dark, slicked back hair.

"Ahh!"

He cursed loudly, coughing and spluttering as the water flowed down over his body, soaking into the waistband of his pants and pooling on the bed around him. Laughter erupted from her mouth. His reaction was everything she wanted and more. He lifted his good arm and rubbed it over the top of his head, sending bloodied water trickling down his face.

"I can't believe you did that."

Faunella jumped back, suddenly unsure of herself. However, his shocked voice gave way to a hearty chuckle, ending in a wince as he jostled his injuries. The pressure in her chest lessened; he wasn't upset.

She grinned, breaking out into another round of giggles when the man flicked the wet cloth in her direction.

"That's the last time I let you be in charge." He smiled. "I don't think I can survive another dunking."

Heart feeling light, Faunella took the cloth from him and gently ran it over his brow.

"No more dunking," she promised. Her hands shook slightly as she ran the cloth down his neck, her nerves getting the better of her as she tried to clean him thoroughly. As she wiped lower, the man stiffened up, sucking in a quivering breath. Faunella's hand stilled, her brows creasing in concern.

"Did I hurt you?"

"No, it's fine."

Faunella considered him for a moment. His breathy voice and grimacing face could surely only be from pain, but he needed to be washed. She resumed her cleaning, resolving to be even more gentle. Her tongue stuck out of her mouth as she concentrated on each stroke over his taut abdomen, slowing even further when his breathing deepened and increased in tempo. Soon, she had almost depleted her clean water supply.

"I'll get some more water," she explained, pressing the last full container into his hand. He murmured a reply, the cleaning having taken his remaining energy. Faunella bit her lip. He was still filthy. The bed bath hadn't really been enough. She shook her head; she couldn't give up now. Before she left, the man upended the last of the water on top of his hair, wiping the last of the dirt and blood out of the dark wet strands. The sight kept a smile on her face as she journeyed to the spring and collected what she needed. She also took the time to give herself a quick wash and have something to eat, so by the time she got back, a chunk of time had passed.

"I'm sorry for taking so long." She stopped abruptly, the sight in front of her robbing her of speech. In the time she had been gone, the man's now clean hair had dried. And instead of the black straight hair from before, his head was now capped with short brown curls.

"It's you."

The words escaped her, shock leaving her breathless.

His lips twitched. "Of course it's me." He tilted his head in her direction, humor lacing his words. "Were you expecting someone else?"

She couldn't respond, her thoughts whirled dizzyingly. It was the same man. The man on the bike who helped the injured girl and tried to help her the night she was attacked. Her eyes darted to the shelf behind her, finding the book he had given her instantly. What were the chances of them meeting again after all this time, of him stumbling into her life right at the very moment she began her final change. She blanched. She had almost left him at the forest's edge, her fear inches away from overwhelming her empathy. He would have died.

"Are you okay?"

His hesitant words shook Faunella out of her spiraling. Swallowing the relieved lump in her throat, she let her body relax. He was safe. This strange man who was somehow attached to her life was safe. She squared her shoulders and shortened the distance between them, her eyebrows softening.

The man glanced around the room unseeing, his tension increasing the longer she stayed silent. Connection flared through her, the knowledge of who he was increasing her compassion.

She reached out with a steady hand and brushed her fingers over his arm.

"I'm okay," she breathed. "And you will be, too."

CHAPTER FIFTY FIVE
DERICK

ERICK COULD STILL FEEL the gentle touches of Fawn's hands from the day before. With nothing to do except lie here, he found himself thinking constantly about the strange woman who had taken him in. After having water poured all over his head, he thought that nothing could shock him more. But listening to Fawn's melodic laughter a second later, the sound so pure and natural—well, that had jolted him more than the cold deluge of water. He was beginning to get a sense of her. She was obviously shy and unsure of men, but there was a playfulness to her that was so at odds with anything he was used to. She intrigued him to no end.

He probed gently at the wound on his shoulder, frowning when his fingers brushed past knitted flesh. Jerking his hand back, he reached behind his thigh to touch the stab wound there. He had been stabbed in the past and knew how long these types of injuries usually took to heal. For some reason, he was healing much quicker than normal. His head swam with confusion as he tried to count back the days since the attack, not knowing how long he had been unconscious until Fawn found him. He could have sworn it had been only a few days since he was in agonizing pain. But it was impossible to heal that rapidly, so he must be missing time.

Derick shook his head, pulling up the blankets that covered his near-naked body. Fawn was out at the moment, gone to wherever she went when she wasn't with him. He hoped she was getting him some new clothes. After he had washed, she refused to give him back his jeans and jacket, and his t-shirt was unwearable after she had ripped it free.

He chuckled, remembering the flustered way she had torn it from his body after revealing his bare skin. There were times when she seemed at least as old as him, but other times he would swear she was still just a girl. That was one of those times.

She lives by herself, so she must be an adult.

Leaning off the side of the bed, he groped around on the floor, searching for something to drink. His fingers brushed up against a bottle, and he grasped it eagerly, bringing it to his lips and gulping down the incredible liquid. As he'd come to expect, he grew warm all over, the tingling going from his mouth throughout his limbs. It had to be some kind of medicine; that was the only explanation. The pressure around his eyes lessened, giving him the first glimpse of light since the attack. Forcing his eyes to blink, he tried to see through the thin, blurry slits. All he could see was green and brown. He waved his hand in front of his face, seeing the blurry color of his skin as it passed in front of his face, but no distinguishing features.

Derick felt a bubble of happiness bloom from his chest. He would finally be able to catch a glimpse of Fawn, to see what she looked like and maybe get some answers about her age and why she was sometimes so reluctant to interact with him. Carefully, he scooted himself to the edge of the bed, gripping the base with one hand and holding the blanket around his waist with the other. He wanted to snoop, but on the off chance Fawn came back and surprised him, he didn't want her to find him stumbling around in his underwear. Bracing his bare feet on the wooden floor, he gritted his teeth and sucked in a breath. Then, with one heaving motion, he pressed himself up, careful to keep most of his weight on his good leg. To his surprise, the movement barely hurt, only causing several dull flares of pain in his shoulder and thigh. He could have sworn he had felt his ribs crack from the violent kicking. He rubbed at his jaw, the growing stubble rough under the pads of his fingers. He should still be in a lot of pain.

Taking a hesitant step, he was flooded with unease. He felt great. It was as if he had been resting and healing for months. But he knew, even with his head injuries, that it couldn't have been that long.

I need to ask Fawn how long it's been.

He looked down beside the bed, where the brown and green bottles blurred by his feet.

And what was in those bottles.

He walked slowly across the floor, his hands stretched out in front of him until he was stopped at a bright green panel. He brushed his fingers over the pink splotches dotted among the greenery, surprised to find that they were flowers. Leaning forward, he placed his nose on one of the flowers, breathing deeply. A uniquely floral scent flooded his senses. It smelt like nothing he had ever smelled before.

First that drink, and now these flowers.

Was everything here simply more? He placed his hands on the greenery, letting out a breath when he felt the soft, bristly brush of leaves.

What the hell? Am I outside?

He turned back around, straining to see through the narrow slits. So much brown, but from what he could see, it did seem as if he was in a house. There were other spots of green throughout the room, bright light coming in from between them.

Windows?

He walked towards one, his outstretched arms meeting the edge of what felt like a lumpy branch. A fresh breeze blew in over his face, and he traced the shape of the gap. It was a window, but it wasn't made out of glass or any traditional building supplies. It felt like the frame was made out of twisted branches. What was this place?

A light thump came from his right, and with it came that comforting feeling of warmth he had come to recognize as Fawn's presence. Clutching the blanket tighter to his chest, he swung around and tried to make his way back to his bed, using the blurry colors of his bedding to guide him. Breathing quickly, he laid down, trying to steady the racing of his heart. He closed his eyes when he heard the soft footfalls of Fawn entering the room.

"You're back."

"I am. I just—"

She broke off abruptly, a stillness replacing her words. Derick turned his head to face her, eyes slitting open, as worry clenched at his chest.

"Is everything okay?"

"You were out of bed," she said, her voice heavy with disappointment.

Derick felt confused at her tone. As much as he hadn't wanted her to catch him snooping, he thought she would be pleased that he was healing so well. He shrugged his good shoulder, pushing himself back up to sitting. The ease with which he moved was night and day compared to yesterday.

"I'm sorry. I was feeling better, and I thought I'd stretch my legs." He moved his head around, trying to catch sight of her through his narrowed vision. "I wanted to ask you how long it's been since you found me?"

"It's been four days."

His blood went cold. That couldn't be right. He touched his shoulder again and stretched his ribs. "Only four days? Are you sure?"

Fawn moved closer, a cream-colored blur coming to crouch at his feet. He felt a gentle touch on his knee over the blanket and reached out to capture her hand. She let out a soft gasp but didn't pull away. He closed his eyes, mind whirling at the implications of the timeline. He had been severely wounded, and while it's possible to heal with medical attention, there was no way he could have improved this much in such a small amount of time.

"What's wrong? Are you okay?"

Fawn's voice was strained, her worry evident in the way she clung to his hand. Derick gave her hand a squeeze, needing the connection to reality.

"How is this possible?" he whispered under his breath. "How did you do this?"

Her hand stilled, tensing and pulling out from his. He opened his eyes again and tried to make out her face. All he could see was a pale oval surrounded by bright tendrils of auburn hair. His breath caught in his chest, the impossible situation coming second at this moment. Reaching out, he touched the vivid color, sliding his fingers down the long strands.

It couldn't be.

It was inconceivable, the chance that the person who saved his life would be the girl who lived tucked within a corner of his mind. But he would recognize that fiery color anywhere.

"Fawn?" His voice cracked, making him flush with embarrassment. He swallowed thickly, trying to find the words. "Are you... I mean, have we..."

For fuck's sake, pull yourself together.

Squaring his shoulders, he straightened up and tried to bring her image into focus. A sharp pain burned in the still-swollen skin, making him wince and forcing him to relax his muscles. It was no use, he couldn't see any clearer. He tried again.

"Do you know me?"

Silence was his answer.

"It would have been years ago." He rubbed the back of his neck, awkwardly trying to see if she remembered their interactions. "I know I don't look like myself at the moment, and I can't see, but..." His voice tapered off, uncertainty filling him.

"The book."

Derick's head snapped up. The words had been quiet, whispered in her lilting voice, but he hadn't imagined them.

"The girl."

Hope filled him. She did remember. He waited with bated breath for her to acknowledge the first time they had crossed paths when he was in his late teens and she was still just a girl. It had to be at least a decade ago, nine years to be exact. He flushed, embarrassed to admit even to himself that he knew the exact amount of time that had passed.

She delicately cleared her throat before nervously speaking, her words almost too quiet to hear. "The crash." But Derick heard. Too full of awe to question her strange tone of voice, he reached out slowly and let a broad grin ripple across his face.

"You do remember."

He stroked down her hair again, reassuring himself that she was real. After all this time, he hadn't imagined them meeting. Who was this girl? This woman saved him, cared for him, and healed him with such speed. It was like a dream. Despite his injuries, he felt a lightness fill him, a sense of peace unlike anything he had ever experienced before, and it frightened him.

"What have you done to me?"

His voice was low, the huskiness of his words coming out like a caress. She didn't retreat from his touch, but the air became thick with tension. Derick rubbed the silky strand, enjoying its softness, and then picked it up and tucked it behind her ear.

The moment his fingers brushed over the shell of her ear, he knew he had done the wrong thing. Fawn leapt backward, a frightened gasp exploding from her mouth like a slap to his face.

"I saved you!" she cried out. "That's all." She lowered her voice, a desperate note of pleading lacing her next words. "Please, that's all you need to know."

His heart was beating so hard. He didn't know what to say. There was more to this than he had ever expected, but the thought of forcing Fawn to open up to him made his stomach clench painfully. The last thing he wanted to do was to upset her.

"I'm sorry." His voice cracked, and he cleared it roughly. "I won't ask anymore questions."

She stood there, a pale willowy figure, faceless in his limited vision.

"Thank you."

She lowered her head, her hair tumbling down to obscure half her body. Derick yearned to touch it again. His mouth felt dry, and his jaw clenched painfully. He wished there was something he could do to put her at ease and get to know her. He opened his mouth to ask her how old she was when her head shot up, turning to face the light of the window.

"I have to go."

No, don't go, he wanted to say, the words pulling at his lips. But years of covering his true feelings had him swallowing his plea, instead nodding and giving her a small smile.

"I'll see you later?" he asked, not able to hide the hopefulness in his voice. "Fawn?"

Her figure backed away from him, the silence stretching out like a rubber band between them.

"I have to go," she whispered, her voice heavy with emotion.

He closed his eyes, not wanting to see her go when things were so tense between them.

I'll fix things when she gets back. I'll make her happy again.

"Wait." A thought occurred to him. He swung his head up and looked for her, not able to see her anywhere in the blurry brown room.

"Don't you want to know my name?" he asked, realizing that she's never once addressed him by name.

Her voice came to him lightly, as if it traveled on the very air around him.

"I already know."

She didn't come back.

He waited all day, drinking and eating the food Fawn kept on the floor next to him. When the night finally fell and she still hadn't come back, he debated going and looking for her, but with his limited vision and the darkness, he decided it would be safer to wait. If she wasn't back in the morning, then he would go and find her, injuries be damned.

He fell into a fitful sleep filled with incredible dreams of strange creatures, moving trees, and whispered words. But most of all, his dreams revolved around a tall, graceful girl. Her shining hair and willowing form captured his mind and his heart. He could still feel the smooth shape of her ear, the soft shell that curved up and ended in a delicate point.

Derick woke up with a gasp, his body sitting up in one lurching motion. He looked around in bewilderment. He was sitting outside on the ground, the trees from the forest rising up around him. The sound of waves crashing into the rocky shore let him know he was back by the coast.

Lifting his arm to run through his hair, he winced at the dull ache in the center of his shoulder. The pain brought back his memories of the past few days in a thunderous rush.

"Fawn?"

He got to his feet, swiveling to look around the lonely forest as if she would pop out from behind a tree at any moment. It didn't take long to realize that he was alone, aside from a small bird staring at him with bright eyes from the fork of a tree. Pursing his lips, he blew a small whistle towards it, making it ruffle its feathers and turn with its back to him. A hint of a smile pulled at his lips, and he turned away, shaking out his limbs. His time with Fawn had a dream-like quality to it, but the remnants of pain were still in his shoulder and leg, each movement reminding him of the surreal experience.

While his vision was no longer blurry, his eyes still felt heavy, as if the swelling hadn't completely abated. He pressed around his eyes, pleased to feel only a slight tenderness. A flash of color made him look down at his body, his mouth popping open at the sight of the bright pink shirt he had on under his black jacket clashing spectacularly with the brown and gray plaid pants he now wore instead of jeans. He shook his head, pursing his lips to stop his smile over the ridiculous clothes Fawn had dressed him in.

Not knowing what else to do, he walked in the direction of the sea, hoping that a passing car would give him a lift back to The Vipers' headquarters. It was too much to expect that Jarred would have left his bike untouched. He clenched his fists, more upset about that than the fact that Jarred had beaten him almost to the point of death.

Unsurprisingly, it took Derick over an hour before someone pulled over and agreed to take him where he needed to go. The clothes he was wearing combined with what he was sure were still some colorful bruises on his face made people speed up when they saw him, not wanting to chance allowing someone so strange-looking into their car. The burly trucker who stopped had taken one look at him and declared, "No funny business, ya hear me?" Derick had simply nodded and stayed silent, staring out the window at the passing forest and thinking of Fawn. He wondered what she was doing right now and where she was. His mind was consumed by her, bouncing back and forth over every interaction the two of them had shared. A heavy weight settled in his chest at the thought of not seeing her again. She had saved his life without saying more than a few words, and he wondered how he was supposed to continue with his normal life now.

The truck pulled up at the end of the street, the trucker not wanting to drive down to the abandoned buildings surrounding the gang house. Derick thanked him with a tight smile and hopped out of the cab, wondering if he could get inside and up to his room before anyone could see him in his current state. Each step toward the old warehouse filled his stomach with lead, his time with Fawn leaving him with a new appreciation for what life could be—no fighting, no breaking the law, and no watching his back in case someone stuck a knife into it.

He hadn't fully realized how bleak his life was until Fawn had shone like the sun and showed him a different, more peaceful way to live. He shook his head. He had barely spent any time with her. He didn't even know her enough to be having these absurd feelings. A flash of movement caught his eye. He scanned the forest behind the rundown buildings until he spotted what had drawn his attention. It was another bird. He couldn't quite tell from this distance, but it looked similar to the one he had seen when he first woke up.

I need to stop all this and get my head right.

He approached the warehouse, swallowing back a groan when Shaun emerged from the building. Jarred was hot on his heels, his scarred face screwed up as he gestured wildly. Derick braced his shoulders and pulled his expression into a hard line, striding confidently towards them while ignoring the slight pull in his leg.

"Derick!" Shaun stopped in his tracks, his face going slack with surprise as Derick closed the distance between them.

"Shaun." He nodded at the man, then turned his steely gaze to Jarred, relishing the way the thin man was staring at him in disbelief, his eyes scanning over Derick's mostly healed body.

"Jarred."

He let iciness seep into his tone, wanting Jarred to know that he knew what he had done and wasn't going to let it go.

"What the hell happened to you?" Shaun stepped forward and clapped him on the shoulder, looking him up and down. "And what in God's name are you wearing?"

Derick opened his mouth to accuse Jarred of his attack, but before the words could come out, he realized how it would sound. How could he say Jarred had almost killed him five days ago when the injuries looked months old and the bruises and swelling on his face were only days away from being completely gone? No, nothing he said would be believable.

Gritting his teeth, he glared at Jarred, swallowing down the curses that he longed to inflict on the other man, not to mention a beating of his own.

"Nothing much happened. God damned drank too much and crashed my bike. Woke up with a mean hangover wearing this." He gestured at his mismatched clothes, smiling wryly. "Don't think I'll be doing that again anytime soon."

Jarred stared at him with narrowed eyes. Derick ignored him, stepping around the two men to retreat to his room.

"If you don't mind, I'd like to change."

Shaun laughed. "I don't blame you. I wouldn't want one of my men being caught wearing something like that." He gave him a nod. "Good to have you back, boy. The place wasn't the same without you."

Derick turned and walked away, not needing to look back to know Jarred's eyes were boring a hole in his back. The men inside greeted him with boisterous cheers and laughter, mocking him for his absence and appearance. It was a relief when he could shut the door to his room and sink down onto the edge of his bed.

He lay back with a sigh, resting his hand on the firm muscles of his abdomen.

Why did she send me back?

He closed his eyes and imagined he was back in Fawn's room, listening to her quiet steps as she prepared food for him or touching his brow when she thought he was asleep. He smiled, remembering her laughter when she had cleaned him, her amusement fading into something sweet, something new between them.

He let out a harsh sigh, irritation running under his skin. Getting back up, he stood in front of his window, the still filthy panes blurring his view of the endless forest.

She must be out there. It's the only explanation.

He could see her now, in a little cabin in the woods, her soft hands brushing at the wavy strands of hair that curled over her shoulder. He closed his eyes again, pressing his forehead to the glass, wishing he could be back with her now.

CHAPTER FIFTY SIX
FAUNELLA

S HE SAT STARING OUT the window, the first rays of morning sun just starting to appear. Her mind kept replaying her last glimpse of Derick. When the night was at its darkest, Amon had pulled Derick's limp form from the room, his power keeping him in a deep sleep. She shifted uncomfortably, a strange hollowness moving within her body. The plan had always been that he would have to leave before getting his vision back. She just hadn't thought it would be so soon.

No, that wasn't right. She let out a heavy sigh and pushed to her feet. She had hoped it wouldn't be so soon, but she didn't have a choice. He'd recognised her almost instantly. She picked up a piece of her hair, stroking it the way Derick had. She had seen the moment he knew it was her. He stiffened up, an almost preternatural stillness settling over him. Her heart started pounding all over again—with fear or excitement, she couldn't tell.

She dropped her hand, shaking the tingling from her fingertips and started pacing the room, nervous energy making her need to move her body. "It's better this way," she blurted to Rafi, Beebe having disappeared not long after Derick. "He might have hurt us. Men like that are dangerous." The words immediately turned to ash in her mouth. "No," she whispered, her voice small. "I don't think he would have."

She lowered her head and closed her eyes, bringing his face to mind. In every interaction, he showed her nothing but care. His low voice was gentle and his smiles made her light up from within. Her lips twitched. After Amon ensured Derick wouldn't wake, Erwin and Flavire dressed him in the mismatched clothes Huxley had come up with. She could still hear his crunching laugh ringing out when he had handed the items over.

Her eyes blinked open. She hadn't felt a connection like this since Lucy. Maybe he really could have been a friend to her. Faunella shook herself out of her head and bounded over to strip the bedding off the bed, determined to clean her home of Derick's presence.

"It's too late now, Rafi. He's gone, and he's not coming back." She paused, her arms full of sea salt-scented blankets. *It was the right thing to do. It's almost time for me to return to Amaranth, my people.* Harnessing the air around her, she created a vortex where she threw her bedding. It snatched in the jumbled material and sucked it out the window. Faunella left her home the same way, not bothering to use her door. The power felt like an old friend, something all the more special due to all the tears and heartache it caused. She eased towards the forest floor, wondering what it would feel like to be among Fae like her, to be able to use her powers without holding back in fear that she might be discovered.

Yes, Derick leaving was the right thing. It's not like he could come with her to Amaranth.

She touched down lightly, then straightened up and squared her shoulders. She had a duty to fulfill, a people to save, and a family to meet.

After she had put her house in order again, she found herself at a loss. Her thoughts kept bouncing between Derick-filled daydreams and imagining what her return to Amaranth might look like.

I'll go and see the Fae, she decided. The decision had nothing to do with asking how returning Derick had gone. She flushed. No, she simply wanted to catch up with how they were doing.

She quickly changed her clothes, pulling on one of her forest outfits. The woven evergreen leaves contrasted nicely against her skin. Tucking her hair behind her ears, she let out a surprised gasp. Her ears had finished their transformation and now curved upwards into firm but delicate points. Her skin heated up as she touched the tips, remembering how yesterday Derick had leaned forward and tucked a strand of hair over her ear. She had torn away, his touch a stark reminder of who and what she was.

Was it fully pointed then, or was it still round like a human?

She didn't know, and the thought of him knowing what she was sent a tremor through her. Pushing the thought away, she made her way through the forest. As the dappled sun reflected off her body, she marveled at the way it made her glow, as if she held a layer of light underneath her golden skin. Things were changing fast for her now. Her vision had improved, she had grown even taller, and her High Fae ears popped out. Her powers lay easily within reach inside her, ready to be used whenever she felt the need. So why did she feel like something was missing?

The clearing came into view just ahead, the light streaming brightly through the surrounding trees. Faunella quickened her pace, her eyes finding the dark opening of the cave easily. After a few steps, she stopped in her tracks, an oily feeling creeping up her spine. Unable to put her finger on what was different about the scene in front of her, she stayed where she was, all her senses on high alert. The forest was still, the clearing ahead was empty, and multiple voices came from within the cave.

Her blood ran cold and a sick feeling of horror clenched at her heart. The voices. They weren't the rustling, crashing sounds of the Fae. They were speaking clearly, each word as clear as if she were talking.

With a sweep of her hand, Faunella pulsed out air, propelling herself up into the nearest tree, pressing behind the trunk to hide herself from sight.

How did the humans find us?

She felt sick at the thought of Derick leading a group of humans into the forest, invading the Fae's deep forest home. Her pulse pounded in her ears, and she forced herself to breathe deeply, calming down so she could listen in to the human's conversation.

"There's no way he could follow us back here. We didn't leave a trail, of course, but we still took the long way to the coast just in case."

Faunella's brow furrowed, not understanding what the humans were talking about.

"Do you think he saw her before he left? The swelling had cleared up a lot from the day before."

"God, I hope not. No hot-blooded human man would be able to resist our beautiful Fawn if he saw her. We'll just have to hope we took him back in time."

Faunella gasped, sliding out of the tree in disbelief. They were talking about her. They were talking about Derick. It wasn't humans in the cave. It was the Fae, no longer speaking in the languages of nature. Instead, they talked like her, and she could understand them.

She walked into the cave open mouthed, looking at the Fae with new eyes.

"I understand you," she gaped out, still awestruck by the change. "You're speaking normally."

They turned to her, ten sets of eyes appraising her body. One by one, they broke into delighted smiles, some of them clapping and Erwin and Violetta came forward to wrap their arms around her.

"You've done it," Violetta sniffed. "Your second puberty is over."

"You're a High Fae now," beamed Amon, his new voice recognisable from the memories that he had shown Faunella.

Faunella hugged her family back, enjoying their happiness, but still confused at the significance of becoming High Fae.

"Wasn't I always Fae?"

Amon scratched at his leafy head, looking around until his gaze landed on Lothian.

"Lothian, why don't you explain the significance of High Fae to Fawn?" He turned back to her, a shadow passing in front of his eyes. "We have much to tell you."

They filed out of the cave, settling into a large circle within the clearing. The Fae kept glancing at her, smiles cemented to their faces. Faunella hadn't realized this was so important to them and felt a hint of pride peeking through her confusion.

"So, I'm a High Fae now," she started. "What's the difference between that and a normal Fae?"

Looking at the elderly Fae, she waited expectantly, allowing him to gather his thoughts as he cleared his throat.

"Back in Amaranth, the realm of the Fae, we were the first species of Fae to exist."

Faunella bit back a smile, Lothian's gravely voice sounded more similar to his tree sounds than she had expected.

"We were simply known as Fae. Over time, a new generation of Fae started to appear. Their powers were not as strong, and their lifespans were shorter than ours. They were also known as Fae, but we—" He gestured around the circle. "—started to be referred to as Ancient Fae."

Ancient Fae.

The term tickled a long ago memory in Faunella's mind. She had heard of the Ancient Fae somewhere.

"I won't bore you with the full history, my dear, but—"

"Once there were humans in Amaranth?"

She finished his sentence, the knowledge pulled from the recesses of her mind.

"Yes, that's right." He smiled at her, his filmy eyes brightening at her interest. "The humans joined with the Fae, creating half-Fae, half-human children. These children were called lower fae. They looked human until their second puberty, when they either stayed as lower fae or changed into what we now know as High Fae."

Faunella's mind bloomed with understanding. The explanation answered all of the questions that had cropped up over the years.

"I was a lower fae?" she spoke slowly, encouraged by the steady nodding of not only Lothian but some of the other Fae as well. "But now I'm High Fae? And you're all Ancient Fae?"

"Yes."

Faunella sat back on her heels, the information swirling around in her mind. She always knew she was Fae, so becoming High Fae didn't seem as amazing to her. She was happy about the extra abilities, but it didn't change who she was as a person nor the way she felt about the others.

"So my parents are lower fae?" she asked. "Or is one of them human?"

"Oh, no," spluttered Amon, waving his leafy branches wildly. "There are no more humans in Amaranth, but the descendants of the humans are still present. Your father is one of those descendants, a lower fae, but your mother is High Fae."

My mother.

Faunella's chest swelled. She had a mother, a mother just like her. A High Fae mother. The thought made her pause, a startling confusion creeping in.

"High Fae," she started, swiveling her head to take in all the Ancient Fae surrounding her. "You mean Ancient Fae." A nervous giggle bubbled out of her, even as she wrung her hands, the slender appendages beginning to slicken. "My mother has to be Ancient Fae because I am, right? You told me I'm the heir to the Ancient Fae Kingdoms."

Amon looked around the group, the tension in the air causing the hairs on Faunella's body to stand on end. He walked over to grasp her hand, holding it firmly in his wooden twigs. Erwin shuffled closer to her side and she felt the whole world take a breath.

"Your mother is a princess of Madivyre, and you, Fawn, are also the heir to that kingdom. You are the heir to both Madivyre and the Ancient Kingdoms."

Faunella drew back, her eyes stretched wide at his serious words. Her heart thudded painfully in her chest, her mouth suddenly dry with disbelief.

"They're in Madivyre? They're safe?"

The words didn't seem real. Her mind ran over her geography lessons, landing on the seaside kingdom with a snap. All these years, she pictured her parents suffering in the Ancient lands, patiently waiting for her to return, now to find out they were safe and healthy, living not just well, but actually as part of the ruling class.

Unconcerned with how she could be the heir to two opposing kingdoms, Faunella could only clutch at her stomach, at the hollow that formed and threatened to consume her.

"You said I was in so much danger that the only option you had was to bring me here to keep me safe." Her words increased in volume, spewing forth with the intensity of her emotions. "But my parents?" Her mouth tripped over the word, but shaking her head vigorously she continued. "My parents would have had no reason to interact with Petrov. The Ancient Fae are so removed from every aspect of Amaranth's society. I would have been safe there." She choked on a sob, belatedly realizing that her eyes had welled with tears, merging the Fae into nothing more than the surrounding forest. "I wouldn't have been alone," she cut off, gasping for breath, as everything she thought she knew was thrust into question.

"Fawn, that's not all. You—"

"Wait, just wait."

Putting up her hand, she swiped at her eyes, swallowing thickly as she tried to get her bearings.

"This is a lot of information right now, and I just need a minute." She looked around at the Fae, their smiles now replaced with concern and pity. "I'm going to go for a walk."

"Alone," she added when Huxley stepped forward and opened his mouth. "When I get back, you can explain yourselves." She didn't bother asking if that was okay, too angry and hurt to care about the Fae's feelings at that moment.

"That's more than okay," said Violetta, stepping out of the circle and giving Amon a pointed look. "You take as long as you need. We can wait until you're ready."

Faunella shot her a grateful smile, then turned and stiffly walked into the trees, trying not to break into a run even though her body strained for her to flee from this latest revelation.

When she was far enough away from the sight and hearing of the Fae, she let her body flop against a tree, leaning her head back onto its bumpy bark. How could they have lied to her all these years? How could her parents allow her to live on Earth for all this time? Didn't they want her?

Did they even know?

That thought was the most frightening of all. Did the Fae find out she was their missing heir and steal her away from her own kingdom?

She pressed the backs of her hands against her eyes to ease the hot sting of tears that threatened to spill. Was every interaction with the Fae a lie, a massive manipulation? No. She shook off the thought. The Fae would have never taken her from a family who wanted her. That would be too cruel.

Faunella longed to have someone to talk it over with, someone that knew who and what she was—a friend. If Lucy were here, she would have understood. And even though she shouldn't, her thoughts turned to Derick, wondering if he had known the truth, would he have offered her a sympathetic ear? She nibbled on her lower lip, hoping and choosing to believe he would.

Like multiple other times during the day, her imagination took over, and she spun a story in her mind, drawing comfort from the images she created. In this dream world she was just a normal girl. Fae—human? It didn't matter, she was simply herself. But Derick was there. Tall and beautiful, he trailed his fingers over her arm before wrapping her in a warm embrace. Laughing, he filled her with a fluttering feeling of joy, and she imagined she would always feel safe and wanted in his arms.

Groaning in frustration, Faunella flicked open her eyes, upset that now, on the edge of her destiny, she should be filled with so many strange and conflicting emotions. She shook off all thoughts of Derick and ground her teeth. She needed more information and knew the Fae would have all the answers to make sense of this new jumbled reality. Pushing away from the tree, Faunella kicked haphazardly at a lone mushroom. The conversation would have to wait, she was too raw and too vulnerable to open herself up to more truths. Rafi wove between her legs, pouncing at the now loose fungi. At least when it came time to learn her history, she could now understand the Fae's words perfectly. Her second puberty was over. Faunella nibbled on her lower lip. She should be happy; perhaps now she would be able to go back to Amaranth, but to what kingdom, she didn't know.

Derick's smile came to her unbidden. Leaving Earth would mean she would never see him again. Not that she was planning to, but the thought of leaving without seeing him one last time had her heart tightening uncomfortably.

Without meaning to, her legs started to take her towards the coast. She played with her power as she walked, firing bursts of air towards fallen leaves, Rafi jumped up to catch them as they drifted back down. His playful antics soon worked to push her worries to the back of her mind, giving her a reprieve from the uncomfortable feelings. They had only walked a short distance when a light chirping call made them both stop and look upwards. Beebe came gliding in from above the trees and came to land on Faunella's shoulder.

"Where have you been?" she asked with mock seriousness, her lips pulling up in a one-sided smile.

Beebe preened her feathers, sending a smug teasing pulse down the bond.

"Beebe?"

The bird puffed herself up and then flitted up to a nearby tree, cocking her head and staring at Faunella with her tiny black eyes. A picture of a brown-haired man staring through a large dirty window appeared in the bond. Faunella reared back, visions not being the normal way they communicated, as they used up a lot more mental focus than simply sending feelings, or sometimes speech.

"You followed him?"

She gave a short chirp.

Faunella pursed her lips, thinking. That meant Beebe knew where he was.

"Can you take me to him?"

Beebe let out a happy cry and swooped away. Faunella hurried to follow her. Rafi stayed where he was, giving a short questioning bark.

"I just want to make sure he's healing properly," she explained, beckoning for him to follow. "That's all, no other reason."

Rafi huffed, jumping up and racing past her, his senses alert to keep Faunella safe from any potential danger from the others past The Edge. Faunella smiled at his protectiveness, then turned to follow Beebe northward, a lightness filling her up the smaller the distance became between her and Derick.

CHAPTER FIFTY SEVEN
DERICK

LIFE CONTINUED IN THE gang like Derick had never left. The only difference was Jarred and his friends kept their distance, bringing him a small measure of relief.

It had been several days since he had returned, and, unable to stomach being around the other men, Derick found himself retreating more and more to his room, staring off into the forest through his freshly washed and repaired windows. A knock came from the hall, and before he could answer, his door swung open, revealing a stern-faced Shaun.

"What can I do for you?" he asked, standing with his legs apart, hands in his jeans pockets to show he wasn't threatened by the older man.

Shaun walked in, his heavy boots slapping on the concrete floor. He sat down on Derick's bed, frowning and reaching under the covers to pull out the book Derick had been reading earlier. He arched his salt and pepper brow at Derick and tossed the book haphazardly to the floor.

Derick kept his face impassive, not allowing Shaun to see his feelings.

"I'll get right to it." Shaun placed his closed fists on his knees, the inky stains from decade-old tattoos marring each finger. "I've heard that during your time away, you've been working with the cops, trying to cut a deal for yourself in exchange for information about The Vipers."

The ground dropped out from under Derick's feet. What Shaun was suggesting was as dangerous as it was outlandish. His mouth fell open, and he couldn't help the scoff that blew past his lips. Shaun frowned and stood back up, placing one hand behind his back.

A tight feeling of warning curled in Derick's stomach, and he took a step back towards the window, his hands outstretched in front of him.

"Look, Shaun. I don't know who you've been talking to, but you've got it all wrong. I'm loyal to you and The Vipers. I haven't been with the cops or anyone else this past week."

If only Shaun knew how true that was. The only person he was near was a mysterious girl living somewhere in the forest, a girl that Derick had begun to think he dreamt up.

Shaun narrowed his eyes, rubbing the gray stubble along his pointed jaw. Derick kept quiet, knowing that nothing he could say now would convince Shaun of his innocence, but that running his mouth would be a surefire way to look guilty as hell.

"I've always liked you, Derick," he said at last. "So, I'm going to give you the benefit of the doubt. But if I were you, I'd watch your back." He nodded to the book on the floor. "Get rid of that shit. It sends the wrong message."

He left and Derick picked up his book, tenderly brushing off the dust and straightening the bent pages. Hiding it from sight, he turned back to the window feeling more alone than ever before. As bad as it was living in the gang, it was all he had known for the past sixteen years. Now, probably due to Jarred, he was losing his long-fought-for position. He placed his hand on the glass, watching the light bounce off the deep green array of leaves that made up the thick forest. She was out there somewhere; he could feel it in his bones. Fingering the fully healed cut on his shoulder, he reminded himself that it wasn't a dream. Fawn was out there in a peaceful haven far from this madness.

Steeling his face, he turned from the window and left to join the gang downstairs, needing to solidify his place before Jarred succeeded in getting him killed.

"Ah, Derick, there you are," one of the younger members called out, causing more than a few eyes to turn his way. "We thought you were hiding away in your room like a little princess trapped in her tower."

The men broke into rowdy laughter, slapping the younger man on the back as if he had said something clever. Derick ignored them, keeping his face in an impassive mask of boredom. He walked up to Jarred, making the laughter die down until there was nothing but a tense silence in its place. Staring down the man who wanted him dead, he addressed the group.

"Thought I'd treat the lot of you to a round at The Locker." He kept his eyes locked onto Jarred as he spoke. "Since my bike's gone, I'm sure Jarred will be pleased to lend me his."

He heard the muffled whispers around him but didn't so much as blink. This was a pissing contest—one he was determined to win. The moment Jarred placed his keys in Derick's outstretched hand, the rest of the men gave a cheer, all getting to their feet and heading out to their own vehicles.

As the space cleared around them, Derick lowered his head, allowing a thin smile to break out on his face. As he looked at Jarred, an urge to make him feel even more pathetic came over him.

"I know what you're doing, and it's not going to work. There's a reason I'm Shaun's second and you're not. That's because Shaun wishes I were his son instead of a sniveling coward like you." He straightened back up, satisfaction sliding up his spine from the mottled red skin that had appeared on Jarred's neck. He turned to leave. "Next time you come for me, you'd better bring more than the four of you."

He strode out of the room, his lips pursed together with the last of his bravado.

After emptying his wallet and solidifying himself back with the men of the gang, Derick quietly slipped out of The Locker, longing for the peace and solitude he would find on the open road. He spent the rest of the day making a large lap around the forest until the sun fell behind the horizon, turning the world black.

When he arrived back at the old warehouse, his heart sank. There were several fires lit outside and music blaring so loudly he heard it from the end of the deserted street. Women and men crowded around the open doors, inside and out, drinking and gyrating together. He could see two separate fights going on, and he wasn't surprised to see that people were betting on the winners.

He sighed, swearing softly as his peaceful night came to a crashing end. Parking Jarred's bike, he threw the keys into a nearby bush, smiling at the thought of him rummaging around to find them. As he moved through the crowd, several women came up to him, pressing their heavily perfumed bodies up against him and offering themselves to him even as he brushed them aside. Their behavior was such a contrast to Fawn's sweet innocence that he felt a pang of longing for her. His fingers itched to run through her soft shining hair, and he would give his right kidney for the chance to feel her gentle hands stroking his brow again.

Finally making his way to the base of the stairs, he placed his foot on the first step, relief washing over him at the chance to be alone. But something made him hesitate, a small, nagging feeling in the back of his mind. He heard the small voice that over the years had kept him from the worst of danger, helped him watch his back and survive in a world filled with murderers and thieves. He turned around and made his way down the lower level hallway, stopping just outside Shaun's office, leaning with his ear turned towards the slightly ajar door.

"So, where was he tonight? He took the boys out for drinks, but they came back without him."

It was Jarred, his voice rife with feeling. Derick gritted his jaw. He knew it was Jarred turning Shaun against him. The little weasel didn't know when to stop.

"Craig heard him talking about how you don't have anything on him anymore."

Derick frowned, wondering what the hell Jarred was talking about. A drawer slid open, followed by the rustle of papers.

"Fuck! It's gone." Shaun's voice was wound tight, rage lacing every syllable.

"He must have taken, deleted, or destroyed the video." Even from behind the door, Derick could hear the restrained glee spewing from Jarred's mouth. They were talking about Shaun's phone. The phone contained the video of him killing Rhett—the phone that he had in no way touched.

Jarred continued his poisoned tirade, each claim more outrageous than the last. Derick seethed. How could Shaun believe the things he was saying? He longed to burst into the room and defend himself, putting Jarred back in line. But Shaun's next words made his skin go cold, and a heavy weight settled in his chest.

"See if you can find him." His gravelly voice was cold, devoid of any feeling. "When he gets back, you and the boys can take him out." He sighed and Derick heard another drawer open. "Do it quick, and do it quiet. I can't have Frank's son messing things up for me now. I've worked too hard for too long to get where I am."

"You should have killed him years ago." Jarred sounded peevish, and if Derick wasn't so worried, he might have scoffed. But the conversation had him reeling. There was something about Shaun's tone of voice that made him think he might be missing something.

"You never should have made him your second."

"You're right." Shaun made a sound, low in the back of his throat. "I should have put a bullet in him instead of the two I put in that security guard."

What?

Derick had heard enough. He stumbled back from the door, his heart pounding. The guard? All those years ago, it was never him? He was never a murderer. Sickness churned in his gut.

I have to get out of here.

He didn't have time to get anything from his room, so he shouldered his way back through the crowd, ignoring the yells and curses hurled his way, all the while fighting over this revelation. Would things have been different if he had known? Could he have lived a different life? He reached Jarred's bike, glancing at the bush and cursing at himself for his stupidity in throwing the keys away. He started jogging along the front of the warehouse, thinking if he could just get into the city, then he could catch a ride with someone and get out of Northaven.

A booming yell made his head swing around. Jarred was making his way through the partygoers, a malicious sneer on his face, and his eyes locked onto Derick's retreating body.

Jarred.

It was like a light bulb went off in his head—the words Jarred whispered into his ear right before he had lost consciousness after his brutal beating.

"It was never you who killed that guard. Your pathetic shot went wide. It was Dad."

He had told him. For whatever reason, Jarred had told him the truth of that night. All the good that did him now. Ducking out of sight, Derick raced down the space between the warehouse and the empty building next door, emerging at a dead run and heading straight for the inky blackness of the looming forest.

Not slowing, he passed the first layer of trees and promptly crashed face-first into a narrow pine. Cursing violently, he picked himself up, ignoring the burning sting running down the side of his face. He could hear Jarred's voice calling for him from the side of the warehouse, so he stretched his arms out in front of him and hurried deeper into the depths of the dark forest.

It took about an hour of steady walking until he could no longer hear the calls of Jarred and his men. It was only then that he finally allowed himself to rest. He had fallen several times and now sported more bruises and scrapes, but his wounded pride hurt more than any of the damage the forest inflicted. If he could just wait out the night, then in the morning he could make his way west and hitch a ride from someone going south.

He buried his face in his hands, flinching when he irritated the open wounds along his palms. The only problem with his plan was that he was sure Jarred, as dumb as he was, would have placed men up and down both exits to the city, leaving him trapped in the forest. With no food or water, he wouldn't last more than a few days here. Exhausted from his escape, he lay down at the base of a tree and tried not to think of his predicament. Instead, he focused on his dream girl, her long auburn hair and sweet soothing voice sending him into a deep dreamless sleep.

He woke with a dry mouth and a stiff body. Groaning, he rolled over and got up, continuing to make his way west. He didn't allow himself to worry about what would happen next; he just concentrated on making his way out of the thick forest. He had never been this deep and found the terrain slow going. The trees were large and grew close together with fallen logs and large boulders scattered throughout. He kept his eyes and ears open for the first hint of a water source, his mouth growing drier with every step he took.

After climbing a particularly large slippery log, Derick tried to continue on but found himself veering south instead of west. A cool breeze blew past his neck, cooling the hot sweat slick on his skin. Groaning in pleasure at the cooling touch, he altered his heading but kept finding himself inexplicably turned around. Frustrated and in no mood to wonder how in the world this was happening, he closed his eyes, took a steady breath in, and stepped forward, letting the comforting pressure at his back guide him south.

CHAPTER FIFTY EIGHT
FAUNELLA

"WHERE ARE YOU OFF to this morning?"

Faunella tossed her hair, feeling a flush bloom on her cheeks from Laurel's question. Beebe had shown her the dilapidated warehouse where Derick was, and Faunella had hidden safely within the forest watching for a glimpse of him. By a stroke of luck, she had seen him through a high-up window, his impressive form taking up a large portion of it. Thankful for her Fae eyesight, she climbed a sheltered tree to raise herself to his level, drinking in the sight of him as if she were once again crouched beside him back in her treehouse. He had healed well, standing straight with nearly all traces of bruising gone from his face, but his eyes looked sad. Their warm hazel depths had sucked Faunella in, making her wish she could creep inside his mind and hear the thoughts that put such a despondent look on his face.

She had been intending to make her way there again this morning and was on her way when she came across Laurel, the Fae innocently wanting to know where Faunella was going.

"Just to The Edge. I felt like seeing what the humans are up to these days. It's been so long since I've gone." She pulled her hair over one shoulder, running her fingers through the strands absentmindedly. "And I know it won't be long till we leave for Amaranth."

Laurel patted her hand, her obscure face contorting with sympathy.

"Of course. You did seem to close yourself away." Her face brightened. "But good for you for getting out there again. Humans are always evolving and creating new things. It will be a shame to no longer be able to witness that."

She turned to go, leaving Faunella with a heavy feeling of guilt for deceiving her. As she watched her leave, she suddenly licked her lips, grimacing before calling out for Laurel to wait. The Fae turned around, her green face open and unsuspecting.

"I don't suppose I could have some berries before I go?"

Faunella blushed, shrugging her shoulders when Laurel laughed. The Fae's amusement sounded strange compared to the natural sounds Faunella was used to hearing.

"Of course," she chuckled as large glossy berries began to bud and grow all over her foliage. Stepping forward, Faunella eagerly began to pluck the berries from Laurel's body, filling the soft bag she pulled out from under her clothing.

"Thanks, Laurel," she said, popping a berry in her mouth and biting down, letting the sweet juices explode in her mouth. "Well, I'll be going."

Racing away with the taste of berries on her lips, Faunella enjoyed the feel of the wind pulling her hair back. It swirled around her body, tugging her baggy sweater to the side and plastering her loose pants to her legs. She was fed, she had her two friends at her side, and with her heritage pushed firmly to the back of her mind, she felt brave and capable. It was such a change from the week before when fear still had her in its hold, keeping her trapped inside the forest.

Coming into her High Fae form made Faunella feel different, stronger and more confident in herself and her abilities. She made a beeline towards Derick's warehouse, humming to herself as she rode the wind.

The forest started to thin out slightly when she was almost to the edge. Faunella quickened her pace and sent tendrils of air floating out around her, even though her new senses were more than capable of hearing any danger.

Just ahead of her on the dirt path, Rafi stopped, his bushy tail stretched out behind him. He sniffed the ground in front of him, his black nose twitching as he took in the scents lining the ground.

"What is it?"

He looked back at her and gave a short bark, turning to the side and snaking his way through two trees.

"Where are you going?" she called softly, not wanting her voice to carry this close to The Edge.

Rafi gave no answer, only sending a flare of urgency down the bond. Faunella didn't want to follow him; she wanted to see Derick. But Rafi had never let her down before and always had a good reason for diverting her attention.

Beebe glided down to perch on his back, catching a ride with him as he bobbed and weaved over the undulating ground. Faunella blew out a breath and followed them, glancing back the way she really wanted to go before putting on a burst of speed to catch up with the animals.

She was so focused on Rafi's weaving form, she almost didn't notice the damage inflicted along the path they traveled, the upturned leaves and smeared dirt on top of rocks and logs. The branches of bushes were bent back and hanging limply off their undamaged counterparts. She glanced up higher, frowning at the smaller branches on the trees around her. They were broken as well, leaving a clear path of destruction through this part of the forest.

Something big ran through here.

"Does someone need help?" she whispered, trying to peer around the thick trees, her improved eyesight useless in the dense forest. Rafi picked up his pace, his little red legs blurring as he pressed on.

Frustrated and a little worried, Faunella stopped. Drawing on her powers more fully, she closed her eyes, sending air swirling past each tree and plant. The air pushed into every crevice, painting a picture in her mind of the shape of the forest ahead. She could see the small figure of Rafi as he flew across the ground, no longer waiting for her to catch up. Sending the air further, she spread it out, marveling at the ease with which it molded to her will. Stiffening her shoulders, she let the air show her the trail made by the damaged branches, urging it forward until at last it enveloped the tall form of a human man.

Faunella let out a gasp, her eyes flying open in surprise. It was Derick. He was back out in the forest. She closed her eyes again, thickening the air to show her as much detail as possible.

He was walking, no, stumbling over fallen trees and rocks. He didn't appear to be injured again, and she sighed in relief, glad he was unharmed. He raised his arm, wiping it over his brow.

He's hot. How long has he been out here?

Biting her lip, she thickened the air around him, gently turning him in the direction of a small hidden stream that happened to be in the direction of her home. Then, with a gentle flick of her hand, she sent a tendril of cool air over the skin at the back of his neck, smiling when he threw back his head, his mouth opening in pleasure.

After a few tries to walk west, he finally gave in to her urging and started towards the stream. Faunella opened her eyes, her heart thudding loudly, and hurried to where he would end up, making sure she kept a light pressure against his back.

Faunella made it to the small waterway before Derick, so she took the time to get herself a drink and wash the warmth from her face. Her ears picked up the sounds of Derick's movements long before he emerged from the trees, but she hurriedly climbed high above the water, suddenly nervous about seeing him again. She left Rafi and Beebe far behind, knowing that Rafi's keen nose would lead him to Derick eventually. So when he stepped into view at last, it was only her and him, alone without anyone near or watching.

Maybe it was because of this that Faunella decided to do what she did, or maybe it was the guiding hand of fate. But whatever it was, the moment Derick had sunk gratefully to his knees and plunged his head into the trickling water, Faunella took a big breath and dropped to the ground, standing on the opposite bank with only a short jump separating them.

He looked up, his eyes blinking past the water as he stared at Faunella. She quivered under his gaze as his hazel eyes locked onto her. Keeping her hands fisted at her sides, she was prepared to fling him away and flee back to the Fae if he did anything she felt was threatening. But he just crouched there, face still dripping water, and looked at her, his chest moving more rapidly with each passing second.

She couldn't move, feeling trapped under his heavy stare. As the air stretched taut between them, she let herself drink him in. His face, now clear from bruises, revealed clear, sunkissed skin, darkened by a faint shadow of stubble growing from his chin and cheeks. The way he crouched only accentuated the width of his shoulders, reminding Faunella that he was much bigger and stronger than her. It should have made her afraid, but instead, it caused the pit of her stomach to clench, sending a strange fluttering feeling reeling through her body. His lips parted, drawing her attention to his mouth, still moist from the stream.

She flushed, lowering her eyes to the space between them.

"You're real."

His words were hushed, quietly murmured over the gentle bubbling of the water at their feet. But it was the awe in his voice that made her look up, eyes wide with surprise. His mouth curved up at the corner, causing small lines to fan out from the corner of each eye.

"I was beginning to think I had dreamed you up. I'd had one too many knocks to the head, and you were a figment of my imagination."

Faunella swallowed dryly, wondering if she had made a mistake in revealing herself to him. His full attention was on her, and she felt vulnerable and seen. But at the same time, she couldn't imagine walking away.

"Still not the most talkative, are you?" He chuckled, getting to his feet.

Faunella stepped back and sucked in a sharp breath. She was only used to him lying down or sitting, forgetting that he was at least a head height taller than her.

Derick's smile fell at her retreat. He raised his hands at his sides and frowned slightly, not trying to move forward at all.

"I'm sorry. I didn't mean to frighten you. I won't come any closer if you don't want me to."

His earnest words rang with truth, and he waited calmly for her to respond. As the silence stretched out, she began to feel embarrassed. He hadn't done anything to make her feel threatened, and he had lived with her in her home for several days. Granted, he was badly wounded at the time; but she was sure that if he wanted to hurt her, he would have made that clear by now. Swallowing dryly, she gave him a tentative smile.

His returning smile lit up his whole face, making the hazel of his eyes shine gold.

"Why don't we start over?" He placed his hand in the middle of his broad chest. "My name's Derick, and yours is?" Holding his hand out towards her, he arched his eyebrow, looking at her expectantly.

Faunella's lips twitched, his playfulness reminding her of the reasons she had felt a connection with him when he was first injured. It was too late to turn back now.

Touching her hand lightly to her own chest, she looked him in the eye. "My name's Faunella."

"See, that wasn't so hard. So, Faunella, what brings you to this part of the forest?"

Before she could answer his amusing question, the sound of something crashing through the undergrowth caught Derick's attention. Faunella looked in the direction of the noise, waiting expectantly for what she had heard coming for several minutes now. But before Rafi and Beebe could emerge from the trees around them, Derick jumped over the water and grabbed her arm, pulling her behind him.

Her heart jolted at his closeness, and a small gasp escaped her mouth.

"Stay behind me," he growled, his voice rough even as his hand on her arm was gentle.

Faunella's mouth fell open. She couldn't understand his actions. His muscles were tense, facing toward rustling foliage as he widened his stance, trying to cover her with as much of his body as possible.

Rafi burst through a large fern, his sleek red coat a blur as he launched himself between Derick's legs and stood, fur on end, at Faunella's feet. Beebe flew from his back, coming to nestle onto her shoulder. Her little beak peeked out from between Faunella's hair.

Sending soothing thoughts down the bond, Faunella reassured the animals that she was okay and not in any danger from Derick. They settled down immediately, surveying Derick with mixed looks of curiosity and wonder.

Derick dropped her arm and spun around to stare at the trio, mouth agape, looking from where Rafi had emerged and where he was now sitting at her feet. Faunella watched him curiously, waiting to see what he would do. From her observations, humans liked animals, though she hadn't seen any foxes past The Edge.

After a moment, his face relaxed, the muscles in his jaw and his neck unclenching as he turned his full attention to stare with confusion at Rafi.

"Is that a fox?"

She glanced down at Rafi, who was obviously a fox, and wondered at his strange question.

"Yes?"

His skin flushed at her quizzical tone and he ran his hand through his warm brown curls, flashing her a crooked smile.

"I'm sorry. I was expecting something else."

Curiosity peaked, Faunella crouched down to scratch between Rafi's ears, watching as Derick's eyes widened when she did.

"Something else?" she asked, her hand stilling when his face darkened and turned serious and he glanced once more northwards.

"I'm in a bit of a mess." He sighed, lifting his head and looking away from her. "The people I live with...well, they aren't very good people." Stepping back, he looked down at her once more. "I'm not a good person either."

Her heart sank at the resignation in his voice, the utter certainty he had about what type of man he was. She could see the sadness in his eyes and had felt the gentleness of his hands. No matter his past, she couldn't believe he was a bad person, no matter the fears she sometimes felt. Connecting briefly with Rafi, she felt the fox's feelings towards Derick—curiosity, excitement, some amusement. There was nothing to indicate she had anything to fear from him.

When she still hadn't said anything or shown any emotion on her face, Derick continued, his brow furrowing slightly.

"I'm in a gang. I've been in it my whole life, but now they want me dead."

Faunella gasped, coming to her feet in one smooth push. Suddenly, his nervousness about Rafi coming through the bushes made sense. They wanted to kill him, the man who laughed at the water she had poured over his head, who hadn't gotten angry once when she wouldn't talk to him, the man who made her breath catch when he touched her hair. She couldn't let him die.

Connecting with the air around her, she pushed it out in a large circumference around them, searching for anyone who might currently be out in the forest.

The area was clear with no sign of anything aside from several nesting birds and a small family of mice.

"They know I'm in the forest, and the man who's been sent to kill me won't stop." His lips curved up into a small sad smile. Reaching his hand slowly towards her, he curled a strand of her hair around his fingers, making all the breath leave her body.

"I'm just grateful I got to see you one last time before I go."

His finger stroked all the way down her hair, his hand pulling back and landing with a slap on his thigh when the long strands ended.

Faunella's pulse thudded. It was too soon. Their brief interactions had only reminded her of the joy she found in connecting with another person, someone other than her family. The thought of never seeing him again sent a wave of desperation washing over her.

"Where will you go?"

She kept her voice even, not wanting to share the depths of her feelings. Not when she didn't quite understand them herself.

He blew out a breath, clapping his hand on the back of his neck.

"Ah, about that. To be honest, I'm not so sure. I thought I'd head to the main highway and try to hitch a ride, but I'm sure Jarred will have men watching out for that. I've been wandering around in here since last night." He waved his hand towards the canopy of leaves high above them. "But the trees are so thick that I think I'm lost. I don't know which way to go."

The thought of being lost in the forest was such a strange idea to her. The abundant trees and each mossy rock were all simply a part of the place she called home. She eyed his body. He contrasted sharply with the muted greens and the warm brown of the forest. His black jacket, jeans, and t-shirt, so similar to when she had first found him, were better suited to life in the city he was from. If he had any chance of getting away from these bad men and making it through the forest, he would need her help.

She shyly looked up into his eyes, momentarily at a loss for words when she got caught in the whirlwind of feeling she saw in them. Wetting her lips with the tip of her tongue, she broke the connection, unable to speak otherwise.

"I could hide you." She dug her toes into the soft dirt, aware she was breaking all the rules that the Fae had set for her. "You could stay at my home. No one would find you there."

Derick opened his mouth, then shut it with a clap. He stared at her in silence for a moment before clearing his throat roughly.

"Look at me."

She looked at his mouth, mesmerized by the shape of it.

"No, Fawn, look at me."

He gently placed his finger under her chin, lifting her face slightly until her eyes landed back on his. His eyes were soft, drinking in every contour of her face. She wanted to look away, unable to bear the concern filling his shining eyes.

"I couldn't do that to you." He released her chin, stepping away and creating space between them. "You're afraid of me, aren't you? Ever since that first day after you saved me." He shook his head, flashing her a weak smile. "I don't blame you. And as much as I'm grateful to you for looking after me, I don't want you to constantly be afraid, not while you're in your own home. I'll figure something else out, but maybe you could show me the way out?"

Derick was right. She was afraid of him, but not in the same way as she first was. She no longer feared that he would hurt her or attack her like the experience from many years ago. Instead, she feared the feelings he made her feel, the shortness of breath when he looked at her, the racing of her heart when he touched her. She had never felt this way before, and it terrified her. But the thought of him leaving and never coming back had her even more frightened. She didn't want to lose him—well, not until she had to. Squaring her shoulders, she spread her feet on the ground and looked him full in the eye.

"I'm not afraid. I can look after myself." She tossed her head, sending a small gust of wind at Derick for good measure. "And I can look after you too. Now, are you coming or not?"

She turned around without waiting for a reply and flounced off into the trees, her heart pounding a mile a minute. It was only when she heard his fumbling footsteps behind her that she slowed down, her lips twitching into a satisfied smirk.

CHAPTER FIFTY NINE
DERICK

ERICK COULDN'T BELIEVE HE found her. The forest was so vast that it seemed impossible for the two of them to be in exactly the same place at the same time. And yet, here they were again.

After sending her animals on ahead, a feat that he could barely believe, she stayed just ahead of him, seeming to know when he slowed down and adjusted her pace to match. He was slowing down a lot more frequently now. He removed his jacket long ago, and a blister formed from his thick leather boots. His stomach gave a hollow rumble. A full night and day without eating was taking its toll.

Faunella was about fifteen feet away, having just climbed up a boulder that had to be at least his height and then half again. The way she scaled the rock face was nothing short of miraculous, her lithe form seeming to fly up the side of it. She stopped when his stomach growled and turned back towards him, her lips curving up as she regarded him.

"You're hungry."

She said it with utter certainty, despite the fact that there was no way she could have heard his stomach from all the way over there.

"How'd you know that?" he called, jogging to catch up and trying not to wince each time his blister rubbed inside his boot. He stared up at the rock face, wanting to climb it as easily as Fawn had. Swallowing hard, he threw himself at the rock, scrambling for footholds and gripping tightly with his fingers. To his utter surprise, he scaled the full height easily. It

451

almost felt like his body was weightless. When he got to the top, he sat on the edge, clenching his fists and discreetly flexing his biceps.

I must be stronger than I thought.

Faunella came up behind him, her presence like a warmth against his back.

"Some things are easy to tell," she said in reply to his earlier question.

Sitting down beside him, she pulled out a small cloth bag from under her clothing. With almost painful shyness, she handed him the bag.

"We can share these if you'd like."

Curiosity peaked, Derick opened the bag and peered inside.

"Berries?"

He reached in and pulled one out, rolling it between his fingers. It was most definitely a berry, but as for what kind, he didn't know. Glancing at Fawn, he was pleased to see her smiling at him. As his stomach gave another rumble, he popped the berry into his mouth.

The flavors were like nothing he had ever tasted before. He rolled the pieces over his tongue, trying to pinpoint exactly what made the fruit taste so amazing. It was tart, making his taste buds tingle before being soothed by the smooth sweetness. It made all his senses come alive and filled his nose with the sweetest perfume.

He groaned around the berry, not wanting to stop chewing even for a moment. Faunella giggled beside him, which made the corners of his mouth twitch upwards. Swallowing with great satisfaction, he turned to her, loving the bright sparkle in her blue eyes.

"What was that?" he asked, reaching in the bag to grab another. "I've eaten a lot of berries in my life, but never one that tasted like that."

She grinned broadly, revealing straight white teeth. Then, reaching over, she took a few berries for herself.

"They grow here in the forest." She popped one in her mouth, mesmerizing him by the way her lips moved as she chewed. "Berries are my favorite, but these berries are by far the best."

"You can say that again."

He leaned back on his elbows as they finished off the berries in companionable silence. He had never felt so at ease around anyone before. The forest was so peaceful, and Fawn had a stillness about her that he had never seen in another person. He glanced at her out of the corner of his eye. She sat with her knees drawn up, her arms hugging them close with such a serene look on her face that he felt his stomach tighten with longing for whatever it was that had made her this way. His fingers itched to reach up and stroke down the smooth contours of her cheek, but he held back, not wanting to mar her luminescent skin with his filthy hands.

She let out a sigh, sucking her lower lip into her mouth to remove any last trace of the berry juice. Derick's eyes fell to the sight, watching the way the soft plump flesh sprung back, still moist from her tongue.

"We should keep moving." She glanced at his legs, which gave him the opportunity to jerk his head away from her face and pretend he had been looking at anything else.

"Sure thing. How far do we have to go?"

She pushed to her feet and worried her hands, her face flushing a becoming shade of pink.

"I'm not sure." Her eyes bounced around, looking anywhere but at his face. "I've never traveled this slowly before, so I'm not sure how long it will take."

Now it was his turn to not meet her eyes. His skin went hot with mortification. He was slowing her down so severely that she had no idea how much longer it would take. He flushed with embarrassment and launched himself to standing, shaking out the tightness in his limbs.

Faunella touched his arm, her slender hand standing out starkly against his tanned skin.

"We'll get there. Don't worry." Her hand curved around to grip his arm, pulling him along with her as she walked. "Try not to step so heavily. There are surfaces for your feet to land on and gaps for your body between the trees."

Derick barely heard her gentle words, and she tried to teach him how to move through the forest. All he could feel was her soft hand on his arm, her elegant fingers pressing and pulling with each step they took. He moved on, no longer feeling the aches of his muscles or the blister on his foot. It was only him and Fawn as they moved through the forest, the trees a green and brown blur as they passed by. When her hand released and fell to her side at last, Derick was ready, sliding his arm along hers until he caught her palm, lacing her fingers with his.

She paused and turned to him, eyes wide with her pink lips forming a soundless *oh*.

"It's easier for me to walk better with you helping," he explained, shrugging his shoulders like it was no big deal, when, in fact, it was a big deal. The feel of her hand in his made his heart race, like he was a teenager experiencing things for the first time again.

Fawn looked at their hands, then nodded, her face serious.

"Of course."

He gave her hand a little squeeze, his lips twitching when she looked at him with such confusion.

"I'm ready to go." He smiled innocently.

They carried on, hand-in-hand, and Derick refrained from stroking his thumb along the side of Fawn's hand. He wondered at her reaction and finally came to the conclusion that this could very well be Fawn's first time holding hands with someone. The thought caused a wave of sadness to wash over him and also a burning curiosity. But he gave in to neither, only focusing on the feel of her hand in his as they journeyed onwards.

"Almost there."

They had been walking for hours. Derick didn't know how Fawn had the energy. She was tall and lean, more so than most of the women he knew, but the way she could just keep on going without seeming to tire was amazing. They stopped several more times since that first time, and each time he grabbed ahold of her hand when they started walking again.

The last time, he had purposely not taken her hand and had felt a rush of pleasure when she reached out and took hold of his instead.

She came to a stop beside a massive tree trunk. He looked around, not understanding why they were stopping when they were so close to her home.

"Shouldn't we keep moving?"

Laughing, she released his hand, turning to pull herself into the tree.

"We're here. Just a little climb and you'll be safe."

"Climb?"

He let his head drop back as his eyes traveled up the length of the tree. It was easily five stories high, with absolutely no sign of a house within. She pulled herself up further, now over his head.

"It'll be okay. Trust me. It's not as hard as you think."

She looked so at ease in the tree, her sweet face sparkling with mirth. He swallowed, stepping forward to place his foot in a rounded knot at the tree's base.

"Wait." He paused, looking up at her past the lowest branch. "You're saying you live in a tree, right?" She nodded back down at him. "But why can't we just go where you had me before? I'm sure that will be easier to get to."

Fawn frowned at him, shaking her head in confusion.

"This is where you stayed before. In my house, with me."

Derick removed his foot and backed away from the tree, his mind whirling at the improbability of it all.

"I was unconscious, Fawn, halfway across the forest. You're telling me that you got me here and all the way up into this tree, not to mention doing all that in reverse, by yourself?"

She looked away, nibbling nervously at her lower lip.

He ran his hand through his hair, hating himself for making her feel afraid, but not able to wrap his head around the crazy facts. He studied her, looking for any trace of something that might reasonably explain how it was possible.

She was tall, but there was no way she was strong enough to carry him. Her skin was luminous, marred only by a smattering of freckles across the bridge of her pert nose. Nothing about her appearance could even remotely explain how she could get him up the tree.

He let out a harsh laugh, throwing his hands into the air and turning his back on her as an errant thought crossed his mind.

"I don't suppose you have magical powers, do you? Super strength, super speed?" He laughed again, thinking of the two wild animals that had followed her around. "And powers over animals, right? They come at your beck and call?"

He turned back to face her, thinking she would smile at his over-the-top suggestions. To his horror, she was bone white, her freckles standing out starkly amongst the paleness of her face.

"Fawn, what is it?"

He darted forward, heedless of his weary muscles, and pulled himself up the tree, coming to a stop in front of her, a branch digging uncomfortably into his back.

"What's wrong? Tell me what's wrong."

He steadied himself against the tree, cupping her cold face in his palms.

"Oh my god, you're so cold."

Stroking down her hair, he tried to get a response out of her. Her stillness frightened him. Even when she was painfully shy, she wasn't this still. Brushing a hair out of her face, he tucked it behind her ear, finally evoking a response from her.

"No!"

Fawn wrenched herself from his touch, hurriedly pulling her hair back over her ear. But the damage was done. His fingers could still feel the arching point of her ear, the touch bringing back a memory that he had dismissed as imagination. The last time he had hooked her hair behind her ear he thought he had felt a point, but without his vision and after his injuries, he had told himself he was wrong. But now there was no hiding it. He had seen it with his own eyes. Heart beating fast and mind struggling to keep up, he reached out again. Pulling back her hair and revealing her delicately pointed ear.

Fawn trembled, her eyes filling with tears.

"You know." Her voice shook. "I should never have let myself get close."

"Know what? I don't know anything."

He reached out to touch her cheek again, but she pulled back drawing herself further up the tree. He followed, not wanting her to leave him over some silly misunderstanding.

"Do you mean the ears? That's not even a big deal. A lot of people have body parts that are different. It doesn't make me think of you any less. I think they're beautiful." He chuckled. "Like a fairy."

She let out a sob and simply flew up the tree. A rough bark sounded from down below, and Derick glanced down. The ground blurred dizzily from his height.

How did I get up this high?

The fox was back, a bright orange blob on the forest floor. To Derick's surprise, he gave a running jump and launched himself into the tree, his sleek body finding foot holds he hadn't noticed on his way up. The sight of the animal climbing the great tree had his mouth falling open in shock. He was so focused on watching the incredible sight that when Fawn's small bird came gliding past his face, he jumped in surprise. His tired muscles cramped up painfully, and his hands scrambled for purchase. But it was no use; he fell backward, gravity doing its job of pulling him back to earth. With his stomach lurching sickeningly, he let out a yell, flailing his arms as if his limbs could save him from the plummet.

The ground approached fast, thick air rushing past him and tearing at his clothes. He squeezed his eyes shut, his final thought was regret that his last moments with Fawn were not good ones. Then, suddenly, he stopped.

There was no pain, no sickening thud from his body striking the ground. His eyes flew open, heart pounding and body slick with sweat.

He was face up, the tree's great canopy far above him. About halfway up the tree perched the fox, its gaze caught by something higher up. He tilted his head, looking for what had captured the animal's attention.

It was Fawn, hands outstretched towards him, her face pinched with strain. He frowned, tearing his eyes from her and looking to his side.

"Holy shit!"

He hadn't hit the ground. He hadn't even reached the ground. All the breath left his body, and he tried to sit up, only freaking himself out more when he sat hovering above the ground.

Slowly, he lowered fully to the ground. Standing, he patted frantically at his body, assuring himself he was still in one piece. With growing awe, he looked back up at Fawn. Panic grew into a near-painful tightness when she stepped out of the tree.

His world stopped, the last thirty-one years narrowing to this exact moment.

How could he have ever thought she was human? Her hair spread out from her body like a flame, showing her otherworldly ears. Her clothes flattened against her, revealing the soft rounded curves of her body, from her long slender neck to the delicate pointed tips of her toes. She was grace incarnate, descending like an avenging angel to judge his blackened soul.

Derick couldn't tear his eyes from her. She was magnificent. The most beautiful creature he had ever seen in his life, and she wasn't even human.

She touched down, landing with a gentle bend of her knees. He watched her approach, heart pounding in his ears. Her skin was still pale, the blue of her eyes accentuated by her wide eyes. The bird came to land on her shoulder, making her seem all the more ethereal.

Stopping in front of him, she didn't speak, letting the silence stretch out into a near-painful tension.

She saved him. She saved him yet again. He was struck dumb, not able to think of a single thing he could say to her.

They stood like that until his pulse returned to a normal rhythm, and his legs began to feel like jelly.

"I think I need to sit down."

Wobbling over to the base of the tree, he placed his hands on the bark and lowered his body back to the ground. Taking some deep breaths, he braced his forearms on his knees and looked back up at Fawn.

Now that he had gotten over the shock somewhat, he noticed the way Fawn was fiddling with her hands. She was obviously worried about his reaction, which was fair enough. But it sent a wave of compassion rushing through his body.

She's still the girl who saved my life. Nothing else matters.

He patted the ground beside him. "Why don't you come over here, and we can talk?" He forced a chuckle. "I don't know about you, but I don't think I'm quite ready to make that climb again."

Fawn's head shot up in surprise, her pale skin regaining some of its color.

"You still want to stay? Even after?" She made a large motion with her hands, gesturing towards him and the uppermost branches of the tree.

He ran his hand through his hair, feeling a bit sick as he remembered the feeling of falling.

"I have nowhere else to go. But if it's okay with you, maybe we could get to know each other a bit?" He patted the earth beside him again, hoping she would take his offer.

She hesitated, but after the bird gave a small chirp, she walked over to him and lowered herself gracefully to the ground. He jolted when the fox jumped from the tree and came to curl up in Fawn's lap.

"So, I take it that you're not human?"

Derick cringed at the question, hating how stupid it sounded the moment the words left his lips.

But to his relief, she didn't seem to mind it. She actually seemed pleased at the blunt question.

"I'm not a human. I'm Fae."

"Fae? That's like fairy folk, right?"

He hadn't read many fairy tales, but he knew the basics. Though, he had never imagined that they could be real.

"Yes. Those stories are about my people, but they don't come to Earth anymore."

Her tone was sad, but she was opening up to him and talking more than he had ever heard. So he carried on with his questions, needing to learn more.

"But you're here. Where are the others?"

Her eyes darted around, looking through the trees as if someone might stumble across them talking.

"Fawn? You okay?"

She flashed him a small smile, her eyes coming back to meet his.

"I'm fine. The other Fae are back on Amaranth, the realm of the Fae. But I can't remember it. I've been on Earth as long as I can remember."

He opened his mouth to fire off several more questions, still utterly bewildered by what seemed to be totally normal for her. But she held out her hand to stop him.

"I can't tell you everything, and there are things in my life that I'm only just finding out. But if you still want to stay, then I should tell you about my friends."

Friends?

He felt an inexplicable rush of jealousy at the thought of Fawn having friends. If one of them was a man, he would have to be blind to not fall for such an amazing person. He remembered how he felt when he last met her and flushed. Even blind, he felt drawn to her, her warm presence attracting him more than just her looks.

"Friends?" he ground out, clearing his throat to cover up his feelings.

"Yes, Rafi and Beebe." She pointed at the animals on her lap and shoulder. "You were right before. I have a way with animals. I can connect to them, and we can communicate with each other through a bond."

The animals. She's talking about her animals.

Relief flooded over him as well as a tight sensation of embarrassment for feeling possessive over Fawn's attention. His first thought should have been happiness that she had other people in her life, not jealousy that she might prefer another's company.

She continued talking about her animals while Derick only half listened, still shaken by her revelation. By the sounds of it, other than the animals, Fawn was totally alone.

"It was actually Rafi that found you that day. He led me to you, knowing that you needed help." She pressed a kiss on top of the fox's head, making Derick envy the animal.

"I've never heard you talk so much."

He said the words out of the blue, enjoying the sound of her voice. She flushed prettily, burying her face back in the fox's red fur.

He smiled, charmed by the way her hair almost exactly matched the fox's coloring.

"Is it because you don't have to hide who you are anymore?"

Fawn pursed her lips, pondering his question. He shifted in place, his muscles starting to burn painfully.

"I think so. It's dangerous for humans to know about Fae. We are only supposed to observe and not be seen." She flashed him a quick smile. "I broke the rules when I saved you." She stood up. "And I'm breaking them now."

He glanced up at the tree, sighing heavily.

"Time to go up?" he asked, knowing the answer but dreading it just the same.

Twisting her hand in a swirling motion, Fawn grinned down at him, her shyness disappearing like the light that was gradually fading around them. A small twister of air pulled at his clothes, and he looked up at her, lips parting at her easy display of power.

"Don't worry." The wind pulled at his body, pushing him to standing. Her eyes sparkled in the fading light. "I can help."

CHAPTER SIXTY
FAUNELLA

H E KNEW. HE FOUND out about her, and nothing bad happened.

Derick was asleep in the treehouse, exhausted after his day of walking followed by the shocking revelation that she was Fae. Faunella watched him fall asleep, her vision allowing her to see him perfectly while the dark of the night kept her hidden from his sight. He asked her a few more questions before he dozed off, not knowing that she could see the happy smiles that kept showing on his face each time she spoke. It made her feel tingly all over that he enjoyed her company even after he found out she wasn't human. He hadn't treated her differently or wanted to leave.

Afterward, his face relaxed, making him look younger. She had crept over and brushed the chocolate strands off his forehead, enjoying the way the gentle curls wrapped around her finger. Then, as the joy had threatened to burst out of her chest, she swung herself out of the window and up to the leafy roof of her home. She chuckled when Rafi jumped on the bed to curl up with Derick as she left.

Beebe came with her, snuggling her small warm body up against her neck. The bird's presence was a steady comfort while she worked through her tremulous feelings.

She looked up at the stars, their light a smattering of color burning their way over the deep of the sky. She sighed, letting the coolness of the night wash over her face, the air softly teasing the small strands of hair around her face.

"He stayed, Beebe."

Her lips curved upwards, a heady euphoria filling her to the brim. Beebe cooed softly beside her, her little striped head beginning to droop.

"I don't have to be afraid anymore. Derick knows what I am. He saw my powers, and it didn't cause anything bad to happen."

The image of Derick falling through the air flashed through her mind. She sucked in a breath, then smiled wryly. "Well, other than that one little thing."

Derick falling brought back other memories from long ago. She had saved Lucy from a similar fate when she was just a child. The thought of her childhood friend still sent a pang of sadness through her, but Amon had been right. Time did lessen the sting.

"I think Derick could be another friend to me."

She glanced down at Beebe and smiled when she saw that her feathered friend had fallen asleep. With great care, she scooped her up and swung herself back through the window. Placing Beebe in her nest, she turned and began to prepare for bed, pausing when she heard the sounds of someone approaching on the forest floor.

Faunella focused on the sound, her ears picking up several different nuances. She flinched, glancing at Derick fast asleep in her bed. It was the Fae.

She knew she would have to face them sooner or later. Taking one last look at Derick, she descended from the tree house and turned to face her gathered family.

"You went back and showed yourself to the human."

It wasn't a question. Amon said the words with such certainty. Faunella briefly wondered how they found out so quickly, but then decided it didn't matter. She had made her decision and would stick to it. Confidence filled her up, making her pull back her shoulders and meet Amon's dark eyes.

"Yes, I did."

The Fae glanced around at each other, their worry palpable. But Amon kept his eyes on her, concern pulsing from him in great waves.

"But why? Why would you put yourself, and us, at risk? He will find out who you are." He reached out a limb to touch the top of her ear. "What you are."

She reached up to clasp his hand, bringing it to rest against her cheek. Amon was just concerned. His love for her was always at the root of all of his decisions and actions.

"He already knows," she whispered, hating the look of shock that filtered over his face, but needing them all to know. "He knows, and it doesn't matter to him. He accepts me for who I am!" She stepped back to speak to the other Fae gathered, her voice rising in volume, passion dripping from each word. "I can't see the harm in some humans knowing about us. Isn't that how it was thousands of years ago?" Raising her face to the sky, she closed her eyes, overcome by the intensity of her feelings. "I've felt alone for so long, and I've finally found someone. Someone who needs me, and I need him. More importantly, I choose him, and I won't let you change my mind."

She looked into each of their faces, the faces of the family who had found and raised her, and felt a hot rush of shame. They were looking at each other, indecision on many of their faces. Her words had done that. And while she didn't regret revealing herself to Derick, the fact that she had broken the Fae's rules and upset them made her feel sick.

"It's not the way we do things anymore, Fawn. The humans have changed too much." Amon shook his head, stepping back from her. "There is much you don't know about the way we do things and why. Perhaps that's my fault for not teaching you better."

Faunella opened her mouth to argue the point. A hard lump formed in her stomach after hearing Amon put himself down in that way, but he held up his hand to stop her.

"But I will teach you now. It's time we finish telling you about your heritage and how you came to be on Earth."

She backed away, her skin heating up and her pulse pounding, though she didn't know why.

"I'm not ready for that."

"It can't wait for much longer. There are things you need to know, and the human only complicates things."

Faunella swallowed, willing her pulse to settle. She knew she couldn't avoid the subject forever. And while information about her past and Amaranth was something she's been wanting to know for years, suddenly the knowledge felt like too much to handle right now. She glanced up towards her treehouse, itching to return to Derick.

"Wait, how did you even know he was here? I know you didn't see us."

"Ha, are you kidding? With the amount of noise that human was making, we could hear him from halfway across the forest." Huxley laughed and slapped Baol across the back, effectively breaking the tension.

Faunella gritted her teeth. "Stop calling him that!" She snapped. "He has a name."

"Hux," Violetta chidded, shaking her head at the grinning rock, before turning her clear eyes back to Faunella. "Of course he has a name, and I'm sure we would all use it if we knew what it was." Her lips drew upwards and she stroked down Faunella's arm. "But he wasn't that bad—just a little heavy-footed."

"And slow," Flavire added with a snicker.

Faunella fired a glare at him, turning so that Huxley got a share of her displeasure.

"He'd been walking all day and night. He's not used to the forest, not like us."

"It's because he doesn't belong here with us." Amon's voice was quiet, his soft eyes holding Faunella's attention.

She sucked in a breath, not looking anywhere but at Amon. As the stillness stretched out, she curled her lips up into a small smile. A deep feeling of certainty bloomed deep inside her chest.

"He belongs with me."

Amon closed his eyes, his branches drooping in resignation. Faunella stayed standing, her back straight and her eyes clear. This she was sure of. Derick had come into her life for a reason, and she wouldn't let him go easily.

A light bubbling broke the silence. Violetta cleared her throat and stepped between Faunella and Amon.

"I think Fawn has made herself clear. I suggest we all get a good night's sleep." She coughed, looking quickly at Faunella. "We can discuss the circumstances of how Fawn came to be on Earth later." Flashing her a smile that didn't quite reach her eyes, Violetta placed her hand on Faunella's shoulder. "How does that sound? We can give you some space and talk when you're ready."

Faunella's body almost drooped in relief. She wrapped her arms around the water Fae and gave her a firm hug.

"Thank you, Violetta."

Violetta squeezed her back, bringing her mouth close to Faunella's ear.

"It won't last forever. Amon's right; there are things you need to know."

Faunella stiffened, pulling back from Violetta's embrace.

"Just give me a few days. I'll listen to it all in a few days." She flung herself up in the tree, waving goodbye to the Fae, who reluctantly headed back towards the grotto.

She didn't know what was wrong with her. For as long as she could remember, she had been wanting answers about who she was and why she couldn't return to her home world to be amongst her own kind. But now, with the Fae practically bursting to give her the knowledge, she was afraid to hear it.

I'm a princess. I have a mother and a father. There is nothing to be scared of.

Despite her thoughts, she couldn't help the thin current of anxiety that ran through her when she thought about how she came to be here. There had to be a reason she had been kept on Earth and why she had to stay in a place where her own kind were unable to walk freely. That reason was just waiting to be revealed, but Faunella couldn't make herself hear it.

Heart weary and her mind heavy, she walked through the entrance to her home. She came to a complete stop when she rounded the curved wall to find Derick sitting up in bed, staring right at her.

"You're awake," she chirped out after an uncomfortable pause. She made her way over to a window, pulling open the curtain to let the moonlight flood in. "Are you okay?"

She turned to him, suddenly worried that something had happened to make him change his mind about her.

"I woke up because I heard voices." He cocked his head, peering at her through what Faunella knew to be a barely visible room.

"Voices?" she winced at the way her voice rose uncomfortably high.

"Well, one voice really. Just yours." Derick scratched at the dark hair growing on his jaw, his brows furrowing. "Who were you talking to, Fawn? I could only hear your voice out there."

Faunella swallowed thickly. She would never have gone out to talk to the Fae if she had known he was awake.

"I can't—"

"You can't tell me."

She drew back, surprised at his expression. He sat still on the bed, absentmindedly stroking Rafi's thick fur. His hazel eyes were trained on her with the barest hint of a smile upon his lips.

"Don't worry. I know you can't tell me everything." He stood up, brushing his hand through his hair as he took the few steps that brought him to stand in front of her. She drew in a breath, unable to look away from the intensity in his eyes.

"But did you mean what you said out there?"

"What I said?"

His eyes darted down to study her lips as she spoke. The inches between them suddenly felt like miles.

"You need me. You choose me." He swallowed, his voice deepening. "I belong with you?"

Now it was her turn to be mesmerized by the curve of his lips. Her breathing became shallow, the air thinning out until there was nothing left to inhale but him.

"Derick, I…"

"Yes?" He stepped closer until she could feel the heat emanating from his body and all she could smell was his rich, woodsy scent.

"I haven't had someone in my life for so long." She tilted her head up to look into his eyes, fighting the urge to step back. The tip of her nose grazed the short bristles on his chin. "I thought you could be a friend to me?"

Something dulled in his eyes, and he was the one to step back, his gaze roving over her face.

Faunella didn't know what she had said to make the light leave his eyes, and she stepped forward to try to explain.

"A best friend. Someone who accepts me for who I am." She touched her ears, suddenly self-conscious, and wondered if she had been wrong about the connection she felt between the two of them.

Derick opened his mouth and then shut it abruptly, a rueful smile forming on his face.

"I can be that." He blew out a breath, reaching out and taking her hand, then bringing it to his mouth. He pressed his lips against her knuckles, letting her feel exactly how soft they were. "I can be your friend."

Faunella's stomach flipped, a tingling warmth spreading up from where his mouth had lingered on her skin. But despite his words, she still got the sense that Derick was disappointed in some way. Not wanting to question his acceptance of her friendship, she gestured to the bed.

"It looks like you made a friend with Rafi as well."

With a chuckle, he spun around, still holding her hand tightly. Faunella didn't pull away, liking the way it felt wrapped around hers.

"I don't think he gave me much of a choice. I'd never been this close to a fox before now, but I'm happy to have him as a friend too." He looked over to where Beebe was fast asleep, her head tucked under one wing. "And the little chickadee, if she wants." He squeezed her hand, turning warm laughing eyes back to her.

Feeling breathless and vivacious with happiness, Faunella returned the squeeze. Letting out a little giggle of her own.

"I already know she likes you, but you can tell her yourself in the morning."

Derick's eyes softened. "You're amazing, Fawn," he murmured, his voice sounding incredibly sweet. "I don't think you have any idea of how special you are."

Her cheeks grew warm, and she looked away from Derick's eyes, unable to form a reply when he looked at her like that.

He cleared his throat, giving her hand one last squeeze before dropping it between them. She looked up, her hand feeling cold now that it was once again empty.

"It's late. We should sleep."

Faunella nodded, clasping her own hands together and walking around Derick to the second room where she would sleep.

"Of course, you've had a big day." She paused at the entrance, not wanting to leave him. "Are you okay? Do you need anything?"

He grinned at her, teeth flashing white in the moonlight.

"Just a good night's sleep, nothing else." He lowered himself onto the bed beside Rafi, never once taking his eyes off her. "I'll see you in the morning."

Heart thudding, she gave him a bright smile, ducking out of sight into the other room. As she readied herself for bed, she listened to him in the other room, her senses on high alert with each rustle of the blanket and deep, breathy sigh. Finally, she lay down, dressed in herwhite nightgown, hair brushed and loosely braided. She closed her eyes, listening to the deep steady breaths of the man in the next room.

"Goodnight, Fawn," he breathed, bringing a smile to her face and a tight, fluttery feeling in her stomach. She rolled over, drawing her blankets up to her chin, and closed her eyes.

"Goodnight, Derick," she whispered back, falling asleep with the smile still on her face.

Faunella woke to excited whispers coming from the other room. She cracked open an eye, amazed to see the sun was already up. She usually woke with the dawn. She must have been more tired than she realized. Turning her head towards the door between the rooms, she listened to the hushed voices, a smile curving over her face. Derick was still asleep, his breathing deep and even. She got out of bed and padded softly to the doorway, her gaze shooting to the open window where the voices were coming from.

Peeking over the ledge was the leafy head of Laurel and the clear eyes of Violetta. They were staring at Derick, quiet murmurs and giggles coming from their mouths.

"What are you two doing?" she hissed, glancing at Derick and tiptoeing over to the window to arch a disapproving eyebrow at the two female Fae.

"We just wanted to get a look at him now that he's no longer covered in bruises," Laurel breathed. "He's very handsome for a human."

"That strong jaw," continued Violetta, her eyes sparkling. "Fawn, what color are his eyes?"

"His eyes? Handsome?"

Turning her attention to the bed where Derick slept, she studied his form. He was relaxed in sleep, his brow smooth and jaw slack. His chocolate hair flopped down over his forehead, making Faunella's fingers itch to push it back. He was pleasing to the eye, his skin smooth and tanned. And the way his arm lay over the blankets, his muscles showing under the short sleeve of his t-shirt, made her skin heat and her mouth dry out.

He is handsome.

She flushed, turning back to the two Fae.

"You two shouldn't be here. He could see you, and you know how Amon feels about that."

"Come on, Faunella. What's his name at least? Then we can stop calling him 'the human' like you wanted. Tell us something. It's not often we get to be this close to such an attractive human man."

They dissolved into giggles again, raising themselves higher over the ledge to see Derick better.

"You two are acting like children."

Faunella undid her plait, untangling the long strands and flicking them back over her shoulder. She sighed, shaking her head slightly.

"If I tell you his name, will you leave?"

Eyes bright, they both nodded. Violetta's water splashed into the room and Laurel lost a few leaves in the process.

"Good." Faunella glanced back to his sleeping form, checking he hadn't woken up. Rafi's nose peeked over Derick's legs. His furry face made Faunella smile. She crouched down beside the window, coming face-to-face with the females. "His name is Derick." She paused, smile turning soft. "His eyes are the color of ripe hazelnuts, like the bark of a redwood in the deepest light of the afternoon sun," she continued, not noticing the way Violetta and Laurel slowly started ducking down out of sight. "He's taller than most humans and taller than me." She sighed, remembering the way she had to tilt back her head to look into his eyes when he stood unbearably close to her. "His hands are warm." Her voice had dropped to a whisper, lost inside the memories of the past day. "They are soft and strong. They make my hand feel small and make my skin tingle when he touches it." Voice trailing off, she peeked over the ledge, finding the tree outside empty of Fae. Letting out a huffing laugh, she pressed her forehead to the ledge, chiding herself for getting so carried away.

"I don't know who you're talking to, but that was a great way to be woken up."

Derick's deep voice had her spinning around on the balls of her feet, still in her crouch, back against the wall. Her hand clapped over her mouth in surprise, color blooming in her cheeks at being caught saying those things about him.

He grinned at her from the bed, his head propped up on one hand as he lay on his side.

"Don't go back to being shy now. We're friends, remember?"

Pushing her embarrassment aside, she raised herself to her feet, her thin nightgown tangling between her thighs as she flounced over to the opposite window. Derick was right. They were friends; there was no reason to be shy around him now.

"I didn't realize you were awake," she chuckled under her breath. "I guess that keeps happening, huh?" Leaning out the window, she closed her eyes, drawing on the warm spark that lived deep inside. Then, with a flick of her hair, she turned back towards Derick, a mischievous smile pulling at her lips.

"Let me show you a proper forest welcome."

She closed her eyes again, drawing on that essence within her body. A moment later, she felt them.

Dozens of soft bodies rode the air currents and beating their small wings. She felt a tug and smiled. Beebe was leading the host. With a warm swirl of air, they descended through the open windows, circling the room in a synchronized vortex of feathers and squawks.

Faunella laughed, feeling their joy as they skimmed past her body. She raised her hands and spun around, her powers teasing the wind and joining in with the swirling frey. In less than a minute, they were gone, leaving Faunella standing in the middle of the room facing Derick, her chest heaving with excitement and small feathers stuck in her windswept hair.

"Good morning, Derick," she panted, finally taking a good look at his face.

Her smile fell, and her arms dropped to her sides. Derick sat up on the bed, Rafi pressed tight against his leg. His face was slack, mouth slightly parted, and his eyes were fixed on her, tracking up and down her body as the temperature in the room seemed to heat up.

"Derick?" she tried, coming closer to him and reaching out to touch his shoulder. "Were the birds too much?"

He jerked away from her touch, dragging his eyes up to her face, a faint flush darkening his cheeks.

"No," he coughed, rolling past her and out of bed. His hands came down to adjust his pants, pulling at the thick fabric. "No, the birds were wonderful." He shot her a strained smile, then ran his hand over his hair, his eyes firmly on the ceiling. "Thank you for showing me that. Your powers just caught me by surprise, that's all."

Faunella wrinkled her nose, not understanding why he kept looking up instead of at her when he talked.

"Are you sure you're okay?" she tried again, once more coming to stand in front of him. She tilted her head to figure out what he was looking at.

A nervous laugh exploded from his mouth, and he covered his eyes, allowing Faunella to have a good look at his soft lips. Sliding his hand down over his face, he brought his eyes down to meet hers. With deliberate care, he placed both of his hands gently on her shoulders, giving her a tender smile.

"I think we should go get something to eat. Why don't you go get dressed for the day, and I'll wait for you here?"

He turned her and gave her a small push towards the other room.

"Okay, good idea." She looked back at him, arching her eyebrow as she took in his rumpled clothing, dirty from the day before. "We might need to get you some new clothes as well."

Glancing down, he took in his appearance, wincing at the dirt-streaked items. Faunella ducked out of sight, a low chuckle bubbling out of her mouth as she went to get dressed for the day.

CHAPTER SIXTY ONE
DERICK

*Y*OU'RE JUST HER FRIEND. *Only a friend, Derick. You need to keep your distance.*

He thought the words over and over, trying to make himself believe them. From the moment Fawn had stood up, revealing her body clad in nothing but that near-translucent nightgown, he had been transfixed. Not even her impressive feat with the birds could make him tear his eyes from the lush contours of her body. She looked like a goddess, her hair careening around her body, her hands outstretched as the wind and the birds swirled around, with her standing in the epicenter. But her body made his mouth go dry and his heart pound with undisguised longing. She stood tall, her limbs long and toned. The translucent material only highlighted the swell of her breasts, each round curve topped with a slightly darker nipple. He had to clench his fists in the bedsheets to stop himself from reaching for her, not cup each breast, run his hands down to the dip of her waist and back over the gentle curve of her hip.

He bit down hard on his lip to try to stop himself from picturing the dark V at the top of her thighs and what he was desperate to do to her if she would give him the chance.

She only wants a friend. Keep it in your pants.

He adjusted himself again, grateful that Fawn hadn't seen him straining in his trousers when she came close to him.

"Please wear something concealing," he whispered under his breath, walking over to stare out the window.

"What was that?" Fawn called out from the other room, her voice slightly muffled.

"Nothing. I didn't say anything."

He let out a breath. He had forgotten about her insanely good hearing. He'd have to be more careful in the future.

Walking around the edges of the room, he marveled at its construction. The floor was large smooth planks of wood, but the walls looked like they were woven in place as the tree grew. He touched the undulating texture, thinking he would have to ask Fawn how she managed to create such a home. Turning around, he opened his mouth to call out and stopped short.

Faunella was standing at the entrance to the room, her long hair pulled over one shoulder and her body covered from neck to knees in a green woven dress.

"Wow," he breathed out, coming closer to inspect her garment. To his great relief, her body was concealed. Those tantalizing curves were hidden behind the strange dress. "Did you make this?"

She nodded, fingering the fabric as a line formed between her eyebrows.

"I make a lot of my clothes. It's not so easy to borrow clothes past The Edge."

"The Edge?"

"The edge of the forest," she explained, still stroking the front of her dress.

"Ah, I see."

He stepped back, taking in the full outfit again. Noticing the way Fawn's large blue eyes stayed locked onto his face. It wasn't the most attractive item of clothing he had ever seen, but on Fawn out in the forest, it did the trick. It made her look all the more otherworldly, and he once again wondered how he had ever thought she was human.

"I like it," he finally said. "It suits you. Maybe you could make me a top to match. I'm sure it would help me blend in while we're in the forest."

When Fawn's face lit up, a wide smile stretching from ear to ear, he knew he had said the right thing. She stopped fussing with her dress and walked around him, snatching up his hand as she moved past.

"I can do that. But first, breakfast."

Faunella dragged him past the curving wall and her assortment of belongings, bringing him to the edge of the doorway. He paused, leaning over and peering down the long distance to the ground.

A warm body pushed past his legs and leapt from the treehouse. He gulped. The fox made that look incredibly easy, and he was a fox for goodness sake. They weren't supposed to climb trees.

Faunella looked over at him and laughed at the expression on his face.

"Going down is easier." She squeezed his hand before releasing it. "I've got you."

Steeling himself, Derick followed her out onto the first large branch, easing himself down with a few guiding touches from Fawn. To his surprise, she had been right. Going down was easier than going up. It definitely made it easier that he wanted to impress her, so he gritted his teeth and made his way down without uttering a single one of his fears.

Despite his brave face, he was still covered in a thin layer of sweat by the time he reached the ground. He pulled the fabric of his t-shirt away from his body. He'd have to shower sooner rather than later.

"So, breakfast?"

Faunella had walked off through the trees. She turned, eyebrows shooting up in surprise before ducking her head with a smile.

"I'm sorry. We have some more walking to do." She bit her lip, staring pointedly at his boots. "Are you going to be okay? Are your shoes comfortable to walk in?"

Derick took in his black boots now covered in a thin layer of dirt. Then his eyes traveled to where Fawn stood, her slender feet playing with the ground.

"They are pinching a bit, but I'm not used to going barefoot. I think that would end up being harder for me."

"Come," she beckoned him forward. "We can just go a little way, then I'll leave you and go collect something for us to eat."

Faunella's 'little way' turned out to be over an hour of walking. His blister was back with a vengeance, and he had two more coming up by the time they finally emerged into a sunny clearing with a stream cutting through it.

He let out a large breath of air when Fawn told him they had arrived. Walking over to lean against a large boulder beside the bubbling water, he sank gratefully to the ground, his feet splayed out in front of him.

"Derick, you..."

He raised his head to look at her, catching her just in time as the finger she pointed to the rock at his back curled into a fist, and dropped back to her side.

"What's wrong?"

He leaned forward, craning his head behind him to study the boulder. It was large and rounded, leaning upon a smaller, flat-topped rock. He couldn't see anything wrong with it and looked curiously back at Fawn.

She shook her head, lips quirked up at the corners.

"No, nothing's wrong. I just thought you might be more comfortable somewhere else."

He shot her a wide smile. She was so thoughtful, but there was no way he was getting up any time soon. His aching muscles wouldn't allow it. Stretching his arms over his head, he rubbed his back against the stone, giving it a slap for good measure.

"Nope, I'm plenty comfortable here." He smiled.

Faunella winced, and then let out a breathy laugh, coming over to crouch at his feet.

"Okay, if you're sure."

Reaching out, she grasped his foot, nimbly untying the laces on his boots.

"Woah, what are you doing?" He tried to pull his foot from her grasp, only managing to assist her in removing his shoe. "You don't need to do that." Leaning forward, he tried to stop her from doing the same to his other foot, mortified that Faunella, a Fae, would lower herself to perform such a menial task for him.

"Please, Fawn." He clasped both of her hands in his. "Stop."

Slowly but firmly, she pulled her hands from his, looking at him from under lowered lashes.

"I want to. You've been limping, so I know you're in pain. I thought you could soak your feet in the stream while I get food for us."

The thought of putting his aching feet into the cool water did sound heavenly.

"You've already done so much for me. I can take my own boots off." He ran his fingers through his hair, trying to figure out how to make Fawn see that it was he who should be waiting on her.

"I wanted to help." She drew back, a slight frown on her face. "Did I do something wrong?"

His heart sank. He was such a fool. Here she was doing yet another lovely thing for him, and all he could do was make her feel bad about herself.

"No, Fawn, no." He tucked his now shoeless feet under his body, scooching forward until he was knee to knee with Fawn. Looking down at her, he itched to wrap his arms around her and pull her close to his body. But he did neither, only reaching out and touching her knee with the tips of his fingers. "You haven't done anything wrong." He groaned, fighting for the words that would clarify how he was feeling. "How do I explain?"

She sat still, her round eyes taking in his every move and his every word.

"Nothing you could do would be wrong," he tried. "It's just, you are so incredible, Fawn. You are tall, beautiful, strong, and kind." Taking a breath, he blew it all out in a big rush. "You're not even human. You're a Fae, for god's sake, a mythical being. You are so much better than me,

Fawn, and it should be me getting on my knees before you, not the other way around."

Faunella's eyes had grown even rounder as he spoke. Her pink lips popped open into a small circle. He shook his head, trying to repress a smile at her stunned expression. Bopping her on the nose, he turned himself around, wanting to give her space to process his words. He removed his socks and rolled up his pants. Using his hands and feet, he moved to the edge of the stream. The moment he lowered his legs into the water, he let out a deep sigh. The water felt even better than he imagined. The coolness numbed the sting of his blisters and lessened the ache from the large amount of walking the past few days.

His eyes closed in bliss at the sensation, and a moment later, he felt Fawn's warm presence move to his side.

"I'm not better than anyone," she spoke softly, her words chosen with care. "It makes me happy to care for others. I saw you had a need, and I wanted to help."

Derick turned his head to face her, finding her sitting with her hands clasped gently in her lap and her head tipped back, staring into the sky.

"I might not have much experience with being a friend, but I do know that friends are meant to be equal. And they are allowed to take care of each other for as long as they can."

Fawn's voice grew heavy, the corners of her eyes seeming to glisten with tears. With a lump in his own throat, Derick reached his hand out and grasped hers, interlocking their fingers and turning his face away.

"You're right." He cleared his throat, startled to find his own voice thickened with emotion. "You can take care of me, and I'll take care of you."

He felt eyes on him and turned to find Faunella looking at him, a wide, toothy smile upon her face.

"Good," she chirped, nodding her head once and then jumping to her feet. "Now, stay here, and I'll go get us something to eat."

She left the clearing, disappearing without a sound into the trees, leaving Derick staring after her, his feelings all over the place.

How does she do that?

After years of keeping his thoughts and emotions in check, Fawn had successfully thrown his carefully crafted composure out the window. Without a doubt, he had felt and said more in the last two days with her than he ever had in the past sixteen years, maybe even longer than that. She had an amazing way of making him feel things deeply, including the way he was starting to feel about her.

"Ah," he groaned, falling backwards to stretch out on the grass. "She only wants me as a friend. Don't feel more."

Closing his eyes, he let himself enjoy the midmorning sun. The warm rays coupled with the gurgling of the stream soon made him doze off.

"Derick...Derick."

The sweet voice pushed in on his drowsy mind. The sound filled him with a warm feeling of pleasure as he relaxed further into the hard bed.

Hard bed?

His mind sharpened, taking in his surroundings with a snap. Beds weren't this hard. They were soft and spongy. A soft hand stroked down his cheek, leaving a tingling warmth in its wake.

Derick's mouth curved up into a smile and he cracked one eye open. He was still in the clearing, his feet submerged while he lay prone on the hard ground. Faunella's face blocked out the sun, her hair ringing her face like a fiery halo.

"You're back."

He sat up, stretching out his limbs. His impromptu nap had done wonders. The aching in his body had faded. His feet felt pain-free.

"You looked so peaceful. I didn't want to wake you."

"No, I'm glad you did. I'm hungry."

Faunella smiled at him, scooting back to reveal an assortment of food on the flat-topped rock beside the stream. There were mushrooms and nuts, grapes, and an apple, all on a bed of dandelion leaves.

"Wow." He grinned, taking his feet out of the water and standing up. "What an assortment." He took a step toward the rock, reaching out to take a grape when he realized that something was different.

"Hey, wasn't there a bigger rock right here?" Pointing to the space beside the flat-topped rock, he glanced around the clearing, seeing nothing but the one rock. "I could have sworn there was a big, round boulder here."

"A boulder?" Faunella's voice was high, her bottom lip drawn up in a pout. "No, I don't think so. There was just the one."

"Really? I could have sworn." He scratched his head, crouching down to inspect the ground. The grass was slightly indented but the same length and color as the surrounding greenery.

A pair of shapely legs came to stand in front of him, distracting him from his inspection of the grass.

"Still hungry?"

He looked up, taking in her body as his eyes made their way slowly to her grinning face.

Huffing a laugh, he grabbed her hand and pulled her down onto the grass with him, using any excuse to touch her.

"I'm ready. What about you?"

Faunella's eyes sparkled, and she grabbed a handful of dandelion leaves, popping them into her mouth and chewing vigorously.

"Of course I'm ready. I've been waiting for you."

The food was different from what he was used to, but he supposed that there wasn't much variety in the forest. Starting in on the food, he watched Fawn eat, his lips pursing as he watched her enjoy every morsel she put in her mouth.

"Don't you ever leave this place?" he asked after a particularly chewy mushroom. The food filled the empty hole in his stomach, but didn't do much in regard to flavor.

She stilled, her hands coming up to stroke at her hair. All at once, the bird flew in from nowhere, coming to land on Faunella's shoulder. The fox was still off doing whatever the animal did when it wasn't with Fawn.

Turning her blue eyes to him, she took a deep breath, her hands stilling and dropping from her wavy locks.

"I've only left the forest twice in my life. Once when I was a child—" Her mouth curved upwards, emotion swimming in her eyes. "—and once a few years later."

The air seemed to turn chilly around then. He rubbed his arms, fighting off the goosebumps that had begun to form. The sun was still beating down on them, so there was no reason why the temperature should plummet.

Fawn's face had grown blank, her attention no longer on him, but directed inwards.

I wonder if...

"Fawn," he said gently, reaching out to run the pads of his fingers down the soft skin of her cheek. "I think you're making the air cold." He frowned, pursing his lips at the reason. "Was the second time just before the third time we met?"

She lifted her eyes to him, her pain visible just below the surface.

"Yes." Biting her lip she tried a small smile. Derick frowned, remembering her fear and the state of her clothes. Not wanting to see her upset, he asked about the first time she left the forest.

"The first time was the best thing I had ever done."

"What happened?" He let his hand drop, bringing it back to his lap.

Faunella glanced around the clearing, taking her time looking through the ring of trees that surrounded them. Finally, she turned her attention back to him, leaning in to narrow the space between them.

"I haven't talked about it before." She bit her lip. "I'm not supposed to leave the forest, and humans aren't meant to know about the Fae, so if I'm seen, it could be bad. But..." She looked around again. Derick looked as well, wondering again what she was looking at. "I was seen," she whispered, eyes brightening. "I was seen, and I made my very first friend." She leaned back, smiling softly at him. "My only friend until now."

Derick felt a warmth in his chest, and he leaned back, not able to stop his cheeks from pulling the corners of his mouth up. Having a friend, while so normal and cavalier to most people, was obviously something special to Fawn. He couldn't blame her. If he really was her second friend ever, then that would be special to him as well. In fact, other than Rhett and a few children from his childhood, he was lacking in real friendships himself.

"I'm honored to be your friend." He looked around for his socks and boots, pulling them over in preparation to leave the clearing to return to the treehouse. "What happened to your first friend? Do you still see them?"

Faunella's face shuttered as she clenched the front of her dress and tilted her head to the side.

"No," she whispered, her voice coming out like the breath of a bird's wing. "She only lives in my heart now."

His heart dropped. Fawn's excitement and joy at having a friend was now so much more understandable. The pain and sadness in her eyes spoke of a loss, a loss like he had experienced when he was younger. He let go of his boots, scratching at the stubble on his jaw as memories of his past flooded his mind.

"I lost someone, too. My friend." He patted Fawn's hand absentmindedly when she let out a small breath, a stricken look on her face. "It's okay. It was a long time ago. I just wanted you to know that you're not alone. I know how it feels to lose someone you care about."

"I'm sorry."

He flashed her a weak smile, shaking off her sympathy. Rhett died a long time ago, and while he grieved his loss, he didn't deserve Fawn's sympathy, not when he was the one to take Rhett's life. He cleared his throat and changed the subject.

"Well, whoever your friend was, I bet she felt super lucky to have you as her friend."

Faunella smiled, her face lighting up with what he hoped were good memories. Pleased to have put a smile back on her face, he turned and began pulling on his socks. The first sock slid easily over his now dry foot, the skin smooth and unmarred. He began putting on the second sock before his brain caught up with him.

"Hold up."

He stripped off the first sock, lifting his foot and peering at the now-perfect skin. Then he did the same to the second foot. Both feet were unmarked with no sign that they were ever blistered.

"How in the world?" He touched the skin in awe, glancing towards the bubbling stream. "Fawn, is this some supernatural water or something? My feet were covered in blisters and absolutely killing me when we arrived here. But now, look." He angled his foot towards her, watching as she blinked slowly, face going suspiciously blank.

Letting out a deep groaning chuckle, he leaned back, watching Fawn look anywhere but at him. Another secret.

"Can't tell me, huh?" He let out a breath, wanting to respect her privacy, but burning to get some answers. "Okay, can you at least tell me if what healed my feet was the same stuff that healed my body when you cared for me the first time?"

She bit her lip, and he could almost see the wheels turning behind her eyes.

"It's the same," she finally murmured, bringing her gaze up to meet his.

"Is the stream responsible for that?" he tried.

Fawn shook her head, scanning the clearing once more.

"It's just a normal stream. Nothing special about it other than it comes directly from underground." She grinned. "So you know it's safe to drink."

"So, something else healed me, but you can't tell me what?" She nodded her confirmation. "Okay, well at least I know I'm not going crazy." Fawn's words reminded him that he hadn't drunk anything today. He moved to the stream and cupped his hands, lowering them to get a drink. From the taste, he knew Fawn had been telling the truth. This water, while refreshing, was nothing compared to the amazing liquid he drank while he was recovering.

"Did you want to go back to the treehouse now?"

Wiping his mouth with the edge of his shirt, he contemplated Fawn's question. Did he want to return to the dwelling? It was the safest place in the forest, but the thought of being cooped up inside all day didn't sit well with him.

"What would you be doing if I wasn't here?" he asked instead, turning the question around on her.

"I would be making something or looking for food to store. I might go for a trip through the forest or play with my powers." With that last part, she flicked her fingers, forming a small round globe of swirling air that quickly dissipated back to nothing.

She laughed, her teeth flashing in the sunlight, and sent a wave of air rushing over him.

Inhaling deeply, he settled himself, still a little in disbelief that magic existed at all.

"I want to do whatever you want to do." Swinging his arm around in a great arc, he gestured to the entire forest. "This is your domain. Show me your life."

Faunella smiled, getting to her feet and offering him her hand. Her animals let out little cries of delight and took off into the trees, leaving Derick and Fawn standing hand in hand under the beating sun.

"Leave your shoes here." She winked at him, causing a flush of heat to race up his neck. "You won't need them where we're going."

With a tug she turned, pulling him past the tall ring of trees. He held on to her warm hand, his feet pounding on the brown earth as she drew him further into the depths of the forest. A chuckle burst from his mouth. Never in a thousand years did he think he would be racing through the forest in bare feet, following a wild fairy who had saved his life, and in the process, captured his heart.

Derick let himself go, releasing the years of wearing a mask and hiding who he was. He let himself feel whatever he needed to feel. Fawn had turned his life upside down, drawing his true self to the surface without even trying.

"Where are we going?" He panted, trusting her to keep them safe.

"Wherever the wind takes us," she called back, her long hair trailing behind her and a warm breeze pushing him from behind.

Losing himself in the moment, Derick let his feet fly, throwing off the cares of the world, if only for a little while. But deep down, hidden in the back of his mind, was that tiny niggling fear that all this wouldn't last. Jarred was still out there, and not even Fawn, with her amazing powers, could stop him from coming.

CHAPTER SIXTY TWO
FAUNELLA

Luckily for Derick, Faunella and the wind kept him firmly on the ground. He had asked to see her world, but her favorite parts of the forest were ascending past the tree line and letting the wind push and pull her with abandon. However, she had seen his nerves when climbing up to her treehouse, and wanted to show him things that would elicit a smile, not make him feel bad.

For what had to be the hundredth time, Faunella glanced at him from below lowered lashes, sneaking a look from the corner of her eye.

He seems happy enough.

Her line of sight traveled down to their joined hands. He still hadn't let go. Turning her attention back to the trail, she bit her bottom lip and slackened her hand, pulling away ever so slightly. Then, like the past two times she had experimented, Derick lengthened his stride, slid his hand more firmly into hers, and tightened his fingers around her palm.

Faunella's lips twitched. It was becoming a pattern. For some reason, he wanted to stay connected. Just to see what he would do, she pressed down on his hand, giving it a quick squeeze. She felt more than saw his head turn to hers, but a split second later he gave an answering tug. Her smile grew wider. She repeated the gesture, not able to help the bubble of laughter when he once again returned the motion.

Never had she felt this way. Even with her beloved Lucy it had never been like this when they had held hands. Lucy was like her heart, filling a hole that had only ever been empty, but Derick had her burning with sensation.

Faunella turned fully towards him, walking backwards so she could study him in detail.

"Is it a human tradition to hold hands?" she asked, giving his hand another squeeze.

Derick flushed and gave her a crooked grin.

"I guess you could say that," he slackened his grip, letting her hand drop loosely between them. "When you enjoy being with someone or are their very good friend." Faunella watched with fascination as his cheeks seemed to darken further. "That's when you tend to hold hands."

"Or when you're helping someone travel unsteady ground?" she added brightly, trying not to show her disappointment that he had released her hand.

Derick ran his fingers through his curls and let out a sharp laugh. "Yes, especially then." Faunella joined in on his mirth, only stopping when his laughter died off and a shadow passed over his features.

"I can't even remember the last time I held hands with anyone."

Faunellas heart twisted. Poor Derick. He didn't have anyone. Even in her darkest hour, she always had the Fae, and although they didn't have flesh and blood, they still held her with care and love in their own way.

A wave of heat at her back distracted her from responding straight away. Swinging around, she surveyed their destination, hoping that she had chosen the right place to share with Derick.

"This is where I like to come if I need to get away or when I'm feeling trapped."

She swallowed past the lump in her throat, feeling like she was betraying the Fae by admitting her true feelings. The bright field spread out at their feet, flat earth turning to sweeping hills which butted up to the far off mountains in the southwest. Faunella took it all in, breathing deeply. Perhaps Derick would understand. Maybe he could relate to her in ways still unspoken.

His comforting weight stepped up beside her, quietly taking in the vista around them. Faunella closed her eyes when his hand slipped back into hers. The feeling of skin against skin was a marvel she hoped to never take for granted.

"I do remember the last time," he murmured as if to himself. His words sounded fragile, soft, like he could barely believe he was uttering them. Faunella stilled, hardly daring to breathe lest she remind him of her presence. She needn't have worried, he continued as if he was watching the memory play out in front of him.

"It was with my mother. I was only a child, too young to fully understand what was happening. If I had known it was the last time I would ever see her, then I might have done or said something different." A muscle jumped in his jaw, the only outward sign of his inner turmoil. "My dad would beat her, sometimes so hard that she would be in bed for weeks."

Dismay filled her, turning her skin cold with the horror of his life. She kept quiet, listening, even as tears flooded her eyes.

"I didn't do anything about it. I was too young, too weak. By the time I was old enough to make a difference, she was long dead."

He turned her around to face him, smiling wryly. "But you don't want to hear about that," releasing her hand, he rubbed at the back of his neck looking embarrassed. "There's nothing pretty about my life."

Faunella swiped at the moisture under her eyes, fighting to keep her emotions in check. "There's nothing about your life that I wouldn't want to hear." She locked eyes with Derick, empathy dripping from each word. She could hear his pain, could feel it as if it were her own. "I know the burden that loss can be, so if you want to share any part of your life with me, I'm here."

His searching gaze bore into her own, and he must have seen the sincerity there because his eyes softened, and his lips tipped upwards. "My mom would have liked you." He let out a long sigh, effectively changing the subject. "Maybe one day, little Fawn," he tucked a stray curl behind her ear, his face gentling even further. "One day, but not today." Stretching out his arms he surveyed the field, forcing a grin at the sun beating down. "Today is too nice to discuss topics like that, and you promised to show me your life."

The curve of her ear tingled from the softness of his fingers, momentarily robbing Faunella of speech. Swallowing, she considered his words. Needing space to avoid painful subjects was something she could absolutely relate to at the moment, so she tugged on the ends of her hair and let him change the subject. Beebe chose that moment to dart from the forest, several distinct pink flowers clutched in her beak.

Oh no. She hadn't even heard the Fae approaching.

Covering up her panic, she flashed Derick a wide smile and gestured to the field even as she moved back into the tree line. "You stay here with Beebe." She swivvled her head, tugging on her bond with the fox when she couldn't see him. "And Rafi. I'll be right back."

Ignoring the confusion on Derick's face, she turned and raced through the undergrowth, grateful for Beebe's warning. It wasn't long before she came upon Flavire and Venek.

"You two need to turn around and go back."

They pulled up short, drawing back in surprise. Faunella glanced over her shoulder, not wanting to leave Derick for long lest he follow her.

"What's wrong?" Venek asked, reaching out a vine and placing it on her shoulder. "Are you alright?"

"I'm fine," she sighed and worked to regulate her tone of voice. It was obvious that, unlike Huxley earlier on at the stream, Venek and Flavire hadn't come to spy. "I brought Derick to the field. He's close, and I didn't want you walking up and being seen."

Flavire frowned and shot a shared look of understanding with Venek. Faunella caught on and narrowed her eyes at them.

"What aren't you telling me?" She ground out. Flavire was the one who answered her, his fuchsia flowers closing their petals to blend in with his greenery.

"Huxley suggested we take a walk this way."

Faunella clenched her teeth, annoyed, but not surprised. He must have lingered behind and seen the way they had come. Flavire grumbled, more upset that Hux had played him so easily.

"Don't worry about Huxley," she said, taking Flavire's hand and giving it a light press. "I'll deal with him tonight."

Venek looked anxiously between the two of them and then towards the sunlit field. "We should go." He swept a vine around Flavire's back, tugging the Fae in the direction of the grotto. "You'll be okay?" he asked, looking back at her with concern.

"I'm safe," she flushed a little at her lie, feeling guilty for not informing the Fae of Derick's situation. They hurried away, and she returned to the field, convincing herself that the men hunting Derick wouldn't find them this far from Northaven.

Faunella stepped past the tree line to find the immediate vicinity empty. She scanned the long grass, sensing contented happiness from her animal friends. They were close. Heart feeling lighter, she followed the connection, her lips curving up when she saw the warm strands of chocolate hair peeking from the middle of the thick brush.

She tiptoed closer, wanting to see what Derick was so engrossed with. He was hunched over with Beebe perched on one knee and Rafi sitting calmly at his feet. Even from the side, she could see the concentration on his face. In his hands, he held a messy jumble of grass and flowers. The sight of him working so hard on something obviously for her had tears pricking at the back of her eyes. She stayed silent, touched beyond belief.

"I think I need some more flowers," he mumbled, reaching up to rub the back of his head. Without hesitation, Beebe gave a musical chirp and darted off, presumably in search of the flowers he spoke of.

Rafi, impatient to have her join them, let out a bark which finally alerted Derick to her presence. His head shot up, the surprise at seeing her melting into sheepishness as he slowly pulled what he was working on out of sight.

"Fawn, you're back," he chuckled nervously, his Adam's apple bobbing up and down. "I was just messing around."

Faunella eased down beside him, pointedly looking at his side. "Messing around?" she asked, arching her brow high.

Realizing he'd been caught, Derick pulled out his hand, letting the sad excuse for a flower crown dangle from his fingers.

"I saw a bunch in your room and thought I'd try and make you one." His voice shook a little as he spoke, further highlighting how much out of his comfort zone he was. Faunella suddenly wondered if Derick was used to being bad at anything.

But he tried to make one for me anyway?

"I love it," she whispered, her voice softening. "Will you let me try it on?"

Derick swallowed audibly, but his hands were steady when he placed the crown over her head. She straightened, reaching up with one hand to lightly touch the assortment of flowers he had woven together. It didn't matter that it was lopsided or several petals were crushed. Faunella loved it all the more for the thought behind it. "It's beautiful." She beamed at Derick, putting all of her joy behind the smile. His eyes never left her face, staying focused on her with an expression that she didn't have the words for.

"Yes it is," he breathed, sending a fluttering low down in her stomach. "So damn beautiful."

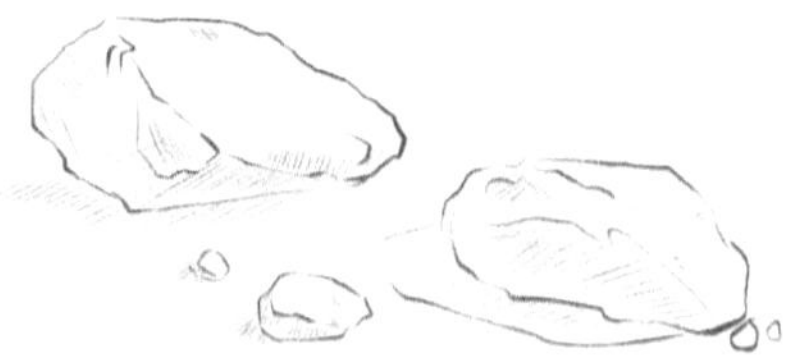

CHAPTER SIXTY THREE
HUXLEY

HUXLEY WAS BACK IN the grotto when Fawn finally made her way to him that evening.

"Where is he?" He heard her ask Baol out in the clearing in front of the cave.

He glanced across at Violetta and the two shared a knowing look. Fawn was not happy, and Huxley knew he was about to get the sharp end of her ire.

"Huxley?" she called into the cave, her voice echoing around the cavernous space. "Come out here, please."

He winced, not liking her cool tone of voice. "You'd better come with me," he hissed at Violetta. "I wasn't the only one out there today, and I'm not taking the fall alone."

With a sigh, Violetta got to her feet, flicking her long hair to the front of each shoulder. The two of them reluctantly made their way to the mouth of the cave, stopping when they came face-to-face with a stern-looking Fawn.

"Huxley, how could you?" she started, her face smoothing out into disappointment. "I was mortified. I'm not a child anymore who can't take care of herself. And I don't need you snooping!"

He scuffed his rock foot into the dirt, much preferring her anger to her disappointment.

"He noticed when you had gone," she continued, throwing her hands into the air. "You're massive, for goodness sake. He might be a human, but he's not stupid. Of course he's going to notice when a giant rock gets up and walks away."

"He was asleep," he argued. "It's not like he saw me leave."

"You know that's not what I meant. Violetta, can you just…"

She gestured towards him, rolling her eyes to the back of her head. He turned to Violetta, narrowing his eyes at the water Fae. Her cheeks became opaque, and she opened her mouth, letting out a thin squeak.

Faunella's eyes rushed back to Violetta, her lips tightening as she regarded the female.

"That's right," she said slowly. "How amazing that Derick's feet were healed after soaking them in the stream." Raising her eyebrows, she stared down at the two of them. "Violetta?"

"We just happened to be there, and I saw his feet." She stepped up to Fawn, grasping her hands. "His feet looked terrible, the poor thing. I couldn't help myself. I just wanted to help him."

Faunella's face softened, making his drop in disbelief. How unfair. Violetta was getting let off just because she did something nice for the human. He opened his mouth, preparing to deliver a scathing retort, when Amon stepped out from between two trees.

"That's enough of that," he said, sending a pointed look towards him. "Huxley won't be showing himself to the human anymore, right Hux?"

"His name is Derick!" Fawn cut in, eyes flashing.

"I wasn't showing. I just…" Huxley threw up his hands, turning to kick the edge of the cave. He just wanted to make sure Fawn was safe with the human. She was sheltered and innocent, not even realizing that the man was interested in her in a romantic sense. He had only observed them for a little while, but even he could see their burgeoning feelings. It was there in every sidelong look, in every touch of their hands.

He gritted his teeth, breathing through his nose to get his emotions under control. He no longer thought that the man, Derick, would hurt her physically, but he feared the damage he could inflict on Fawn's heart.

Fawn turned to Amon, craning her head to look up into the tree Fae's face.

"I thought I was clear last night when I asked for some space. I'm not in any danger from Derick."

"We can respect that," Amon ground out. He nodded his head in Huxley's direction, making him swallow thickly at what was about to come out of Amon's mouth. "But Huxley mentioned that you and this Derick—" he frowned slightly at the name. "—were forming an attachment."

Faunella's head whipped around, turning her large round eyes to him. He flinched back from her accusing stare.

"I don't know what Huxley thought he saw, but we are friends, nothing more."

"Be that as it may, the fact of the matter is that the longer time goes on, the closer the two of you will become." Amon placed his leafy hand on the side of Fawn's face, turning her back to face him. "So, we no longer have the luxury of time. You need to hear what we have to say."

Huxley felt more than saw Fawn tense. The subject of how she came to be on Earth obviously scared her. He didn't think she remembered anything from when she first came to be with them, but obviously some repressed trauma from that event had stuck with her, leading her to try and avoid any mention of that time.

Stepping forward, he reached out to touch her smallest finger, forgetting about her anger towards him. He just needed to be close to her, hoping his presence might somewhat lessen her fear. She swallowed audibly and curled her fingers around his hand, holding fast as she gave a tight nod to Amon.

"Tell me now, then." She lifted her chin. Only the slight quiver in her hand betrayed her real feelings. "Nothing you can say will change things between me and Derick."

Amon glanced around the clearing, making sure that the other Fae had gathered and were present.

"You remember we told you that you are also heir to the kingdom of Madivyre?" Fawn stayed silent. Her body tensed as she waited for Amon to continue. "That is the reason you were sent to Earth." Amon let out a breath. "It had nothing to do with you being the Ancient Fae heir." Faunella's hand tightened around his, the strength of her grip making him glad he was made out of stone. "Fawn, you were sent here to die, a feat that would have been accomplished if it wasn't for us finding and healing you. She wanted you out of the way so that she could take your place as the heir."

"She? Who is she?" Faunella ground her teeth, her words coming out tight.

"She is your aunt. Your mother's sister."

"How do you know all that? Why would you think that?" Her voice broke, the words thin and high. Out of the corner of his eye, Huxley saw the other Fae draw closer, their faces mirroring what he knew to be on his. Grief.

"I know because I was there," said Amon, his voice tinged in sadness. "You were so small, so young. It's no wonder you lost the memory."

"But why would she do that? Why would she want me to die?"

"People do horrible things for the chance of power," came the gravelly voice of Lothian from the direction of the cave, causing everyone's eyes to settle on where he stood. "But that's not the whole of it, child. There is more."

"More?" she asked, turning pain-filled eyes back to Amon. "What more could there be?"

"Your family haven't given up on you. Queen Nyssa, your great-grandmother, has set guards in the South Forest where you disappeared with the hope that one day you might return." Amon's voice quieted, sorrow dripping from his words. "They have been waiting for you all this time." He glanced around at the gathered Fae, including Huxley who couldn't stop the frown that marred his forehead. "But we decided that we could protect you more than your family could."

CHAPTER SIXTY FOUR
FAUNELLA

A MON'S WORDS ECHOED AROUND and around her head.

They decided—*they*.

She snatched her hand back, dropping Huxley's stone fingers like they were covered in acid.

"My family wanted me this whole time. They have been waiting for me this whole time?" The words came out like ice between her gritted teeth. Her worst fears were true. The Fae had taken her from her family—from her kingdom, and hidden her away. A cold emptiness settled low in her chest. All those years on Earth wasted when she could have been safe in her parents' arms.

Her power stirred. It picked up the current of air around them and strengthened it, turning it into a living thing that she could wield. All around her, the Fae stepped back, except for Amon and Huxley, who stood their ground. Faunella felt no fear; she was well beyond her earlier years of letting her power rule her emotions. No, this was all her. Her magic flexed, flattening the grass in the clearing with a single thought. Her next thought thickened the air on either side of each Fae in her sight, effectively making them immobile.

Her breath came faster, the questions in her mind as erratic as her actions were purposeful.

How could they do this to her? Who were they to have made this decision? She closed her eyes and rubbed her temple, trying to sort through the jumble of emotions. But anger and disappointment held her firmly in their grasp.

It was one Fae, one family member who wanted me gone. The rest of them would have protected me—would have loved me.

Something tickled the side of her leg. Her eyes flew open and dropped down to find the source. Erwin stood about a foot away from her, held tightly by her air. One small green limb stretched out from his body, held there through a will that was stronger than the power she was wielding. His face was contorted with what Faunella could only describe as grief, as he fought with every inch of his being to connect with her leg and offer her comfort.

Her chest softened. Curious, she released the air around just him, still upset enough to hold the others tight. Without the restriction, Erwin jerked forward, his body slackening in relief. He didn't wait more than a moment before launching himself at her and wrapping his arms firmly around her legs.

"They wanted you, Fawn," he cried out, his words dripping with anguish. "How could they not? You were the most precious thing I had ever seen, but your aunt came so close to killing you." He choked back a sob. The sound tore through her angry heart. "You have no idea how close." He buried his face into her knees, the motion muffling the rest of his words. "Please, don't hate us. We tried our best. We only wanted to keep you safe."

Faunella lifted her eyes from his quivering body, scanning the immobile Fae around her. Their faces wore similar expressions of sadness, ranging from deep guilt to pained grief.

With a sigh, she released her magic entirely, letting the Fae fall free.

Despite her anger and churning emotions, she was determined to keep hold of the conversation, not allowing Amon to take charge. As expected, the tree Fae stepped forward, limbs outstretched.

"Stay where you are." Eyes flashing, she lifted her chin and stared unflinchingly at Amon. "I'm mad at you." She flicked her gaze to the others. "I'm mad at all of you." Her nails dug into her palms as she struggled to keep her voice even. "You had no right to keep me from my family. No matter your reasons, you should have told me the truth."

Amon's mouth opened, his lips beginning to form the words to explain. Faunella's hand shot up, one finger outstretched to cut him off before he could speak.

"Not yet."

She would let them try and excuse themselves soon, but not before she got her feelings out. The Fae shuffled uncomfortably but didn't try to interrupt again.

Feeling more in control, Faunella took a moment to gather her thoughts and sort through what was fiction and what was fact. However, as she ran through the information given sporadically over the years, she couldn't land on one concrete reason that the Fae had done the wrong thing. Sure, they had taken her from her family, but to protect her. They had hidden her away in this forest away from humans.

To protect me.

Her ire dimmed, reason momentarily overriding her emotions. Frustrated with her chain of thought, she gritted her teeth and tried to reignite the flames of her anger, recalling the years of pain and loneliness, every moment that she felt 'other.' But through the dregs of her mind, images began to flash by, one by one, coming faster and faster: Huxley surprising her with a shiny wrapped sweet, his face bashful when she expressed her joy, hours spent with Flavire out in his meadow and his utmost patience teaching her how to weave the most beautiful flower crowns, Amon holding her tight and growing taller than the tallest tree, all to share a peace filled moment watching the sun descend.

The moments kept coming, seemingly endless in number. Erwin, Baol, Violetta, Baeroot, Venek, Laurel. Even Lothian had a place. Faunella sucked in a breath, startled to find that her throat had thickened. She blinked past stinging eyes and took in the Fae waiting patiently for her. They had raised her, had taught her. The lessons on how to rule, and how to be a good queen, were all thanks to them. And if not for them, she would never have met Lucy or Derick.

I'm still angry. They kept me from my family. But the anger was less than before, simmering quietly under her skin. As she took in all their faces, Faunella felt her stubbornness ease. Crouching down, she unhooked Erwin from her leg and wrapped her arms around his mossy body.

"You can explain now."

There was a collective sigh of relief. Tentatively, they moved to surround her, reaching out with vines and limbs and stones to place their hands upon her. Their closeness eased something inside her, but after a long, steady silence, she realized that no one was saying anything. Raising her head, she searched until she found the right face.

"Amon?" She nodded at him, letting her eyes soften fractionally. "Tell me."

"You are right. We decided to keep you from your family. Perhaps that was wrong, but we had our reasons." Faunella stayed still, working to keep the emotion off her face and let Amon explain.

"The first reason was we couldn't be sure your family would keep you safe. Your aunt used powerful dark magic to cover her tracks, and the Ancient Fae have been hidden for so long that we didn't know if we would be believed had we come forward to accuse her." He paused, fear flashing across his face. "Also, revealing ourselves to the Fae in Madivyre would have brought the attention of Petrov to you and your family."

At her stricken expression, Amon frantically continued.

"Maybe we made the wrong decision, but you were so close to death when we found you, and you were so small and defenseless. I didn't want to risk losing you."

His use of the word 'I' didn't go unnoticed by Faunella. As much as she didn't like being kept away from her birth parents, she could see that

Amon's intentions were true. All through her life, he had only ever tried to keep her safe, even if that now caused her pain. He looked away from her, his own eyes looking suspiciously wet.

"And the second reason?" she asked, turning to Lothian for the answer.

"Ah, that's when things get a bit more complicated." He stretched out his pale limbs, sending a creaking noise screeching out through the stillness of the night that had fallen. "It ties into the first reason somewhat." He mulled over his words, considering each of them before speaking. Irritation began to pull at Faunella's chest, and she willed herself to be patient. Lothian continued. "I will try to keep things brief for this retelling. Now, where should I start? Ah, yes. Back—"

"This is going to take all night," Huxley cut in, frowning at the elderly Fae. "Sorry Lothian, but I think short and sweet is the way to go." He turned his severe face to hers and gave her back a gentle pat, his face softening a touch.

"You've known for a while that our lands are dying because of Petrov, who isn't our rightful ruler. We told you that you couldn't return to Amaranth to claim the throne until you were older, and that's because Petrov doesn't want to give up his seat of power."

"You told me he was dangerous, and it wasn't safe for me in Amaranth yet." Faunella's brows furrowed. "How did you know I would be in danger from him?"

Huxley barked a laugh. "That's easy. When the king died, instead of looking for and finding an heir, the usurper Petrov took over ruling the kingdoms and has been content to let our lands and people suffer. Why would he do that if he cared about anything other than power?" He huffed, looking around at the other Fae as if daring them to contradict him. "Petrov is a massive ass who most likely would have killed you rather than allowing you to wait out your second puberty to see if you would become High Fae and take your rightful place as queen."

Great, another person who wanted her dead. She ran Huxley's words over in her mind, her attention catching on a particular part.

"What does being High Fae have to do with me being queen?"

"Only High Fae can rule," said Lothian, shooting Huxley a disapproving look. Amon stepped between them, blocking Lothian from Huxley's view.

"Yes, well," he coughed. "You had an above-average chance at becoming High Fae. But on the small chance you didn't, then you would be denied your seat on the throne in both kingdoms."

Faunella forgot everything else—forgot that her aunt wanted her dead, an Ancient Fae who she'd never met would rather kill her than give up the throne. All she could focus on was the absolute unfairness that a lower fae, one without powers or the physical attributes of a High Fae, would be denied something that should be rightfully theirs. In all her studies, she had never come across this rule.

"What is wrong with lower fae? What could be so bad about them that they would be denied their heritage?" she ground out. Frowning at the Fae as if they were personally responsible.

"There is nothing wrong with them," piped up Flavire. "But, they are essentially human. In Amaranth, humans are seen as lesser. It's the way it's been for thousands of years."

"What's wrong with humans? I was a lower fae—essentially human, until recently. There was nothing wrong with me, and nothing changed inside when my body grew to be High Fae. I'm still the same person I always was."

Awkward silence filled the space. Faunella felt a deep disappointment that the Fae couldn't see what was wrong with how things were done in Amaranth.

"I think we are getting off track a bit."

Faunella looked up at Amon, biting her lip as she considered everything she had been told tonight. Knowing there was nothing any of them could do about the inequalities regarding the lower fae, she decided to address some of her other concerns.

"Why now?" She adjusted her position on the ground, crossing her legs comfortably. "What's to stop my aunt and this Petrov from trying to kill me anyway?"

The Fae followed her lead, lowering themselves to the ground around her, but Huxley answered her question.

"You're powerful, Fawn. You're old enough to understand the dangers, and you're strong enough to kick some Fae butt if you need to."

"Huxley!" hissed Violetta, wacking him lightly on the arm. "She's going to think she has to fight for her life when we go back."

Faunella's heart started to pound. The thought had never occurred to her. She loved using her powers, but she wasn't sure if she could bring herself to hurt anyone with them. She had a flash of memory—the night sky was filled with birds, their talons outstretched, followed by the yells and cries of human men. She swallowed thickly. Maybe she could defend herself if she needed to.

"Fawn, we're not sending you into battle."

Amon's words drew her attention back to him.

"I'm telling you this now because we need to start preparing how we will return to Amaranth. We need to be careful how we play this, as the situation is complex."

The conversation had circled back to the beginning. The reason for the Fae's insistence to tell her becoming glaringly obvious. Her heart sank.

"You're finally taking me back."

I'll have to leave Derick.

The thought blew past all her other concerns. Derick needed her. But so did the Ancient Fae back on Amaranth, and her parents were waiting for her. The pressure to save an entire kingdom while fighting to survive attacks from two fronts had a cold sweat breaking out on her skin. She felt she was being pulled in three different directions, with no say of her own.

"What about Derick?"

"I'm sorry, Fawn." Amon's eyes softened in sympathy, his leafy branches wilting as he spoke. "I tried to warn you sooner, but the human will have to stay here on his own."

Leave Derick? Panic took over her body, her pulse quickened and her breath caught in her chest. He had told her that he was in danger. The men chasing him wouldn't give up. They would track him down and kill him if they could.

"I can't leave him," she cried out, jumping to her feet. "They will catch him. They'll catch him and hurt him."

Her heart pounded violently. Her body vibrated with the need to protect him. The thought of two Fae wanting to kill her was nothing compared to the fear she felt at potentially losing Derick forever.

Strong wooden limbs wrapped themselves around her, picking her up and holding her close.

"Fawn, what do you mean? Calm down, and tell me what you're talking about."

Amon's voice finally got through and she turned her tear-filled eyes to him, voice cracking as she explained the danger Derick was in and she had taken him in to save his life.

As the words poured out of her mouth, she felt a weight lift. It felt so good to be honest with the Fae. Keeping things to herself only made her skin itch, as if the secret was trying to burst free.

Amon listened silently, his eyes growing wider the more she spoke. When she finally finished, he held her close, swiveling his head from side to side as if the humans hunting Derick would burst into the clearing at any minute.

From her vantage point in his arms, she looked at the other Fae. Flinching at their fearful expressions.

"You should have told us sooner," Amon murmured. Faunella's brows pulled together at the hypocrisy.

"Erwin, Baeroot, Venek. I need you to head north. Keep to the shadows. If there are any humans in the forest, then we need to know about it. Huxley, Violetta and Baol, spread out around the treehouse. If those men do manage to get close, I don't want any of them near Fawn."

Faunella's mouth fell open. Amon spat out instructions left and right, his voice strong and booming. She sat quietly in his arms, upset and grateful that even when she was angry with the Fae, she could depend on them.

"I need to get back to Derick," she whispered to Amon, the two of them standing still amid the flurry of activity among the rest of the group.

"I'm taking Fawn home," Amon called out to the others. "No one sleeps until we figure out where those men are."

As his final word faded from hearing, Amon was gone. Flying through the trees, he held her close. Despite the fact that she was more than capable of getting home by herself.

Faunella allowed him to take her, knowing he needed to ensure that she was safe and also because she needed the time to sort through her turbulent emotions. So much had happened in such a short time. She was finally allowed to return to Amaranth, but instead of a joyous homecoming, she would have to be on her guard, prepared to defend herself if she needed to. Her heart thudded painfully in her chest. She didn't want to fight. She wasn't even sure she wanted to go anymore. To leave would mean Derick would be left behind. Eyes prickling painfully, she breathed through her nose, trying to fight off the tears that threatened to come.

She had finally found another friend, someone different and special, and now she was being asked to give him up. It wasn't fair.

Amon slowed down, causing her to look around in surprise. They had made it to her treehouse quicker than normal. Amon must have been traveling faster due to his stress. He paused under her tree, beginning to stretch himself upwards.

"Wait, what are you doing?" she hissed, wacking him on his branch arm. "Derick will see you if you take me up."

"At this stage, I wouldn't care. Nothing matters more than keeping you safe."

She frowned at him, wrenching herself out from his arms and landing lightly in the other tree.

"Don't be silly, Amon. I'm in no danger climbing the tree." She shook her head, clucking her tongue. "I'm sure the men after Derick are far from here. What are the chances they could find us?"

"That's not a chance I'm willing to take with you."

He looked down on her with warm eyes, reaching out to tuck a hair behind her ear. She smiled, grasping his hand and giving it a quick squeeze before starting to climb the tree.

"Go," she mouthed, shooing him away when he still hadn't moved after a few moments.

With one final look at her, Amon reduced his size and disappeared back into the forest.

Letting out a tired sigh, Faunella finished the climb, pulling herself wearily into her home. Her emotions were still all over the place, and all she wanted to do was see for herself that Derick was asleep and safe. Then perhaps she could collapse into bed and hide from her problems with the unconsciousness of sleep.

She stepped into the room, eyes lifting to the bed. It was empty.

Blood freezing in her veins, she spun around scanning the room frantically for any signs of Derick. He was gone.

"No, no, no."

Her breathing began to come faster. All she could hear was her erratic pulse pounding in her ears.

They've taken him. The men found him and took him away.

She raced to the bed, picking up the blankets and flinging them to the side as if his large form was hidden underneath. Collapsing down onto the bed, she let the tears come. The long night, coupled with finding Derick missing, took its toll.

She didn't know what to do. If she couldn't even figure out how to save one human man, then how could she be expected to rule two kingdoms while trying to stay alive?

Burying her face in her hands, she cried out her frustration, feeling the tight pressure under her ribs ease from the release.

"Fawn? Are you okay?"

Her head flung up with a snap, eyes training on the large figure easing himself through the window. Beebe flew in after him, followed by Rafi a moment later.

Faunella looked at him, realizing all at once that the three of them had simply been sitting outside on the tree, something that she did often herself. With a sob of relief, she ducked her chin again, pressing her fists to her eyes as a fresh wave of tears ran down her face.

Footsteps raced across the floor, followed by a warm hand on her knee, making her cry even harder.

"What is it? Tell me what's wrong."

The panic in his voice made her look up, her vision blurry as she stared into his worried face.

"I thought you had gone," she choked out, her words haltering. "I thought those men found you and took you away."

Wiping at her nose, she blinked past the moisture in her eyes, taking in the beautiful contours of his face.

"I was so afraid," she whispered, reaching out and touching his cheek lightly. The short, dark hair under her fingertips was rough to the touch, and for a moment, she let her fascination take over.

"I'm not going anywhere," Derick said, conviction in every word.

Faunella flushed and looked away, withdrawing her hand from the intimacy of his skin. Derick reached out and captured her hand in his, then without taking his eyes from her, he cupped it and pressed his lips to the center of her palm. Her heart tightened as he held it there for what felt like forever, his soft lips warm and smooth against her sensitive flesh, the stubble growing on his cheeks and jaws a delicious contrast to the tender pressure of his mouth.

It was all so much—so strange and wonderful. Faunella's breathing quickened, even as her tears threatened to spill once more. She didn't know what to do with all these feelings.

"It's not you who has to leave," she whispered, whimpering when his tender brown eyes traveled to hers, surprise shining in their depths.

She closed her eyes, not able to bear the look on his face. His hand slid to her wrist, drawing her upwards until she was standing beside the bed. The skin on her arm tingled as his hand inched higher, sliding up her bare arm to wrap around her back. His other hand did the same, and all at once, he tightened his arms, pulling her body flush against his wide chest.

"Don't cry," he murmured against her hair. "Please don't cry."

Faunella stilled, her body sinking into his comforting warmth. The soothing strokes of his hands against her back made her want to press herself even closer. She turned her head slightly, her nose pressing against the soft skin above his collar. Heart pounding, she snaked her hands behind his back, inhaling deeply as she did. He smelled so good, an organic smell that made her think of the sea. His hands continued stroking, sending jolts of pleasure down her back. Sighing deeply, she nuzzled into his neck, breathing in more of his unique scent.

Without meaning to, her lips connected with his skin, making them sear with warmth. Derick stilled, his hands clutching at the back of her dress.

"Fawn."

He breathed her name as he slid his head backward, only stopping when his nose was pressed to the side of hers, his lips brushing her flushed cheek.

All Faunella could focus on was the sound of their breathing. His warm breath tickled the hair by her ear, and the feel of her breasts pressed into the strong muscles of his chest. Her mouth went dry, and a fluttering feeling started low down in her stomach. She couldn't utter a word. She couldn't even think, so focused on the feel of his mouth so close to hers.

Letting out a pained groan, Derick released her dress, but instead of letting go, they flattened on her back before sliding up to tangle in her hair. He threaded his fingers through the strands to cup the back of her head with a gentle pressure. A breathy sigh escaped from Faunella's parted lips. Every fiber of her being was alive with sensation, filling her with an unbelievable awareness of each touch of his skin against hers.

With the utmost control, he tipped her head back, angling their faces and gliding his mouth over to press against hers.

Her world narrowed to the feel of his lips on hers. The warm softness as he sealed them together, his mouth pulling at her lips, making the tender skin come alive with wonder. She sucked in a sharp breath, softening beneath him. He applied more pressure, sliding his lip between hers, and deepened the kiss.

It was like nothing she had ever felt before. She felt a heady rush as his other hand came up behind her neck, holding her in place as he sucked her lip into his mouth. His tongue slid over the plump flesh, eliciting a moan from deep in her throat at the jolt of heat that ran through her. The thought briefly occurred to her that she should try mimicking his movements, but before she could experiment, he pulled back.

Though their lips were apart, Derick kept their faces pressed together, panting heavily in time with her own harried breaths.

"Fawn."

He started talking, his deep voice sending a quiver through her stomach when a movement to the left caught her attention.

All the air left the room. Faunella flung herself back, tripping over the bed in her haste to get away. Disoriented by the frantic movement, she underestimated the force of her retreat, whacking the back of her head against the wall.

"Oh my god, are you okay?"

Derick leaped forward, holding out his hand to help her up. But she could only stare wide-eyed at the window into the disproving face of Amon.

513

CHAPTER SIXTY FIVE
DERICK

"**O**H MY GOD, ARE you okay?"

They had been locked together, experiencing the most amazing kiss of his life. He didn't even know how it had happened. One moment, he was comforting her, and the next they were locked together, her slender body soft in his arms.

But then she had pushed him away, flinging her body so violently backward that she cracked her head against the wall, making him wince at the contact.

He placed his hand on her shoulder, the other one stroking down her bright curls to check for injury.

"Faunella, are you hurt?"

She wouldn't even look at him, her face pale in the moonlight trained on the uncovered window. Brows furrowing, he turned his head, looking to see what had caught her focus. As his eyes adjusted further to the dark, he saw several tree branches poking over the window ledge. Scanning the dark space revealed the knotted whirls of a tree.

I think a branch has fallen on the window.

He opened his mouth to ask Faunella if she had heard the crash of the tree hitting the side of the house when the tree twisted, deep groves opening to turn dark shining eyes on him.

A strangled yell flew from his mouth as the wooden face appeared.

Pushing in, the branches grew at an alarming rate, and the tree opened a wide groove that looked like a mouth, letting out a deep rustling creek.

"Holy shit!"

It's a tree! The tree is alive, and it's coming for us.

Without another thought, he threw himself in front of Faunella, pressing her back into the bed and holding his arms wide, his mind boggled at the terrifying sight in front of him.

"Fawn, get out! Use the other window and climb down. Quick! I'll hold it off."

The tree stopped its advance, studying his stance and making another light rustle. His heart was pounding. There was no way he could fight off a goddamn tree, but he would try if it would give Faunella a chance to get away. She still hadn't moved.

"Go, Fawn," he demanded, reaching back to try and give her a little push.

The tree didn't like that. It speared out a thin branch, wrapping it around the hand that had connected with Fawn, and emitted a high-pitched screech.

Derick couldn't move. His hand was locked in the grasp of the tree creature. All the breath left his body, and he stilled, preparing to make his last stand here. Firmly between Fawn and this creature. It would be an honorable way to go.

"Leave, Faunella, and don't look back," he whispered before grabbing hold of the branch that held him, needing to release himself if he had any chance of giving Fawn enough time to leave.

"Let him go, Amon. He wasn't trying to hurt me; you know that."

Faunella stood up behind him, using his shoulders to push herself up. Derick shook his head in disbelief. Surely she hadn't spoken to the tree, her voice calm, if not slightly exasperated.

"What?"

He tried to ask what the hell was going on when the tree suddenly released him, retracting a few feet from where he stood. He rubbed at his sore wrist, not taking his eyes off the creature, but feeling like he was missing some vital information.

"Ah, Fawn? What's going on?"

She stepped lightly off the bed, coming around to stand at his side, and took his hand. Inspecting his wrist, she frowned, turning her head towards the creature.

"You could have broken his wrist," she hissed, lowering his arm and discretely stepping in front of him.

Scared of the danger the tree possessed, Derick wrapped his arm around her middle, pulling her back until she was flush against his chest.

The tree rumbled, its limbs twitching as if it would shoot out and attack again.

Faunella stroked his arm, twisting around until he could feel her eyes on him.

"Derick," she started, her voice gentle. "This is Amon. Amon raised me. He's my family."

He dropped his head, finally taking his eyes off the tree—off Amon. Faunella was grimacing up at him, her wide eyes apologetic as she placed her hand on his chest.

"If you could let me go, I think that would make him feel a lot happier."

"If I could...a lot happi—"

Her smile grew, and she pushed out of his arms.

"I'm sorry I didn't tell you. It was important for them not to be seen."

His stomach clenched painfully as he focused on one word in that sentence.

"Them?" he choked out, still unable to get a breath. "There's more?"

"Ah, yes." She tucked a ribbon of hair behind her ear, wincing slightly. "There are a few of them. But I can tell you about that later. For now, I'm sure there has to be a good reason why Amon would reveal himself at this moment."

She turned towards the tree, still staying close to him, for which he was grateful.

"Amon?"

Amon started rattling off an assortment of indiscernible noises. His mouth moved, and his face changed with feeling. But all Derick could hear was an assortment of creaking and rustling.

He concentrated on breathing through his nose and keeping his face neutral. Fawn wasn't scared of the tree—quite the opposite. Some part of him knew that he shouldn't be afraid. Unfortunately, no matter how much he willed himself to remain calm, he couldn't stop the frantic beating of his heart or the slight tremor in his legs.

"Where?" said Fawn, her voice insistent and her body becoming rigid. The tree responded, prompting Fawn to suck in a sharp breath. "That close?"

The fear in her voice had him stepping forward, keeping the tree in the corner of his eye as he reached out to touch her arm. She turned fully to him, her eyes shining in the moonlight.

"The men, the ones who are after you? They're close." She kept her eyes on him, only turning her head slightly to direct her next comment to the tree.

"Amon, can you give us some space?"

Frowning, she listened to his reply. Derick watched in disbelief; she seemed to understand the strange sounds perfectly.

"Don't be silly," she said and lowered her eyes, the skin on her cheeks darkening.

Another rustle.

"Are you sure?"

A high-pitched creak.

"Okay, but go now."

Derick kept his eyes on Faunella's face, shuddering when he heard the tree's limbs slide back over the window frame. His muscles were so tense, his jaw aching from how hard he had been clenching his teeth.

"It's okay. He's gone now."

Faunella rubbed his arms, warming the skin with gentle circular motions. With a relieved sigh, he stumbled backward, catching Fawn's hand and pulling her down as his legs gave out and he sat wearily onto the bed.

"What was that thing?"

He shook out his hands before wiping his moist palms on his shirt.

"He's a Fae, like me."

"But he's a tree person, thing." He ran his fingers over his face, anxiety starting to creep up the more he thought about Amon. "You could understand him. He talked to you, and you talked back to him." Struggling to breathe again, he sucked in short shallow breaths, trying to get enough oxygen to his starved lungs.

"Derick, it's okay. Just breathe deeply."

Fawn slid off the bed, coming around to kneel between his thighs. With great tenderness, she cupped his face in her palms, lifting his head until he felt a sweet breeze cool his face, the air slipping into his mouth and gliding down to fill his lungs. All at once, his mind sharpened, clearing enough that he felt embarrassed for his actions, rather than justified.

"I'm sorry." Placing a hand over one of Fawn's, he held her hand to his cheek. "You said he was your family?"

He continued to breathe the fresh air and concentrated on Fawn's lips, curving up slightly as she regarded him.

"That's it. Keep breathing. I'm so sorry about that. When I was abandoned here, Amon and the other Ancient Fae found me and saved me." She frowned, her eyes unfocusing for a moment before she continued, her voice considering. "They raised me here in the forest. They are the only family I've ever known." She shook off the expression and let the corner of her lips quirk up. "I know they can look a bit frightening, but they're harmless. They wouldn't hurt a fly."

Derick remembered the way that Amon had gripped his arm and grimaced. He wasn't so sure that was true.

"If they are Fae, then why are they here? And why did he look that way and not like you?"

Faunella blew out a breath, flicking her head so her hair was out of her eyes.

"It's a long story, and we don't really have time. But to answer your questions quickly, they were sent to Earth ages ago to observe humans. They do look like me, except they are Ancient Fae, so a little different. Their bloodline means they can transform into things of nature. Because they were in those forms when their king died, they can no longer take back their High Fae form."

"A High Fae? That's what you are?" She nodded. He went to ask another question then remembered what she had said about their limited time.

"Wait, why don't we have much time? What did that Amon say to you?"

She stood up, drawing her hand out from under his. As she moved away, the calming air cut off, leaving him breathing normally, no longer hyperventilating.

"He said quite a bit." Biting her lip, she parted her hair into segments, weaving the long strands together as she spoke. "They found the men after you. They are only a short distance away to the north." She pointed out of the window that the moonlight shone through, finding north easily. "They want to take me back to Amaranth, the Fae world. But it's too soon for me to return, so we need to figure out what to do with the men so it's safe for us here."

He got to his feet, glad to see that the tremors had passed. He hadn't registered what Fawn said earlier on, brushing over the fact that Jarred was drawing close because of the bigger issue literally just outside the window, but now he could appreciate the urgency.

"How far away did he say they were? Do you know how many men are coming?"

"He didn't say how many there were, only that they were very close."

Derick scratched his chin, remembering that morning when Fawn had told him the stream was close.

"I'm assuming these other Fae are just as fast as you?"

Faunella shrugged, looking at the ground but not able to hide her smile.

"Almost as fast."

He chuckled, loving the fact that she was quicker than the other Fae and knew it, but that meant Jarred could still be over an hour away. The chances of him heading in the right direction weren't that great. He walked to the window, peering out as if he could see more than the silver-tipped tops of the trees stretching out to the horizon.

"I've put you in danger, Fawn. I should have run far away, no matter the risk to myself."

"Don't say that." He felt her move closer, her steps no more than a whisper. "I wanted you to stay with me," she breathed, her voice soft before placing her hand on his back. "I knew the danger."

He quivered under her touch, wanted to turn around and pull her into his arms to resume what Amon had so thoroughly interrupted.

"The Fae will help us. We can figure out what to do and then we can stay here safely, together."

Derick longed for what she said to come true, to be free from his past and start a new life with Fawn at his side. It was a life he hadn't dared to dream of. But there was only one problem.

"What about Amaranth? You said they wanted to return home?"

"Well, yes. But I can't leave you."

He turned around, heart leaping and simultaneously falling. She felt the same way; he was now sure of it. She wet her lips, drawing his attention to her mouth.

"They need me to go back, but I won't. I'll stay here with you."

He studied her face, and his heart fell more. She would rather stay here, hidden in the forest for the rest of her life, than return to her own world where she would be free to be herself without worrying that she'd be seen. She would give that up for him.

He reached out, running his finger up the soft point of her ear. She would never be free here. Always hidden, never able to have friends or experience anything the forest didn't provide.

No. That's not the life he wanted for her.

She closed her eyes, a soft smile on her face, and leaned into his touch. *God, she's so beautiful.*

He stepped back, needing distance from her before he changed his mind and allowed the Fae to deal with Jarred, leaving him free to grasp this fantasy life that he was so desperate for. Cause that's all it was—a dream, a fantasy, that a man like him didn't deserve.

Mind made up, he cleared his throat and pasted a smile on his face.

"So, what do we need to do next?"

Faunella opened her eyes, straightening up and giving him a hesitant grin.

"We need to go down to convene with the Fae."

"Isn't it safer for us up here?"

"Well." She looked away, darkness spreading across her cheeks. "Amon wants us down where they can keep an eye on you."

Derick drew back, surprised that they would think he would ever lay a single hand on Fawn. She was something to be treasured, something precious to be protected. There was no way he would ever harm her.

"They think I would hurt you?"

"Not hurt me," she whispered, still not meeting his eye.

All at once he realized what they were afraid of. He felt his own face redden when he remembered what Amon must have witnessed. If the Fae were her family, then it was almost as if he had been kissing Faunella in front of her dad.

"Oh," he croaked out, scratching the stubble on his chin while trying not to smile. "I see."

Fawn looked up, relief written across her face. "Good. Well, let's go then." She started to walk to the door, looking back to make sure he had followed. "I do need to warn you. The Fae can be a bit protective of me. Try not to be scared though. They won't harm you."

He gulped, suddenly wishing he had a drink. But he followed her out of the treehouse and started the long descent to meet the rest of her family.

CHAPTER SIXTY SIX
FAUNELLA

FAUNELLA DROPPED LIGHTLY FROM the tree, keeping her eyes on Derick as he climbed down after her. She was pleased to see he had made the descent easily, even though his skin was still pale from the meeting with Amon.

With a heavy thud, he landed on the ground next to her. Immediately, he stepped closer and rested his hand gently on her lower back. She blushed, looking around to see if the Fae could see. Amon stood beside another giant tree. It was easy for her to see, but by the blank expression on Derick's face, she knew he couldn't see him. The moonlight couldn't permeate the dense foliage of the surrounding trees. Glancing around, she looked for the others.

"Where's everyone else?"

"Are you talking to me?" Derick asked before Amon could reply.

Amon frowned, stepping forward and poking him in the shoulder.

"No, she's talking to me."

"Amon!" she hissed, keeping her voice low. "You know he can't see you." Turning to Derick, who was grimacing and rubbing at his sore shoulder, she placed her palms on his arms, letting him feel that she was there.

"I was talking to Amon. I'm sorry. I know you can't see in the dark. But if you could, just stay quiet and I'll figure out what's happening."

She stayed still, holding her breath when he blindly reached forward until his groping hands landed on her shoulders. Then he smiled. His lips spread wide, showing his teeth.

"Whatever you say."

He leaned forward, and Faunella's heart leapt into her throat.

Surely he's not going to—

Stopping short of connecting with her face, he furrowed his brows, lowering his voice to a hushed whisper.

"Could you do me a favor, though? Could you let me know if that tr—if Amon comes near me again?" He winced. "I'm still a bit freaked out."

A smile pulled at her own lips. Derick angled his head, waiting for her answer.

"Of course. I'll let you know what's happening." She arched an eyebrow, knowing that Amon could hear every whispered word they said. "I'm sure Amon won't come near you again."

Derick sighed in relief, straightening up and letting his hands slip off her shoulders, one coming down to catch hold of hers.

Amon huffed, staring pointedly at their joined hands. Flushing hotly, Faunella stuck out her chin.

"He can't see, and I'm assuming we're going somewhere?"

"Yes," said Amon, now all business. "Back to the grotto. All the others are there, aside from Venek. He's trailing the men until we decide what to do."

He reached out as if to pick her up, then stopped, his eyes flicking to Derick.

"I can walk with Derick," she quickly said, wondering why she felt so awkward being with Derick in front of Amon. "You go on ahead. We'll be right behind you."

She took a step, and Derick stepped quickly after her, stumbling before righting himself.

Amon groaned, slapping his hand against the trunk of the nearest tree.

"You'll never get there if you have to go at the human's pace." His branches swayed and rustled in agitation. "Give him to me. I'll carry him."

Faunella flinched back in surprise, then after a second, she narrowed her eyes suspiciously. Huxley was usually the trickster in the group, but Amon had made his dislike for Derick clear, and she was wary of his sudden generosity.

"What did he say?" Derick whispered over her shoulder.

Biting her lip, she studied Amon for another minute before letting out a breath and turning her head to talk to Derick.

"We need to go to the cave where the Fae live. It's not far, but with your inability to see in the dark, it would take longer than normal." She shrugged, giving his hand a squeeze. "Amon suggested he carries you so that we get there faster."

Derick's face dropped. The color that had returned to his face disappeared again.

"We can just walk if you want to," she softly spoke into his ear. She could almost hear his heart pounding.

"No," he croaked out, clearing his throat and giving his head a little shake. "It's safer for you if we get there faster."

The fluttering in her stomach started up again at his words. He was obviously afraid, very afraid, but trying so hard not to show it. He took a deep, steadying breath, then angled his head upwards, slightly to the right to where Amon stood.

"Is this cave a good place to hide? Will Fawn be safe there?"

Faunella pursed her lips and tilted her face to look at Amon. The Fae was studying Derick curiously, his expression thoughtful.

"We can barricade the entrance so no one would even know it's there." He stood even straighter. "We've done it before."

It had only been once, years ago when she was still so young. But Faunella could remember it vividly. Her free hand fluttered against her leg, the motion grounding her. It was the day she had found out who she truly was, what she was destined for—Queen.

She banished the thought and turned to Derick, relaying word for word what Amon had said.

Seemingly satisfied with Amon's words, he gave a short nod. "I'm ready." With one last squeeze of her hand, he let go, stepping forward and clamping his eyes shut.

Fighting a smile at his tense body, she looked at Amon until she caught his eye.

"Be nice," she mouthed.

With one sweeping movement, Amon lunged forward, scooping Derick up into his limbs. Other than one small yelp, Derick stayed silent, his body rigid in Amon's hold.

"We'll be there soon," she called up, biting her lip and feeling terrible for feeling like laughing. "I'll be beside you the whole time."

She looked up at the treehouse and felt for the connection between her and her animals. Before she could summon them, Amon shook his head.

"Get them to stay behind. I don't want them to get in the way."

Respecting his decision, she sent a request through the bond, asking the two of them to stay in the treehouse until she told them otherwise. Then, wasting no more time, they headed for the grotto.

They made it there in record time. The moon was directly overhead, which lit the clearing enough that Derick should be able to see better once his eyes adjusted. Unfortunately, that meant he would see the other Fae gathered in the clearing.

"We're here," said Amon, depositing Derick abruptly on the ground as far away from Faunella as he could.

Derick held out his arms to steady himself, scanning the clearing and blinking as he took in the dark shapes gathered in a loose circle.

"Fawn?" he quietly called, his face pinched with worry.

She hurried to his side, cupping his elbow to steady him. "I'm here."

He let out a breath, relaxing briefly before a loud grinding caused him to stiffen up. Faunella rolled her eyes, stepping closer to Derick and murmuring under her breath.

"Remember what I said about the Fae. Just try not to be afraid."

"Were my eyes deceiving me, Amon? Or did I see you carrying the human?" Huxley let out a barking laugh, coming closer to where they stood. "I know you like humans, but I didn't think you'd want to cozy up with one."

"Knock it off, Hux. Unless you wanted us to take half the night, I didn't have a choice."

Erwin shuffled over and stepped around Huxley, smiling up at Faunella.

"I'd like to meet him, if that's okay?" He screwed up his face a bit before glancing around at the other Fae. "I know it's bad timing, but we have a bit of time."

Out of all the Fae, Erwin was probably the least threatening, and things would probably go a lot smoother if Derick wasn't so afraid.

"Do we have time for introductions?" she asked, looking at Amon for approval.

He dug his roots into the ground, cocking his head and closing his eyes. One by one, the other Fae fell silent, including Faunella. They all listened for the sounds of intruders in the otherwise peaceful forest. She couldn't hear anything, even with her Fae hearing. However, Amon was the most connected with the land, and the final decision would be his.

"I can't hear them," he said at last. Letting out another heavy sigh, he nodded at the Fae. "Go on then, but keep it brief."

The eager faces of the Fae around her made her skin prickle with happiness. Most of them surged forward, ready to meet Derick. Only a few stayed back, staring at Derick with suspicious eyes. Huxley, though, was a real cause for concern. He stepped up, a wicked smile etched on his face.

Faunella kept her eye on him, stepping even closer to Derick.

"The Fae want to meet you before we get started on deciding how to keep us safe. Is that okay with you?"

Derick smiled weakly, his eyes darting around at the Fae surrounding him. "How will I understand them?"

"I'll tell you their words, and you can just talk to them normally like you did with Amon before."

"Alright."

Faunella nibbled on her lip. Her chest was tight with tension. She wanted the Fae to like Derick as much as she did, and she needed Derick to not be scared of the Fae. They were her family, and she couldn't have the most important people in her life not getting along.

"Erwin, you first."

Hopefully, Erwin, with his sweet, gentle nature, would pave the way for the more severe-looking Fae. She shot a glance back at Huxley, not liking the gleam in his eye.

Erwin leapt forward in an explosive motion, latching himself firmly around the entirety of Derick's leg.

Faunella jumped in shock, her mouth flying open as Huxley erupted into raucous laughter.

Arms wheeling, Derick stepped back on his free leg, his jaw set as he righted himself. Erwin laughed, letting himself down and scrambling up to sit on top of Huxley.

"I'm sorry, Derick," he wheezed. "Huxley said we needed to break the ice and that laughter was the best way to do that." He grinned broadly, reaching down to slap hands with Huxley.

Faunella translated, scanning Derick's face anxiously. To her immense surprise, Derick's lips quirked up at the side, and he let out a breathy chuckle.

"Well, it was better than meeting Amon for the first time." He winced, squinting around the clearing looking for the tall tree. Faunella blushed, remembering what Amon had seen.

The Fae laughed, even the few that had stared at him with suspicion. Faunella began to hope that this would all go well, then Huxley stepped forward.

"You're pretty big for a human. Almost Fae sized, I'd say." He smirked. "But not as big as I was."

Derick raised his eyebrows. "Huxley, I presume?"

"That's right." Raising his arm, he smacked Derick on the chest. "But we've met before."

"We've met before?" Derick turned to Fawn, confusion lining his features. "Fawn?"

Faunella felt her face burn with embarrassment. She had been keeping so many secrets from him, and now she would be exposed.

"Well, actually, you've met Erwin as well."

"What? When?"

"Do you remember the boulder that you could have sworn was in the clearing by the stream?"

Derick turned back to Huxley, looking him up and down with his lips slightly parted.

"That was you?"

"That's right. Had yourself a nice little rest, didn't you?"

"And Erwin?" he asked, stepping away from Huxley with a nervous chuckle.

Faunella's blush deepened.

"The first time you were here," she started, rubbing her hands together. "When you were injured and you needed to...you know. Well, Erwin's the one who helped you."

The Fae all snickered as Derick's face darkened, his hand coming up to brush over his head.

"All right, that's enough. The rest of you can introduce yourselves later."

Amon stepped forward, his voice ringing with authority. The Fae backed off, chattering amongst themselves as they moved to their places in their normal circle.

Faunella slipped her hand into Derick's. Her palm tingled at the contact. Peering up at him, her lips curved into a small smile.

"It's over for now." She bumped her shoulder into his arm. "You did so well. I just know that with a bit of time, they will love you."

His face fell.

"Don't they want to go back to their world?"

"They wouldn't want to leave me. They will stay on Earth as long as I'm here."

Derick's brow furrowed, a pained expression crossing his face. She opened her mouth to ask him what was wrong when Amon started the meeting.

"As you all know, Fawn has befriended this human, Derick. Unfortunately, he is being hunted by some of his own kind. For what, we don't know. Regardless, having humans in the forest who are on the hunt is extremely dangerous for Fawn, not to mention, it makes it more likely that we will be seen, a fact strictly forbidden by the late king."

Faunella translated Amon's words for Derick, flushing whenever he said anything negative towards him. Amon sighed.

"While it is too soon to take Faunella back to take her rightful place, we still need to make the forest safe until such a time when we are ready to leave. So, I propose that we encourage the humans to leave and hope they don't come back until after we have gone for good."

He scanned the group, a twinkle in his eye.

"If no one is opposed to the plan, I suggest you all come up with ways we can scare off the humans without revealing our presence."

Faunella's stomach clenched as she relayed the final message to Derick. Then she stepped forward, making sure to keep any weakness from showing.

"I'm not going back," she announced, raising her chin when the Fae simultaneously sucked in a breath. "The plan sounds good, but when it's over, I want to stay here." Looking over her shoulder, she smiled tenderly at Derick "With Derick."

The shocked silence was enough to make her heart start pounding, her palms growing moist as she waited for their reaction. Unsurprisingly, it was Amon who broke the silence.

"It's been a long night, and dawn is approaching. I suggest we take the rest of the night to get some sleep, and we can talk more in the morning."

Faunella burned with confusion. Amon didn't sound angry. He didn't even sound shocked. She wanted to ask him why, to demand that he tell her she had a choice in this instead of just brushing off her desire like she was still a child. But before she could form a clear thought to ask, he continued.

"Baol, you and the Fae of your choosing can go out and explain the plan to Venek, then start putting some ideas into motion. Remember, don't be seen."

Baol grinned. "Come on, Huxley. I can't think of anyone more perfect at setting traps and pulling pranks than you."

The other Fae started filing into the cave, urging Fawn and Derick along with them. They herded them into the opening, and she watched as Amon remained outside the cave, turning his back and keeping watch.

Without knowing why, sadness flooded over her, and all she could do was hold tight to Derick's warm hand, letting them be swept away.

CHAPTER SIXTY SEVEN
DERICK

THE BRIEF MOMENT OF light in the clearing had disappeared back to utter darkness. He was pushed and jostled into the cave, unable to fall due to how tightly he was pressed up against the Fae creatures. He was still uneasy around them, but it was hard to be terrified of things that acted so casually, so much like normal people.

Holding tight to Faunella's hand, he trusted her to keep him safe, focusing on the feel of her smooth skin locked around his rough palm. Before the crowd released him from their herding, he felt moisture seep through the back pocket of his jeans. With a startled yelp, he lurched towards Fawn as something gave his ass a firm squeeze.

"Holy hell. What was that?"

Faunella dropped his hand, leaving him suddenly alone in the darkness. The sounds of nature rose up around him, the bubbling of a stream, the rustling of leaves, the faint snapping of wood.

"Violetta," Fawn choked out, her voice bursting with amusement. "I know," she continued, replying to some indecipherable sound. "But you can't just go around grabbing at people."

The bubbling, splashing sounds continued. He stayed still, fearing to move lest he run into another Fae.

"Yes, he is."

"What did they say?" he asked, leaning forward towards where Fawn's soft voice had come from. He felt her warmth as she stepped closer, her sweet scent invading his senses.

"She asked if you were mine," she said in her quiet voice, filling him with a hot rush of feeling.

He struggled to keep the smile off his face, losing the battle when he felt his cheeks lift.

"Ah, so no more touching?"

He tried to keep his tone light, not wanting them to know how much her words meant to him.

"No, not by Violetta," she breathed, threading her hand back through his.

Derick twitched in his pants, heat running through him at the double meaning in her words.

Keep it together. She's an innocent.

He let himself be dragged a little further into the cave until Fawn stopped, tugging at his hand so he would sit down.

"We should sleep." She let out a yawn, giggling at herself as it ended. "I'm so tired."

Conscious of the fact that she could see him, he forced a smile to his lips, not letting the weight of sadness show on his face. Even now, he was contemplating staying, not wanting to leave her side, even for a moment.

"Can I hold you while we sleep?"

He heard her intake of breath and imagined her blue eyes going wide, her cheeks likely flushed.

She wriggled around, making small scuffing sounds on the ground. Derick held his breath, waiting until her movements stilled. She shyly whispered, "Yes," just before he began reaching out blindly to feel for her. Landing on her arm, he moved down until his hand stroked over her rounded hip. She was lying on her side, facing away from him.

Pulse racing, he lowered himself to the ground, tucking himself around Fawn's curled form. Slowly, he eased his arm under her neck, sucking in a breath when she sighed and pressed her body back into his. Careful not to touch her anywhere that would bring her family down on his head, he wrapped his top arm over her body with the utmost tenderness, to lay flat against her thrumming heart.

They lay in silence, Fawn's breathing beginning to deepen.

"Fawn?" he murmured against her hair.

"Mmm?"

"What did Amon mean before when he said you have to go back and take your rightful place?"

She yawned, curling up even tighter. Derick waited, needing to know the answer.

"The queen," she mumbled, her voice heavy with sleep. "I'm meant to be their queen."

His entire body locked up. Any chance of him staying with her vanished like a wave upon the sand. A deep resolve came over him as he held her in his arms. He wouldn't be the one to hold her back. His mind was made up.

As the minutes passed and Faunella's body slackened further, he lifted his head, placing a gentle kiss on the back of her head.

"You will make a great queen," he breathed, sliding his arm out from under her. "You saved me in more ways than one and showed me what life could be." Closing his eyes, he breathed in her scent one final time. "I don't regret a single second."

With dawn only just beginning to lighten the sky, there was just enough light for Derick to feel his way out of the grotto. He wished he could have seen her beautiful face one last time.

It would be slow going, but hopefully he would reach Jarred and the other men before Faunella awoke and figured out where he had gone. As he stepped into the still dark clearing, a shadowy tree unfurled and turned to face him.

His heart leapt in his chest until he realized it was only Amon, then it began to beat in an entirely different way. The Fae were putting so much effort into keeping him and Fawn safe, but he couldn't let them stop him from doing what he needed to do.

"Amon," he murmured, craning his neck to look up at the Fae.

The Fae responded, creaking out something that he couldn't understand. Luckily, the pointed limb back into the cave was clear enough.

"I'm leaving."

Amon lowered his arm, staring at him curiously.

"She's only staying for me." He lowered his head, his voice thickening. "She doesn't deserve a life of hiding away. She needs to be with her own people, and she's too good for me anyway." Straightening up, he gritted his teeth. "I'm taking myself out of the picture. Those men, they want me. So, I'll let them have me."

He stared Amon down, waiting for the Fae to respond. His heart pounded as the final obstacle to his plan deliberated if he would let him die.

Finally, after what seemed like an eternity, Amon stepped forward, clapping his heavy limb on Derick's shoulder and bowing his head.

Derick shuddered, his life now counting down with only a matter of hours left on the clock. He blinked back tears, swallowing past the heavy lump in his throat.

"Just tell her I did it for her, and she was worth it."

He stepped out from under Amon's arm, clearing his throat and scanning the dark tree line.

"Which direction?"

After one final moment, Amon lifted his limb and pointed Derick towards his retribution.

CHAPTER SIXTY EIGHT
FAUNELLA

S HE DIDN'T SLEEP FOR long. The last thing she remembered was being wrapped tight in Derick's arms, a deep happiness filling her up with his solid warmth spreading through her back. She flicked her eyes open, the hard ground sending an uncomfortable ache through her shoulder.

The sunlight dancing on the walls of the cave greeted her. She stretched out languidly, giving a small mewl of pleasure as the stiffness of her body melted into hot tension. Feeling better, she turned her head, preparing to wake Derick and find out how he had fared in his sleep. She wondered if, after they returned to her treehouse, he would want to continue sleeping side by side. After years of sleeping alone, she had relished his closeness.

To her surprise, he wasn't beside her.

"Derick?" she called out in a hushed voice, scanning what she could see of the cave. Most of the Fae were still asleep, with a small handful missing.

Maybe he's with them.

Getting to her feet, she bit her lip, trying to ignore the quiet ringing deep inside her chest. Walking past the resting Fae didn't take long, her hurried steps leading her directly to the clearing.

"Did you see where Derick went?"

Amon drooped, turning his tall body around until he faced her.

"Fawn," he started, the word dripping with sadness.

She stepped back, startled, her pulse beginning to increase its rhythm, even more so when Amon stepped forward with his arms outstretched, his familiar face pained.

"He wanted to go."

"No," she breathed, backing away from him. "He wouldn't do that. We were friends. There was a plan."

The ringing in her ears grew louder, making its way through her body as she struggled to understand what Amon was telling her.

"He didn't want to put you in danger. Sweetheart, he would have only held you back." Amon kept moving towards her, backing her towards the cave. "Try to accept his sacrifice." He looked to the sky, nodding at the sun's position. "The other humans should be on their way out of the forest and out of our lives. You'll be safe now to make your choices without having to consider him."

Faunella's blood ran cold. She stopped moving, looking up at Amon with horror.

"What did you do?

He looked down, not able to meet her eyes.

"What did you do, Amon?" she yelled up at him, her voice ringing with fear.

He turned his pleading eyes to her, his body wilting even further. Faunella held her breath, almost vibrating with tension as she waited.

"I let him go," he whispered, regret lacing each word. "I let him go take himself out of the picture."

The roaring in her ears made her shake with fury.

"But he'll die."

Her voice came out cold and inhumane, making Amon step back in shock, eyes widening.

She continued, stepping forward with her eyes narrowed.

"What I do with my life is not up to you." Pain flared with each step forward she took. The effort it took to not run directly to Derick had her body flaring in agony, but her anger would not be contained. She was barely tempering her anxiety for Derick's fate.

"My life is my own, and who I choose is up to me." She stopped, arms clamped to her side as she stared up at the Fae who had been like a father to her. Pain flickered across her face. "How could you, Amon? He was mine."

Then, unable to withstand the pull any longer, she spun on her heel and launched herself into a sprint. Her anger at Amon pushed aside as each step she took had Derick's name pounding through her mind.

Her teeth clenched with effort as she pushed as much of her powers into her mad dash through the forest. The air pushed at her back and slipped under each foot, propelling her forward as she narrowly missed crashing into the trees that stood in her way.

Please be okay. Please be alive.

Her breathing became ragged, her body pushing itself past the point of her endurance. A tiny seed of hope started to bloom. Her efforts had paid off. With her Fae hearing, she caught the deep sounds of men talking. Pulling on a fresh burst of energy, she pushed herself further, angling towards the men.

She didn't even consider stopping and observing what was happening before intervening. Her panic over Derick had her entirely focused on rushing in to save him. She couldn't lose someone else, not again. So, with a final gust of air, she pushed herself through some low-lying branches, coming to an abrupt stop as she took in the scene in front of her.

"Oh my god! Fawn, no!"

Derick's one good eye stared at her in horror, his words distorted due to the cut running through his lips.

Faunella froze, her heart continuing to tap out its frantic rhythm even as she caught her breath. Derick was being held between two men. He was on his knees, wearing only his jeans. She let out a sob as she took in his body, the thin slices that dripped blood down his chest and stomach, and the giant purple bruises, slowly spreading over his ribs. He looked just as bad as he did when they first met, except now the beating wasn't over.

She turned her eyes to the men, narrowing them to thin slits. Derick was still alive. She arrived in time to save his life. But the fury crawling up her back told her that the men who had harmed him had to be punished.

"Get away from him," she hissed out, her voice low with that cold stillness.

Three of the men had already turned towards her when Derick called her name. But now the final man turned, the knife in his hand glinting as it caught the light. His black jacket, the same as the others, was stained with blood, and his pale hair was slicked back.

All at once, Faunella stumbled back, her knees going slack as she took in his face. Apart from a few silver scars spread across his face, the face that had haunted her nightmares for years was unchanged.

"You!" he exclaimed, his eyes bright as his tongue darted out to lick at his lips. "Look boys, it's the one that got away." Something dark flickered in his eyes as he looked her up and down, making her shrink back as he leered. Absent-mindedly, he wiped the blade and put it in his pocket. "Our forest girl. Come back for more of this?" He clutched roughly at his crotch, jerking his hand up and down. The men behind him laughed, and Faunella realized with mounting fear that these were the same men from that night so long ago.

"Don't even look at her!" Derick spat, straining against the men who held him. "Faunella, get away. Just leave." His voice steadied out, his one eye serious with meaning. "Go home."

His words pulled her out of his shock, giving her legs back their strength. He wanted her to go back to Amaranth, away from this world. But she couldn't do it. She couldn't leave him. For Derick, she would be strong.

"Oh, I see what's going on here," Jarred said, clutching his bloody hands to his chest. "Derick and the forest girl have fallen in love," he said in a sing-song voice before laughing and sneering between the two of them. "How did you like my sloppy seconds, huh Derick? The boys and I had our fun with the girl years ago."

Faunella tried not to flinch as his words brought back the terror of that night, but Derick didn't hesitate. The skin visible under his spilled blood drained of color, and his good eye sharpened.

"You'll never touch her again. You put your filthy hands on her, and I'll cut them off."

With a deep bellow, he reared up, wrenching his arms from the grips of the other men. Then, screaming a curse, he launched himself at Jarred, knocking him to the ground and swinging his fists at the smaller man with a feral roar.

Faunella clapped her hand over her mouth. Worry for Derick rooted her in place as he continued to viciously beat the man on the ground, his ferocity at odds with his wounded state. Within moments, however, he gave a guttural groan and collapsed, his hand coming to press against the side of his abdomen.

"Fucking prick," Jarred spat, scrambling to his feet as he gingerly touched the tender flesh on his face. In his hand, he held the long serrated knife, its blade dripping with Derick's blood.

Faunella couldn't wait any longer. She shut her eyes and let her power fill her. Ignoring any residual fear from the men, she pulled at the soft, gentle feeling she felt when she was with Derick. Letting it fill her up and make her strong. Derick clutched at his side, his head raised to look at her even as the blood gushed through his fingers.

"*Run.*"

He mouthed the words, his eye shining. Then he looked away, trying in vain to get up, grimacing with every movement. He only made it to his knees before his body gave up, unable to move any further.

Watching this all unfold, Faunella's power swelled with emotion, growing bigger than ever before. Her anguish over Derick's pain and the intensity of her feelings for him had her heart swelling in her chest. The air started swirling around her body, pulling at her clothes and raising her hair up until it flowed around her in the wind. In that moment, she knew that she loved him. The love was small, a gentle whisper of friendship and affection, something to cultivate and breathe life into until it could bloom into something stronger. But she felt it.

Jarred stalked around behind Derick, gripping his hair and roughly pulling his head up.

He won't touch him again.

She stepped forward, eyes flashing. "Get your hands off him."

Jarred locked his eyes on her, frowning at the sight before him.

"Jarred, maybe we should leave," one of the other men said, uneasiness coating each word.

"Yea, remember what happened last time with the birds?"

A second man stepped forward, pulling at Jarred's sleeve, his eyes darting to the side as the wind picked up, the air now pulling at their clothes.

Faunella smiled, feeling powerful at the fear she was eliciting from her abusers. In the back of her mind, she could hear the approaching Fae, but she stayed focused on the humans in front of her. They deserved all her attention.

Jarred stared at her a moment longer, fear and confusion passing over his face. With his free hand, he touched the silver scars on his head. With a sick satisfaction, she realized that they must have been inflicted by the birds the night they had met.

In one smooth moment, she raised her arms high, her palms together, and then threw them to the ground, sending out a shockwave that blew all four men back. Their bodies crashed into the trees around them, and to her delight, she heard more than one sickening crack.

Derick blinked in surprise, still kneeling in place and untouched by her power. She let her magic subside, her heart racing as hope grew in her body. The men started to get up, letting out hoarse cries and groans as they cradled broken limbs. One by one they stumbled away, leaving

Faunella and Derick alone. The Fae were getting louder, only moments away from bursting into the now flattened area.

It's over.

"You saved me again," wheezed Derick, slumping over in pain.

"Oh, Derick!"

She raced to his side, placing her hand against the stab wound and catching him so that his head rested over her shoulder.

"It's going to be okay. We can heal you from this. Just hold on a little longer."

He coughed, letting out a gurgling cry when the movement jostled his wounds. Then, suddenly, he stiffened. Warning Faunella only seconds before she heard the shuffling steps behind her.

The whole world stilled, time slowing until it barely moved. She turned her head to look towards the sound, then felt Derick's arm slip around her waist, twisting them in one desperate movement. The sharp crack of a gunshot rang out, and Derick jolted as he finished their rotation, until she was the one facing where Jarred now stood, a small black object pointed at where her back had been.

Derick's hand released her, falling with the rest of his body to the ground.

Faunella's vision narrowed.

She didn't see the Fae burst through the trees. She didn't notice the look on Jarred's face as he saw her family before he turned and ran. She only saw Derick, his face slack, his chest no longer rising and falling.

She fell forward. Her fists pressed against the hole through his chest. He didn't move.

He was dead.

An all-consuming pain tore through her. She couldn't breathe. All the air sucked into her body, pressing her together as she began to fall apart. Was it always her lot in life to lose the ones she loved? First Lucy and now Derick.

Gathering her remaining energy, she lifted her head and closed her eyes, letting hot tears snake down her cheeks as she cried out her pain in a heart-wrenching wail. She pressed both hands to Derick's chest and let her power explode from her. Losing Derick had her body so ablaze with fervent agony that she needed to escape. She needed to get away from this reality. Power flashed around her, building in intensity as it ripped through her with each frenzied cry, her heart tearing itself in two. Then, between one breath and another, she released it, unable to bear another moment. Her power pulsed out, gathering both her and Derick into its energy and winked them out of existence, leaving the Fae staring at nothing but the bloodstained ground.

PART SIX

Whether High Fae or Ancient Fae, the law remains the same— A lower fae, regardless of their heritage, may not inherit the throne in any Kingdom.

Furthermore, if a Fae chooses to join with a low fae, they will forfeit their right to rule.

—Law 56 of the Protection Order

<u>Furthering from Law 56 of the Protection Order</u>
After the time of the second puberty, those who remain lower fae are to be treated in such a way that demonstrates their tainted lineage. The threat of non-magical blood spreading throughout the realm is too great to allow these lesser fae access to our higher positions. Therefore, any High Fae who degrades themselves to join with a lower fae shall be forbidden to hold any position of authority, regardless of their own bloodline.

These fae are to support the High Fae as their betters, serving until such a time that they prove their worth to Amaranth.

As always, our focus remains on increasing the diminished magic the humans caused long ago.

—Excerpt from the High Fae Covenants, Vol. 3

AMARANTH

CHAPTER SIXTY NINE
SOLANINE

"**I**T IS IMPERATIVE THAT you defer to the ruling monarch when you are in their territory. You must also respect their heir, but when you are a queen in your own right, then they must defer to you."

Queen Nyssa continued droning on about fair trade agreements and proper etiquette between the rulers of different kingdoms.

Solanine inwardly rolled her eyes. She was so sick of listening to her grandmother tell her over and over what to expect when she takes over as the Queen of Madivyre. The seaside kingdom would be better off when she finally got her chance to rule.

She shifted restlessly on one of the padded seats in the queen's council chambers. It was just her and the queen in the room today. The other council members were, thankfully, not present for this lesson, which usually meant that Solanine would get out faster.

Murmuring vague noises of approval, she tuned out the queen's voice and instead wondered how long it would be before the old bat died. Solanine took in her grandmother's slightly lined face and elaborately styled graying hair. Though the Fae was nearing her eight hundredth year, she still held herself with the grace and poise of someone half her age. Solanine gritted her teeth, hiding her resentment behind a decidedly bland smile.

At this rate, she'll never die.

A loud pounding on the door snapped her out of her musings and stopped her grandmother from talking, the monotony of her sentence cutting off abruptly. They both turned to look at the large double doors at the other end of the chamber when they were suddenly flung open.

Flinching slightly as the doors crashed back into the wall, Solanine glanced at her grandmother, eagerly waiting for her to berate the Fae who would dare enter the queen's council room without permission.

Looking back to the door, she watched as an out-of-breath guard came running into the chamber. Her eagerness fell when she saw that the interrupting guard was none other than her grandmother's favorite, a lower fae named Harrigan. Turning up her nose, she sniffed in disdain at the fae's presence. It was a pity that the fae was Harrigan, not only because of the fae's unclean blood but because her grandmother was less likely to talk down to the older guard than she would have if it were one of the younger, fresher Fae guards.

Curious as to why such an experienced guard would make such a mistake, Solanine paid more attention to him than she usually would.

His face was bright red, and his brown salt-and-pepper hair was sticking to his sweaty brow. He looked like he had been traveling fast as his clothes were torn with bits of twigs and leaves caught in the leather straps of his uniform. Solanine turned fully to face her grandmother, not quite knowing how the queen would react.

"My queen."

Pausing to bow sharply, the disheveled guard strode towards the large table where the two of them sat. The queen stood smoothly, her face showing her worry for the guard, but her voice was strong when she spoke.

"What is it, Harrigan? I'm sure it must be important for you to totally dismiss protocol and burst into these chambers without waiting to be summoned."

"Yes, Your Majesty."

He paused to take a shaky breath, his eyes wide with shock and excitement.

Something inside Solanine's chest tightened by what she saw in the guard's eyes. Suddenly worried, she leaned forward slightly, clutching her hands together under the table.

"Queen Nyssa, we have found something in the South Forest. An injured human man appeared near where we were stationed by the portal tree."

Solanine's hands loosened slightly at his words. She let out a breath of relief, chiding herself for jumping to conclusions.

"There was a Fae with him." Harrigan continued, pausing to stare directly at the queen.

The world around Solanine slowed down, coming to a complete stop as his next words echoed loudly in her ears.

"She said her name was Faunella."

ACKNOWLEDGEMENTS

I cannot believe I made it to the point where the last thing I have to do is thank all the people who have helped me. It is a surreal feeling.

But let's get right to it.

First off, I would like to acknowledge myself for completing this story from start to finish, even when I didn't trust that I could. My husband delights in calling me a "ninety percenter" as I quite often complete the bulk of a project, then burn out and lose interest. Well, take a look hunny! I got it done 100% this time!

However, secondly, I have to thank said husband. Without his encouragement, unfailing love and support, I really would have given up a long time ago. Doug, thank you for letting me hide away from you and the kids, and thank you for letting me spend all our money. I couldn't imagine a better cheerleader to keep me excited. Never once did you complain about the time I devoted to this; the answer was always yes to anything I needed. You fed me, forced me to shower, and lovingly rubbed my hands when they ached from typing. You read this book more than anyone else, maybe even me, and each time you gushed about how wonderful it was. I don't know what I ever did to deserve such an unfailing husband. Thank you from the bottom of my heart.

Then I have to give credit to my critique partners, A.N. Caudle and R Lynn Hanks. My girls. Even though we are worlds apart and writing completely different books, the two of you have shared with me the highs and lows, picking me up when my self doubt got the best of me. I am so grateful to the two of you for sharing all your love and skills.

Before I get too far into the thanking game, I wanted to make a special mention to Matt Froggatt. Matt is a friend and fellow writer here in New Zealand. When I first had the idea for Fawn, I messaged him to let him know I was starting a book. Then I wrote my first 800 words and promptly gave up. If it wasn't for Matt messaging me every few weeks and asking me about my writing progress, I don't think I would have started back up. So thank you Matt for your annoying check ups.

Throughout this journey I have had some terrible beta readers, and one specific one who set me off my course for a very long time, but I want to take the time now to thank the good ones, the ones who gave me their time and feedback. You all helped shape Fawn into the book it is today. I can't mention you all, but Michelle and Alex, I want to thank you personally. Michelle, you were the first person to fall in love with Fawn, and your encouragement kept me going for a long time in those early drafts. And Alex, your enthusiasm was like a cool glass of water to my pessimistic soul.

Charis, Nikki and Keira. You three also get a special mention. Out of all the beta readers, you three loved this story so much and believed in me enough to put together my street team. Without you three, I probably wouldn't have anyone to read this book. Thank you all, and I hope you'll be with me for at least the next two books!

Finally I want to thank my children. I doubt that they will read this, but maybe one day they will pick up my first book, flip to the end, and see how much I appreciate them. Whether you have children or not, I'm sure you know how much time a mother gives. So when I tell you that my children were so wonderful at giving me the space to write, you know what a sacrifice that was. They helped with cleaning, they made dinners, and they played quietly on the other side of the house so I could create. They sacrificed their time with me so I could pour my energy into this book, and for that, I am beyond grateful. To Tyler, Thomas, Theodore, Katherine, Elizabeth and Sebastian, I love you so very much. Xxx

553

book, and for that, I am beyond grateful. To Tyler, Thomas, Theodore, Katherine, Elizabeth and Sebastian, I love you so very much. Xxx

ABOUT THE AUTHOR

Laura lives in New Zealand, the birthplace of Middle Earth. By day, she works in a small local fabric store, and by night, she wrangles her six children into bed so she can write.

From an early age, Laura dreamed of becoming an author. Now, at 32, she has realized that dream and published her first novel, *Fawn*.

With the support of her loving husband Doug, she plans to one day live in a large house in the country so she can write in nature and live out her *Anne of Green Gables* life. Laura loves to read and is passionate about all aspects of living. With the first book behind her, she will forge ahead and continue writing books that touch the heart.